Praise for
GAIN

"Ambitious...the most accessible and straightforward of Powers' novels thus far....The most emotionally affecting work Powers has done to date."
—Michiko Kakutani, *The New York Times*

"With *Gain*, Richard Powers launches his own strong bid for entry into the canon of America's best novelists, delivering a work both epic in scope and universal in emotional resonance."
—David Livingston, *Detroit Free Press*

"This is a harrowing and powerful novel, uncompromising in its depiction."
—Joan Mellen, *The Baltimore Sun*

"An acclaimed, accredited genius....There are many moments when the ideas absolutely dazzle."
—Adam Begley, *The New York Observer*

"*Gain* is Richard Powers' attempt to make up this lost ground in one great pole vault; to loft the novel of American enterprise over the old swamps of socialism, Darwinism, and absurdism into a new place. And he succeeds."
—Walter Kirn, *New York Magazine*

"The elements of a major novel, and *Gain* only confirms that Powers is, in fact, a major American novelist."
—Adam Kirsch, *The New Republic*

GAIN

RICHARD POWERS

GAIN

PICADOR USA
NEW YORK

Picador® is a U.S. registered trademark and is used by St. Martin's Press under license from Pan Books Limited.

For information on Picador USA Reading Group Guides, as well as ordering, please contact the Trade Marketing department at St. Martin's Press.
Phone: 1-800-221-7945 extension 763
Fax: 212-677-7456
E-mail: trademarketing@stmartins.com

Library of Congress Cataloguing-in-Publication Data

Powers, Richard, 1957–
    Gain / Richard Powers.
        p.   cm.
    ISBN 0-312-20409-4
    I. Title.
    [PS3566.092G34   1999]
    813'.54–dc21   99-18955
                                                                CIP

First published in the United States by Farrar, Straus and Giroux

First Picador USA Paperback Edition: July 1999

10   9   8   7   6   5   4   3   2   1

GAIN

Day had a way of shaking Lacewood awake. Slapping it lightly, like a new-born. Rubbing its wrists and reviving it. On warm mornings, you remembered: this is why we do things. Make hay, here, while the sun shines. Work, for the night is coming. Work now, for there is no work in the place where you are going.

May made it seem as if no one in this town had ever sinned. Spring unlocked the casements. Light cured the oaks of lingering winter doubt, lifting new growth from out of nothing, leaving you free again to earn your keep. When the sun came out in Lacewood, you could live.

———

Lacewood's trace began everywhere: London, Boston, Fiji, Disappointment Bay. But everywhere's trail ended in this town, where folks made things. Some mornings, when the sun shone, history vanished. The long road of arrival disappeared, lost in the journey still in store.

At first, the town subsisted on the overhauled earth. Wild prairie weeds gave way to grain, a single strain of edible grass, grown on a scale that made even grass pay. Later, Lacewood graduated to human wizardry, thrived on alchemical transformation. Growth from bone meal and bat guano. Nourishment from shale. Breakthroughs followed one upon the other, as surely as May followed April.

There must have been a time when Lacewood did not mean Clare, Incorporated. But no one remembered it. No one alive was old enough to recall. The two names always came joined in the same breath. All the grace ever shed on Lacewood flowed through that company's broad conduit. The big black boxes on the edge of town sieved diamonds from out of the mud. And Lacewood became the riches that it made.

Forever, for anyone who would listen, Lacewood liked to trot out the tale of how it tricked its way into fortune. At its deciding moment, when the town had to choose between the sleepy past and the tireless nineteenth century, it did not think twice. With the ease of one born to it, Lacewood took to subterfuge.

The townsfolk felt no qualms about their ruse, then or ever. If they felt anything, it was pride. They laid their snare for the fifth Mr. Clare, the namesake president of an Eastern firm that had lately outgrown its old markets. Clare Soap and Chemical was heading West, seeking new hosts. The fifth Mr. Clare was looking for the ideal site to build the burgeoning business's latest plant.

Douglas Clare, Sr., secretly preferred the aroma of Lacewood to the scent of Peoria. Lacewood smelled clean and distilled. Peoria was a little too unctuous and pomaded. He liked this place for a number of reasons. But he kept mum, sporting the indifference of a cagey suitor.

The fifth Mr. Clare could not say exactly what he was looking for in a future site. But he always claimed he'd recognize the place when he laid eyes on it. Even that most resourceful businessman could not call this location central. But the country's growth would yet center it. Lacewood sat on train lines connecting St. Louis, Indianapolis, and Louisville. It lay a reasonable freight haul away from Chicago, the West's lone metropolis. And land in this vacancy was still dirt cheap.

Lacewood decided to doll itself up, to look like what it thought Clare wanted. Weeks before the visit, the town began papering over its crumbling warehouses with false fronts. Every boy over ten turned builder. The mayor even had two blocks of plaster edifices erected to fatten out anemic Main Street.

For the duration of the company tour, the town rented an old Consolidation locomotive. It ran the engine up and down the line at frequent intervals, rearranging the consist for the sake of drama. The freight even discharged a much fussed-over load at the suspiciously new station. Ten hours later, it returned from the other direction and hauled the crates of gravel away.

Clare and his advisers saw through the whole charade. One glance told the Easterners that the decaying antique hadn't seen service in over a decade. Peoria had run much the same stunt. And its fake façades had been fancier.

But necessity drove Lacewood beyond Peoria's wildest invention. Long in advance of its August inspection, Lacewood dammed up its sleepy little stretch of the Sawgak, just upriver of town. Ordinarily, the pathetic trickle didn't even dampen the dust on a muskrat's whiskers. But for four glorious days in the heat of late summer, the town council built itself a junior torrent.

At key intervals, Lacewood posted several fishers who passed as either entrepreneurs or sportsmen, depending on the light. With uncanny regularity, the anglers struggled to land a series of mighty northern pike: fat from off the land, food from nothing, from honest labor.

The fact that *Esox lucius,* the species these men pulled like clockwork from the synthetic rapids, had never on its own accord strayed south of Minnesota touched Mr. Clare. He admired the industry, the pathos in the stratagem. He could work with these people. They would work for him.

He glowered throughout the length of the inspection. He shook his head continually. At the last instant before heading back to Boston in his private Pullman—whose builder, up in Pullman, Illinois, had recently created an ingenious live-in factory town that supplied all his employees' needs—Clare acquiesced. Sighing, he accepted the massive tax concessions proffered him in perpetuity, and closed the deal.

And that's how Clare Soap and Chemical came to stay.

Years later, just in time to stave off the worst of the Great Depression, the globe's largest producer of earth-moving equipment dropped its world headquarters down in Peoria. Caterpillar played for more than fifty straight profitable years and ran up its annual sales to over $13 billion by the game's twilight, at century's end.

But Lacewood never complained. Without Clare, the town would have dozed forever. It would have stayed a backwoods wasteland until the age of retrotourism. With Clare, Lacewood grew famous, part of an empire of three dozen production facilities in ten countries, "making answers, meeting needs."

Lacewood joined the ride gladly, with both feet. It got the goose it bargained for, and more. For over a century, Clare laid countless clutches of eggs whose gold only the niggling would stoop to assay.

———

———

May, just before Memorial Day, just this side of millennium's end. Up on North Riverside, on the good side of the river, a Lacewood woman works her garden. A woman who has never thought twice about Clare.

Sure she knows it: the name is second nature. Traders on the Frankfurt Bürse mouth "Clare" at the mention of Lacewood, the way they point and go "bang" whenever they meet someone from Chicago. Teens in Bangkok covet anything bearing the company's logo. Whole shipping-container sunrooms in São Paulo are emblazoned with it. The firm built her entire town, and then some. She knows where her lunch comes from. Which side of her bread bears the non-dairy spread.

She drives past Clare's Agricultural Division headquarters at least three times a week. The town cannot hold a corn boil without its corporate sponsor. The company cuts every other check, writes the headlines, sings the school fight song. It plays the organ at every wedding and packs the rice that rains down on the departing honeymooners. It staffs the hospital and funds the ultrasound sweep of uterine seas where Lacewood's next of kin lie gray and ghostly, asleep in the deep.

She knows what it makes as well as anyone. Soap, fertilizers, cosmetics, comestibles: name your life-changing category of substances. But still, she knows Clare no better than she knows Grace or Dow. She does not work for the corporation or for anyone the corporation directly owns. Neither does any blood relation or any loved one.

The woman kneels in her garden, kneading her fifty square feet of earth. She coaxes up leaves, gets them to catch a teacupful of the two calories per cubic centimeter that the sun, in its improvident abundance, spills forever on the earth for no good reason except that it knew we were coming.

Some nasty bug has already begun to nibble her summer squash in the bud. Another goes after her beans. She responds with an arsenal of retaliations. Beer to ward off slugs. Lemon-scented dish soap in solution, spritzed liberally to counter beetle insurgencies. Home remedies. Stronger measures when strength is needed.

She transplants flowers outdoors from their starter beds. The work is play; the labor, love. This is the afternoon she slaves all week for. The therapeutic complement to the way she makes a living: moving families from starter homes into larger spreads.

Spring releases her. The early oriental poppies unwad like her children's birthday crepe. The alpine columbine spread their two-toned trumpets, an ecstatic angel choir. Every growing thing looks like something else to her. Her mind hums as she weeds, hungry to match each plant with its right resemblance.

Tight, hard globes of Christmas ornament relax into peonies. Daisies already droop their tutus like sad, also-ran, Degas dancers. Bleeding hearts hang in group contrition. She urges them on, each to its colored destiny. No human act can match gardening. She would do it all day long, if she could.

The ballet school sponsors. The ones who pay for the TV that nobody ever watches. The annual scholarships for the erector-set kids at the high school. The trade-practice lawsuits she hasn't the patience to follow, and the public service announcements she never entirely understands. The drop-dead-cute actress who has the affair with the guy next door in that series of funny commercials that everyone at the office knows by heart. The old company head who served in the cabinet during World War II. She hums the corporate theme song to herself sometimes, without realizing.

Two pots in her medicine cabinet bear the logo, one to apply and one to remove. Those jugs under the sink—Avoid Contact with Eyes—that never quite work as advertised. Shampoo, antacid, low-fat chips. The weather stripping, the grout between the quarry tiles, the nonstick in the nonstick pan, the light coat of deterrent she spreads on her garden. These and other incarnations play about her house, all but invisible.

This woman, forty-two years old, looks up into the gathering May sky and wrinkles her nose. Yesterday's *Post-Chronicle* predicted azure. But no point in second-guessing yesterday, with today coming on like there's no tomorrow.

Her seedlings are further along than Memorial Day could have hoped. A dollar twenty-nine, two spritzes of lemon dish soap, and a little loving effort can still keep one in squash all summer.

The woman's name is Laura Rowen Bodey. She is the newest member of Next Millennium Realty's Million Dollar Movers Club. Her daughter has just turned seventeen, her son is twelve and a half. Her ex-husband does development for Sawgak College. She sees a married man, quietly and infrequently. Her life has no problem that five more years couldn't solve.

A woman who has heard, yet has not heard. And on this day, no one but the six people who love her gives her a moment's thought.

———

Business ran in the Clares' blood long before the first one of them made a single thing.

That family flocked to commerce like finches to morning. They clung to the watery edge of existence: ports, always ports. They thrived in tidal pools, half salt, half sweet. Brackish, littoral. They lived less in cities than on the sea routes between them.

Clare was, from the first, transnational. Family merchants traded in England for the better part of a century, specializing in a bold shipping commerce that ruined and made their fortunes several times a year. Each generation refined the gamble. Jephthah Clare drank in gambling with his mother's milk. He gambled the way he breathed.

Jephthah fled the mother country in a hurry, on a wager gone wrong. He left in 1802, the year the aristocrat du Pont, escaping the French turmoil, set up his gunpowder mill in Delaware. Jephthah Clare ran from a more prosaic chaos: not wrongdoing, exactly, but failure to share inside knowledge of a collapse in sugar beet prices with an excitable trading partner upon whom he had just settled a considerable shipment. After his house in Liverpool burned, Jephthah thought it wise not to await further repayment.

He, his wife, and three small children sailed unannounced. They stowed away on one of Clare's own packet traders. For the length of the crossing, the family slept on a cargo of Wedgwood Egyptian stoneware. The pain of the passage eased as soon as they and the plates disembarked upon India Wharf, in Boston, America. That thorny pallet of freight paid the family's way toward a comfort that outlasted all memory of the uncomfortable voyage.

The greatest meliorator of the world is selfish, huckstering Trade.

—EMERSON, "Works and Days"

Jephthah Clare cared not where he landed, so long as he could reach the all-delivering ocean. He sold his Wedgwood plates and leased a countinghouse adjacent to Long Wharf. Starting with that one salvaged packet, rechristened the *Rough Bed*, he commenced one of the most lucrative schemes in the long and august history of commercial laundering.

France and Britain, eternally at war, blockaded each other's colonial trade. Clare sent the *Rough Bed* down to Jamaica and loaded it with coffee and molasses. He called these barrels back up to Boston Harbor, where they became, by the magic of paperwork, American coffee, American treacle. These he could then take to London, where the pinched combatants paid hand over fist for their deliverance. In the interests of fair play, he now and then took American rum to Le Havre, courtesy of Guadeloupe.

This dress-up game lasted for a full four years. Jephthah Clare extracted his markup both coming and going. When the belligerents at last closed down the trickery in 1807, Jephthah cursed Jefferson's embargo and turned smuggler. For every ship impounded, two more came in to pay the bribes and ransom, with a little bit left over.

That margin secured him a house in Temple Place. From this base, Jephthah strolled out daily to his favored haunts in Merchants Row. He struck deals in Topliff's Reading Rooms. He traded gossip in the Exchange, learning which packets had come in and which were overdue. He waited for the semaphores from Nantasket to reach the sentry on Constitution Wharf with word of the *Favored*, the *North Port*, the *New Jerusalem*.

When the embargo at last grew too risky to flout, Clare fell back upon longer runs. He dispatched New England goods to the Oregon country. There he exchanged his stock for furs. These furs he sent across the Pacific, to Canton, where his hong could not get enough of them. Furs bought tea in profuse bouquets. Tea came back home at a profit sufficient to buy ten new shipments of cheap New England goods. For truly:

The one thing Home cannot supply
Is that which hails from far away.

The sheer markup of distance sufficed to begin the whole self-enriching triangle all over again.

The world had to be circumnavigated before the humblest washerwoman could sip from her ragged cup. The mystery of it all sometimes visited Jephthah at night. It played in his drafty thoughts as he and his uncomprehending Sarah lay under the eiderdown in their timbered bedroom, tight against the night's worst incursions. He, the Oregon trapper, the Chinese hong: everyone prospered. Each of them thought he'd gotten the better end of the deal. Now, how could that be? Where had the profit come from? Who paid for their mutual enrichment?

The port of Fayal, in the Azores, turned whale oil into wine. A trip to the Sandwich Islands sufficed to change percussion-cap rifles into sandalwood. Everyone everywhere wanted what was only to be had somewhere else. Jephthah shipped Dutch herring to Charleston and Boston cod to Lisbon. For a while, he made a fortune selling white silk hats from France to New York gentlemen, until his competitors bought up a shipment and gave them away free to Negroes, discrediting the style.

Yet the man who moved these goods around the globe could not sell to Ohio. The prospect had no profit in it. The nine dollars that moved a ton of goods from Europe to Boston moved that same ton no more than thirty miles inland.

But on the sea, Jephthah engaged in the entire range of merchanting. He owned some ships outright and hired others. He bought and sold on his own account, acted as another's commissioned agent, exported and imported, traded with jobbers and factors. At times, he even vended directly to shopkeepers. He shipped and insured and financed, open to any deal or part thereof.

A memory for trustworthiness and great patience for paper labyrinths saw him through many setbacks. Competence returned cash, and cash bought competence. Jephthah handled cotton and indigo and potash. But above all else, he dealt in risk. Profit equaled uncertainty times distance. The harder it was to haul a thing to where it humanly belonged, the more one made.

Jephthah loved best those deals that others deplored. He joined a venture to ship ice to Martinique, lately ravaged by yellow fever. In this, neither altruism nor profit moved him. He took on the trade simply because all his fellow merchants considered it mad. Whatever the mind of man stood unanimous against probably had some merit to it.

He tithed to charity, an easy speculation in both good and bad weather. It carried almost no downside risk, while the potential upside was considerable.

Ten percent of a thousand might conceivably swamp the thousand a thousandfold in returned investment. Ten percent of nothing, on the other hand, cost a man nothing.

———

THINGS TO DO TODAY

Sixteen rectangles run across a two-page spread, bordered like a colonial sampler. Each carries one imperative underneath a familiar package.

Rise and Shine
(Viva-cleanse)

Be Fruitful and
(Multi-pli Maxiwipes)

Put On a Happy Face
(Clarity Pore Purifier)

Tie One On
(Infinistik)

Make Some Noise with Those
Pots and Pans
(Slickote Surface)

Put Your Best Foot
Forward
(Leather Lifts)

Provide for tho Common Defense
(Compleet Daily Supplements)

Shed a Little Lite on the Subject
(Fat-Fighter Spreads)

Clear the Air
(Blue Spruce Vapogard)

Soothe the Savage Breast
(Gastrel Caps)

Hit the Road, Jack
(All-Weather Gravel-Grippers)

Hold Everything
(Lok-Toppers)

Bring Home the Bacon
(Heat 'n' Eat)

Cover All Your Bases
(Clareglow No-fume Enamel)

Clean Up Your Act
(Sterisol)

Party 'til the Cows Come Home
(Partifest Non-dari Treats)

The Consumer Goods Group
CLARE MATERIAL SOLUTIONS

———

At last, conflagration came home. Embargo failed to keep Europe's blood from America's doorstep. But Jephthah Clare saw, even in Mr. Madison's War, new chances for expansion. The old tithing speculator spread his risks, taking his certainty from the world's confusion.

When his high-seas routes began piling up losses, he placed himself in the service of the United States and turned to privateering. He passed along to the government a share of the spoils his ships picked from slower British merchantmen. This pirate tax bought both his nation's blessing and its weapons.

War's end found the family with markets in burghs that had not existed until the chaos of 1812 sprouted them. Only Irénée du Pont, whose gunpowder mills held his belligerent country captive, came through the conflict sadder about peace.

One by one, Jephthah honed his sons to begin life's journey as sassafras and come back home as sterling. He sent Samuel, the eldest, to sea to graduate. Resolve, the middle boy, finished his education in the business, apprenticed to the countinghouse. Jephthah's first daughter, Rachael, went to a Liverpool cotton factor in exchange for ten years of favorable credit.

American-born Benjamin attended Harvard College, even finishing a degree. Business steady, Jephthah let his youngest drift into advanced study of Botany. The mere existence of such a field instilled in Jephthah a scornful pride. Two other American-born Clares failed to outlive the school of their infant diseases.

Clare and Sons had only to hold up their hands and let the magic skein of trade loop itself around their outstretched fingers. Nothing new arose along the self-replenishing arc except the *ad valorem* matching of the needy with the need. But whatever value the Clares added by moving goods to their proper locales, the events of 1828 conspired to negate. In that year, all liquidity threatened to evaporate.

The laws of God shipped cotton to Liverpool and sent it back to Boston as whole cloth. The laws of the fledgling Senate rose up and inquired: whither, and why? Could not government simply say how much a thing would cost, and thereby make worth's rivers run down hills of our own devising?

But the Tariff of Abominations turned on its makers, erasing twenty years of native industry in one stroke. Sowing protection reaped disaster. Prices for raw materials and fabricated goods exploded overnight. Yankee commerce burst in air as convincingly as Key's celebrated bombs. Tax now sucked all advantage from Clare's intricate system of interlocking runs. The voyages out paid too little to foot the crippling return leg. Receipts failed to pay off costs. Trade no longer even broke even.

Clare the Elder grinned at having lost the last roll of the dice. He made ready to deliver himself to earth's long deficit. For his wife, he arranged what hedges against destitution he could. Then he headed for the coffeehouses on Long Wharf to wait for the winds to change. He left it to his sons to tidy up the last entries in Abomination's double ledger.

Funerals are for the living. Her mother liked to say that. More times than Laura cares to remember. Death was different, a lifetime ago.

She leans in to the mirror, trying not to block her own light. It should be easier, making up in full daylight. Her eyelids say otherwise. She closes one, touches the tip of a pinkie to adjust the indigo. They used to go to a funeral every other week, when she was little. Kind of gone out of fashion these days.

She lightens the lines at her eyes' east and west, wresting her girlhood's gaze back from its wrinkled halo. She stares into the silvered glass, looking for herself at age ten. Hearing: *Funerals are for the living.* Thinking: *Funerals are for my mother.*

She tries to imagine her father in a dark suit, shaking hands, standing about looking solemn. Bearing a coffin or driving in the cortege. Doing the heavy lifting, that bare minimum of the joint tenancy contract that males always get away with. But he does not come back to her, even that much.

Her mother runs all her memory's funerals. Baking the stupid spinach casseroles. Washing the picked-over plates that people leave all over the dead person's home. Shushing the shrieks. Keeping the collapsing widows from flinging themselves into the open dirt hole. Visiting the deserted, three times a month for the rest of her own abbreviated days.

Laura worries her mascara brush through miniature arcs. She flicks her lashes like a fresco restorer, returning what time has hidden. She tilts her head against the harsh fluorescence, and suddenly that missing girl stares back at her, caught in mid–girl's thought. *Funerals are for my mother. I'll never have to do any of this. Look at polio. Look at smallpox. Disease is just a passing holdover from when we lived wrong. It's all been a terrible mistake. My parents and their friends: the last generation that will have to die.*

She looks again, and the girl is gone. Her face has become her mother's, despite the blush. She sports her mother's little tics and turns. Her voice is her mother's, even this afternoon, trying to console Ellen, telling her that funerals were for the living.

Her first must have been Uncle Robert. Laura, maybe eight. Her uncle, a T-shirted ex-Marine in those three stray Polaroids. A healthy ten years younger at death than she is now.

Would you like to go to the wake? that voice, now hers, asked her.

The question, too much to answer.

That's fine, sweetie. Sometimes people like to remember others the way they . . .

No, no: her horror, squeezing up into her throat like puked sour milk. Panic jamming the exits, like a crowd in a burning theater. Wake? They're going to try to *wake* him?

Later that year, the funeral of a man at church who got electrocuted in a lake in Wisconsin. Distant enough to turn out without much distress. Laura and little Scotty, starting middle school, there just to learn forever never to swim in a thunderstorm.

After that, her last surviving grandparent, her father's mother. A merciful death, by any measure. Surely better off, wherever she was going, than in her body during its last four years.

Worst was her mother's sister, a closed-casket car wreck. The death was easy. What it did to the living almost killed her. Watching her mother in her grief. The woman she knew best in the world, an utter stranger. Her mother's own funeral was a blessing in comparison.

Then Don's mother, who even before Laura and Don got married liked to send Laura Christmas cans of high-fat Virginia nuts signed "Love, Mom." That absurdity of the surgeon's: the operation was a success, but she died in recovery.

The thought strikes her as she finishes her face. As she makes her lips look as if she has done nothing to them. Ellen's first funeral, and she's already twice as old as Laura was at her first. But Laura's first was a vague abstraction. Ellen's first is her girlfriend Nan.

Everyone knew, and no one admitted. Nan at the end, almost invisible. Away most weeks, until Laura lost track. The last four months, chasing specialists, up in Minneapolis, out in Boston. Then wasting at home, eclipsed in her growing bed, body a brown curl of hair snipped and laid upon the pillow.

The girl that died was half the size of the girl four years ago, the one Laura met when she sold the Liebers that split-level on the rolling lot across from what was then still cornfield. Ellen had come on the last house visit prior to closing. The real estate agent's braided, same-age kid: probably helped nail down the deal.

The two girls hated each other. Some altercation involving one of them flinging the other's Malibu Ken Grungewear out the Aerostar's window. A year and a half later, they were inseparable, swapping wardrobes all the way down to each other's favorite shoes and socks. Nan still used shoes, still walking then.

Ellen's port-wine birth stain, meeting Nan's almost imperceptible limp. *Say anything about either one of us and you're toast.* An unspoken mutual defense contract, binding them together for life.

But birth stain lifted. Four trips under the laser lightened Ellen's shame. Plastic surgeons burned her crimson temple back to normal. Nan cheered the emergence of her friend's belated beauty, even as unstoppable rot ate away her muscles.

Ellen was their designated emissary, in the last months. Their runner, their diplomat, their spy. Launching forays for both girls into the kingdom of boys and boy products. Returning her awful intelligence reports at regular intervals. Seeking advice, long after Nan could reply. Nan, paralyzed foal, bent in the bed sheets, peering up through unfocusing disks, gurgling her guttural placeholders for delight.

Laura followed Nan's downward progress, in all the things her daughter wouldn't tell her. All the scraps from silence's table. The specialists were a bust. Nan weakened with each meal she failed to work down her throat. Her muscles frayed like shoelaces tugged on beyond their allotted span.

The grapevine passed along the updates, with all the meticulous attention it pays to the grim. No one could claim ignorance. But no one followed out the girl's curve to the only place it could land. No one once practiced for this early graduation.

Tim refuses to go to the service. "I'd rather remember her how she was." In fact, he'd rather stay home and play on the computer. He's been logging way too many on-line hours these days. Laura needs to start rationing him, force him outside, get him a bike or something equally archaic.

She chooses a natural, leafy scent that will not clash with massed funeral bouquets. Ellen is a mess. "Honey, not a sweatshirt. Don't you want to look nice?"

"No."

She wants to look the way they used to look. She wants to wear what they wore, when they wore things together.

"Let me at least fix your hair."

"Don't you dare touch it," Ellen threatens.

Late, they scramble to the funeral home. Laura scrapes the front bumper on the curb, pulling up too hard. They find two metal bridge chairs at the back, for the overflow crowd. Ellen slams down, begins instantly to pulp her program to shreds. Folding and refolding, a desperate origami attempt to flush the leaden words into flight. Laura sneaks sidelong looks at her, every three minutes. Her daughter's neck droops forward like an aster in September, choked under pollen's profusion.

The preacher—who obviously didn't know that little girl from Eve—delivers from the makeshift pulpit every Nan Lieber story that he could collect from grief. Fierce Nan, insisting on a block and tackle for the tree house. Imaginative Nan, inventing elaborate tales of her past lives. Studious Nan, just before leaving school for good, entering herself as an exhibit in the student science fair.

The memorial seems designed for no purpose but to torment the survivors. Laura watches the stunned parents up front, slack in emergency's sudden vacuum. The stoic living kids next to them. The stranger doing the eulogy tortures them all with trophy portraits they'll never now be free of.

They sing the girl's favorite songs. They read from her favorite books, then her letters. Funerals are for the living, to punish them for all that they've failed to do for the dead.

Ellen refuses to go to the graveside. Laura would sit in the car herself, if she could get away with it. The casket could be carried by two underage pizza delivery boys. The baby brother himself could place it high up in the crook of a tree for safekeeping. This package not sold by volume. Some settling of contents may occur during handling.

The words spoken on the world's rim scatter mercifully in the spring air. Impatiens line the neighboring stones, flowering already, a week further along than hers. Forced in greenhouses, probably. Earth falls on the girl, as softly as the girl falls into the earth.

Don skulks awkwardly at the back of the mourning ring. Light blue suit, so wrong that it's not even worth being weary over. Permanent press, permanently wrinkled. Guilty obligation brings him here. Here for their daughter's grief, at least, if never for her triumphs. Laura gestures toward the car, trying not to hold his eyes. She gives them fifteen minutes. Too generous by five.

They follow the parade of mourners back to the Liebers' house. The house Laura sold them, how long ago? *Convenient to all locations.* A cruel joke, now that it has become the median strip of a major thoroughfare. A LumberLand sprouts from the farmer's headland that once fronted them. A hulking Computer Toys mother ship and 120,000 square feet of Food Universe set down across the widened intersection.

Stoplights march down an empty Broadway out to nothing on the horizon, a sight gag until the next expansion, four months from now. Harbingers of Phases III and IV, future transformations already planned well out into the next millennium. Wishes in a fairy tale that malevolently come true.

It's all private interests on the planning board. The town's four richest land-grabbers, jiggling with the zoning. The Liebers will never get out now, never recover the price she got them in for. Stuck forever in a three-bedroom split-level, Nan's bedroom an unbearable, uncleanable shrine.

Laura pulls up at the curb. They walk up the driveway, past the Lieber car, bumper sticker reading: "My Child Is an Honor Student at Lacewood West." Laura and Ellen enter the perfect place, head into the kitchen by instinct. There, Laura helps set out the breads and cakes, the dips and vegetable sticks. Ellen stands staring at the high-tide watermarks of growth penciled on the inside of the doorframe: Greg, age 8. Greg, 16. Nan, age 10. Nan, 11. Growth's Christmas Club balance, socked away, compounding for the future. The leapfrog laddering of days.

Adults pass through this branded doorframe, stopping to offer Ellen sounds of non-binding kindness. Laura takes Ellen's shoulder, turns her away from the doorway's stripes, tries to steer her back into the gathering. Ellen, not even furious, shrugs off her grip. Inconsolable now, unimpeachable. Gone for good.

Laura wants to tell her a truth bigger than the one she has just discovered. She wants to tell her daughter to give thanks for this first unlikelihood and say goodbye. But any words would be worse than the captions in real estate brochures. Finally, you just have to see the place. She gives Ellen a mother's hardest gift. She leaves her alone with disclosure.

They drive home through the no-man's-land of the north side of town. They skip past the new multiplex cinema, where famous actors play a variety of young adults with heroically surmountable handicaps. You can go your entire life without thinking twice about, say, Scottish nationalism, or astronauts, or those people trapped in that horrible mine collapse. And suddenly there are a dozen movies about it. In the air, somehow.

They pass the new Herefordshire subdivision, and the Clear Stream one. That little ski hill they're making out of all the artificial lake dredging. Two new interstate inns go up beside the Old Farms strip, for no reason that Laura has heard of. The town is exploding, without any good explanation.

They take the west route, past Clare Research Park. Mistake. Ellen gazes at the palace of swept steel and bronzed glass.

"Will Nan's father go back to work tomorrow?"

"I don't know, sweetheart." Meaning yes.

Laura watches the hatred form in her daughter's eyes. Hatred of everything. Of all business as usual.

Ellen snarls like a baffled house pet, wrongfully punished. She says nothing the whole way home. She even refuses to push the garage door opener, a ritual pleasure since forever.

Tim has gone out, miraculously, leaving no message. Laura, alone, drifts to the computer. She closes the windows from her son's games, begins to massage last week's contact tickler file. Ellen sits picking at the macramé table runner until it's ruined. Silent, frozen, giving her answer to life's exam: it's not worth getting close to people.

After some time, Laura looks up. "Ellen." Patient. Defensive.

The girl shrugs: it's self-evident. Beyond arguing. She takes the stairs slowly and closes the door to her room.

The girl is so young, too young to hold on to today's rage. So many more pencil marks ahead of her, each leaping from the last's shoulder. They will crawl up the doorframe, around the molding, out the window, and off. And Nan, frozen, small, will fall into the past. She will stay behind, preserved, a tiny museum mummy, shrinking each year by inches, until she vanishes.

The Blairs are asking one hundred thirty-two for the Cape Cod on Windsor. Nate Webber will make some kind of silly counter in the neighborhood of one oh two five. The trick will be keeping the Blairs from having a pique fit, while bringing them down enough to make Mr. Webber feel he's getting away with something.

Laura spins the mouse in tight, idle circles. She watches the cursor's ghostly vapor trail dart across her screen. *You'll see,* she apologizes to her child, now upstairs with the door closed, well out of earshot of this silence. *Someday. The dead want nothing of us but that we live.*

———

The winds of trade never did change for Jephthah Clare. Life's point drained from him as his seaborne trade withered under the tariff. A furious ingenuity, if not dementia, settled into his mind.

He took to living at Topliff's, trying to interest financiers and captains in mad ventures to escape taxation, visionary risks that made the Lord of all Creation seem a mere jobber. Shipping soiled laundry across the Pacific for scouring. Serving up muddy tortoise sweetmeats to France. Hauling African termites to Canada to clear the northern forests. All Clare needed was backing.

He died still awaiting those backers. It fell to Clare's sons to devise a practical plan for surviving Abomination. Samuel chafed against the injustice. America, he raged, had fought the Revolution over a tax now dwarfed by the one it levied on itself. Resolve, his cooler brother, pointed out that a second revolution would probably be prohibitively expensive.

The punitive tariff aimed to protect New England's infant textile industry. The fully integrated Waltham model factory brought whipper, willow, picker, lapper, breaker, winder, finisher, drawing frame, double speeder, stretcher, carder, throstle spinner, speeder, warper, dresser, loom, bleacher, printworks, cutter, sewer, and sundry other intermediaries into a continuous operation. Steam, water, thundering machinery, and small girls' hands took production from fiber to finished garment. And tariff meant to shepherd that garment to market.

Yet the tax wiped out all potential export profit by making it too expensive to haul any cargo back. Ships could not pay for themselves if empty for half their time at sea. The age of the all-purpose merchant was ending. Trade had lost its status as favored child. Law now preferred the bastard manufactory to the pedigreed countinghouse. Yet how could manufacture flourish, without trade?

Some solution, Samuel insisted, must exist. A God that fashioned a mind capable of conceiving salvation while denying it that deliverance would have long since derived all available amusement from the arrangement and closed up shop. Resolve agreed, but added only that the burden of salvation lay not with the Creator but on their own ingenuity.

What trade good might still command prices inflated to twenty times its real worth? Resolve put the question to Benjamin, whose interest in the practical concerns of his older brothers was exactly nil. The youngest son had sought in Harvard a refuge from this same family business that now tapped him for answers.

But *Vanitas* was always *Veritas*'s most driven student. Benjamin took the tariff problem across the river to his students' quarters in Brattle Street, Cambridge. He rode back to Temple Place some days later with his reply: the only imports that tariff could not wither were those absolute necessities. Twenty times invaluable was still invaluable.

Several disastrous cargo runs proved this conclusion wrong. For nothing could be counted a necessity in this newfound land. Any foreign-supplied need, rendered so exorbitant, quickly gave place to cottage commerce. Self-reliance tolled the death knell of sale by extortion.

Benjamin returned to his tropical phyla, more than ever convinced of commercial futility. But while sketching the *Vanda* orchid's leaves, their ever-higher laddering conversions of light's energies, he grasped in a blink the perversity of economics. He looked upon that place where money parted from value, where polishing might bring out the best knot in the American grain.

Ben returned to Boston with the prize his brothers sought. The answer lay not with necessities but with their very opposites. Frivolity: the only merchandise whose sales could survive a frivolous increase in price.

This time, the market bore theory out. Most of the family's packet runs now lost money with foolish consistency. The small but intriguing exception involved an unlikely import called Pech's Soap. Pech's Cleansing Ovals cured an itch that Americans did not even know they had until the scratch announced it.

Pech's Soap, in its native England, was a mild toilet soap for the middle classes. Unlike domestic soft soaps, it left no residue on the skin. It smelled citified, proficient, slightly tart, slightly sweet. Smooth, consistent, sophisticated, it glowed a pleasant, pale orange. Beyond that, it was just soap. Clare and Sons would not have touched the product, but for the need to fill their empty holds upon return from London.

No one in his right mind would pay to import soap. Waste fats, potash, and brine: a household produced soap as the body made excrement. Importing taxed soap made as little sense as bottling spring water or charging a fee for air.

But on this side of the Atlantic, the Tariff of Abominations suddenly marked up the banal into the realm of luxury. Pech's Soap grew exotic, exclusive, foreign without the taint of immigration.

Samuel and Resolve's promotional strategy resembled Jesus swearing His disciples to silence over the latest miracle. The impertinent price bore witness to some hidden amplitude: the perfect, extravagant gift. For objection to extravagance could not hold out against something so practical as soap. Pech's left on the skin the cachet of forgivable indulgence, the corsage of a giddy night of courtship dried and pressed into the family Bible.

In a land where a third of everything ownable lay in the hands of a mere one percent, the very ruinous price of import produced a premium that domestic soapmakers couldn't duplicate. Too, purchase had something antinomian to it, a vote against the tyranny of majority rule. Freedom of choice meant freedom to choose economic irrationality. Available in the United States of America by exclusive arrangement with Jephthah Clare and Sons, Long Wharf, Boston.

For two brief shipments, Pech's Soap helped to offset the Clares' mounting losses. But the windfall was not to last. Imitating importers fought for a sliver of Clare's elite niche, finding products to peddle that were just as English and machine-perfect. And the flood of imitations defeated the very exclusivity that Cleansing Ovals had so briefly serviced.

As Tocqueville, the French chevalier, was just then discovering, no blooded aristocracy matched the economic meritocracy for harshness.

———

Soap is a desperately ordinary substance to us. It is almost as omnipresent as air and water. It is so common that it is difficult to imagine life without it. Yet soap is probably the greatest medical discovery in history . . .

Not until modern industry came along to demonstrate the virtues of mass production did soap become the property of all the people.
    —*Into a Second Century with Procter and Gamble*, 1944, no author

———

Crowds forever packed the public landing, within spitting distance from the slip where Clare's packets tied. They must have milled there in force the afternoon the *Sea Change* came in and the Irishman Ennis and his wife set foot in the New World.

The harrowing crossing had been but a pleasure cruise, compared to the privation it freed those two from. All the way out, man and wife celebrated their escape from bondage. For seven years, Robert Emmet Ennis had been another man's indentured servant, bound "to abstain fully from drink and fornication and theatre and all other excess . . . and to serve his Master gladly in all requests both day and night." In exchange, the grubbing English master had kept the letter of his word, instructing Ennis "in the fine art of chandlery."

For half an ocean, nothing could touch the pair. They sailed to a place where their own labor would reap their own increase. Soon the strength of their backs and the force of their spirits would settle the measure of their fate.

This thought took them three-quarters of the way to Georges Bank. There Cathleen began to defecate what, by landfall, became a stream of silty water. But by the time they entered Boston Harbor, Cathleen, delirious with fever, thought she was entering the Kingdom of God on earth.

Her annihilated body held out until it touched soil. And on the public dock of that sweet prospect, amid a crowd not so much indifferent as busy, Cathleen Ennis succumbed to fulfillment and dehydration.

Her husband camped out by the wasted corpse. He stood watch over her, smoking a clay pipe, studying the three hundred yards of America he could see. Their life together here, in this all-possible place, had come to this one, impossible end.

Your wife is sick, a concerned merchant slowed down enough to inform him.

My wife is dead, Ennis assured his new countryman.

After a while, the harbormaster demanded he remove the corpse.

Where? Ennis asked. Why?

The Charitable Irish Society helped the man find lodging in the North End, walking distance from the pier where his wife had come to port. As charity cases went, Ennis was a king. He had both a little money and a stock in trade: magic beans of no small worth in this fairy-tale place. All he now lacked was a reason to go on living.

The warren that he lived in crawled with the unemployed. Machines had eliminated some. Others had lost the scramble for employment to their fellow desperate thousands, streaming in through all the country's ports. Only the promise of unlimited land—the hopes of another lottery farther West— siphoned off the squalid overflow and averted certain revolution.

A month sufficed to teach Ennis the ropes. No social pyramid was more steeply pitched, more needle-tipped than this one. America rigged the race for the swift. Ennis no longer cared to win that race. But he owed it to the memory of his wife, the myth they once shared, not to be eaten alive.

He sank his entire remaining purse into equipment, a starving man spending his last dinner dollar on a new recipe. In a ragged lot behind his building, he hung a cast iron kettle with wooden sides above a boiling pit. The frames, molds, and wick plaiter filled his rented room, taking up the space his wife would have lived in.

———

MEETING THE CHALLENGE OF A GRAYING AMERICA

Two older but distinguished men in tennis outfits, at the net, rackets at rest, shake hands after a fierce volley. The drier one jokes, "Another set?"

The other pants gamely, "I thought you'd never ask."

A male voice-over intones, "By early next century, more Americans will be retired than will be working."

Blackout.

Investment Services

CLARE MATERIAL SOLUTIONS

And so one frigid night in 1830, a bull Irishman trawled through Temple Place toting on his back a wooden wedge full of candles. He'd found those privileged enclaves of the city where no one had boiled their own animal fats for a generation or more. Some nights, those neighborhoods favored him with a sale. For every class of people needed clear and lasting light. And those with some leisure used more light than most.

Resolve Clare answered Ennis's knock on that discreet, Federal-style door. He made to send the peddler away before the latter could begin to hawk his wares. But Samuel, noting the poor man's shoes, intervened. He purchased the modest minimum that politeness allowed. The peddler thanked the men and pushed on into the frozen black.

No sooner did their door shut upon night than Clare's sons fell to arguing. Resolve upbraided his brother. Hadn't they agreed to guard against unnecessary expenses until some fresh cash came in?

Samuel demurred. Nothing was necessary if not candles.

Not these candles, his brother argued. We have a stock of good light.

We are not yet so destitute that we can't help those less fortunate than ourselves.

We will be, Resolve insisted, if we take to throwing good money after cheap tallow dips.

The candles turned out to be no cheap tallow. They were no luxurious spermaceti, either. Yet they gave off a hard, cold light. Firm to the touch, they burned almost as slowly and cleanly as the best-boiled whale oil.

More than once, Resolve asked his brother how much they had paid for the sticks. Samuel, more than once, shook his bewildered head at the answer.

For the space of a week, Resolve kept a vigil. He could not remember the precise day or hour the Irishman had come through. There was no means of finding the man again except to watch the street and lie in wait. Days went by, and the chandler did not return. Their parsimony had driven him away.

Only by chance did Resolve find his quarry. He saw the Irishman from afar, toting his candle wedge near the fish market. He chased down the peddler and identified himself: a customer who had bought a few candles from him some weeks before.

Ennis immediately offered to refund the purchase price. Some defect of wick or wax might somehow have escaped his examination.

And just as quickly, Resolve knew what he was dealing with.

From whom did you buy these? he asked.

Ennis thought a moment. The words came out one by one, like tapers cracked from the mold. He sold for no man but himself.

You made these candles?

The question brought Ennis up short. Who wanted to know? They were good candles, his jaw contended.

Resolve offered to buy all the candles upon Ennis's wedge.

The bid only fired Ennis's suspicion. He agreed to a sale, but for not a penny less than the price previously agreed upon.

The words both bewildered Clare and confirmed him. Could the fellow make soap as well? A good toilet soap? At—at something of a commensurate price?

Ennis snorted. Could a horse make mules? Soap and candles were the same line of work. In fact, his stearin candlemaking, as a happy by-product, produced a red oil that would make a better soap than half the rubbish that people in these parts got away with selling.

Saying even this much, Ennis fell into horrified silence. He stood penitent, swinging on that flapping barn door, watching his mare bolt happily down the lane.

Resolve smiled and asked if he could see the man's candle works. Ennis refused.

Resolve smiled again and asked if Ennis cared for a drink. Ennis did not.

That red oil, Resolve asked, stone-faced. The words caused his antagonist to study his shoes and drift off.

Resolve inspected Ennis's carrying wedge. He calculated the cost of rendered fat, the number of candles a lone man might make, the hours in a day, the time it would take to sell as many candles as one could carry. He did several quick products in his head. He extrapolated outward, to include the costs of this man's apparatus. He then figured how much cheaper these stearin candles might come into existence at, say, ten times this man's production rate.

Sight unseen, Resolve Clare offered to buy all the equipment Ennis now owned, plus a figure that would comfortably cover all Ennis's costs for a year.

The Irishman stared at him. You want to give me this? This money?

My brother and I, yes, would like you to come into a business with us. Making candles. And soap.

Surely this mechanic was the kind of man who saw that a right fit needed no preaching. Yet Ennis insisted on thinking. He thought so long that Resolve began to recalculate. Then resignation clouded the laborer's face. At last, Ennis declared that he would take the cost of his equipment as well as the suggested salary. But he demanded a third, smaller sum, up front, in cash.

For a long time afterward, it irked Resolve. Not the pitiful extra sum that Ennis had held out for. The Clare brothers paid Ennis's demand without a second thought. But Resolve hated the idea that he had misjudged the man. He would have staked the Clare reputation on his sense that this Ennis was above bargaining. But the man had bargained.

Time, that universal solvent, dissolved the mystery. Resolve learned the truth some while after the three men set up shop and produced their first joint slab of soap. Ennis had held out for the most specific of capital investments. The pitiful sum just covered the cost of digging Cathleen Ennis a real grave.

OUR GET UP AND GO
JUST GOT UP AND WENT

How would you like
- to run your lawn mower . . . on garbage?
- to power up your computer . . . with light?
- to light your whole house . . . with bacteria?
- to take a little joyride . . . on hydrogen?
- to play your favorite hits . . . with nothing but the heat of your hand?

A man stretched out at the beach watches a woman in an apricot one-piece plunge into the surf. He holds a tiny portable radio between thumb and index finger. Through the earpiece there issues a tinny but unmistakable "Getting better all the time."

The Energy and Fuels Group
CLARE MATERIAL SOLUTIONS

Two weather-beaten men gossip in line in front of Laura at the Bounty Mart. They must be farmers. They have that natural-history skin. Farmer's tan—beet red from the top of the wrist to the middle of the upper arm, and ivory above. They've come in from the outlands, like the accidentals that stumble bewildered upon her finch feeder. They've wandered back into town to be hospitalized or die.

So odd to her: Lacewood, with its billion-dollar money machine, sitting in the middle of this scattered Stone Age tribe. Farmers always fill her with vague shame. She, an amateur gardener, a dabbler in drippy slipperworts and lilies, a potterer whose most useful crop is chives, having to mince around the real growers, the only people on earth whose work is indispensable.

How do they live? Homesteading in those hundred-year wooden boxes on their little knolls in the middle of nowhere. The houses go onto the market now and then, when all the children die or move to Chicago, selling out to inevitable Agribiz. She brokers them now and again. Tons of white pine wrapped around a sump pump sunk into a hummock. Irreplaceable. But not much of a market, except for Sawgak junior faculty who want to get back to nature.

She wouldn't know how to talk to these men if one turned around and chatted her up. All she can do is take from them. These boxes of multigrain cereal. The corn dogs that Tim eats unheated, right out of the pouch. Ellen's tubes of fat-free whole wheat chips. The nonstick polyunsaturated maize oil spray. The squeezable enriched vegetable paste. The microwave tortillas. The endangered-species animal crackers. Everything in her cart, however enhanced and tangled its way here.

The line is slow. The cashier pages her supervisor for the fourth time, pleading for anyone with authorization to come unjam a bungled card payment. With infinite patience, the cash register commands, *Please make another selection*. The customer jabs repeatedly at a touch screen where a package of cold cuts does two-and-a-half gainers in holographic space.

On the magazine rack in front of the register, next to the free booklets of the monthly Next Millennium Realty listings, an issue of *Trends* beckons to her. Cover story on the New Spirituality. As the wait turns eternal, she starts to read. Former drug-abusing wild teen star says it's time for America to reexamine its values. Sexiest man alive divorces supermodel and turns Buddhist. Maybe something Ellen would read. Nothing better to do, she lays it on the belt with her other offerings.

The farmer in front of Laura, wearing a Deere Moline cap, says, "Right here'd be a great place to open a supermarket."

Without losing a beat, the Archer Daniels Midland Company Decatur cap next to him replies, "You'd make a killing."

The usual, resigned abiding that people who make their own way reserve for the weather, collective idiocy, and other things beyond their control.

Nothing Runs Like a Deere asks *Supermarket to the World*: "Doing any gasohol this year?"

"I'm in for about a dozen, fifteen. You?"

"Well, I don't know. They're all of a sudden making this big gluten push, you see?"

"That's part of that Europoort B.V. angle they're trying to pull off. You blink your eyes, and bingo. It's kickbacks all over the globe."

They pay for their pouch tobacco and reconstituted orange juice and disappear, chatting about futures pricing and getting one of those clip-on cellular modems so they can receive commodities reports while out hoeing the north forty.

Laura's turn. One by one her goods glide over the laser enfilade and surrender their bar-coded secrets. The name of each item appears on the LCD panel in front of her, like a teach-your-child-to-read machine. A machine voice chants each price out loud like hymn numbers.

"Paper or plastic?" the fifty-five-year-old bagger asks her. What is she supposed to say? Liberty or death? Right or wrong? Good or evil? Paper or plastic? The one kills trees but is one hundred percent natural and recyclable. The other releases insidious fumes if burned but requires less energy to make, can be turned into picnic tables and vinyl siding, has handles, and won't disintegrate when the frozen yogurt melts.

She panics. "Whatever is easiest," she tells the bagger, who grimaces.

On the way to the car, she catches herself limping. Hanging on the cart, favoring one side. It's a sickness. How she always gets everyone else's symptoms. Psychosympathetic. Choking to death on Don's asthma. Laid up with her colleagues' migraines. Or that nightmare on Elm Street: working for months to sell Bill Mason's split-level cinder block bunker while all the while trying not to mimic his speech impediment.

Now Nan. Laura, favoring her right side ever since the funeral. But was it the right leg, where it started, or the left? No sooner does she wonder than both legs start to throb.

A universe of things can go wrong with you. More all the time. When she was twelve, science had conquered all the diseases. Now look at the place. And the cost of the smallest accident: five days in the hospital—that weird thing with Tim's joints that they never diagnosed—would have wiped her out if it hadn't been for the Next Millennium group emergency coverage. How can people out west of the tracks live? Just going to the dentist must ruin them. She still hasn't paid off the kids' last trip. Still recovering from the shock of learning that the past tense of "floss" is "fleeced."

Behind the wheel, her arms start to feel cold, like Nan's after the clot settled in. She manages to make it home without incident. Fortunately, she hasn't started copying other people's crazy driving tics. She talks to the aggressive cars, backs them off, keeps them in their lanes. Man, woman, or machine:

everyone becomes "Ludwig." Nice going, Ludwig. Hey, Ludwig, it's my turn. An old habit of her mother's, picked up without her realizing.

The bagger used plastic. In the kitchen, the counter overflows with this week's haul. Three people, one week, eleven plastic sacks. She's going to build an addition. Maybe expand the dining nook out past the flower beds.

"Hey, guys. Salvation Army's back."

She hears Tim clicking in the next room, little soundblasted caissons rolling along, punctuated by subvocalized profanities. The war, going wrong on some encroaching front.

"Timmo? Ellie? I said, 'Hey, guys . . .' "

A "Hey, Mom" emanates from upstairs.

From the computer: "Yeah, okay. Whatever."

Ellen comes down to inspect the booty. She roots through the sacks, extracts a new requested commodity. Peanut sheets. Laura is not sure what problem the sheeting of peanuts actually solves. What was wrong with yesterday's peanut concept? The little oblong things? Or butter, for that matter? Sheets must be more manageable. More predictable, somehow. Flatter.

Anyway, they make Ellen happy. No mean feat, these days.

"Way to go, Mom. Bodacious." She peels off the first page of rubbered goober and pops the corner in her mouth.

"Ellen!"

"What?"

"I used that word less than four weeks ago. And all you could do then was roll your eyes at me."

"That was you, Mom."

"What's the difference?"

"It sounds stupid and pathetic when you use it."

All adulthood the enemy, since Nan died. For failing to intervene.

"You could help put some of this stuff away, you know."

"I could."

"In the cabinets, I mean. Not your gullet."

"What difference does it make? It all ends up in the toilet, eventually."

Laura says nothing. Nothing she can do for her daughter but limp with her.

It's not all grief. Raging hormones were already kicking in, even before Nan. Things will probably just get worse for another ten, fifteen years. Once her daughter turns thirty, they can be friends again.

Another volley of cybernetic mortar errupts from the study. It ends in a commanderly expletive, decidedly not "Nuts." Tim was better off in the hammering-ants-with-Wiffle-bats stage than in this one. Not so great for the ants, but at least Tim got some exercise. Worked his muscles. At least the bat was real.

Ellen disappears upstairs, squirreling away the peanut sheets. Lining her private nest with them. She buries her grief in fan 'zines, music with deeply suggestive lyrics Laura hopes she doesn't understand, and long phone conversations.

The last harvest burger brought in, Laura pours a Thirst-Aid for Tim and a loganberry-kiwi seltzer for herself. She takes the drinks into the computer room and sets them next to the speakers, using the mouse pad for a coaster.

"So, General. How goes the war?"

Tim twitches his shoulders. A deniable shrug.

"Hey, buster. I'm talking to you. Give me the order of battle, at least."

He takes his eyes off the screen for a second, inspecting this bizarre sneak attack. He sighs, the most he has moved anything above the joystick elbow all morning.

"This is a Stuka. This here is, like, Warsaw."

"Warsaw, Poland?"

"Just Warsaw."

The Stuka looks to her like a winged saltshaker. Warsaw looks like two ranch eggs over easy. She can see nothing more than a ragged, rushing, panning, zooming blur. Colored dots sloshing around. A tapeworm's-eye view of the dog's GI tract after he's gotten into a dish of bridge mix. Every so often, some digital Göring screams "Jawohl," and there's this bloodcurdling death rattle, like a lawn mower hitting a section of chain-link fence.

"What's that?"

"What?"

"That horrible noise."

He smiles. The most pleasure she's given him in days.

"Those are the 88s. We're movin'."

"Moving?"

"Movin' now, puss."

She thinks of a house she sold last month. That subdivision out north of Fairview, just airlifted in by helicopter. The new couple, Clare executives, and their little daughter. She stood in the treeless, bald lot with them. Across the lunar landscape, a common flicker clung and rapped at the polyurethane, simulated-wood-grain gingerbreading, completely baffled. Couldn't sink a hole and wouldn't give up. Living things never know when to.

"Sucker doesn't know what I'm doing. Rearin' back on his heels. Puss."

"Don't say 'puss.' Who doesn't know? Stalin?"

He takes his fingers off the buttons to glare at her. *Stalin?* "Rosen. That stupid sucker."

"Don't say 'sucker.' Rosen? You mean *Andy* Rosen? In Warsaw?"

"Jeez, Mom." Get an ethos. "Yeah. In *Warsaw*." The soundblasted digital signal for total disgust. "No. Jeez. Like . . ." Where to begin? "Like, he's on the modem?"

"You're using the modem to—?"

"You said if I paid for half of the local calls on the second phone, I—" He slams down the joystick. Rage starts to flare out of him again. "This sucks. Unfair. Why the hell do you think I got that stupid job taking those dumbass Citizen's Shoppers—?"

"Okay. Chill out. I said, *chill*." Maybe the nurse is right. Maybe she should consider that medication. "I didn't say you couldn't. I just didn't know you could."

"Could what?"

"Andy is playing this same game, on his machine, while you . . . ?"

"Duh, Mom. And right now he's wiping my butt. So, if you don't mind?"

"Oh. You mean me. It's called a diversionary tactic. Andy said he'd pick up the other half of the phone bill if I'd . . ."

She lets the joke fall into the silicon ether. Five seconds later, squeezing the trigger, Tim registers. He rears his head back and snorts. "Whatever."

He could be blitzkrieging anyone, there on the other end. Andy Rosen, his dad, some strange digital hitchhiker he's picked up from some bulletin board. Master of the Universe seeks fast-shooting companion with good communications skills for chat, file exchange, and occasional Eastern Front apocalypse.

She finally understands the appeal of the computer revolution. In virtual reality, no one can tell that you're twelve.

At day's end, she thinks, we'll all be disembodied. Mobile microcomputer puppets doing our shopping and socializing. Human heads pasted onto modem bodies. Insert your face here. Like those billboards that Next Millennium posts everywhere around town. Pictures of all the agents, half photo, half cartoon. Hers is a black-and-white passport photo superenlarged and stuck upon a generic fairy godmother torso complete with wings and magic wand. She sits on a haystack of sparkling bullion, underneath a caption reading, "Good as Sold." The kids wince every time they drive past the thing.

Her virtual billboard sits out above the parking lot in front of the Member's Discount Club. The store's $25 annual screening fee nags at her conscience, but there's just no cheaper place. Tonight's dinner, in fact, is a Member's

Exclusive. The Cool Juice comes from Bounty Mart. Bounty's the easiest place to reduce the fat and cut back on the sodium. But all the rest is Discount Club: the fifteen-bean Old Almanac soup, the skip-dippers, the frozen melon medley.

She's probably saved close to a fifth of the meal cost right there. And if Tim and Ellen let her get away with that twice a week, there's your membership costs back in a little over a month and a quarter.

But you gotta pay to play. Ante up: that's the catch. Hard to put aside a little bit for the future when the present is eating you alive. She's heard that folks from the west side will check into motels on hot days to beat the heat. Three weeks, and you'd have your air conditioner. But who's going to suffer through three weeks to get relief?

"A cyst is like a little ball of water," she tells the kids, over dessert. "They make a tiny incision. They hardly even have to use a scalpel."

"They just Shout it out," Ellen cracks.

Tim sneers at her. "Idiot."

"Geek."

"Guys. Please. I'm going in next Tuesday. You'll just go stay with your father."

When they go to sleep at last, she tries to catch up on the New Spirituality. But she can't stay with the article. A horrible thing, on the late show. Why do they rerun such nonsense? Some arrangement where the parent company owns a print of the film and the subsidiary cable racket doesn't have to pay royalties.

First you lose five sons in a war. Then someone goes and makes a feature film about it. Then they rerun the monster at midnight, forever. Until every child of every mother falls.

———

The scorn of his former business partners would have killed Jephthah, had impossible packet dreams not already claimed him. At least death spared the old man the indignity of his sons' fall. He did not have to witness Abomination drive a flourishing trading family into bastard handiwork.

Clare's sons had once sold Pech's Soap by the shipload. They knew the jobbers and middlemen. The paths of bulk distribution were to them like favorite country lanes. But neither ever imagined stooping to make the cakes themselves. Yet still, the drop from trading to making was less inglorious than the drop that awaited them if they did not find some way to make a living.

Prejudice crippled their venture from all sides. No bank would underwrite such a naked wager. No tooler stood ready to build the plant the brothers envisioned. Overnight, they learned the lay of the land: local manufacture had endless suitors, but no one wanted to marry it. Clare's soap, like American Business at large, threatened to expire, crushed under its own start-up costs.

Ennis brought his new owners to his North End tenement. He swore the Clares into a secret brotherhood. They toured the newly purchased candle works in the shed out back. Despite the crudity of the works, Ennis's knowledge of fats and oils flowed through each cranny. Once a man knows what he is doing, the Irishman declared, he can do as he needs.

The maxim struck both Samuel and Resolve with all the force of truth. Ennis's stearin process placed him well out in front of his rival Boston chandlers. He showed the Clares the closed boiling vessel where he split tallow in the presence of a few percent lime. The lime, Ennis guessed, started the process that heat and steam then finished.

Into this turbid boil Ennis sprinkled just enough sulfuric acid to dissolve the lime salts and precipitate them out as sulfate. Up from the resulting sea of glycerin floated the prized fatty acids. Ennis skimmed off the desired layer, clarified it, and clarified it again. He poured out the result into holding pans and waited for the fatty acids to crystallize into a lovely magma.

This he split again and pressed, squeezing out the liquid red olein oil from the solid stearin. He melted, purified, and poured the stearin into his molds, through which he drew his cleverly plaited wicks. Cold water set the molding. He cracked the finished candles from their molds and packed them into his wedge. The rest the brothers already knew.

While Resolve examined each mold and pan, Samuel looked over the scraps that Ennis referred to as his "books." Together, the Clare sons discovered how Ennis was able to make so wonderful a product and to sell it so cheaply.

The product's quality came from Ennis's innate perfectionistism. He lovingly repeated each purification beyond the point of visible improvement. Resolve asked about the value of such fastidiousness. Ennis scowled and declared that he would never let a cloudy product out his door.

As for these candles' remarkable price, the answer was even simpler. Ennis had been systematically selling at a loss. He could not bring himself to ask more for his obsessive craftsmanship and superior chemistry than the going rate for inferior light. And he refused to do the math and see where business was taking him. The Clares did the projections for him. Had they not come along at that moment, Ennis would soon have been unable to make sufficient candles to cover the cost of his rendered fat.

The Irishman defended himself. He had been building up casks of the by-product, olein. When the cash ran out, he planned to do something with his stockpile of red oil.

What? Resolve asked. Make a perfect soap that you could go and sell below cost?

Yes, Ennis insisted, without saying anything. Lose money honorably, until some wealthy backer came by and salvaged him.

—From *A Tale of Soap and Water: The Historical Progress of Cleanliness,* by Grace T. Hallock. Copyright 1928, the Cleanliness Institute. ("Review copies free to school administrators. $12 per 100 in lots of 25 or more.")

Soap appealed to Samuel because it put the purchaser next to godliness. Resolve liked it because the purchaser used it up.

Scavenging what they could from the North End candle works, the brothers and their Irishman rebuilt the workshop on a larger scale. They moved the equipment out to Roxbury, closer to supplies of rendered fat. The new factory combined candle- and soapmaking, feeding the scraps of the one to the other's maw.

Resolve and Samuel commissioned a huge, iron-bottomed soap kettle. They built the best crutcher, tanks, frames, and drying racks they could. All three men scorned false economy, each for his own reason. Profit depended on the efficiency and quality that only superior equipment would give.

The plant's dedication was a select affair, involving just the three of them. Ennis allowed himself half a flute of the christening champagne and sang a song his wife had loved, called "May Fortune Smile." Samuel prayed for the Lord's benediction, then set a modest production goal for year's end. Resolve, surveying with pleasure the first fruits of their labor, looked out over the new equipment and cackled a joke about Mrs. Whitney and her husband's interchangeable parts.

Saponification was a complex affair, a delicate marriage of science and idiosyncrasy. The four-day boiling process involved much poking, prodding, and tasting on Ennis's part. He determined the exact ratios of lye to red oil with a mix of algorithm and whim. He killed and caught the stock, steering the kettle back and forth between alkali and fat the way the old Clare captains navigated the Strait of Magellan.

He gauged the soapy strings adhering to his stirring paddle, awaiting the exact moment when the soap grained and salted out. He cut the steam and drew off the salt lye and glycerin, letting his broth set like a temperamental soufflé. He lyed and boiled, boiled and lyed, awaiting strong change, the moment when the mass turned transparent and became another animal.

When the curds rose up like polar bergs, he cooled the mixture for several days and again decanted it. The batch settled into a parfait of soap, caustic nigre, and sedimented lye. In this standing rainbow, each crudeness floated to its own level. He skimmed the soap off the surface like scum off a pond. He washed off the impurities, pitched and finished the purified mass.

Until this point, he let no Clare near the broth. One cook: that's all that the world itself had taken. One skilled pair of eyes and hands, one nose, one tongue. Out of the kettle and into the crutcher, the soap became public domain. Only then did Ennis trust the others to mix and frame and dry and slab and cut. For by then the recipe was done.

The resulting slabs were a mystery to behold. Here was a substance, grease's second cousin. Yet something had turned waste inside out. Dirt's duckling transformed to salve's swan, its rancid nosegay rearranged into aromatic garland. This waxy mass, arising from putrescence, became its hated parent's most potent anodyne.

To make their first run, they paid cash for a quantity of fine rendered fat.

Thereafter, they sought suppliers who would trade good tallow for excellent soap, a pound for a pound. As their process made two pounds of soap for each pound of introduced fats, they would have half their run left over to pay for alkali, keep the equipment repaired, and put bread on their own tables.

Only when Resolve gazed upon that first readied ton did he consider their odd position. Their own customers would be their chief competition. Caked soap was still an expensive substitute for the slippery paste that every home could yet make as a matter of course. The Clares' soap had to teach thrifty New England how smelly, difficult, and undependable home soapmaking had always been.

To distribute their wares, Samuel and Resolve resorted to their old handlers. But these ancient family associates turned a deaf ear to the fledgling firm. The distributors knew the Clare family only as good merchants. Not one trusted such a late-day change of life, this willful descent to the mechanical ranks.

Weeks passed while the three men waited for some jobber to step forward and purchase any chunk of their stock, even on credit or commission. Desperate, Samuel drew up, at his dinner table, a crude advertisement which he ran in several trade circulars as well as the *Boston Directory*. The square of print bore much the same message as the wooden sign that hung upon the side of their shop:

J. CLARE'S SONS
JUSTICE AND SPRING STREETS, ROXB.

2ND DOOR NORTHWEST

MANUFACTURER & WHOLESALER OF ALL IMAGINABLE

SOAPS AND CANDLES

UNGUENT TO CLEANSE THE MULTITUDES   LIGHT TO LIGHTEN THEM

HIGHEST PRICES PAID FOR TALLOW

———

Chemistry is the art of separating mixt bodies into their constituent parts and of combining different bodies or the parts of bodies into new mixts . . . for the purposes of philosophy by explaining the composition of bodies . . . and for the purposes of arts by producing several artificial substances more suitable to the intention of various arts than any natural productions are.

—WILLIAM CULLEN, c. 1766

Whole lifetimes went by, with no sign of a sale. Ennis told the Clares they must lower their price. Resolve pointed out that no purchaser had even gotten close enough to inquire about pricing.

The afternoon of their first buyer, Samuel manned the shop alone. With the modest warehouse already threatening to burst, Ennis and Resolve had gone off to an ashery on the south coast, to secure potash at a good, bulk price.

Seeing a visitor after so long a drought, Samuel naturally assumed that the man had wandered in off the street to ask for directions. As it happened, the fellow actually did want soap. But he wanted a pitiful two pounds.

Samuel very nearly told the man his mistake: this was a manufactory. They dealt only in quantity. But given the trade until that date, two pounds *was* quantity. In the end, the gaping future suggested to Samuel that it might be wiser to go ahead and hack off a paltry piece from the slabs out back and proffer explanations later.

He wrapped the cut chunk and took the man's pittance. Only then did the customer ask to have the soap delivered. Samuel faltered, tried to pretend that delivery was a matter of course. The customer gave him a name and a street address. The street was in Charlestown, all the way across the water.

Truly God meant to sport with this enterprise. Samuel closed down the shop and spent the rest of that afternoon shepherding the anemic chunk to its destination. He could not, at first, find the obscure house, and so did not acquit himself of his delivery until nightfall. With riding expenses and lost shop time, that first sale cost the shop more than the costliest of Ennis's retail excursions.

Not long after, a prominent grocery factor, Matthew Fox, paid a visit to Justice and Spring Streets. He thanked the Clares on behalf of his cousin in Charlestown for what appeared by all accounts to be a very passable soap for both laundry and personal use. And well delivered, too, Fox winked at Samuel. He then placed a trial order for a thousand pounds of candles and a hundred forty-pound boxes of soap.

The Clares filled the order from inventory without problem. And with each crate that began moving out the door, word of the crates' contents shipped as well. Other factors and jobbers followed. But the Fox orders always remained privileged.

Another profit followed from that first commission. Samuel's eye in time settled upon the factor's daughter, Dorcas Fox. A suitably long courtship converted love into its market equivalent. Samuel married Dorcas, joining the Roxbury firm to its factor's family: the dowry of vertical integration.

Resolve, ever skilled with the books, calculated the total loss of Samuel's half-day junket to Charlestown. He prorated and projected. At last he declared that the service had left them a solid five cents in the red for that day. He mounted five large cent coins in an expensive oak frame. And for as long as he lived, on the wall of each subsequent office he in time occupied, Resolve Clare hung this framed keepsake, the five lucky cents the company had lost forever, in the course of that first sale.

———

Ninety-eight percent certain.

When Ellen reports the probability to her father, he flies off the handle.

"What do you mean, 'Ninety-eight percent certain'? Certain of what?"

"Search me. Certain that it's a cyst."

"That it's . . . ? You mean they don't even know it's a cyst? This is total idiocy. I thought they said—"

"Okay, okay, Daddy. It's a cyst."

"Then ninety-eight percent what?"

"Percent sure."

"Percent sure of *what*?"

"Stop harshing on me, Daddy."

"Harshing?"

"Don't yell at me. I didn't do anything."

"I'm not yelling." Furious, because he doesn't even know who to be angry at. "I'm not yelling. Sure of what?"

"I don't know. Sure that everything's gonna be cool."

"Well, why didn't they just say everything's going to be cool?"

"Because . . . how should I know? I knew I shouldn't have told you anything. Mom didn't tell me to tell you, you know. I could of just lied to you. Made something up. Would that have made you happier?"

"All right. Don't get excited. Don't get excited. Just tell me one thing. Was it someone at Mercy who told your mother that number? Did they say 'ninety-eight,' or was that just an estimate she told you guys, based on what the doctor—"

"Dad. I'm gonna scream. Know what that means: 'scream'? Just leave me—"

"No, I won't just leave you—"

"Just forget it. Okay? Lose it. It's only a number. It doesn't mean anything."

Her mother's head for figures. "It means—"

"It means they're saying the operation's not a big deal. So don't turn around and make a big deal out of their saying that it's not gonna be a big deal."

"That's supposed to make everybody feel good? Ninety-eight percent?"

Ellen storms from the room. Don doesn't bother to stop her. She can't tell him, anyway. Can't explain to him why doctors stoop to saying such crap. They say it because they think it comes across as some kind of professional reassurance. Cheerful, meaningless, and unprosecutable. That's what you get when your whole health care business is driven by fear of malpractice. They can't say *Shut up and relax,* as in the old days, because Suzy Homemaker has become Susan Super Health Care Consumer, and won't accept a professional's word as answer.

There's a woman gyny involved somewhere. Why not ninety-seven? Why not ninety-nine and forty-four one-hundredths? At least then the prognosis might float.

With Laura's head for statistics, it's completely possible that she doesn't realize that 98 percent means that "certain" is going to be wrong one week out of every year. Means that two people out of every hundred are going to come out of the procedure on a platter. Worse odds than going to 'Nam was.

It figures. The Laura that Don met, two decades ago, was a mathematical midget, an absolute arithmetic microcephalic. She could divide two numbers and not be surprised when the result was bigger than both numbers she started with. The woman couldn't even figure tips. Not even 10 percent, even with a good wind at her back. He tried to show her. But she just claimed that decimal points made her nervous.

When she wanted to get a job, Don helped her. They didn't need the money; he was doing fine. But she needed something, just to feel good about herself. He looked up tons of jobs she could get into without too much fuss. He drew up entire lists for her. *Real estate,* she finally decided, out of pure perversity. Just to be contrary.

Laura, he told her. *Get real.* Square feet, carrying costs, taxes, financing, percentage points, amortization. She'd be wretched. Worse off than she already was.

She insisted she'd be fine. Laura knows best. Always.

Of course she bitched and moaned throughout the whole year she sat in that damn school. What in God's name is a logarithm? How do you compound? But before he could even get out half of the answer, she'd start laying into him. Finally he had to quit helping altogether.

Then, of course, she had to trot out all the large-caliber emotional guns. The silent treatments at home and the shouting matches in front of their friends. Turns out he was always a controlling and manipulative personality. From the start, secretly trying to dominate her, run her life.

He put up with the antics for the time it took her to get the certification. He figured she'd get sick of it, give up, and choose a more realistic profession. But against the astronomical odds, she actually started to get the knack of calculation. Little gold stars on the homework. She graduated in the top third of her group.

How many honor students does that make in all? he teased her, for old times. To lighten things up. And she even smiled at that one. But about a month after graduation, the feces really hit the turboprop. She put on the little Millennium jacket, hung out the shingle, and discovered that she actually *liked* all that calculation crap. Hey: it's true what those public service commercials are always saying. Numbers *are* our friends.

She told him that all the trouble she'd had with adding and subtracting up until then might have been *his* fault. He never let her do any of the household computations. He always tried to protect her from the mortgage and the monthly statements. He kept the 1040s all to himself, every year, never let her near them.

He asked her why in hell he would have insisted on sweating out a Schedule A by himself if he thought for a second that he could stick her with half of it.

Because numbers were power, she told him. He made math seem harder than it really was. All these years, telling her she couldn't calculate, in order to cripple her and preserve his monopoly on decisions.

Yet for someone so badly crippled, she recovered nicely. Her grasp of figures in court had impressed him. When it came to the algebra of shafting, Laura was MIT material.

All right: so she can count to forty-two. So she can compound forty-two at .00274 percent per annum, ad infinitum. She knows that forty-two doesn't have to be old. But she has let herself get old. She's a half century if she's a day. And it's her own damn fault.

She lives wrong, from block to tape. From hair spray to toenail polish. If she paid attention to half the things he'd told her over their fifteen-year relay race to hell, she wouldn't look like her own mother already. He'd like to see her figure out the annual rate at which her weight's appreciated, since Tim's birth. Talk about your balloon mortgage.

He's four years her senior, but nobody ever thinks so. Their friends were always surprised, when they told their ages in public. He's kept himself up. That's the difference between them. Cross-training. Antioxidants. Halve your calorie intake and eliminate your saturated fats.

To Laura, health is an abstraction. "Why do you waste your time with all that running? How many miles do you want to go? Aren't you going to *get there* one of these days?"

No good trying to tell her he does it for his health. He once tried to explain it to her, using statistics. Never again. You can't change your number coming up, she just kept saying, no matter how many times he tried to say no, but you can change your number.

Now this cyst thing. In the end, you run out of evidence that doesn't sound like "I told you so." Not that she's brought it on herself. But you do have to take responsibility for what happens to you. To pay the check for the meal you've eaten.

That idea always eluded her. All fatalism to her. Sparrows falling. He tried to put it to her in her terms. Your flowers do better when you water and fertilize them, right?

"Some do. Others don't require fertilizing, Donald."

He tried to say he wasn't talking about fertilizer. He was talking about basic effort. Preparation.

She countered with her typical contrary bullshit. "Some plants do better than others, no matter what you do."

She probably thinks that 98 percent means 98 out of 100 people having partial hysterectomies are going to be fine, regardless of their surgeon or anesthesiologist or level of post-op care. She's probably done nothing at all to see who's cutting on her. Probably hasn't read a single word about ovarian cysts, or taken the first step to see if her gynecologist knows what the hell she's doing.

Don waits until Ellen leaves for her dance orgy and Tim heads out to his weekly Internet group crack session. Then he calls the hospital. Makes up some fumbling excuse about insurance company questions and misplacing the papers. He says, "This is Mr. Bodey."

When the receptionist asks, "Oh, you mean her husband?" he just grunts.

Despite Laura's total laissez-faire attitude toward her own life, everything does seem to be in order. The tests all indicate a benign fibroid mass on her right ovary. No biggie. A quick incision and sayonara.

Tim misses his curfew. He's in deep mischief. Again. The kid is living on virtual time. It's impossible to discipline him, when he lives at his mother's.

Between the two of them, he and Laura have failed these kids. They've failed to give them consistency, the one thing that every kid wants and needs.

Ellen comes home first. She sees Don lying in wait, and tries to make a break upstairs.

"Night, Dad. Had a great time. Catch you tomorrow."

"Ellen—"

"Don't want to talk about it, Dad."

"You can't not want to talk about it. Because I don't want to talk about it either."

She spins on the landing and pulls her hair. "Daddy. You're absolutely stark-raving me."

"Are you done yet? You don't even know what I want."

"I know what you want."

"What do I want?"

"Okay. All right. I surrender. What do you want?"

"Can you call your mother and say good night?"

Relative prosperity encouraged Resolve to follow his brother's example and marry. Samuel's choice of Dorcas Fox brilliantly united the firm with its distributors. Resolve set his sights even higher, upon the ultimate business match. He courted and won a mate who would lend the firm an aura of social respectability.

Julia Hazelwood played dawn to Dorcas Fox's faithful dusk. The niece of Elbridge Gerry, former governor of Massachusetts and Madison's Vice President, she'd suckled statesmanship with her mother's milk. She owned by birth what her husband could only purchase.

Where Dorcas ratified her husband's life with an invisible hush, Julia ruled Resolve by rowdy voice vote. Her modest frame exuded stature, and her reedy voice intimidated with the sound of its native intelligence.

Beyond all doubt, Resolve loved his wife. They fought fiercely, lived apart for months at a time, reviled and refuted and rebuffed each other. But theirs was a love match. Each scared the other into becoming more than either would have been alone. At times, they lost all common language, all mutual words. Fifteen years separated them in age, a span during which the world had overhauled itself into an unprecedented place.

Yet they understood one another. For above all else, Julia Hazelwood seconded the only truth Resolve ever swore to. She knew that the job of mankind lay in making much where there had been nothing, turning deserts into gardens, replenishing life's spent paths.

Julia was a freethinker, and she did not much converse with God. For God had said what He had to say to us very early on. Go forth, be fruitful and multiply, and have dominion over the earth. Beyond that, what was there to discuss?

Clare's Sons dutifully multiplied. They extended themselves through the flow of credit. They assumed their distributors' risks and passed them back to their suppliers. In an era when a fifty-dollar bill issued in New York returned forty in Maine on a good day, Clare's Sons broadened their contracts by the unprecedented practice of accepting distant bank notes at near–face value. Where needed, they resorted to cashless barter.

The crates went out, each marked with the Clare "C." Wholesalers sold the crates to stores of many stripes. And the stores, in turn, hacked from the slabs exactly the amount of soap that any one life's week required. Shopkeepers sold the cakes of anti-fat like so many wedges of immaculate cheese.

Protected for the moment from British undercutting, the Clares' patient spider spun. Cholera to the south, uprising in Philadelphia, even the burning of New York served only to increase Boston's need to ablute. By the mid-1830s, it seemed that if Clare's Sons could survive Emperor Jackson and the nation survive Nullification, the factory venture might very well pay for itself two or three times over by decade's end.

The Clares could not have profited more handsomely from their damnation. They sank into manufacturing at the precise moment when the railroad broke loose. The new, self-propelling engines began to fling mankind outward, and the expansion sucked all business along in its wake.

The first engines seemed to run mostly on hope. Rail cost outrageous sums to lay, a massive sink of both capital and labor. Trains were slower and less reliable than the creatures they competed with. Locomotives eternally exploded, setting fire to fields, boiling clientele alive by the hundreds per year. Extorted by canal companies, foreign interests, and politicians alike, the start-up railroad companies nevertheless plowed into the frontier, as inevitable as the grave to which all expansion leads.

The Clares, like rail, sought subsidy in wishful thinking. And wish proved the very stepfather of growth. Necessity had forced trade to cultivate the infant nation's industries. Soap made a virtue of that necessity. The Clares soon discovered that driving their own machines flat out was cheaper than letting them stand idle. Cost could be shared over greater volume. The more candles and soap Clare's Sons sold, the more return per pound they saw. By the time their kettle reached full capacity, Samuel and Resolve managed to set aside enough cash to hire on a few men. More hands resulted in more boilings, which made for still greater and cheaper quantities.

Ennis worked the changes. He stoked the blistering kettle, minded the coils, and tapped off the spent lye. He tinkered and tested, all the while humming to himself "The Lament of the Irish Emigrant." He employed every avuncular Erse trick he had to boost yields and turn out a neat soap as pure as any other. When he could increase the kettle's crop no further, he asked his employers to build another.

They brought a second kettle on line, larger than the first. Soon this kettle, too, minded by the new men, was boiling flat out. And crates marked with the Clare "C" continued to speed healthily out the door.

I need a new beast, Ennis declared. Something grand and unheard of. One that won't be old-fashioned by the time we've finished building it. I need a profound, magnificent monster of a new process.

Resolve eyed him with splendid superstition. What kind of process?

Well now. Have you heard tell of the Harrowing of Hell?

Resolve had not. And he reacted poorly upon learning the details.

Ennis mapped out the uses of the experiment. The increased volume would give them hard soaps with new oils: olive, palm, and cocoa-nut from plantations in the Malay and Africa and Feejee. They might learn to make a cheap castile, a mottled, a yellow rosin. In time, they would possess the capacity and expertise to mill fancy toilets—a rose, a musk, a bitter almond, a cinnamon.

The owners approached their baby brother Ben. They spelled out the flagrant plan: a kettle that could boil 30,000 pounds at one go. *Will it work?* Resolve asked the Harvard man.

Benjamin demurred. Sirrah's the chemist. I study plants.

It works in miniature, Ennis defended himself. It'll work bigged up to life-size.

For some time the brothers mulled over the gamble. At last they accepted the inescapable conclusion. The only way to make money is to spend it.

Samuel found a British-born mechanic to build the monster kettle. Anthony Jewitt had come to America as a young man with the idea of retiring by fifty and spending what remained of his life reading drawing room novels. By skill and effort, he managed to avoid starvation, and then some. But his foundry work left no time for reading of any matter. By the time Clare's sons entered his life, Jewitt had all but abandoned fiction.

In the empty lot adjacent to the Roxbury works, Jewitt built an open shed, three stories tall, to house the towering cauldron. Then he went about the task of casting the considerable stewpot. Neighbors came to marvel at the construction. Competing soap manufacturers from Boston and beyond came, too, first to spy and finally to laugh at Clare's self-prepared funeral.

Jewitt and his employers brought the monster into production in 1835, the afternoon the Liberty Bell cracked while tolling the death of Chief Justice Marshall. In fact, as Resolve later remarked, their kettle greatly resembled the said damaged goods, only inverted. And much, much larger.

———

In a crude block print, a cadre of the dead, replete with flowing gowns and tresses, rises up from holes in the ground. The recent corpses gaze astonished at their newly spotless limbs, the Last Judgment's supreme windfall. Beneath the image, a caption beseeches:

BE CLEAN IN THE EYES OF CREATION.
FOR HE IS LIKE A REFINER'S FIRE,
AND HIS GRACE LIKE FULLER'S SOAP

J. CLARE'S SONS
JUSTICE AND SPRING STREETS, ROXBURY
2ND DOOR NORTHWEST

———

Ennis's hell-harrowing kettle left its mark upon the Columbian landscape. Its fires sparked an economic lift-off that changed the Clare operation as profoundly as splitting and decanting changed your garden-variety grease drippings into *Savonnettes au Miel*.

For the first time, the name Clare circulated as part of the commodity it brokered. Clare's Soap offered the old quantity of self-reliance by another, more manicured avenue. It emitted a whiff of purity that one could smell even above the crust of horse droppings that fouled ankles from Noddle's Island to Southie.

The tax that forced them into manufacture gradually vanished. Years too late, Congress admitted that the tariff was a bipartisan swindle, one that backfired at disastrous cost to all parties. The fledgling native enterprise that had fared best under protectionism was Nativist riot. Belatedly, the over-steering skippers of the ship of state phased out the Abomination.

The tariff had killed shipping. Now repeal threatened to kill shipping's replacement. One by one, the economic props fell away, until nary a crutch remained. The high-water mark of protectionism receded, making way for a tidal surge of cheap imports. Yet to everyone's surprise, the House of Clare, even with all its struts kicked out, did not go crashing to the ground.

Habit had made a place for Clare in the lives of its customers. Habit, Service, and that most elusive quality, Quality. For in the two-way miracle of trade, their clients, too, had prospered. New goods entered their lives by virtue of exchange, goods in greater profusion, costing steadily less. Perfectly molded stearin candles; perfectly pressed olein soap. People—and more of them each year—grew to see these dependable goods as household familiars. Wholesalers liked the crates stamped with Clare's "C." And customers liked the moderately priced cakes hacked from those comforting slabs.

But with prices falling, profit receded. Resolve suggested they follow the widespread trend of short-weighting. Samuel reacted in horror.

We have not yet begun cheating our customers, Samuel declared.

Resolve grinned at his brother's righteousness. But he soon realized how fine a selling point the stamp of "Real Weight" had begun to make.

With rising volume, their station rose. Yet a rise in status only agitated Resolve.

We will never be anywhere near as famous as the Tappans, he worried aloud.

Samuel reassured him. Our wives know us. Our children will answer to us. And we'll never get mixed up in as many social caprices as those fellows.

Ennis got along equally well with the two older Clare brothers, as different as the men were. But he saved his adoration for Benjamin. He loved to harass the fellow, just for sport. Young Clare supplied endless recreation. The boy spoke more languages than was healthy for a person. That university of his was a staggering waste. Its library boasted how many books? And not one had a working theory of poverty. All the combined thinking of Harvard's finest had yet to discover how to keep the Irish in Ireland.

Botany did not seem a real subject to Ennis. What use is all that school chemistry, he chided, if you waste it on plants? Come work with us. We'll teach you some chemical chemistry.

But the college graduate's science remained the Irishman's secret envy. Ennis commissioned Master Ben to bring him a world of journals, on the most urgent of topics: the chemistry of oils and alkalis, scent and solubility. Ben hunted down the appropriate tomes. The boy made good those years invested in meaningless study by reading Ennis the scientific German and French. Ennis, in turn, instructed Ben in the way agricultural chemicals really behaved, outside the laboratory, in the crucible of experience.

Together, they isolated the source of soap's action. Ennis supplied the facts and Ben the explanations. One side of the filmy substance mixed readily with water. Somehow soap's microscopic shape—Dalton's atoms?—fit hand in glove with the inner shape of that fluid. By contrast, the other side of this slippery go-between meshed just as nicely with the greases and oils upon which water ordinarily remained unpersuasive.

So soap stood, a Janus-faced intermediary between seeming incompatibles, an interlocutor that managed to coax mutually hostile materials onto speaking terms. It removed grime by smoothing the way for the insoluble to be taken up into solution. Such the two men concluded, between themselves.

Ennis was a genius in the truest sense. He held an iron grasp on simplicity. His mind let ideas fall like water to their lowest basin. Then he made good on those ideas. For each school-chemical insight he gleaned from Ben, he had Jewitt build him a machine. Or rather, he got Samuel to get Jewitt to build, as the English mechanic and the Irish chandler would not speak directly to each other.

The Clare manufactory's happy dream of growth shot awake in the Panic of '37. Briggs Cotton Brokerage of New Orleans collapsed, pulling down the national pyramid of fiscal speculation. In the space of two months, the Clare brothers watched depression bankrupt forty thousand men and reduce more to starvation. The escalating crash drove ready cash from circulation and closed every New England mill except Stevens at North Andover, which survived by doubling working hours and increasing production.

With textiles dead, the whole region threatened to fold. Men who just last year had busied themselves with drilling Jerusalem's new seed now plowed themselves under, resigned to the long, all-winnowing winter.

Resolve and Samuel refused to wait passively for disaster. Instead they sallied out to circumvent it. For if any healing charm against disintegration existed, it was light and scent. Candles and soap, if not depression-proof, remained resilient enough to weather the storm. Volume might vanish and cash sales fall off as sharply as the great auk. But people still needed the things Clare's Sons had to give.

From their debtors, the Clares extracted food transfers, trade credits, and whatever various instruments of forgiveness they could secure. With this makeshift scrip, they settled up with their suppliers, for their suppliers had no choice but to take what they could. When pinch came to punch, Samuel and Resolve paid their workers in soap. All the soap their laborers' ragged dependents could ever hope to use.

What cash they could secretly stockpile went toward acquiring defaulting competitors for as little as ten cents on the dollar. The fewer the rivals lasting until recovery, the easier recovery would come. The Clare sons moved through the massacre, picking opportunities for philanthropy like the Lord's Passover angel spotting unmarked houses. All the while, Samuel bargained with and rebuffed their own creditors, stalling these financiers until one by one they, too, went under, with no one to take up demands for payment.

This nationwide misery trickled steadily downward, in that direction most favored by gravity. Depression gathered its scapegoats, some of whom Benjamin described in a letter to Boston from a field excursion to the South:

> I cannot ascertain precisely how many are affected, but the resettlement of the Civilized Tribes touches even those who own houses, who work the land as we do, who trade in our currency and worship as we have taught them. We send them many hundred miles, on foot, in the dead of winter, the sick, the aged, the women with small mouths gnawing hungrily at their spent bodies. They number not fewer than forty thousands in my estimate, and if the half of them survive to reach the deserts we have set aside for them out West, it will only be by virtue of the Government's count . . .
>
> On route from Atlanta, I found it my misfortune to witness a band of these forsaken. I cannot tell you what an ill-making education it is, to travel by rail at maniacal speeds, to stop for the night at another wayside inn, with its requisite print of General Jackson embarking on yet another heroic dash to save New Orleans, shimmying onto his charger, smoke emanating from nostrils (those of the horse, not of our General), and then to turn from this comfortable scene to see, through the window of the public room, a column of creatures struggling to build a makeshift church and altar, from which a Cherokee preacher might exhort his hopeless fold to remember the delivery of the Children of Israel from bondage!
>
> *Whose art thou? and whither goest thou? and whose are these before thee?* I asked myself at that moment, searching to revive in my soul some vestige of the religion these lost men yet practice with such surety . . .

Back in Boston, the recipients of this letter each resorted to his private reading. Ennis worried for the boy's safety among savages. Samuel feared for his younger brother's doubting soul. Resolve vowed to make the wayward philosopher join the firm and earn his practical living, immediately upon return.

But that return took the youngest Clare son some time. Ben did not come straight home, but made a four-year detour, shipping out from Hampton Roads with the United States Exploring Expedition to the southern polar regions. Quietly and quickly, before any other Clare could thwart his intentions, Benjamin accepted a position on the nation's first scientific voyage.

Nor could any Clare, in his wildest mercantile fantasy, have imagined that from such remote wastes would come the firm's salvation.

———

The full moon shines above her empty house. Tonight's blaze is so bright it almost tricks her nasturtiums into syncopating their circadian rhythms. Moonlight the width of a halogen spot pierces her bedroom window. Such a moon, were she home in bed, would keep Laura awake all night.

At home, she would lie stretched out in moonlight's cool puddle. Lie on her abdomen—no sign of pain; not even tender—gazing out at the tops of her trees. Her skin would explore these sheets of wrinkle-treated Wamsutta, sheets that, to her mother's soul's horror, she hasn't had to iron in years.

The sky is an indigo blue swirled with night cloud, like a fabulous Fabergé Easter trinket. The moon lasers a hole in the side of this egg's shell, through which God could blow out the runny yolk of the world.

Lying in this empty bed, head just below the sill, she could scan the peaks of her Scotch pines and Lombardy poplars. She and Don bought this house because of those poplars. How they throw about the midnight moonlight. Summer nights, it feels like her very own coastal cottage, even here, even in Lacewood, a thousand miles from the nearest sea.

How can Lacewood live, so far inland? The best that developers can do here is to set fake lakes lapping at the shores of new subdivisions. All the latest living communities, even the strip outlets, named for nonexistent water. Baytowne. Harbour View, with that silly little sailboat logo. Insane, of course. But anything vaguely nautical is easier for her to sell. And so the state is littered with invisible inland seas.

The moon that soaks her sheets glints, too, on these artificial whitecaps. Fabricated cornfield maritime beckons beneath her window, a view she isn't even home to indulge in tonight. And this is her ocean deliverance, the closest she will come to her fjord, her coastal opening.

She left the window open just a crack when she checked into the hospital.

Otherwise smells accumulate. Unpleasant odors, when the place is closed up. Probably radon, too.

The breeze that flushes these rooms imports its own aromas: stubborn lilacs and stultifying magnolias. Ozone from dry lightning, forty miles distant. Swiss almond decaf from the new coffee shop, half an hour from its red-eye opening. Organophosphates wafting in from the south farms. Undigested adhesives slipping up Clare's smokeless stacks. The neighbors' gerbil food and scoopable cat litter wafting over her fence in two parts per billion.

But mixed together in the air's cross-breeze, these smells sum to a short-hand for freshness. The day's background radiation. The scent that pine and poplar sprays, too clean in their chemical mimicry, can never quite emulate.

The house sits empty now, the scene of local evacuation. Her bedroom dark, except for the green light of her abandoned VCR, still blinking twelve, as on the day she took it from the box. Downstairs, her major appliances go on quietly working, keeping their programmed vigils. Delinquent burglar alarms ring the property, electronic sentries she never learned to activate, despite her husband's repeated efforts to train her. From her hospital bed, she hopes their mere existence will act as a deterrent. Ward off the easily impressed robber.

Someone might walk into her unguarded house and pillage it. Might pull up in a Mayflower van, posing as professional movers. Neighbors would take it in stride: the broken Bodey family, off on their next pilgrimage. Banks or the government might exercise eminent domain, rescind all the belongings that the three of them laid claim to. Reclaim all things durable or fleeting, natural or invented.

Everything she owns could disappear in her absence. Everything could vanish, from great-gran's priceless filigree to the cubic zirconium pierced-ear posts that Tim wrapped so patchily for her last birthday. Ellen's CD collection, the runaway hits now such passé embarrassments that only the most indiscriminate looters would take them. The computer, with its four game-years of *Panzer Attack* and its two real-years of irreplaceable client files. The Toshiba and the Westinghouse and the Sanyo. The records and canceled checks. The carpet smells. The Wamsutta sheets, faithless in moonlight, ready to serve whoever might steal them.

What happens to stolen things? Could she stumble across her own clothes someday, in an innocent resale shop? Does the fenced piece of filigree still carry her great-grandmother's ghost? Does the purchaser of hot data take over her clients? How much can a wallet photo of her kids be worth to a thief?

When the airplane ticket with your name on it disappears, the seat flies empty. Does the world get poorer when a hundred-dollar bill falls down a sewer? For that matter, does the world get richer when we strike gold or cut down trees?

What does it mean, to *own* something? Twenty-two hours of work equals one mulching mower plus shipping, handling, and tax. What is "handling," anyway? How much can such a thing really cost? Can someone work for nothing? What rises or falls in the country of human ransom when a fireproof safe goes up in smoke or a coffee maker arrives free in the mail? How do insurance companies decide how much to give you when starting you up again from scratch? How often can you start from scratch? And what about stopping from scratch?

She asks herself these questions, the ones people ask only on light-flooded nights, when comforts go ephemeral, threats solidify, and the town unmoors on its self-dug seas. She imagines herself wandering between her house and this hospital, where she lies on white percale. In her thoughts, she walks down to the old part of town, under much this same moon. Her mind strolls past the Riverton Mansion, where the Lacewood Historical Society, time's ground squirrel, digs up its stocks of artifact buried in bygone winters.

She's taken the kids once or twice. Townies can visit the museum for free. The mansion is a century-old, fossilized version of the Bodey split-level. Filled to the brim with fetish and talisman. Downstairs is a reconstructed apothecary shop from 1876. Its shelves sag under canisters, once the keepers of life-or-death cures, now collectible Sotheby's gewgaws.

Upstairs, in the nursery, the porcelain beauties in bloomers pout. The wooden palefaces and redskins stand erect in clothespin circumspection. The dumbwaiter that once transmitted the hour's urgencies is fused fast. Smoky, Gilded Age oval frames, like monster convex lockets, all bear restored portraits of heirs and heiresses. The pantry overflows with Depression glass, magnificently obeying the law correlating a decline in affluence with bursts of artistic fervor.

How long ago did she last take the kids through? An idle Labor Day four, no, five years already. She parked them in front of the hand linen press. The coal stove. The little toy horse. She asked them all the right questions. How in the world did they ever build these things? Make them work? Everything from zero. Think what it must have taken to . . .

But the kids wouldn't rise to the invitation. The thought was as lost as those archaic crafts—as carving or casting or filigree.

For the three of them live in a house trapped in its own made things, hard on the coast of a man-made ocean. A house whose uses she only sees tonight because she is not there. She looks up from her percale raft at the hospital clock. In squared red bars, it reads: 3:08 AM. Around her mechanical bed hum meters and dials, each one cold with purpose.

———

On the sixteenth of January 1840, a year and a half after the U.S. Exploring Expedition drifted from the Hampton Roads slips, Ben Clare's ship the *Peacock* sailed within sight of a new continent. The Assistant Scientific stood on deck, drawing the scene into his journals. His otherwise empirical hand capitulated on that day to dread and wonder. Sketch after sketch probed the pitiless expanse of field ice, while the black bowsprit beneath him plowed on into blinding white.

Passed Midshipman Eld had seen land first, from the rigging. Eld, the man who made a mockery of the Scientifics' efforts. Who slaughtered a mass of birds to demonstrate their lack of prior human contact. Who kicked half a rookery of *Eudyptes chrysocome* down a precipice on Macquarie Island, because the penguins had pecked at his trousers. Eld, the ass, held in contempt by all aboard ship, now promoted to a deathless landmark.

All that day, in mounting despair, the crew had sung that dirge of a fuguing tune, *Idumea*. Kentucky Harmony, United States Sacred Hymnody, on that Republic's fledgling mission to the sole place where commerce had not yet penetrated:

> *And am I born to die,*
> *To lay this body down?*
> *And must my trembling spirit fly*
> *Into a world unknown?*
>
> *A land of deepest shade*
> *Unpierced by human thought,*
> *The dreary regions of the dead*
> *Where all things are forgot!*

But after that day's momentous discovery, these same lines seeped up from the gun deck, bruised with American ingenuity. Some blasphemous bosun's mate uncorked his lungs in an airy magnum, lyrics for a newfound land, here at the edge of the known globe:

And was she borne to sigh?
To have her body ploughed?
And must his trembling finger fly
Into her patch so proud?

Embargoed sailors toasting a harlot's trade goods, a score of degrees south
of the last idea of woman. No song was what it was except through the
alchemy that cunning humanity worked upon it. Yet all human invention,
however impious, begged the same grace. *Forgive this song that falls so low
beneath the gratitude I owe. It means Thy praise, however poor. An angel's song
could do no more.* And God, in His arsenal of ironies, might yet find it in His
heart to forgive men their deep and leeward progress into unknown regions.

Surely He forgave the joy of a nation that dared such an enterprise. Congress's grandest hopes for the expedition fell short of the glory now in hand.
If any of the squadron made it back to port, years from that moment, they
would bring with them such a return on Washington's investment as never yet
rewarded government money.

Rumor of a southern continent had flown for years. But rumor vanished
into fact when Commander Wilkes entered Eld's mountains in the voyage's
log. Now humanity lived to drag foot onto that new land and mark it, to step
into the impossible place before surrendering one's hostage body to death.
The urge for a worthless souvenir grasped the crew more fiercely than drink
seized a Temperance signer. On the thirteenth, when the *Peacock* anchored
on a berg larger than Boston Common, the men had descended to scuffling
over odd chunks coughed up from the ice from the earth's outermost peaks.

For several days, Clare had fought to keep his journal writings worthy of
an assistant collections specialist aboard this exploration. Yet the scientific
truth remained: no man save the few aboard this empirical armada could
credit the uncanny region. A hellish barrier of ice blasted them with ruined
cloisters, icy crenellations and caprices, wind-masoned ogive vaulting,
sculpted follies through whose mighty fissures flocks wheeled.

Life in these latitudes teemed so profusely that it startled even Dr. Picker-
ing and Mr. Rich. Botanist and zoologist alike fell back, embarrassed by their
insufficient catalogs. Monster fish hauled from great depths harbored yet
more monstrous half-digested specimens in their entrails. Unnamed animal-
cula massed in numbers sufficient to employ the Scientifics until the end of
their days.

Well above the crow's nest, fairy pinnacles gaped down on the ship, spattered like a candle left in a windy casement. In front of Clare lay the immea-

surable solitude of terra incognita. The polar region. And not a hole in the earth's crust as far as sextant could see.

Not that anyone in the expedition had ever credited the theory. The voyage was never more than another unholy alliance, a marriage of convenience in the Go-Ahead age. From the start, the Hole in the Pole was the solely owned idea of John Cleves Symmes—the Newton of the West. *To all the world!* Symmes wrote:

> I declare the earth is hollow, and habitable within; containing a number of solid concentrick spheres, one within the other, and that it is open at the poles 12 or 16 degrees; I pledge my life in support of this truth, and am ready to explore the hollow, if the world will support and aid me in the undertaking.

John Quincy Adams had seen enough in Symmes's rant to shepherd the exploration through a Congress so hostile that some legislators considered the mere idea of national backing unconstitutional. But the nation sought a higher presence in the southern seas, and a hunt for the polar hole captured the public's imagination enough to make a voyage seem cheap at the price.

The Scientifics proved willing to use the Hollow Earth to secure funds. The Navy, in turn, exploited the Scientifics. Finally the whalers, in that great food chain, fed happily on the Navy's vested interests. So long as research's goal fell in sea-lanes so full of shrimp and fish, commerce was a great believer in research.

To Ben Clare, fresh from Cambridge's lecture halls, Symmes might as well have been one of those tattooed priests of the god Tangaloa that so fascinated Mr. Hale, the philologist, during ships' landfall in the Samoan group. Clare rejected all of Symmes except his philosophical refrain: *Light gives light, to light discover—ad infinitum.* No one knew just what was plausible in this world, what laughable, what tragic, what obligatory, what contemptible. But man possessed the means to find out. Discovery was man's duty, until all the earth's surfaces were lit.

Now the hole had been definitively filled, and in its place stood mountains. The globe stood fleshed out, the map completed. *Thy sea is so great, and our craft so small, O Lord.*

Ben Clare gazed out on the whited, virgin landscape, for a last moment, still free of human visit. He debated the use of this new land the way, as an undergraduate, he had wrestled with every issue under the sun. Resolved: The President ought to renew the Bank's charter. Resolved: Botany merits the creation of its own formal professorship. Resolved: Land should be made available to any able-bodied, enfranchised man at no cost beyond settlement. Resolved: Old Zip Coon is a very learned scholar. Below his feet, the prurient *Idumea* gave way to a lustier *Blow ye winds, high-o. They say you'll take five hundred sperm before you're six months out. Blow ye. Blow, boys, blow.* The notes flew out upon an antarctic breeze, froze, and fell back to the antipodal ice.

In the days following the sighting of land, Clare occupied himself with organizing the specimens taken from South America and New Holland. He helped the geographers haul their magnetic equipment onto the pack ice. On the twentieth, he watched a cetacean hurl itself fully out of the water while a predator killer hung locked to the thrashing jaws. Two days later, Mr. Eld succeeded in capturing a colossal king penguin. As the Commander later wrote:

> He was taken after a truly sailor-like fashion, by knocking him down. The bird remained quite unmoved on their approach, or rather showed a disposition to come forward to greet them. A blow with a boat-hook, however, stunned him . . . He showed, on coming to himself, much resentment at the treatment he received . . .

Overnight, the *Peacock* received the same treatment at the hands of the malevolent region. She was alone, having lost contact with the flagship *Vincennes* and the others some time before. While endeavoring to evade a floe that materialized under her bow, the ship came about, colliding so violently with a second ice mass that the stern seemed entirely stove in. No longer steerable, the ship drifted into the ice. They drove stern foremost into the ice barrier. The second blow finished off the rudder, broke two of the pintles, and shattered both braces.

The wind chose that moment to revive, and despite spars fitted out along the hull, ice set upon them as dogs on a stricken doe. The ship slammed into a berg towering above the mastheads, grounding her larboard stern. Impact tore away the spanker boom and stern davit while crushing the stern boat. The knee that bound davit to taffrail broke off, carrying with it all the stanchions as far as the gangway.

By blind fortune, the ship canted into the last free water, missing by inches the fall of an ice crest that would have atomized it. Luck seemed to spare them for a worse fate: slow death upon whatever floating waste they might lash to. While danger threatened, the crew had acted with a mechanical competence. Now they fell to considering the destinies each would face alone. The Pole, it occurred to Benjamin Clare, late of Clare's Sons, Roxbury, indeed bore a hole deeper than all cartography.

Ice condensed around the hull, threatening to crush the ship and reclaim the keel's slit. Clare looked on his white mausoleum. He would never decompose, but would enjoy the corporal eternity sought by all industry. The ship, after centuries of pressing, would someday work back up through the ice layers to be coughed up at the feet of later explorers, a square-rigged diamond.

Desperate, the crew employed a berg as a lee helm, performing with the efficiency of those already lost. Benjamin joined a boat aiming to run out a line to swing the ship's head toward the last capricious wisp of open sea. He stood mere miles from the earth's static axle, so close to the Pole that the air lost all convection. He affixed himself to the rope that would either free the ship or tie them like bunting to a coffin. He wrapped the cable through his hands and pulled.

Some minutes passed in the motionless tug-of-war. All terror over the disintegrating *Peacock* vanished, like the visions of an opiate dream. A perfumed thread entered Clare's nostrils: an old, lifelong friend. Yet he had never smelled its like. A scent wafted upon him, a redolence for all the world like the smell of a forgotten existence.

For seventeen months, the stench of sail had attacked him without respite. Each day was a carnage of tainted foods, island incense, brine-soaked winds, overripe fruits, acrid invertebrates rotting on the deck, putrefying soft-bodied conches that the captain would not allow below. He lived smothered in flesh, ten dozen men who laved by lunar calendar, if that often. Fetid fragrance had so ruled his every inhalation that the thing he smelled, out on the ice, was the sachet of scentlessness: air before the employment of lungs.

He worked the idea out, as the crew fought to tether the ship from oblivion. This atmosphere grew so gelid, the spin of the earth so still, that air's larger molecules—those smells that otherwise relentlessly bombarded human nostrils—here dropped frozen to the pack ice, awaiting a thaw that, in some distant future, would awaken olfaction.

The ship's fate now became a matter of indifference. The Benjamin Clare who had signed on with the first U.S. Exploring Expedition eager to serve in his capacity of collector and cataloger of plants, that son of Harvard who awaited the day when human triangulation would fill every empty spot on the map, perished out on the pack ice of newly christened Wilkes Land, finished by his first whiff of nothing.

Frenzy and fluke somehow combined to shove the *Peacock*'s prow loose into the last free cleft in the ice barrier. At midnight, the sea rose and the ship shot down a canyon no broader than its own width. While crags crashed against both gunwales and the crew clamored with activity, Clare savored the taste of the thing he had taken into his lungs. He joined in the celebration at the ship's deliverance. He, too, waved mad flares, shot his pistol, poured out wine on the pack ice that had spared them. But the trace nosegay lingered in him, a postmortem sense of the senses' lie.

———

A postcard pokes out of a book at bedside, marking the progress through a current paperback. The card is perforated to be trimmed down to a recipe, its thumb tab reading: "Healthy Chinese Vegetables and Noodles":

½ pound rice noodles

SAUCE

3 tablespoons rice wine
1 teaspoon sesame oil
2 tablespoons tamari

2 teaspoons cornstarch
½ cup broth

1 tablespoon vegetable oil
1 tablespoon fresh ginger, slivered
4 cloves garlic, chopped
1 cup sliced mushrooms
1 cup snow peas

1 red bell pepper, sliced
1 cup sliced water chestnuts
2 cups sliced bok choy
1 (8-ounce) can bamboo shoots, drained
½ cup sliced carrots

Prepare noodles as directed. Meantime, blend sauce ingredients thoroughly. Over high heat, heat oil in wok or nonstick pan. Stir-fry ginger and garlic for ½ minute. Add mushrooms; stir-fry another ½ minute. Add remaining ingredients and fry 2 minutes. Drizzle with sauce; let cook 2 minutes. Add noodles, stir briefly, and serve. Serves 4. 350 calories, 12g protein, 60g carbohydrates, 6g fat. No cholesterol!

Beneath these instructions is a color picture of the finished meal. Behind the perfect dish, a broken fortune cookie: Use what you have; work for what you need. *At bottom, next to the* Copyright © 1997 Attention Grabbers Marketing, *two tiny icons proclaim:* PRINTED WITH AMERICAN SOY INKS ON RECYCLED PAPER.

On the back of the card—Bulk Rate U.S. Postage Paid, Lacewood, IL Permit No. 534—*arranged to fall within the recipe card's outline, the* Next Millennium Realty *logo adorns a picture of* Laura Rowen Bodey, Broker, GRI,

CRS. More than just an agent. Because your home is more than just a house. Call your friend in the business.

Three phone numbers—office, home, and toll-free—carry the clause This is not intended to solicit currently listed properties.

You don't have to sail halfway around the world to enjoy this delicious and healthy Chinese dish. And you don't have to look anywhere else to enjoy the best real estate service available. I can make your move easy and comfortable. You'll be home safe, whenever you're coming, wherever you're going!

———

The *Peacock,* reprieved, made for Sydney Harbor. Their last communication with the Commander had the *Vincennes* and *Porpoise* setting off for a survey of Disappointment Bay, one of the happiest-named of the map's newest features. By landfall in the Feejee Islands three months later, Clare had shaken the scent, but not the carcass that it marked.

Truly the Feejees were Botany's Eden. For three months, Clare enjoyed near-continuous unearthing. He collected what the great Asa Gray later classified as the new genera of *Brackenridgea* and *Draytonia*. He helped Brackenridge draw and describe *Maniltoa grandiflora,* the thimbithimbi tree. His steady hand proved invaluable, not just to the botanists, but to the ethnography being done by the vessels' zoologists and philologists.

He collected many magnificent Feejeean war clubs and ceremonial paddles, later bequeathed to the Peabody. Each ritual engraving represented an inordinate overhead, given the item's function. The New Englander shrank from this irrational richness of carving while simultaneously thrilling to the appalling waste.

Surely, he asked an island warrior, there must be a more economical manner with which to propel a canoe or bash in a head.

More economical, the native conceded. But not as convincing.

This handiwork bore some fuller utility to it than Clare's eye could discern. The Baroque, tortuous adornment of cudgeling: no maker could hope to turn a profit on such an object. But use supped more broadly in the islands than it did in the land of measure. A war club more elaborate than a railroad locomotive, taking more time to make: it begged the same question that his whiff of scentlessness had. What, in the final face of things, was the use of use?

Clare put it to his fellow Scientifics that the races of the world ought to be approached in the same objective spirit as one might approach a new species.

True, the inhabitants of these islands were, as the Commander noted, "in many respects, the most barbarous and savage race now existing upon the globe." But therein lay their peculiar importance.

Clare reveled less than the Commander in the "considerable progress in several of the useful arts" that the islanders had made since contact with the white man. For the day would come, and lamentably soon, when the makers of these astounding clubs would grow as docile as the Christianized Tongans, and present as little interest to the investigation of diversity. They would pass from the earth like some great, flightless bird, and any further attempt to know their ways would be akin to recovering from a magnificent but fossilized plant the facts of its prior existence.

Clare relayed to the Commander, for inclusion in his *Narrative*, the Feejean myth of racial origin. By native tradition, all men were born of the same primordial couple. The Feejeean was firstborn, but wicked, black, and naked. The Tongan came next, only partly bad, and therefore whiter and better clothed. The Papalangis—white men—came last. The best behaved, they were awarded many clothes, immense ships, and great freedom of movement.

In the islands, the squadron exercised its chief commission: compiling a reliable cartographic description of an area whose riches had previously been sealed in ignorance. For want of reliable maps, the ships plying these channels had paid greatly. Trade could no more survive in a map-free world than the world could survive without trade. For weeks, the tedious task of surveying spun out the reefs' corona. The crew added no end of features to the storehouse of geography: Peale's River, Budd's Forest, Rich's Peak.

But mutual growth demanded more than maps. Some half a dozen years earlier, natives had slain seven crew members of an American brig, the *Charles Doggett*, cooking and eating their Negro. Whites had traced the crime back to a powerful island royal. International cooperation required the Wilkes expedition to demonstrate that the massacre of white visitors could not go unpunished.

The murderer turned out to be a resourceful nobleman named Vendovi. When the fugitive eluded one group of seamen, Captain Hudson designed a fuller plan for his capture. The officers of the *Peacock* prepared a feast aboard ship and invited all the native luminaries to attend. The promise of gifts and lavish entertainment proved too much to resist. For even the High King of Feejee coveted the most worthless trinket of New England manufacture.

Ship's fireworks astonished the audience. A magnificent Jim Crow theatrical performed by the ship's tailor provoked wide admiration. The banquet consumed, the local nobility made to depart. Captain Hudson then informed them, with apologies, that they were all hostages pending Vendovi's surrender. The natives agreed that Vendovi was a dangerous man who had to be brought to justice.

A warrior agreed to go to the village of Rewa and take Vendovi by surprise. After his departure, the King asked for a draft of ava, to soften his confinement. Ben Clare combed the botanical specimens on board and produced some *Piper methysticum* to brew the calmative. The grateful King asked Clare if he were a plant doctor. Clare equivocated.

The two men exchanged botanical knowledge. Clare copied into his journals the infinite uses to which the natives put each plant species. Marking Clare's interest, the King produced an herb pouch full of stems, leaves, and seeds. A rhizomous tuber of unknown genus attracted Clare's attention.

The King called the root by a name that meant either *strength* or *use*. Clare noted the King's claims in his journals, as interested in the plant's fictive attributes as in any real properties. The root possessed a faraway smell, an astringency that Clare would not have been able to detect until a few months before.

Vendovi's capture, according to Wilkes's *Narrative,*

> shows the force of the customs to which all ranks of this people give implicit obedience. Ngaraningiou, on arriving at Rewa, went at once to Vendovi's house . . . Going in, he took his seat by him, laid his hand on his arm, and told him that he was wanted, and that the king had sent for him to go on board the man-of-war. He immediately assented . . .

Brought aboard ship, Vendovi confessed to the assembled chiefs his complicity in the murder of the white sailors. He expressed some regret at having eaten the Negro, whose flesh had tasted of strong tobacco. The Captain put Vendovi in chains and freed the King and court, once again explaining why their imprisonment had been necessary,

> for he would have thought it incumbent upon him to burn Rewa, if Vendovi had not been taken. The king replied, that Captain Hudson had done right; that he would like to go to America himself, they had all been treated so well; that we were now all good friends, and that he should ever continue to be a good friend to all white men . . . They were assured of our amicable disposition towards them so long as they conducted themselves well; and in order to impress this fully upon them, after their own fashion, presents were made them, which were received gratefully.

The King, in turn, lavished on his captors the gratitude of reprieve. On Clare he pressed the moist rhizome from his herbal kit, the one with the hollow, astringent scent.

After the Rewa affair, relations with the islanders degenerated. The squadron burned the town of Rye in retaliation for the theft of a boat, and resorted to punitive shelling with twenty-four-pounder Congreve rockets those populations that would not be subdued in any other fashion. Warriors on Disappointment Minor invited Clare and two other plant collectors into the reef at spearpoint. Two officers, including the Commander's nephew, died in the skirmish on Malolo.

The expedition pressed on to safer anchorage in the Sandwiches, where Clare explored Honolulu. But when the *Peacock* later ran aground in the mouth of the Columbia River, Clare lost the best of his own work forever. The ship, so narrowly spared destruction by ice, wallowed into the mud and expired in what soon became a pitifully well mapped grave.

In the *Peacock*'s demise, Peale lost his whole natural history library as well as a vast collection of Lepidoptera. The great Dana also lost extensive notes and priceless crustacean specimens. Fortune hit Clare hardest of all. He fished from the wreck no more than a quarter of his papers and not a single collected plant of any importance, with the exception of the root given him by the Feejeean King.

This stroke of fate punished Clare. In the wreck he lost all chance to add to science's legacy. He made halfhearted attempts to start new journals. He began a grammar for Chinook trading jargon, but his lack of philological training proved insurmountable.

Among the Spokane people, the amateur anthropologist did, by accident, produce a minor prize, dutifully recorded by the Commander for a later public. Chief Silimxnotylmilakabok, whom the expedition christened Cornelius, told them

an account of a singular prophecy that was made by one of their medicine-men . . . before they knew anything of white people, or had heard of them . . . "Soon," said he, "there will come from the rising sun a different kind of men from any you have yet seen, who will bring with them a book, and will teach you every thing, and after that the world will fall to pieces."

These words haunted Clare's journey back across the Pacific to Manila. They darkened his passage through the Mindoro Strait and drove him to a flurry of unproductive energy in the Singapore Roads, where the Commander was forced to sell the weathered *Flying Fish* into the booming opium trade.

Musing on the Spokane prophecy, Clare grew possessed of an urge to communicate with the prisoner Vendovi. The old island savage had sat languishing in the brig, America's captive, for the year and a half since Fee-jee. During this time, the only person who knew enough of the prisoner's language to be able to converse with him had been Vanderford, the Master's Mate.

Clare studied with Vanderford, to learn what he could of the savage's tongue. Vanderford, however, took ill before transiting the Cape of Good Hope. He died and was committed to the deep before teaching Clare sufficient grammar to be intelligible. The passage across the Atlantic found Clare and Vendovi in a repeated dumb show of frustration.

Vendovi lived on in strangeness until the ships drifted into New York Harbor. Looking on the metropolitan skyline, he died of a sudden burst of incomprehension. Clare all but followed him.

The voyage came to an inglorious close. A healthy chunk of the expedition's ethnographic collection eventually wound up in the capable hands of P. T. Barnum. The aging ships were privatized or broken up for parts. The public grew indifferent to the fleet's discoveries. Expansion had long since outgrown the excursion.

At day's end, the chief legacy of the expedition lay in its charts. With them, fabled locales fell into fact, hurrying the world toward a society of universal trade. The expedition added more miles of coastline to the world than any other single venture. Aside from a few spurious islands drawn by a disgruntled midshipman, the charts were appallingly accurate. One hundred years later, the American invasion of Tarawa employed a map that Ben Clare had helped to draw.

History came to remember Commander Wilkes for sparking international calamity during the Civil War by whisking two Confederate commissioners off the British packet *Trent*. Captain Hudson ended up commanding the ship that laid the first transatlantic cable. Clare lived on, immortal, in a rhizomous bulb of *Utilis clarea,* named for the man who noticed a pungency that set it apart from all the species it resembled.

The priceless zoological treasures fell prey to the raids of Washington souvenir hunters. The public picked over the stuffed creatures. Plants lost their labels. Museums and zoos skimmed off what they wanted. After much loss, government intervened. Thereafter, even the wife of His Accidency, President Tyler, was denied cuttings.

What remained of the rummaged collections formed the core of the infant national museum. An ancient *Encephalartos horridus* cycad in the U.S. Botanic Garden still survives, the lone living remnant of the expedition, aside from Clare International.

Late already, even before fate screwed them royally.

Don tells himself as much with each new wallowing boxcar. Would have been late anyway, even if God and the Illinois Central hadn't chosen this exact moment to engineer the longest freight in creation since that interminable peace train song that Laura used to play throughout the first four years of their marriage.

His fault. He hadn't allotted enough time to pick up the kids at their schools and haul them back across town. The hospital—no more than five, six blocks from West High. Shouldn't have taken more than ten minutes, max, the way he planned it.

His plan was already a shambles, well before this little kicker. Maybe he's stuck in nostalgia, some image of the Town That Time Forgot. Like, a place where you just *drive,* from start to destination, no complications, no surprises, no fucked-up stoplights, no Emmett Kelly work crews sticking Band-Aids on collapsing infrastructures, no in-your-face work-stoppage public servants picketing the hood of your Toyota.

What happened to that manageable, mid-sized town they used to live in, where everything still worked the way it was supposed to? The one with the intact tax base, where they fixed the potholes, where you could drive anywhere in ten minutes?

As it stands, if the cattle cars and chemical cars and car cars shuffle off to Topeka by the top of the hour, they'll be in the recovery room right around five after. Exactly forty-six minutes. He's reached the stage of life where everything takes forty-six minutes as an absolute minimum. It takes forty-six minutes to walk down to the goddamn mailbox.

Ellen counts out loud: "One-huuu-ndred-three . . ." Her aristocratic heiress routine, bored out of her skull by the stupidity of existence. But making sure to share the tedium with everyone, generous soul.

Tim's quit trying to get her to shut up and has moved on to trying to talk right over her. Don's given up even going through the motions of policing them. Five more minutes, plus whatever the rest of the train takes. Just get them to the hospital, and their mother can deal with them.

Tim says, "Wonder what's inside those metal canister thingies. Probably radioactive waste or something."

"Rubbish," Don says. "They don't ship radioactive waste by train."

"Sure they do. They do! All the time."

"They don't just sling radioactive waste around the country, through cities and—"

"Sure," Tim taunts. Like it's a fact of growing up, and his dad's in some kind of denial. "How else're they going to get it from one place to another?"

"They don't. They just leave it where it is."

"Great. Okay. So what do *you* think is in those things?" Like he's just happy, having any kind of conversation with his father. Even this one.

Ellen says, "One-huundred-twenty-fi-ive . . ."

"Those whats?"

"*These*. The submarine whatchits. The Imperial Storm Trooper ones."

"They're all empty. This whole train is just some old guy's hobby. Have you ever heard of anyone actually shipping anything by train? What do you think we have airplanes for? They just keep these trains around to make things look quaint, and to harass people who have to get—"

"And to lug around the stuff that the pilots won't touch," Ellen chimes in, smelling blood. At least she's stopped counting.

Just to spite him, Tim calculates the total bulk of all the freight being hauled past them. How many thousands of dead cows. How many cubic milliliters of explosive fuels. How many Nissans. How many tons of polyvinyl whatever. The kid knows how to estimate.

Don says nothing. Just stares ahead, through the cars, at the other side of the tracks, a place whose existence he has begun to doubt. He considers having an asthma attack.

Ellen nudges Tim in the ribs, a broad gesture visible even in the rearview mirror. "Daddy's pissed."

"He's not pissed. Pissed means drunk."

"Does not. That's *shit-faced*." Semi-suppressed giggles, covert glances monitoring to see if she's over the line. She *knows* she's over.

At least the two of them have the excuse of actually being children. The only guiltless people in the culture of permanent adolescence are the adolescents. All day long, he has to deal with exactly this kind of acting out. Gets it from colleagues and donors alike. They all want to stamp their feet, throw a little tantrum, and get away with it. And his job is to stroke them for doing so. Good boy. Clever boy! Now just write me the check, will you?

Every other lunch, he has to listen to some smartass drawl, "Say, Don. Why do you call what you do 'Development'? Don't you think you oughta just call it 'Fund-raising'?" So pleased with themselves. So proud of their Midwestern caginess, guffawing with bits of baby back rib stuck between their teeth, baby back rib that Don pays for. His job is to laugh along, make the potential bene-factor feel that he's Milton Berle.

And after a hard day's development, he's supposed to go out on some big-budget adolescent fantasy date with his current girlfriend. Forty-six years old, and he's got a damn girlfriend. A twenty-eight-year-old arrested-development girlfriend who can't stand his kids because he lets them get away with all the crap he won't let her get away with. A girlfriend who's jealous of his ex-wife, and an ex-wife who hates him for spending their entire marriage oppressing her.

Terri, last night, calling three times with the same old rag until he just let the machine take it. "Don? Don, pick up. I know you're there." And again this morning, twice, threatening to break things off if he goes to see his ex-wife in the hospital. He should have asked to get that threat in writing.

"Terri," he reasoned with her. Mistake one. "The woman's having an oper-ation."

"Not my problem."

"Ter. It's not like I'm getting back together with her or anything." Not a Democrat's chance in hell.

"I don't *care* if you get back together." Even over the Princess phone, he could hear her stamping her Mary Janes on the shag. Only you can prevent nylon fires. "I just don't think you should see her right after her operation."

He doesn't think so either. But he can't very well not. Certainly Laura's boyfriend isn't going to be much help on this one. For starters, the man's wife might wonder why he's hanging around Mercy for his evening's entertainment.

Besides, the kids want to see her right away. Or: ten years from now, they'll want to have seen her right away. And who's going to take the kids there, if not him?

They're thirty-six minutes late pulling into the parking garage—that extor-tion racket and major supplemental source of hospital income. Which means they're thirty-nine minutes late getting to post-op. The place is a hotbed of sepsis. You can feel the stress hormones accumulate in little pools that slosh around the ankles of the people in the waiting room. Families and friends, rocked or reprieved at the rate of one new verdict every ten minutes.

A great social equalizer, this room. Farmer, college counselor, banker, the whole factory gamut from fork operator up to division manager. The upper-level corporate guys probably have their own underground hospital some-where. But everybody else has to wait his turn, civilized, each wrapped in his own consequences.

The three of them enter the waiting room, impostors just slipping in to pick up a routine All-Clear. Tim latches on to an issue of *Computer Entertainment*. The magazine occupies him for a full twenty seconds, until he notices that it's two months old. He throws it aside in disgust. Ellen camps out in front of the waiting room TV, tuned, for some godforsaken reason, to a hospital soap where some straight doctor has just tested positive for HIV.

Don goes to the desk and reports in. The idiot nurse tongue-lashes him. "The surgeon came by to make the report ten minutes ago. We don't have the time to do everything twice, sir."

Don grins and dutifully eats the abuse. It comes easy to him. How he earns a living. The nurse makes a big, victimized point of resummoning the surgeon. The surgeon is a woman, and something of a piece, even in the surgical scrubs. "I'm the ex-husband," Don says, trying for extra credit.

The surgeon flashes a relaxed, easy smile. She greets the kids, shakes everybody's hands, then says, "Well, Mr. Bodey, your wife has cancer."

Dr. Jenkins continues to stand there talking, but someone has hit the mute button. Don hears only a few words. Something about a big cyst on the right ovary and a little one on the left. Or vice versa. And the big one was fine but the little one had this small, foraging wet spot on the surface.

This Jenkins woman just doesn't seem to be saying what she's saying. Cancer. She smiles at the three of them, asking, "Is there anything else you need to know for now?" The way the pretty cashier at the Style Barn cocks her head and says, "Will that be all today?"

Ninety-eight? he wants to ask. *What about the 98 percent?*

But he says: "That's all, thanks."

Dr. Jenkins disappears to her next case. In a flash, Ellen's all over him. "What does that mean, Daddy? Mom has . . . ?"

Tim says nothing. He won't even look up.

All Don can think about is having failed Laura. Blowing the only real favor she's asked him since they split. Could you get any important details following the surgery? She didn't want to miss anything while still doped.

The news promotes them to floor seven. Oncology. He's never even thought about the word, and now it's his. They walk stunned, in a dream, ending up in front of 7020, the number somebody has scrawled on a piece of paper for them. But Laura is not there yet. The floor nurses deflect them to another little waiting room, different dated magazines, same daytime hospital soap.

Don jumps up to check the room every ninety seconds. Each time, someone on staff sends him back to the waiting room. "Somebody'll come get you when Miss Bodey gets set up."

Set up? Who will know to come get them? Miss Bodey? Is that what the chart says?

He is returning to the waiting room, shagged off the floor for the sixth time, when he sees her. She's on a gurney, being rolled out of the elevator. He does not recognize her. They've done something to her face. She's all puffy, slack, serene. There's something else wrong with it, too. She's smiling.

She swims up to see who this is, staring at her. And she's smiling at him. She tries to take his hand, missing. She squeezes his three fingers, affectionate with terror. Harder than she has ever grasped him. She hasn't a clue what's happening. She hasn't the faintest idea of where she is, or what she is, or why.

"Don. Don." She swings his hand back and forth as the nurses begin wheeling her gurney down the hall again. He lopes alongside, unable to extract his fingers from her grip.

"What did they say?" she remembers to ask. "What did they tell you?"

"Dr. Jenkins said the surgery went very well. She said they're going to take you to this room down there at the end of the hall, where they're going to get you set up and then she says you can . . ."

She waves him off, exasperated. Donald. Not the time. Not the place.

"Which side was the cancer on?"

He doesn't know. They told him, and he's forgotten. He picks an ovary. "The right," he tells her. "It's on the right side." Fifty-fifty odds now seem absurdly generous.

———

A suite of magnets adhere to the refrigerator, their points comprising a Little Dipper:
- Scott Tissue: The Trouble Began with Harsh Toilet Tissue
- Cracker Jack: 5 cents. Surprise Inside
- Lysol disinfectant: Infection . . . the sly and deadly enemy of every home
- Eight O'Clock Bean Coffee: Ground to order
- Raid: Kills Bugs Dead
- Lighthouse: Armour's Family Soap. Premium for Wrappers

Collectibles from five decades, enamel on metal, they yellow in simulated age. Each holds in place some receipt, ticket, or reminder. Underneath the last—a lighthouse advancing through the foaming waves, scrub brush in one hand and a bucket reading "Show me dirt" in the other—a note reads: Mom, Post-Op, Mercy, 3:30 Wed.

Benjamin Clare returned to a Boston overhauled during his years at sea. He brought back little to show for the voyage but a sample of his namesake plant, the living contraband he was supposed to have surrendered to the government catalogers.

The world's change is forever occluded by our own, so intent is the heart upon its private voyage out. At first, Ben felt that something had happened to *him* while he was away. In fact, he had stood still, while the world of his brothers had disappeared forever into its replacement.

At thirty, he suddenly found himself obeying Jesus' stipulation to take no thought for the morrow. For the morrow—that dream of progress his countrymen woke to—had gotten away from Ben in his absence. The morrow had grown tendrils beyond any vintner's power to cultivate.

Jephthah Clare's sons were the last generation to assume that time would bring no fundamental changes to the game of existence. But on some unknown afternoon during Ben Clare's long voyage, a new two-stroke engine had somehow split the future from its mother tenses and set it up, like some ingrate rebel colony, on independent soil.

The country did itself over in steam. Steam: the world's first new power source since the dawn of time: so slight, so obvious, so long overlooked that no one could say whether the engine was discovered or invented. A separate condensing chamber and governor—twinned iron planets rising to dampen with greater drag the faster they spun—with these small changes, time took off.

Life now headed, via a web of steam-cut canals, deep into the interior. No later chaos would ever match this one for speed and violence: the first upheaval of advancement without advance warning. The back-pressure of governed steam erected in railroad. Schuylkill, Delaware, Mohawk, and Hudson: every Valley exalted, and every hill laid low. Rail threatened to render distance no more than a quaint abstraction. America at last split open its continental nut. Populace consolidated; the week vanished into hours.

In turn, the energies released by this energy launched ocean steamships and set machine presses stamping out the tools needed to make their own replacements. Infant factories forged a self-cleaning steel plow, which beat a reaper, which called out for vulcanized rubber, which set in inexorable motion a sewing machine that left half of Boston out of work, turning upon itself, poor against poorer.

The patented spread of power sprang New England from its Puritan swaddling. Never very good with mere abiding, the Yankee made his escape into this giddy game of ever-accreting crack-the-whip, still diligent, still mindful, still industrious. The windbreaks against old pilgrim winters, the stockades of hard-won subsistence were now mere antechambers for more stately mansions.

All the resourcefulness that simple survival once required now came free for reinvestment. Like a maturing treasury bill, Adam's expiring curse called out for new capital targets to absorb it. For the first time in history, it seemed that life's weight might lift a little before this generation passed away.

This dream moved into the Clare works during Ben's absence and took up residence there. Jewitt had begun to tinker with the steam engine, learning how to make that beast do useful work. Already he'd succeeded in forcing gaseous water to drive a shaft powerful enough to mill and extrude soap. This same automated crank seemed capable of propelling the very engine of history.

This was the churning landscape that Ben Clare fell back into, from out of his Antarctic scentlessness. He cleared quarantine and returned to Cambridge in August of 1842. He spent two months simply trying to reorient himself. Much had he traveled in the western isles, but could only look with silent and wild surmise upon the sight of home.

He left to some future Plutarch the task of sorting out Whig from Democrat, Clay from Calhoun. He left the parties to fight each other the way the city's rival volunteer firefighters fought each other for the privilege of putting out a blaze. He saved the full horror of his bewilderment for Development in all its naked glory.

He learned of that hatter's son, self-schooled Peter Cooper, busy changing the American landscape more than any single person since the founders. Cooper's metal tendrils now pushed outward from the Hub like threads from the universe's germ cell. Each year lengthened the track's probe. Trains snaked West, toward the endless grass, at last conquering for Boston its first real agricultural base.

He discovered the Tappans' nationwide credit agency. To his horror, Ben heard how, for a small fee, these men would determine which of humanity was worth monetary risk and which was not.

He read of the collapse of a nearby mill on the Waltham model. Two hundred girls died inside. He could not keep track of the accelerating factory explosions in Brooklyn and Baltimore. He only noted that the industrialists always managed to escape prosecution on the grounds that their works had done more cumulative good than harm.

Facts bombarded him. A printer in Alton, Illinois, had been killed for defying the abolition Gag Rule. A mob consigned his presses to the bottom of the Mississippi. Congress had just granted the portrait painter Morse $60,000 to continue his telegraphic research, providing he spent at least half the money on systematic investigations into animal magnetism, where the big payoffs surely lay.

Replete with news, Ben crossed over the river to pay his respects to industry. He walked through Boston's burial grounds in a calculated dream: Copp's Hill, King's Chapel, the Old Granary. Graves: yesterday's ritual devotion had become today's real estate lament.

In Milk Street, he passed a new ready-to-wear clothier proclaiming "Shirts for the Million." Swaying in the sea breeze, the shop's shingle read: "Naked Was I and Ye Clothed Me." Surely it ought to have read: "Consider the Lilies of the Field." For in Ben's understanding of industry, human enterprise now doomed itself as inexorably as air dooms iron.

At Temple Place, he found his brothers hard at their labor. They took the prodigal out to Roxbury, for a tour of what had grown into a small pod of structures. Soap, too, had built its own head of steam, and candles profited from the memory of recent desperation.

The Clare works had expanded beyond all recognition. Ennis's monster kettle now seemed almost modest by the day's standard. Resolve stocked a small store to cater to his workers' needs, extending them advances against their wages. Some workers got together in their slow hours, late in the evenings, once a week, for self-improvement sessions. Samuel even published their writings, the marvel of European visitors. Americans were not amazed: of course their very factory laborers would rise to poetry.

While Ben had been at sea, Clare's sons perfected an imitation of the marked-up English soap they had briefly imported. With scale and machinery, costs began to fall like oaks at a homestead. The homegrown look-alike came to market at a good price, selling to those who lacked only the right accoutrements to pass themselves off above their station. Samuel and Resolve vended the look and feel of wealth without the expense.

Time had dredged and widened the old distribution channels. The firm now sold as far out as Concord. Slabs and sticks even found their way into towns that four years before could not have purchased anything, let alone rehabilitated waste fat.

New ingredients raised the quality of the Clares' wares. Soda ash gave them a more consistent product. They had to import it from the hated English, who cornered the magical Leblanc process, making cheap, superior alkali from sulfur and salt water. But the Clares were in no position to argue. They now made half a dozen laundry and scouring soaps, not to mention the toilet variety. For reliability at that volume, they would have bought supplies from far more unsavory peddlers.

Ben nodded politely throughout the tour, as if he followed his brothers' explanations. In truth, both the enhanced techniques and the expanded marketing now exceeded his grasp. He noted only that his brothers had shaken off the shame of manufacture. They would not return to merchanting now if they could. Lather now lent luster to the name Clare.

The bemused botanist listened intently to the intelligences. He smiled when it seemed appropriate. He wagged his head, that field scientist's gesture for mystified impatience with material particulars. Business had been a cipher to Benjamin even before his watery passage. After island ethnography, trade now struck him as an arcane branch of religion.

A short tour of industry, he figured, would repay the tedium incurred. Suffer the family enterprise's anatomy, for it buttered his bread and paid for the good that would transcend it. Obeisance came easy on this delicate visit. He could listen all day and into tomorrow, if that was how long the tour of the works took. And after the tour, he would come into fat's inheritance.

For he planned to continue the vegetal studies begun in the Pacific basin. He hoped to build a Cambridge hothouse where he might cultivate the root given him by the King of Feejee. He had begun a paper for the National Botanic Society, weighing the evidence for those many claims the Feejeeans settled upon his species. And for all that, he would need his third of the family capital.

Money? His brother Resolve pretended to reflect upon the request. By all means. The older man pushed his sibling on ahead of him, off the factory floor, up to the bookkeeping office. With a show of quiet method, Resolve dropped the ponderous, brown-ribbed register onto the head clerk's desk and levered it open.

Where do you suggest we find this surplus cash? Exactly which department would you recommend debiting? Here, here: tell me how to itemize the cost. Where to enter the outlay into the ledger. Over what period to amortize the expense.

Ben tested his brother's gaze. There he saw all the words of any possible challenge, already heard, discounted, and dismissed. Merely giving suit to his case would lose it. His brother waited for him to choose: defeat by silence or the humiliation of speech.

Would not, Benjamin risked insisting, would not an investment in his education be worth something? Wasn't knowledge the principal from which all other interest flowed?

He appealed to Samuel, the weaker businessman. Wasn't knowledge of God's creation the reason why we store up riches here at all? As merchant had fathered manufacturer, so should manufacture father scholarship. Wasn't that God's hope for us here on this earth, His laboratory?

Samuel demurred.

Resolve shut the tome and restored it to its shelf. Knowledge. Your pearl of great price. We only sent you to university in the first place in the mistaken belief that the cost of your edification would someday cease to be a drain and begin to return something to the family's current account.

Ben set his bloodless face into a mask. What, then, do you propose I do with myself?

The question was academic, the answer available long before education. What does life ever propose that one do, but come work?

S, R, & B CLARE
SOAPS, CANDLES, & ALL THINGS THERETO BELONGING
JUSTICE & SPRING STREETS, ROXBURY

HE THAT HATH CLEAN HANDS SHALL GROW STRONGER AND STRONGER

She's still asking that first question, years later, when she wakes with tubes all over her. Which side is the cancer on? As if it mattered. As if Don or the doctor or anyone else cares. As if her ovaries know her right side from her left.

But her right side knows why her left asks. She woke in a panic, not for the disaster already handed to her, but for the one still hidden. Cancer: okay. She half expected it, going in. Too clean; too reassuring. A 2 percent chance of catastrophe.

She remembers bobbing up from the truth serum milkshake—thiopental sodium, fentanyl, tubocurarine, halothane—in a state perilously close to knowledge. The concoction left her with a continuous sense of micro–*déjà vu*. She heard the word "cancer" a good two seconds before the surgeon pronounced it. Maybe it was still the drugs, but she found herself thinking, "All right. I can deal with this. I'm an adult." And for a second or two, she thought it might even be true.

She digested the horror with all the ease of downing nouvelle cuisine. It's the aperitif she gags on. She woke from her long nausea sure she'd fallen into one of those amputation stories where they misread the X ray and take the wrong leg. Laura Somebody-else, a stranger's chart accidentally switched with her own. While she let her attention slip, ignorant medical personnel were busy committing colossal mistakes on her.

All the magazines agree: health care is now the patient's business. Responsibility falls squarely on the care receiver. And there she was, sleeping on the job.

Her nose now sprouts a tube, like one of Tim's *Star Wars* creatures. It itches; she picks feebly at it like some declawed cat. She vomits up the last of the anesthesia, convinced that they've taken the good cyst and left the bad one inside her. She badgers the nurses until one of them checks the chart. "Mrs. Bodey, everything was bad. They've taken everything."

Someone sponges her off. Another gets her into a clean gown. Still a third—or maybe it's always the same nurse, recycled—hooks her up to sugar water and electrolytes, with a little anti-nausea chaser. Order of narcotic on the side. Self-administering, they call it. Hit this button every time you think you need some morphine.

She pretty much keeps her thumb locked on the joystick. Like Tim strafing Warsaw. But some sadist has disabled the flow, rigged it to deliver a new trickle only at ten-minute intervals. Patient-administered, but machine-approved.

Whenever the machine thinks she's ready for another thimbleful, it beeps. After an hour, the beep itself is enough to give her a little imitation rush. But the rushes don't last. She asks a nurse to check if there's been some mix-up. "Are you sure there's really morphine in the bag? I don't know. Maybe it's 7022's supper."

The smallest movement makes her wish for death. She never imagined that pain on this scale existed.

She keeps asking anyone in white what she's supposed to do now. But apparently she's just supposed to wait. "Just rest up," someone tells her. "The doctor will come explain everything tomorrow."

After two hours, they come force her to walk. Something about her staples, possible peritonitis. She can make no more than token motions. Get upright, grab the rolling IV hat tree. Gag, retch, collapse, prop herself back up, take two baby steps. Mother, may I? Yes you may.

After four hours, they try her again. This time, she can get to the door of the room and take three steps down the hall before circling back around and crashing.

The kids drift in. She tries to rally herself, joke with them. "Your mother the cancer patient. You'll never have to turn in homework on time again."

Don's there, too. Every ten minutes, she tells him he can go home if he wants. Every time the morphine machine beeps. Finally he does. And finally the pain goes home a little, too.

Long after nightfall, she has the impression of Ken hovering by the bed. Saying what he always says: "I can't stay long."

Laura tells him what she always tells him. Go before anyone sees you. A few minutes later, the visit vanishes into hallucination.

She lurches asleep. In her dream, Nan, Ellen's dead girlfriend, comes back home to get her annual height measurement. Her mother stands her up against the inside of the kitchen doorframe and makes another pencil mark. Only this one is lower than last year's.

They wake her up every couple of hours to get her vitals and check the catheter.

The next morning she waits some more. Waiting: the one skill you get worse at with practice. At eight, the nurses tell her, "The doctor usually makes rounds at nine." At ten, they say, "She's sometimes as late as six or seven." Someone checks; Dr. Jenkins is operating again today. Somewhere, another woman is waking up surprised.

They give her a plastic respiration toy. An accordion plug that bobs up and down when she blows into it. She is supposed to blow into it as often as she can. Something about pressure on the diaphragm, keeping her insides from gunking up. It makes her think of those carnival tests of strength.

Don takes off from work to come by. "So, what's happening?"

"I've got cancer," she tells him. "That's what's happening."

"That's all? That's all you know? I have some questions here. When is the doctor supposed to come?"

"Somewhere between three hours ago and eight hours from now."

"I'm going to go find someone who can give us a little satisfaction."

Laura groans. "What do you mean, Don? 'Can I speak with your manager, please?'" The way it works in his organization. In all the organizations he is used to dealing with.

"Yeah. What's wrong with that?"

She says nothing. She squeezes the button. The button does nothing.

"You think this place isn't a business?" Don asks her.

"Not that kind of business."

"Not *what* kind of business?"

Not the kind that cares what its customers think, she would say. If she cared enough to say it.

They throw silence back and forth at each other until the gyny surgeon comes in. She has traded her scrubs this morning for a short, canary-yellow dress. Gorgeous, shocking, in this ward. Cheery to the point of obscene. Laura has forgotten that yellow exists. She wonders if maybe it's okay to be reminded.

She looks over at Don. He's got this helpless, fretting look on his face. Fighting off the salivation reflex. Poor man. Life is way too complex for some souls. He's going to die without ever knowing what hit him.

"How's it going?" Dr. Jenkins greets Laura as if they're old sewing circle friends. Which they are, now.

Laura tries to grin. She holds up the morphine button, toasting with it as if it were stemware topped off with champagne.

"Good. Let's just have a look at that belly." Jenkins eyes Don. "Could you step outside a moment?"

Laura snorts. Mirth rips through her, canceling all pleasure.

The wound is fine. Hurting like hell. Doing what comes naturally. The doctor fetches Don, who comes back in without a peep.

"Well, the operation went very well," the beautiful canary says. "No visible signs of malignancy remaining in the abdomen."

"You mean she's clean?" Don asks.

Dr. Jenkins smiles at him. This semester's precocious kid, trying to trip her up with the old teaser about the three travelers splitting the hotel room and losing a dollar somewhere along the way.

"There's no visible tumor left after debulking. That doesn't mean that there isn't occult disease loose somewhere in the system."

Laura isn't keen on having her system referred to in the third person while she's still in the room. And occult disease doesn't sound all that hot to her either. She's still not crazy about the ordinary kind.

"How can you tell?" Don asks.

"Tell what? If the disease has gotten loose somewhere else? I took the omentum and peritoneal washings. They're in the lab right now. If they come back positive, then we can figure that some cells have gotten loose."

Laura's eyes close. "I have an omentum?"

"Not anymore." Dr. Jenkins laughs.

"Do you expect them to come back positive?" Don sounds like Laura's lawyer.

"I think it's likely."

"How likely?"

"I'd say there's a 90 percent chance that one or the other will come back positive."

Laura feels the thought flash through Don's mind. But he declines to make the kill. Probably can't kill anything yellow. Instead, he asks, "You're sure you got the whole tumor?"

Massively professional: "Quite sure."

"Say the washings come back positive," Don says. As if he knows what "washings" are. Maybe it's just as well. Left to herself, Laura would not ask anything. This way, she learns more than she wants, and doesn't have to take the blame for discovering.

"Let's say some cells are loose," Don says. "What does that mean?"

"That means the cancer is Stage Three."

"And if not?"

"Then it's a Stage One. Stage One C, technically."

"What happened to Stage Two?"

The man is hopeless. Laura bleats. But she still doesn't open her eyes.

When she does, Don is sitting across from her vacuum drain, scribbling everything down into a legal pad the color of the surgeon's dress. Asking how to spell "serous cystadenocarcinoma." Trying to keep his eyes off the pretty hemline. Poor soul. She's going to have to remind him, soon, tomorrow. They're less than friends, now. The contract's been canceled. He owes her nothing.

Jill Jenkins leans lightly against the empty bed next to Laura's. She seems to be telling Laura to wait some more. Longer. Wait for the lab tests. Wait until tomorrow. Tomorrow: the only lever long enough to dislodge today.

"You'll need a few months of chemotherapy," the doctor says. A handful of system-wide poisonings. Half a year of vomiting and hair loss. "The specialist in Indy will decide what chemicals you will get. How much, and how often. Maybe your doses will include that new drug everyone's so excited about," Jenkins chirps. "The one they're making from tree bark. One hundred percent natural."

Laura can't keep from staring at this woman's legs, either. They remind her of the waxed fruit in that upscale food boutique in Next Millennium's office park. A dollar an apple, catering to young professionals who would never stoop to anything so déclassé as packing a lunch. How old can Dr. Jenkins be? How long will she stay ripe without refrigeration? How old should you be before you get really sick?

Outside, a freight runs past the new hospital parking expansion whose construction Laura fought. The train heads north, through the rotting neighborhoods Millennium never deals with. She begins to imagine herself in another life, indigent, penniless, victimized. But well.

Silence interrupts her fantasy. Jenkins has stopped explaining things. The doctor is waiting.

Laura hears herself speak, from inside a shortwave radio set. "What is the cause?" She cannot say *of ovarian cancer*. She cannot say *of this*. "Is it genetic?"

She just wants to know how much of this is her fault. Whether she should have done something. Might still do something. Whether she would have had to go through this even if she lived better. Whether Ellen.

"Sometimes." The doctor frowns. "Nobody really knows for certain."

Laura feels Don's fury, even through her sedatives.

"Which is it? *Sometimes,* or *Nobody knows*?"

"There was nothing wrong with me," Laura interrupts. "A little tenderness."

No warning signs at all. *How could that be?* she wants to ask. But she doesn't know what a warning sign looks like. Something like in the midnight reruns, when the pretty girl coughs while skipping rope, which means she'll be history by the next commercial break.

She wants to ask, *How long do I have to live?* But the words seem rude. You can't embarrass the physician that way.

"What are my numbers?" she says, instead. The phrase sounds calm. Almost sophisticated, once it's out in the open.

"Laura. Listen. People with ovarian cancer die of ovarian cancer."

What does that mean? Can, might, must? She tries to remember what exactly she needed to know. Should she quit her job? Forget about building that deck? Get the gutters cleared out as quickly as possible?

Don starts asking about prognosis. About five-year survival rates if she's a One versus if she's a Three. How does he know to ask these things? He must have prepared. He must have expected the worst, long before she knew what the worst was.

"Is there anything we can read that might help?" The man sounds like a brownnosing student. The topic interests him way too much. Laura doesn't want to read about it. She just wants it gone.

The doctor summons a nurse, who produces a couple of pathetic hospital pamphlets: *Diet and Cancer. Chemotherapy and You.* Dr. Jenkins also recommends a memoir written by a celebrity actress, one that sold well, even before the comedienne's death.

Disgust plows Don's forehead. A comedienne's memoir: worse than worthless. They need facts. Medicine.

"So." The surgeon taps Laura's chart. "Anything else I can answer for you?"

What do you mean, *else*?

"Are we asking the right questions?" Don asks. "Is there anything we should ask you that we haven't?"

Dr. Jenkins grins again. "You're doing just fine. I would give your questions . . . an A minus." She excuses herself. She leaves the room, a blazing flower, off to give more people the same message.

As soon as the surgeon disappears, Don starts in. He's got everything planned. Indianapolis. Medline searches. Second opinions. Dietary supplements. Second-look surgery.

"Don." *Go home,* she wants to say. I can't deal with you and this at the same time. "Don, I appreciate what you're trying to do. But I'm not your wife."

He flings his hands up—*fine.* He holds that wronged gesture in the air, as if he's playing a tree in the grade-school play. When he brings his paws back down, it's to shove the scribbled-over legal pad into his attaché case and close it quietly. He rises, chilly, at a great distance.

"You're still the mother of my children."

———

When we devote our Youth to God
'Tis Pleasing in his eyes
A flour Offered in the bud
Is no vain saCrafiCe

Eliz. Clare daughter of Samuel and Do. Fox
Clare wrought this Work in the y^r 1843

Soap's summons cut into Benjamin like a scythe loose among the crops of high autumn. He moved into the Roxbury works shortly thereafter, attacking agricultural chemistry with an ingenuity that hoped to wipe out his personal debenture forever. To settle education's bill and balance his ledger, Ben deeded his life to the company until such day as the lucrative virgin secret at last surrendered itself to research.

He studied the boilings, sped the splittings, and rang the changes. He calibrated his test instruments to match the sensitivity of Ennis's eye and tongue. His botanical notebooks now swirled with chemical radicals. He sketched, in symbols, those metallic salts that formed when alkali worked upon fatty bodies. Every mark he made in his private papers became company property.

Benjamin, who still followed the New England horticultural journals, alerted his brothers that a local competitor, Haggerston, was going about claiming that a mixture of 2 lbs. of his whale-oil soap with 15 gallons of water provided a most efficacious solution for ridding the world of the sawflies that infested roses. Thaddeus W. Harris's *Treatise on the Insects of Massachusetts, Injurious to Vegetation* brought the bug-killer to wide attention:

> Mr. Haggerston finds that it effectually destroys many kinds of insects; and he particularly mentions plant-lice of various kinds, red spiders, canker-worms, and a little jumping insect, which has lately been found quite as hurtful to rose-bushes as the slugs or young of the saw-fly . . .

Harris urged readers to wage an all-out war on caterpillars: men in the front lines and women in supply and logistics; their weapons, brooms and pails; their ammunition, soapsuds.

> [I]f every man is prompt to do his duty, I venture to predict that the enemy will be completely conquered in less time than it will take to exterminate the Indians in Florida.

A soap that could double as agricultural pesticide: Benjamin alerted his brothers, sporting the funeral pall of one who has just spied out his own obsolescence. But a few hasty tests confirmed that Haggerston's soap in solution could do nothing that Clare's could not.

Samuel and Resolve further commissioned Ben to find a cheap and feasible process for recovering waste glycerin. It irked the New Englanders to be discarding, as a corrupt by-product, quantities of a substance that fetched handy sums on the import market. Ennis declared the project a fool's errand, like turning dross to gold. He thought it the perfect occupation for "school chemistry." Benjamin agreed.

The ends of Ben's transmuting labors began to outrun the confines of chemistry. In his heated imagination, the fatty origins of this endeavor now converted themselves to the noblest ends. He dreamed a dream of conservation and utility, substances ingeniously made to answer to the varieties of human use. On the day the First Laborer set aside for rest, Ben mined, in place of the nostalgic Psalms, more delivering words, texts such as Dana's *Muck Manual* and Goodrich's *Enterprise, Industry, and Art of Man.* "I was dozing by my evening fire-side," he read in the Preface of the latter,

> when one of those hasty visions passed before my mind, which sometimes seem to reveal the contents of volumes in the space of a few seconds. It appeared as if every article of furniture in the room became suddenly animated with life, and endowed with the gift of speech; and that each one came forward to solicit my attention and beseech me to write its life and adventures.
>
> The portly piano, advancing with a sort of elephantine step, informed me that its rosewood covering was violently torn from its birth-place in the forests of Brazil; its massive legs of pine grew in the wilds of Maine; the iron which formed its frame was dug from a mine in Sweden; its strings were fabricated at Rouen; the brazen rods of the pedals were made of copper from Cornwall mixed with silver from the mines of Potosi; the covering of the keys was formed of the tusks of elephants from Africa; the varnish was from India; the hinges from Birmingham, and the whole were wrought into their present form at the world-renowned establishment of Messrs. Chickering & Co., Washington street, Boston.

If Chickering could turn the world's rough rootstock into that celestial ditty-player, Ben Clare determined to turn the rootstock's rootstock into the notes of a vaster symphony. In his kettle the globe's scattered garden gathered and reconstituted itself, Cornwall and Brazil, Maine and Potosí bubbling up some new and unimaginable Boston of restless and advancing matter.

Chemistry was not the means to soapmaking. Soapmaking was, rather, a means toward the consummate chemical end. To that goal, the elements moved from one incarnation to the other the way that the seasons, variously advantageous, moved through the eternally renewing year. If Nature were no more than eternal transformation, Man's meet and right pursuit consisted of emulating her.

Change paid regular visits to the factory at Roxbury. But it also came to take tea at Temple Place, sipping profusely. Ben's sister-in-law Dorcas Fox,

Samuel's helpmeet, unwittingly brought about the family's first major business rearrangement.

For her whole married life, Dorcas ably discharged the conjugal duties expected of her. Her shadowy stasis made possible her husband's eternal going. She brought the enterprise of domesticity onto a profitable footing.

The joint partnership exacted a toll on Dorcas ever stiffer than its usual excise. She changed religions for Samuel's sake, giving up more than he ever imagined. Fortune promoted her from petty retail to a dizzying Hill society that she never comfortably navigated. Sepsis harvested two infant sons. Anodynes prescribed to treat a nervous disorder after childbearing left her with a perpetual flinch and a constant roaring in her ears.

To these vicissitudes of an industrialist's wife she never objected. Her balance in sorrow and joy remained negotiable. But once or twice, over a quiet supper with their surviving children, she wondered out loud whether the family was not, in their style of life, in danger of serving two masters.

Devout Samuel always reassured her. There was but one Master. Their factory gave work to two score of His most destitute. And their soaps made His cleanliness available to persons of limited means.

But was it not wrong to profit from such work?

If they had been committing some wrong, Samuel assured her, they could not have stayed in business so long. Prosperity only proved how fully they satisfied the wishes of both God and men.

Did not Jesus say to take no thought for the morrow? asked the wife.

He did, conceded the husband. But there He spoke against unhealthy aggrandizement. As for our ordinary lives here, no good had ever entered into this sorry world but through the labor that God Himself, since the Garden, has bequeathed us for our own good.

Such was the education of their three children: the honest table talk, man and wife grappling with the terms of their existence.

In bad months, Dorcas's demon was not prosperity but destitution. Then, too, her steadfast husband consoled her. One learned by adversity just what the world demanded. Hardship would teach them how to bring to market those qualities that best met the clamor of human need. The lean years called out for the vociferous Nay of faith, even as the fat years called out for a modest and pious enjoyment.

To Samuel, even the history of the firm formed nothing short of a moral sampler. They had turned the Tariff of Abominations into a new beginning. They had weathered the Panic of 1837 and nursed the sapling business through absolute drought. They paced the developments of their fiercest competitors with bright notions of their own. Surely the Lord had clothed them with salvation, and they ought to rejoice in goodness.

What other blessing but wealth allows us this liberty and leisure to entertain His many bounties? Samuel certained her. Come, my girl: we cannot banish ourselves from the hutch while still making off with His eggs!

And the warm subtleties of Samuel's arguments would once again bring Dorcas peace.

Then one day in the autumn of 1844, when the earth's newly reaped battlefields reeked of the mechanical war between McCormick and Hussey, Dorcas underwent what an outsider might have thought a surprising conversion. In the space of an evening, the wife of growth grew inconsolable.

In the chill excitement of that fall's harvest, almost by chance, the words of amateur preacher William Miller fell upon that woman's ears like seed upon the readiest of soils. A slender broadside published by the Millerite corporate organ, *Signs of the Times,* came into Dorcas's hands. She read how Miller, after years of extensive study of the Book of Daniel, discovered that the sanctuary was about to be cleansed. The bodily advent of Christ was at hand. The world would end at the stroke of midnight, October 22, 1844.

This was not Miller's first deadline for the end. But to Dorcas, hearing the proclamation for the first time, the words made and unmade creation. They clarified, in one swift syllogism, why all earthly things had been so full of pointless sacrifice. Dorcas lived with the words in silence for as long as she could. Then, before the first frosts rimed the squash and the leaves reddened, she called Samuel's attention to their imminent destruction.

Silent partner in so many cunning contracts, Dorcas now offered her husband a business option. Samuel could give up his share of the expanding engines, dispose of his hank of pretty wampum, and join her in this last, glorious venture for which mankind was made. Failing that, she would leave for the new heaven and earth without him.

For the choice confronting them was non-negotiable, the deadline for divestiture, absolute. The hour had come, the one that no man could know. Man no longer owned tomorrow, let alone the day after. No time remained to fetch the prices that their lives sought. The smart trader would unload now, at market value.

For three days, husband and wife pored over Miller's material. Samuel picked at the tract, looking for fallacy but finding none. The two appraised the autumnal authentication visible all around them. All the auguries added up. No other explanation for events was as complete as Miller's, as detailed, or as likely.

Samuel woke to his wife's urgings. Suddenly, he counted them lucky, and more than lucky, to receive such irrefutable warning just days before being caught with excess inventory. That sere, crisp night when he fully accepted, Samuel came home from the factory and embraced his wife, the instrument of his preparation. He blessed her and his children for their service. With a speed and efficiency testifying to the ephemerality of all goods, he began to order his estate.

It was time to dispose of worldly property and settle earthly accounts. Candles and soap had once been humankind's best weapon against time. But now time had run out. Soon, in a few days, time would be no more. And humankind would no longer need manufacture.

The turning of fat to soap, of labor to cash, of wilderness to rail-served settlements merely predicted in miniature Miller's final transformation. All added value was God's, and man's most frenzied and sophisticated enhancements were but pale dress-ups of this original.

Samuel now lived for heavenly reorganization. Without a blink, he signed over his share of the business to his brother. Dorcas wondered aloud whether they ought, in good conscience, to saddle Resolve with the damnation they now so narrowly avoided.

But Resolve seemed ready for the saddle. No other family branch agreed to join the ascension, and Samuel could not bring himself to sell out his equity to some consortium of strangers. Damnation seemed the greater of two brotherly loves.

On the predicted, gusty October night, all manner of men donned ascension gowns and waited. Legend says they sought out the highest points they could reach. Some mounted hillsides, like loving flocks. Some advance scouts of the Saved even climbed to their own roofs, to speed by a few seconds their joining the fundamental merger.

Some hundred thousand more merely waited quietly, hands held, linked in a circle of family and friends, alive to imminence and completed in this their vigil. And a million other unbelievers no doubt hedged their bets with a watchful head-bow, in the event of some secular miscalculation.

Samuel and Dorcas, with their surviving daughters and infant son, waited in the vanguard. The sweep of the minute hand moved them forward, toward the very borders of expectation. Robed for arrival, they pushed up against the world's last midnight. Faith bumped up against its furthest meridian.

The moment they blundered toward was not fear. And the moment they awaited was not hope. Patient, convinced, prepared, they accepted the hour. No longing, no regret, no belonging. They felt no joy at deliverance, nor anguish at the errands left undone.

Everything up to the click of midnight was *becoming*. Beyond midnight, there would be no more becoming. Everything would only *be*.

Histories agree that in the instant for which Samuel and Dorcas and thousands of other Millerites waited, nothing happened. But histories look for revelation in occurrence, rather than in its more likely dwelling. For something did, in fact, happen on that stroke of midnight: an exchange as subtle and strong as any within human purchase.

In the early hours of October 23, Samuel and Dorcas Clare, Elizabeth, Mary, and baby Douglas descended from the upper room of their house, still stubbornly theirs. They walked back through the obstinately undissolved foyer, emptied at last of the waking nightmare of deliverance. And they looked out, like returned Crusoes, upon the manufactured world.

———

They send Laura home. Except it isn't home anymore. As soon as the van drops her off, panic closes on her like the automatic garage door.

The place is rotten with cut flowers and pretty, printed Get Wells. The kitchen spills over with trays of roasts and casseroles. Her kids will not touch any of the food that anxious neighbors have prepared for her return. Her kids do not eat irregularly shaped meals. Her kids would not recognize a roast if one bit them.

She, of course, is not yet past broth and bouillon. Tomorrow, a little clear soup; the day after, maybe some pureed potato. All those days in the hospital, desperately trying to fart. To pass just a wee little bit of gas to prove that her GI tract was working again. All she wanted was to be off the IV, take a little something in her mouth. Go home, where well-meaning people have piled up mounds of brisket.

The place is much bigger than it was. She gets lost, creeping on the way from the bed to the toilet. She lies sedated, unable to remember how the kitchen and breakfast nook connect, or if they even do.

The house has suffered much water damage in her absence. The rooms have all warped like delinquent cardboard, as soggy as an unsupervised soufflé. The wallpaper gives her vertigo.

All her square footage goes massively irrelevant. Utility room, laundry room, rec room, study, den. How many things must one person do? How many rooms does anyone need to do them in?

All this space: it's never been anything more than an obligation to fill it.

And the filler, all her carefully coordinated furniture: so cozy a nest once. Now lifeless twigs, the rotted rigging of a ship in a vacuum bottle.

She must have been mad. Had some crazed idea that the house would be her safe haven. Would always take care of her. She's spent years taking care of it, keeping up her end of the deal. But now, at the first called debt, the house gets ready to renege.

She lists in her head all the people she has to tell. Searches for ways to avoid telling them. She can't even manage the backlog of the last few days, the thank-yous for all the gorgeous hothouse mums. Going back to the office seems worse than jury duty. The requests for details, that vaguely excited show of distress. Hands consoling her, hugging her shoulders. Colleagues shouldn't let colleagues hug other colleagues.

She lies in bed at 3 a.m., the sawtooth trough across her ruby abdomen throbbing like a digital alarm. The yanked nose tube has left behind a permanent phantom scratch, and her PICC line lies coiled and taped to her collarbone. Junior, floating tumors may be loose in her system, ready to anchor and flare back into production. She must do something. But they leave her with nothing to do. She lies still, trying to kill the stray cells by the power of her concentration.

She's under orders to keep her dressings clean. Come in on Wednesday to get the staples yanked. Thursday for more blood work. Go to Indy in another week to get the chemo regimen settled on. As soon as possible, she must start the first drip. Other than that, they tell her to go slow, try not to burst her evacuated gut.

"Life as usual," Dr. Jenkins prescribes. "The best thing for you."

"Life as . . . ?"

"Live, Laura. But easy. Do what you always do."

And what was that, again? Houses. Go sell a few houses. She wants to start with her own. Get the best lump sum offered and move into a hotel. The kids would love it. Daily breakfast buffet. Swimming pool. Maid service. Slumber parties with unlimited jumping on the beds.

Sell everything. Sell the sport utility vehicle and give Ellen a year's worth of limousine fare. Sell the desktop machine and get a notebook, so Tim could hack his way through basilisks without having to get out of bed. That Mrs. Jensen over on East Prairie died of ovarian cancer.

She gets a driver's license renewal form in the mail. She sticks it to the refrigerator with the Raid magnet. She'll run up to the DMV as soon as she can twist a steering wheel and press a pedal again at the same time.

She walks by herself, but slowly. Damn baby steps everywhere, as if she's

Method-acting a geriatric. Cleaning the bathroom is out of the question. Even making microwave popcorn is an ordeal.

She puts it off as long as possible; then, one morning, she slips back into the office. Next Millennium. The Dream Finders. She sells a few houses, or tries to. The best thing for her. Colleagues' hands linger on her shoulders only for half an afternoon. People fuss a little, kindly. It's as if she's fallen off the Nautilus machine and twisted an ankle. The only C-word anyone uses is "condo."

Only gardening gives her some relief. Pruning the cosmos, she almost forgets herself, except for the throbbing gash in her gut. She plucks the first cukes and peppers, the ones she can reach without leaning. She would sink some narcissus bulbs for next spring, but it's way too soon, and she cannot bend over. Can't get all the way to the ground. Besides, perennials seem too obvious a plea bargain.

In the evenings, she tries to watch her old favorites. Her head still snaps back at the funny lines, the quirks of character. But no sound comes out of her mouth. She surrenders her responses wholesale, to the statistical averages of the studio audience.

Private confusion she might bear. But everything stays so plain, so *ordinary*. Standard order of business. That's the strangest thing about illness. Her body's betrayal changes nothing. The standing, routine pileup of diversions. How disorienting: here, now, all these weird familiars. Nobody sees, so regular is life. Nobody knows what's blossoming inside him.

She'd play dumb, if that could protect everyone. But people catch on, despite her best efforts. Cashiers eye her warily: sure you want all this stuff? The bag boys no longer bother asking her paper or plastic. They choose for her, the bag that will give her the most for the moment. She selects entrees by prep time. She stops buying thick magazines.

Ken calls furtively, early in the morning, when the kids are going to school and he knows she can't talk. "We'll talk soon. About everything."

Don't you see? she wants to shout at the receiver. There's nothing to talk about. Everything's handled. Taken care of. Just fine.

The children feel the hypocrisy of routine worst of all. Ellen will not forgive her. She bikes to cheerleading practice, furious that Laura won't forbid her to go. Furious at the stupidity of the disease that crashes her year, just when she was about to win probationary membership in the Populars.

Tim sits at a corner of the cluttered table, cursing the year's last homework. Laura can't tell him what's going on. She does not know, herself. All she can do is fall back on pretense. Life as usual.

"What's the matter, sweetheart? What'cha working on?"

He slams the book shut and tosses it, knocking over a stack of back mail she hasn't answered. He starts to cry, his face a twisted mask, denying its fat tears.

"Fucking poem."

She stares at him. At the word he's unleashed between them. Begging her to haul off and slap him. Wash his mouth out with soap. Needs her to rise up, a fury of parental force, indignant, undiminished, stronger than ever. To let him know in no uncertain terms that there'll be no getting away with murder, just because she's history.

Even here, she fails him. "Let's see," she says, quietly. Takes the chair beside him.

He will not shove her the book. Does not move either toward her or away. Just sits there, like a stone saint of incoherence, pilloried.

She gathers in the anthology, already beaten to felt by generations of seventh graders. *A Nation's Many Voices.* How many nations, made and unmade, since she had to read Longfellow. Since anyone has read Longfellow.

She flips through the alien, new earth. All the new women and Indians. All too late, too long after the fact. They'll put the poems in the book, sure. But no one's going to give back the 1.2 acres with lovely older structure they just spent their future to acquire.

"Where are you?" she asks him, already lost.

He spits a violent airburst through his lips and hurls one uncomprehending palm shoulderward. The hand drops to the book, still protesting its innocence. It roots out the offending text like a dog after badgers. His finger freezes, pointing. A guiltless martyr to Whitman.

"Crossing Brooklyn Ferry." She remembers it vaguely. It seems to be a four-page, hundred-fifty-line poem genetically engineered and irradiated for both freakish size and an unnatural shelf life. It must have slipped into this child's anthology through some complex scheme of laundered literary kickbacks.

She tries to negotiate with the monster at her son's gates. *Flood-tide below me! . . . Clouds of the west . . . Crowds of men and women attired in the usual costumes, how curious you are to me!*

Somebody has gone completely stark raving. Make that three people: the poet, the editor who included it, and the sadist teacher who has assigned it.

"Oh, honey!" . . . *you that shall cross from shore to shore years hence . . .* "What are you supposed to do with it?"

Do? He stares at her, blankly. Oh. The assignment. Trash the assignment. Not even worth kidding oneself over. "Supposed to say what it's fucking about."

"Tim. That's enough. Now. I mean it." Mean what? Mean: stop saying that word you know I can't make you stop saying.

"Come on," she tells him. "Whistle while we work." How bad can things be, really? Surely a kid faces harder things in this world than poetry.

Still: *The certainty of others, the life, love, sight, hearing of others.* Not exactly what Laura bargained for. She was never very good with words. Always hated English, social studies, all those invented topics. She couldn't wait to become an adult. When things would be real.

She stares at the commodity stretching across these pages. Somehow, she's become a working adult. Somewhere, she's learned: nobody makes a living. There are no other topics but these impenetrable, urgent fakes.

Others will see the shipping of Manhattan north and west . . . Fifty years hence, she reads. She has to take the poet's word for it. *It avails not, time nor place—distance avails not.*

She hasn't the first clue. It's like doing some kind of Martian archaeology. She's in badly over her head. She looks at the page for something to say. Her son stares at her.

She might have liked the stuff, if only she'd had the time for it. Once, at twenty, she memorized a Dylan Thomas that electrified her. One that promised all the comfort she needed to keep herself afloat when her hour came. She stored it up, her maximum armor. No harm could have the upper hand, so long as she recalled those transforming words. Recalled, and stayed twenty.

She tries them now, in her mind. A jingle, the height of irrelevant adolescence. She imagines herself declaiming to her oncologist. Reciting for the night nurse who handled her bedpan, the bored candy striper who brought her Jell-O on the polyethylene tray. Up the morphine a smidge, while I rage against the dying of the light.

Someone wrote her poems, once. Ancient history, now. That boy who fell for her, when she went back to school. Took her for one of the callow bobby-soxers she shared a locker with. Refused to see the obvious: that she had two kids old enough to be this kid's kid sister and brother. Shy, ugly, anemic. And he wrote her a whole sequence of, were they actually sonnets? Laura by morning, noon, and night.

She kept them for a couple of years, to spite first Don and later Ken. Saved them in the jewel box with her dad's old sapphire tie tack. Because the only other lines men had ever given her were apologies.

Tim drums on the table. A nervous, driving grunge beat, ready to explode. She tries to read faster. But the faster she goes, the less she gets. She cannot hear the words above her son's table-thumping. A hard sell, Tim. Like one of those house-hunters, desperate for you to read his mind, figure his every need, and fix him up with perfect lifetime lodgings, today or sooner.

I am with you, the dead man says. *And know how it is. Just as you feel when you look on the river and sky, so I felt, Just as any of you is one of a living crowd, I was one of a crowd, Just as you are refresh'd by the gladness of the river and the bright flow, I was refresh'd, Just as you stand and lean on the rail . . .*

Now she remembers this guy: a long-winded, total mystery. Even back then, way back when she was in peak explicating form. Big, bearded guy, a vaguely menacing Santa whose endless diatribes always bored her stiff and hurt her head. On and on, the numbing catalogs, every line beginning the same, trying to reassure the reader that he hasn't wandered off entirely.

She remembers something about the poet's sexual inclinations. "Is the teacher who gave you this a man or a woman?"

Tim snorts. "Nobody's really sure."

Modulo arithmetic would be easier. Analytical statistics. Linear programming. But this is Laura's penance, her act of contrition. Here: these endless repetitions, the man-loving man droning on about nothing anyone can make out. The perennial miscalculation of a teacher's last gift before summer vacation.

She will tell her kid all the wrong answers. Hopelessly muddle these lines for him, forever. She will bring down the wrath of education on him, cost him the college of his choice. But she will at least sit with him now, today, while sitting is still possible, until the verse is done.

"He seems . . . He's trying to talk with everyone who is ever going to be taking this boat. The boat he's taking. People fifty years later." A hundred. Or ever so many hundreds of years from now.

"Well? What's up with that?" Who the fuck takes boats anywhere?

"This ferry in New York, in eighteen fifty-something. Six. He's trying to imagine . . . all these lives. All these different times. All occupying the same place."

"Why?"

Why? She flips back through the poem. Her end-of-term exam. Surely the answer must be in here, somewhere.

I . . . Saw how the glistening yellow lit up parts of their bodies and left the rest in strong shadow . . . Look'd on the haze . . . on the vapor . . . The white wake left by the passage . . . The flags of all nations . . . I alone come back to tell you.

"Because . . ." she stalls. "Because he . . ."

Because this day's rush stands still and means nothing. Because we are all crossing from nowhere to nowhere. Each fluke life packed on this deck, lost, like every other. *These and all else were to me the same as they are to you . . . What is it then . . . the count of the scores or hundreds of years between us?*

She asks him hoarsely, "She wants you to say what it *means*?"

That I was I knew was of my body, and what I should be I knew I should be of my body. His teacher cannot possibly know what the poem means. Not unless his teacher is already sick. Unless she, too, already has the aerial view. Her own tumor.

"Forget it," Tim sulks. "I'll take the F. Let the bitch kick me out of school on my ass."

So be it. What does it matter, the future? Nothing. Everything. She won't be there. Teacher won't be there. Nor Tim, for that matter. The poet didn't even make it this far.

She looks down at the dead page. He's still at it. Interminable farewell catalog. *The dark threw its patches down upon me also.* Upon him? *Also.* She reaches across the dark patches, cuffs her cub behind his ear.

"Fucking auto mechanic?" Mom asks.

He looks up, dazed. Then he grins, smirks in misery. "Forget that noise. I'm starting my own company."

"Software?"

She gazes down over the rail at a bottle message, a world where even words are once again a growth industry. *Burn high your fires, foundry chimneys! . . . Thrive, cities—bring your freight, bring your shows . . .*

"Software," he cackles.

"Sure," she tells him. *Expand, being than which none else is perhaps more spiritual, Keep your places, objects than which none else is more lasting.* "Great idea. You'll clean up. Make a mint."

We use you, you objects, and do not cast you aside—we plant you permanently within us, We fathom you not—we love you . . . You furnish your parts toward eternity . . .

"Just remember to support your mother, in her old age?"

AN UNDERGROUND RIVER

Under the ground a River went,
A River went, a River went,
And folk in towns were well content

For underground *a* River *went,*
To fill the bathtub brimming up,
To wash the streets, to wet the green,
To fill the jug, to fill the cup,
To wash the clothes and dishes clean.
Under the ground a River *went,*

And folk *in* towns *were well content.*

—GRACE T. HALLOCK, *A Tale of Soap and Water*

———

On that evening when Dorcas cowered with Samuel in their upper room, Resolve's wife, Julia, busied herself with her own imminent arrival. While Dorcas Clare waited, doomed by a pamphlet announcing the arrival of Christ embodied, Julia Hazelwood Clare labored over a pamphlet of her own, one agitating for the annexation of Texas. She prayed in print that God would match the nation with an hour worthy of it. Hope for an American future lay in War with Mexico.

The Rio Grande marked but one of the frontiers Julia advanced upon that evening. In the business of print, she'd long before learned that her words sold in proportion to their audacity. Readers throughout town awaited the next stroke of her boldness, few if any realizing that "J. H. Clare" was one sprung precociously from the captivity of her sex.

Had Resolve been able, he would have bottled the woman's insights and peddled them through retail channels. He loved the low overhead his affiliate brought with her. All she needed to carry out her calling was something to make a mark, a place to sit, and a woman to raise the children that her husband got her with.

J. H. Clare spent little energy defending the rights of women to walk on hind legs. Not that she feared detection: the problem simply required too brute a solution to hold her interest for long. She saved her keenest syntax for two chief addictions: democratic vistas and the Machine.

She nursed an incurable weakness for ingenuity. The steamship was her Hermes, the arc lamp her Apollo. She promoted the extension of the National Road between the Virginia coast and Columbus, Ohio. She rhapsodized for three dense pages on the virtues of the Whitworth system of screw threading. She urged all her devotees to have their portraits taken with the new imaging lenses.

But for J. H. Clare, the engine that most sped civilization toward its providential future was the telegraph. In early editorials, she praised that obeisant electromagnet as the shatterer of the rules of space under which the old world operated. She relayed with approval Richard Henry Dana's words, "This is incredible. My faith is staggered!" But where the average journalist took to electrified stuttering, Julia announced mankind's deliverance from scarcity, ignorance, waste, and chaos.

Prior to this metaphysical invention, Washington and Baltimore stood sundered in their knowledge of each other by a fixed forty-mile ride. Rail drastically cut this barrier, but could not remove the vicissitudes of passage. Then the fateful, steely finger on the Capitol floor moved its distant mate in the B&O station office in ghostly synchrony. Time was dead; things could be known in the moment they happened.

The dull click of the coil carried for Julia all the charged declaration of religious awe. The flat affect of indifferent dot and dash flowed forth in a magnetic magnificat. In Julia's gospel account, the brace of codes flushed into the open air became democracy's duck shoot. She counted her readers blessed to be present on creation's eighth day. Yet the first utterance to travel across the wires struck her as almost irrelevant.

Yes, the Divinity had chosen that moment to revise the rules of His firmament. But *What hath God wrought!*—a text proposed to Morse by a woman— framed too humble an exclamation. For God's work was as nothing compared to what America meant to do now with her Promethean fire.

God, with the help of man, had thrown open a hidden portal in the side of distance. America had destroyed in one key-tap the baffles that had for so long checked the human race. Place, locale, no longer made one jot of difference. The mere existence of the device threw open to expansion the whole compass rose.

For how many eons had insurmountable geography impeded man's business? Now the new American race had burst those shackles. Now it could couple its energies in one overarching corporation, one integrated instrument of production whose bounty might grow beyond thwarting.

Here was the fabled, self-refilling magic beaker. The entire country could grow rich on a fraction of its prior labor. Every mile of wire produced enough surplus advantage to pay for the wiring of another mile. At wiring's end, all the wealth left over would better us beyond imagining.

Julia composed repeated editorial paeans to the breeding of electric messages. She compared their proliferation to the golden propagation of wheat: one seed turned itself into ten. Ten became a thousand. Only now the force of the sun and the fuse of the rain lay entirely in our hands. And the sower no longer had to make the choice between today's enjoyment and tomorrow's growth. Seed corn and feed corn were one and the same.

These delirious proclamations brought fire from various quarters. George Templeton Strong ruthlessly mocked her "millennium of gutta percha and copper wire" well into the fifties, delighting as J. H. Clare's pet Transatlantic Cable dissolved under the pressure of "superincumbent water." The strangest of bedfellows joined Strong in this attack on Julia's optimism. Henry Thoreau sniffed:

> We are eager to tunnel under the Atlantic and bring the Old World some weeks nearer to the New; but perchance the first news that will leak through into the broad, flapping American ear will be that the Princess Adelaide has the whooping cough . . .

But Julia lived longest and laughed last. The first message to span the globe in a fraction of a second was, she granted, a bit of bombast: Queen Victoria opened the link to her apostate colonies by proclaiming, "Glory to God in the highest, peace on earth, good will to men." Yet hard on the heels of this fatuousness came the first utterance of substance. John Cash, a London merchant, cabled his New York agent the immortal words "Go to Chicago."

But years before that transatlantic drama unfolded, J. H. Clare already saw the spark of America's technology ignite her politics. This noble experiment of enlightened self-government had awaited just this moment when its virtues could be dispersed through virgin territory by rail and wire. Steam and the factory system diffused a material well-being through those lower echelons of society upon whom the miracle of the vote depended. Steam-driven mills might make a Republic whose Capitol would be just as self-propagating as the industrial capital that forged it.

Industry's raw inputs were endless, the land fecund enough for any machine dream. And where favor had stinted in natural advantage, agricultural chemistry now offered a way to sow yesterday's dragon teeth and reap tomorrow's reconstituted legions. The Go-Ahead age managed, as Emerson said:

> by means of a teaspoonful of artificial guano, to turn a sandbank into corn.

Clearly, civilization's torch had passed to the North American Rome. But as with any healthy new soap works, the Republic of Invention had to grow to prosper. Julia's mental map of the country bleached toward one inevitable hue, filling out its natural borders between the Rio Grande and 54°40'.

She did not spoil for a fight, but neither did she shrink from it. A readiness to come to blows was the best way to avoid having to do so. The American Diplomat, at seventy years, was now old enough to negotiate from strength to strength. A nation come of age possessed no greater peacemaker than power.

"For whom was this continent meant," Julia wrote, "if not those most capable of developing it?" Prosperity was its own legitimization. The harvest of America fell to those best able to process the windfall. America's very bloom called out for the country to take up her rightful borders.

The call for Texas made Julia the Democrats' unlikely mouthpiece. But her husband forgave her the alliance, too busy prospering to worry much about Jackson's heirs. Resolve left the political pennies to his wife, preferring to mind manufacturing's pounds. He trusted she would, ultimately, look out for the works' best interests.

When the Mexican War at last broke out, Julia hugged its opportunity. J. H. Clare grew famous as the analyst of the assault upon Mexico City. She discredited the reports of invisible Mexican guerrillas sniping upon our troops and disappearing down arroyos into the undergrowth. Such were the invented phantoms of psyches too terrified to face the future. And those well-meaning senators who condemned the war as immoral managed only to give aid and comfort to our enemies.

Outcome, as always, proved the morality of her cause. She deeded the war's last word to that American captain who said, "I knew I could not be wrong, so long as the enemy in large numbers were ahead."

She took undisguised delight in Santa Anna's words at the fall of Chapultepec. She wrote how the marionette general had learned the error of crossing those who had returned him to power. The Yankees, Santa Anna declared, would storm by force the very batteries of hell. But in J. H. Clare's editorials, the Yankee didn't need to storm hell in order to rout it. He had a skeleton key to the back door. "God," as Santa Anna's chief of staff declared and Julia concurred, "is a Yankee."

American enterprise, according to Julia, already doomed the Mexicans, long before any shot had been fired. Reaper, power loom, hydraulic crane, and steam hammer beat the Catholics, not to mention the mass-produced Colt. She linked destiny and device, for to Julia, ingenuity and democratic expansion were the twinned poles of a single sphere. From this spinning globe would flow beneficence such as only lunatics and prophets had heretofore imagined.

On slavery, she held enlightened views. A mispricing in the labor auction could only hurt business, in the long run. Bondage's hidden costs sent false signals to the market that were better corrected than masked. Besides, the chained Negro was simply not necessary. Advances in agricultural machinery would render labor-intensive field work obsolete. At the same time, paying laborers a reasonable wage—made possible by the greater profitability of larger-scale farming—would create a new class of consumer ready to absorb the goods that production unleashed.

The country needed to think beyond the life of the plantation. And if the South failed to accept the inevitable change, Julia publicly promised that industry would vanquish the wayward agrarian with half the North's machinery tied behind its back. She predicted, too, that Armageddon's real beneficiary would be large-scale manufacture. And on this account, she was dead right. After the war, she forced the government to concede her authorship of the plan to lay siege to Vicksburg. J. H. Clare: Savior of the Union.

At first her columns warned against the rush for gold. Even where that pretty metal leached up to the surface, it offered no real prosperity. But soon Julia realized that the flaxen will-o'-the-wisp, if worthless in itself, sang a siren song that would lure the industrious race deeper into its greater habitation. Those who followed in gold's wake would then tap the true resources required by destiny.

Her theory of that destiny took her far afield. With access to brother-in-law Ben's notes, she wrote the first popular history of the Wilkes expedition. Her book credited the American scientists of that expedition with inventing the theory of evolution. She further accused foreign countries of stealing the charts so carefully assembled during that voyage, and disparaged the U.S. government for letting them do so. She lamented the unfair competition our South Sea whalers faced from the British and Dutch fleets, so handsomely subsidized. She claimed that the voyage unwittingly proved that the Indians were not the original inhabitants of America after all but stray Pacific islanders arriving in a chance gust that they never fully capitalized upon.

Of national expeditions in general, she declared:

Our ancestors, pressed by the adversities of their harsh homeland, set their keels upon hostile seas and in the solemn spirit of enterprise chased the westward passage of growth's glorious orb toward a garden that awaited any who gave themselves to its cultivation . . .

In like manner, so long as a single plot of soil on the knowable map remains unexplored, no children of commerce and liberty can refrain from contributing to its revelation.

In short, her nation was a yearning schoolchild, memorizing verse.

Those children over whose recitations she personally held sway learned early on to keep their iambs piping to her unforgiving tetrameter. None of her four children was allowed to stuff bun in mouth without first committing to heart and spouting couplets to life's grand gravity.

Her first surviving boy, Peter, received her endless favor simply for living. His birth ought to have been her death, and she loved him all the more for their mutual reprieve. Ever sickly, Peter Clare hadn't a prayer of living up to the expectations inflicted on him by maternal love. No better outlet for his accumulated sense of inadequacy existed than business. Even in the solitary nursery, the child's life was an elaborate game of farmers, grain, hens, and foxes, each needing to be shuttled back and forth across adversity's stream in the exact order that survival demanded.

Her other children detested her, each for private reasons. She drove her daughter Emma from the house for marrying a labor reformer. Electa, the unwed poetess, fought a violent, running, but finally unsuccessful battle to escape that same abode. William, the baby, Julia barely acknowledged. He saved up his revenge for over half a century, springing it upon the busy object of his needs only after she died.

But to Resolve Clare, God could have given no greater gift than this woman. They married in fortune and clung to each other all life long, like flood victims clutching their waterlogged policies. By stroke of incalculable luck, the manufacturer latched on to the one woman of his era who saw that history called out, above all else, for a better cake of soap. In fact, Julia led *him* to the gradual realization that what was good for soap was good for America. And better still: the other way around.

———

A woman stares frozen into the lens. Inert, motionless: a ravishing oval, hair a consummate cowl. The face is an artist's adamantine composite that would perish in unfiltered air. She sweeps one hand to her eyes in a perfect arc, devout and robotic.

The hand launches into a cosmetic ritual, touching up some eyelash flaw so small it escapes the lens's notice until her ethereal applicator brush addresses it. The hand disappears, returning to fix the hue, to balance the saturation in her cheeks' alabaster. Her skin responds, the color of a bloodroot hiding under forest cover.

The camera peels slowly from the plane of her gaze, revealing that this creature has been gazing into a mirror. Tangent to her own image, her profile solidifies into a pout, a glacial smile. She inclines toward the mirror in a crook almost intimate, almost confiding, flirting with her shadow. Her white sheath falls in a shower of crepe. Her hand snakes back up to appraise a lip, mystify it.

A disembodied voice—male—speaks from another dimension. The voice is pastoral, reflective, sagacious. "Some things you can only say with the one look that will say them."

The hand subsides. She leans in to the mirror a last time, tilting her head a little wryly at the effect: she could now kill anything that breathes. She nods once, a brief "Let's go" to her reflection. Then she rises and floats out the door of the powder room, a walk as composed as the grace she has worked upon her countenance.

The camera follows her into an elegant dining room. She slides into a plush booth across from a suited man doing his best not to whimper. They resume the meal that neither has touched, fingering no more than the stemware, tangling their slant glances, interrogating each other with suppressed peeks, a question hanging between them.

They rise to go. He swings an ankle-length vicuña coat to his shoulders and helps her on with her slight wrap. On the street, after an awkward pause, they pull apart to their separate cars. He succumbs to desperation, a little flick of the forearm, inquiring. She tilts her head and lifts those perfectly penciled eyebrows: who knows? Life is over long before it comes clear.

The camera catches her in her car, making up again in the rearview mirror. Two stoplights, and she is overhauled. The conversion is complete. Her features soften and flaw; her hair relaxes. Alabaster shifts into Harvest Peach. Somehow she changes clothes from courtesan-spy white to hunter-green flannel.

She pulls up to a house the epitome of management. Garage opens at the first entreaty of infrared. A girl of eight waits for her in the kitchen, leaps into her arms, nuzzles the face that gives up none of its layered evidence. She hugs back, pure love.

Brushing back the child's hair, she scoots on, into the den, leaping onto the denimed armchair quarterback there. Her laughing husband returns her embrace.

The whole story unfolds in just under thirty seconds. In their roughhouse clinch, the flannel woman's purse falls open at her feet. With one hand, the same expert snaking limb, she reaches down and closes the clasp on a cake of blush hiding there.

The voice-over returns, arch now, everything understood. "Some things you need never say at all.

"Face by Clarity. For as many looks as you have lives."

The specialist in Indy is a joke. His acne-faced intern comes into the room where Laura sits on the examining table in her flimsy hospital gown. He asks all the same questions she's already answered for the recording nurse. Twenty minutes later, the nervous boy comes back in and starts all over.

"I'm sorry," Laura tells him. "You've done me already."

"Yes," the boy intern stammers. "The doctor will be right in to see you."

She sits on the table forever, shivering in her sheet. Near-naked, in this sterile room, thinking of math. Is math a boy thing? Tim can do it. Maybe even better than his father, and Don has numbers coming out of all orifices. The two of them: batting averages, yards per carry, cruising velocity, kill ratios, angles of fire, square footage of recently conquered territory.

Girls just don't learn to think in numbers. Everything about math makes Ellen crazy. She hates the entire concept, more than Laura ever did. Playing right into the whole damn stereotype. Probably thinks some good-looking doc will balance her checkbook for her. Handle all her five-year survival rates.

The omentum and washings have come back negative. The second time in as many guesses that her hometown woman gyny has rolled wrong. Surely doctors have to do lots of math? Dr. Jenkins had three semesters of calculus just to get through pre-med. Probability and statistics must be Gerber for her. She knows the odds against two ninety-something percents going wrong.

At least the bank error is in Laura's favor this time. A massive break. She's one for two in long shots. But the reversals give her whiplash. Now she doesn't know what to do with any of her numbers.

Don's fed her a small library of books and pamphlets. Quizzes her over the phone, as if knowing the right answers is her only reliable safeguard. What kind of cancer do you have? *Serous cystadenocarcinoma.* What stage is the cancer? *Stage One C.* It's worse than the bloody Baltimore Catechism.

"How do you know you are a One C?" Don asks.

"Cancer limited to the ovaries. No ascites. Negative peritoneal washings."

"No, no, no." It makes him nuts. He'd slap her knuckles with a ruler if he had one. "Positive washings would guarantee that you *are* a One C, minimum. But *you're* a One C because the tumor was topical."

"Topical?"

"On the surface. Have they told you your five-year prognosis?"

But that's where things get a little tricky. That's what she hopes the specialist in Indy will clear up. Her five-year chance of survival requires what they call multivariate analysis. Age of patient, cell type, stage, presence of ascites, tumor differentiation and grade, disease volume prior to surgical debulking, amount of subsequent therapy . . .

She was always too timid to march for Liberation back in the seventies. Back when Liberation was still something you marched for. But she would march for segregated girls' math classes now, the last decade before the naughts, if separate classes could make girls better with the odds.

If only numbers were like perfumes. If every probability had its distinct color. That, she could have gotten. Some equation to map cancer recurrence rates onto different scents or shades. She tries on a 90 percent five-year survival. An 80, a 70. Down such a function's slope, the room browns out from teal to tobacco to tar. The air goes from rose water to chrome to exhaust.

When the specialist does turn up, he clearly hasn't seen her chart. The pimpled intern, in tow, shoots her embarrassed looks: *I gave it to him. Not my fault.* The specialist has written the definitive textbook on ovarian cancer. Definitive today, anyway. The text is called *Ovarian Cancer*. But the specialist can't even find Laura's tissue samples.

He looks at the intern. He looks at Laura. "Your tissue samples must still be on the way to our lab."

Laura says, "Mercy sent them in. Days ago."

Some part of the doctor's brain seems to hear her words. He smiles, without looking at her. He finds the lab work. He explains to her that she has ovarian cancer. That the surgery removed all visible tumor. "The slides show your tumor to be Grade Three."

"Dr. Jenkins at Mercy told me I was a One C."

He smiles again, patiently. "That was Stage. This is Grade."

"What does that mean?"

"Well, it means the tumor has about a 40 percent chance of recurrence."

"No. I mean, how can you tell it's a Grade Three?"

"Well, I'll grant you that the measurement is somewhat subjective. If you give the tissue samples to any three pathologists, they might not all give it the same classification."

She has no idea what he thinks she asked. "I mean, what *is* Grade Three? What does it mean?"

"Oh." Now her question is just a nuisance. Barely worth answering. "Grade is an indication of how clean the edge of the tumor is. How well defined. How aggressive."

In other words, how long before it takes over.

The specialist continues, while writing into her file. "You'll need to do half a year of dual-agent therapy. Taxol plus cisplatin. And by the way, we don't know for certain whether you are Stage One C. Even though your washings are negative, there is still some chance that you may be Stage Three."

Her head throbs; a vein slaps at her temple. She hears in the words a trapdoor opening onto enormous space.

"How can that be?"

"We have no lymph node section. We'd need to test a couple of nodes in order to get a definitive staging."

"Can't you get them?" She doesn't even know what she's asking for.

The idea of a controlled commando raid intrigues him. He considers it, but shakes his head no.

"We could try to snip them in a laparotomy. But with a cancer like yours, you've only got a one-quarter chance of positive nodes. So the risk of another surgery isn't worth finding out what risk group you're in."

Surely she will drown in numbers. She plugs these new ones into the formulas from Don's pamphlets. She seems to have a three-quarters chance of having as high as an 80 percent five-year survival rate. But that means a one-quarter chance of having a five-year survival rate as low as one in five. And do you figure that 40 percent recurrence rate, or is that already factored in?

"Doctor," she says. Louder than she expected. "What am I looking at?"

The specialist smiles and flips back over her charts. She assumes they're her charts, anyway, and not the next patient's. "The recommended chemotherapy for a Stage Three is six months. Stage Ones usually can get away with half that." He shrugs. The ball is in her court. How lucky does she feel?

She agrees to the harsher order. Half a year of hell, to be on the safe side.

"Fine," the doctor says. "You'd like to do the six months?" And into her chart he pens, *Patient elects for* . . . "Is there anything else we can help you with?" he asks.

"Yes." Of course not. "What causes . . . why do I have this?"

"Now, that's a very natural question. Almost everyone who comes into this office wants to know the answer to that one." He grins, indulging her understandable human frailty. "I wish I knew the answer. Ovarian cancer does follow at least three distinct hereditary patterns."

"No one I'm related to has ever been near it."

The specialist shrugs again. The gesture falls on his shoulders like a favorite windbreaker. "There's also some evidence that provoking agents, either combined with or inducing an alteration in the immune system . . ."

She tries to pay attention. But she has a fair amount on her mind. She comes back in time to hear him wind up. "The important thing is that you come back in half a year, after the six doses, for a second-look surgery."

"What will that tell?"

"Well, you may be right. There's some debate about whether invasive second-look surgery is reliable enough to merit the possible complications."

No, she wants to say. *No, no, no.* It's like talking to the kids while they're watching videos.

She promises to come back in six months. She'd promise anything. She just wants him to leave. Go take care of someone else. She wants to dress, get warm, go home.

Ken is cowering in the waiting room, treading in ever-tighter circles. He looks up at her as she enters, his face like a knee whacked by a little rubber tomahawk. The next instant, he is all concerned smiles.

She was against Ken's driving her out in the first place. But she needed him. He gave her the perfect excuse to turn down Don. Not much of a trade. Now he cringes with concern, between impatience and indifference.

"Come on," she says. "Let's get out of this place."

She drags him down the catwalk onto the flyover. They take the glass elevator up to the coded parking lot. The specialty center suddenly strikes her as a giant, state-of-the-art, cancer-fixing factory that enjoys a regional monopoly. The medical equivalent of one of those assembly lines in one of those constantly breaking 16 mm films they used to show in tenth-grade social science.

Why did she have to drag all the way out here? Sitting there in that sheet, and the specialist didn't even look at her abdomen. Couldn't they have done this by fax? By Second Day Air?

"Can we do a little sight-seeing?" she asks Ken. "While we're here?"

"Honey. It's Indianapolis."

The difference between Don and Ken flashes upon her. Don used to say, *Get real, honey.* Ken likes to say, *Honey, get real.* Seemed like a small improvement to her, once.

She makes him drive around the Soldiers and Sailors Monument. Past the Benjamin Harrison Home. Lockerbie Square. The fake-Gothic cathedral. The Indianapolis Motor Speedway and Hall of Fame Museum, which perks him up a little. He actually gets out of the car for that one.

Okay, so it's not Paris. But there's a famous deli not far from downtown that people back in Lacewood always carry on about. They will go load up there, while she still feels like eating. The only time in her life she doesn't have to worry about watching her weight.

She orders the famous Reuben, so famous it has some kind of proper name. She orders a slice of chocolate cheesecake as well. It's probably great. She makes Ken eat it. "I can't afford the calories," he says. Then sets a land speed record downing it.

He drops her off in front of the house. He lingers a little in the car. Wants to say something. He pets her, feels her hair. Like he's going to miss it. Like that's what brings this whole thing home to him.

All she can do is stroke his hair back, down behind the ear, where he has gone dead and bristly, as white as some expensive sheet of paper before anything's been written on it.

Ellen's waiting. She's seen her mother in the car.

"Shameless public display of affection."

"Don't start," Laura warns her.

"And with *that* man." The girl stares at her mother, waiting for a full account. Refusing to ask for it. "Well?" she says at last. "What did the experts say?"

"Well," Laura begins. "The tumor is a Grade Three."

"Wait, wait. I thought the doctor here said it was Grade One."

It stuns Laura: her daughter. Her daughter has been paying attention. "No. Yes. That was *Stage*. This is Grade. And we don't even know that I'm a Stage One, for certain."

The teenager slams a hand to her forehead. "Oy. Okay, okay. What's Grade?"

"How smooth the edges are. How well defined—"

"No, Mom. Mom. Just tell me: is it a good thing or a bad thing?"

Don calls, way too late. Well after ten, that cutoff hour he himself has declared as off-limits for them. He's so excited he barely asks how it went out in Indy. "She was supposed to take your lymph nodes," he blurts out.

"The specialist said something about that. How did you—"

"It says so. Plain and simple, in the National Institute guidelines."

"About needing the nodes for a complete diagnostic—"

"That's exactly it," Don says. Proud of her for staying with the point. "She didn't close the back door. You were lying there, open, on the cutting table, and she didn't take them. Even though the guidelines say she's supposed to."

"It's done, Don. There's no point in—"

"I think we have solid grounds for a lawsuit here."

As good as winning the lottery. The Daily Double. A present from Don to her, to make her happy. Compensate.

"Go to bed, Don." *And don't forget to wake up,* she refrains from adding.

She sits in the kitchen, alone, after the rest of the world has called it a day. The stuff that the coffee machine has patiently kept warm all day has condensed into a chewable acid. She dumps this tannery sludge down the sink— the working woman's Drāno. Or maybe Drāno is the working woman's Drāno. No matter. She starts a new pot.

She starts a new list, too. Two cracked storm windows. The gutters on the north side. The upstairs toilet tank seal. Everything else can wait until after winter.

The ceiling above the den gives a little pop in settling. First time this season. She should switch to decaf, but doesn't. She cleans the counter, waiting for the Peruvian beans to brew. She wipes into oblivion the diet pop rings and the bits of Pop-Tarts rind. *Toasted,* as Tim says these days. *My whole life, toasted.*

When the coffee is ready, she pours it into a Millennium mug that reads: "Own Your Dream." Adds a slug of milk—2 percent, for the heart. Then some brown sugar. Life is short. Who's counting?

She sits at the butcher-block table that gave her so much pleasure when she bought it. That extra leaf that hides away in the middle. She takes the credit card calculator from her purse and sticks it under the fake Tiffany lamp, to activate the solar cell. She tears the top Post-It off the cube by the fridge and picks up the magnetized flower pen. The Post-It shows a little cartoon character holding a pencil twice the size of his marshmallow body. He's saying, "Never put off 'til tomorrow what you can bury forever in a To Do list."

She tries to turn this into an interest rate problem. Mortgages, amortization, points: things she can follow. But it will not go. Three-quarters times 80 percent, plus one-quarter times 20? Or maybe you take the good chance minus the bad chance. Or maybe you have to find a number, say, three times closer to four fifths than it is to one.

As the pamphlets say: the numbers stand for groups, not for individuals. What does it mean, an 80 percent chance of surviving? Eighty lives out of the hundred hypothetical lives that she might lead will make it past their mid-forties? Or maybe it means, repeat the next five years forever, and on average, a fifth of her will die.

The numbers mean nothing. Still she insists on reaching a number, any number, by bedtime. Some definitive digit, right or wrong.

She thinks of that box up in the attic, two flights above this kitchen, a floor above her waiting bed. Her life's cardboard safe, containing the whole paper trail leading from her girlhood to this table. Last she checked, she still had every report card anyone ever served her with. She could find it now, if she wants, that one from age eight, where her third-grade math teacher sums her up in a looping hand: "Laura is slow, but not always accurate."

Typed for life, from out of the starting gate. Nothing ever changes. Slow. Not always accurate. But persistent as the day is long. Persistent as her own cells.

———

Clare's Sons have always sold their candles a full sixteen ounces to the pound. We invite you to ascertain the truth of our stamp of "Real Weight" by submitting our product to your own scales.

J. CLARE'S SONS
Justice and Spring Streets, Roxb.

———

After the world stubbornly refused to end, Resolve welcomed Samuel back into the business. Never again on equal footing, of course. Samuel expected no such absolution, even from his most charitable Maker, let alone that Maker's flawed reflection, his brother.

Samuel and Dorcas returned to commerce's fold chastened but unrepentant Adventists. Granted, the world had missed the latest deadline for its demise. But who would be so foolish as to conclude, from one respite, a world without end? Visitation was merely delayed. All mankind became stakeholders in Creation's impending completion. Had not the Lord Himself said, "This generation shall not pass, till all these things be fulfilled"?

But for Resolve, the practical question remained: Just which generation had Christ referred to by "this"? At the end of the day, all business would indeed be futile. But until such a time, time was of the essence. So long as Now and its consequences belonged to two different tallow lots, why not let the cooker boil for a few more business cycles? The trick was to keep working, so long as there remained time to liquidate before final evaporation.

Upon Samuel's return, the brothers settled into a simple routine. The two senior partners so trusted each other that they no longer crossed paths. Samuel stayed in the plant in Roxbury, overseeing the quality of the goods issuing from it. He seldom set foot in the Boston office. Nor did Resolve often feel it necessary to travel to the factory to inspect the processes. In fact,

Resolve rarely saw the crates and wagons his brothers assembled. But he kept them routed, and found them new destinations.

Resolve took charge of the business. The business now summed to much more than its five major parties. Thirty men and women labored under them. But still no candles cracked from their molds, no soap from its frame except through the combination of Jewitt's monster cauldrons, Ben's chemistry, Ennis's seasoned recipes, Samuel's benevolent direction of the workforce, and Resolve's raptor-like eye on the wholesalers' correspondence.

The firm was like some frugal bank client, reinvesting its dividends in itself. The brothers had long honored a de facto pact not to draw out from the compounding stockpile more than three thousand a year—fifteen hundred for Ennis and Jewitt. Slowly they were getting rich again, richer than the glory years of merchanting. But wealth depended on the provision that they not touch their kingdom.

A dollar sunk into new heated dryers returned a dollar ten cents in increased productivity. A new squad of men to work the acid baths, brought on at $100 a head per year, added $150 a head of new soap and candles by the same period's end. The freed Negro, battered on all sides, would generally work for next to nothing. And there were always jobs, amid the reeking fat, where a Negro's presence would not disturb even the most sensitive of whites.

When cash found no immediate outlet in capital improvement, Resolve once or twice bought up a local competitor, put it out of business, and stripped its inventory of usable equipment. For a time, the works enjoyed the growth of a strapping toddler. Wider distribution and greater efficiency kept them redoubling every four or five years. And a 16 percent growth rate per annum only served further to feed new economies of scale. Each time they increased their daily tonnage by half, it cost them half again what it cost on the last occasion.

The age of the cottage industry was over. The number of Boston chandlers and soapmakers had declined steadily, although the area's population had boomed since the firm's inception. Those few dozen outfits that remained boosted output and pared costs to the marrow. Jewitt's bold kettle—forever nicknamed *Clare's Funeral*—spared the Clare works this shakeout and brought them into industry's next stage. And by and large, the Clares got there just one step before the next outfit down the road.

For his part, Jewitt typified the new industrial tinkerer, the inventive hero, the man of the future. He out-Yankeed any of the native-born. His silent treatments now extended well beyond his antagonist, the Irishman. He stopped talking to all of his colleagues, except to show them his schematics and explain his plans.

Jewitt's Roxbury plant annex was a forest of belts and bearings. He packed the manufactory with self-stringing wicks, self-pouring vats, and self-releasing molds. He perfected his steam-driven soap crutcher, finally sending to its grave the old hand-churning hickory rods. Jewitt squeezed so much use from each square foot of manufactory that the growing number of employees found it difficult to maneuver inside the buildings.

Ennis cursed the fastidious Englishman's each act of mechanical progress, even though he benefited from the inventions as much as anyone. For years, Ennis had to rise at four in the morning to light the kettle fires. When Jewitt's steam boiler coils changed all that, the Irishman's gratitude consisted of railing against the wizardry.

For all his ingenuity, Jewitt's most profitable invention scraped the bottom of technology's barrel. He rigged up massive block tables with hinged overlays strung with piano wire. Slabs of soap were made to roll onto these tables. Then the stoutest laboring men yanked on the wire-rigged hinges, cutting several blocks at one go. A second set of wires strung at 90 degrees produced scores of discrete, one-pound chunks. The chunks then slipped off the cutting tables to be crated and sold in any quantity, over any distance.

The new cutting process changed the way that product passed through the plant. Flexible, rational, better-regulated: the "bar" proved the biggest boon to margins of all Jewitt's innovations. Had the Clares paid him by percentage of return, he could have retired with enough years left to read every gloomy parlor novel ever written.

Mid-century prompted the Clares to take stock and examine the overall health of their holdings. Together, the men mounted a comprehensive inventory, forecasting the fate of their group labors. They calculated and projected, sampled and surveyed. Owners and agents went over their library of ledgers. How solid were the sales of their various soaps and ten kinds of candle? Did each carry a price the market would bear? Were the machines and hands being used to maximum advantage, at the lowest possible costs? How ready was the company to undergo a new round of strong change?

The numbers revealed a concern healthy enough to trundle along for many seasons to come. But mere persistence wasn't good enough for Resolve. His genius lay in seeing that progress demanded the destruction of much that had once been considered wealth. Manufacturing, like the very project of civilization that it advanced, was a snaking, torrential Shenandoah beyond anyone's ability to dam. The waters had constantly to leave behind the landscape they drained, if ever they meant to reach open sea. So, too, any forward-looking enterprise had to be ready to cast off what had once been its mainstay. Hanging on to spent ways was a pro forma suicide.

Resolve persuaded his brothers to quit making cheap tallow candles. They broke up once-gainful equipment, their former pride, for scrap. They stopped production of the Fair Grade and the Extra Fair Grade, the last scouring soaps still made by the old potash method. They committed to superior soda ash, however much that indentured them to English alkali. They concentrated on their German mottled, whose red veins proved how little water the soap contained; their yellow rosin laundry soaps, good for the hardest waters; their palm oils, with their pretty violet scent; and of course, their star toilet brand.

They severed ties with now-unprofitable outlets, those glories of the canal age that rail had siphoned off. They pitched their lot with the chaotic spew of new lines, cuts connecting the Hub with Albany and Vermont, routes like the Champlain and St. Lawrence, promising endless frontier. Rail freed them to serve all sorts of previously isolated customers. They hired commission brokers in Baltimore and fought to break into New York's murderous market.

They also joined the fray for the Western customer. The crushing of Mexico—Julia's pet cause—resulted in their shipping an additional ten thousand pounds of candles and soap around the Cape every two months.

Lard moved off the premises by the tierce, the keg, and the pail. The years had been good to lard oil as well. Pig and cow fat, pressed prior to splitting, yielded rivers of precious grease. When burned in special lamps, the oil produced a light acceptable enough for the Clares' own factory floor. When Ennis discovered how to convert the stuff into the perfect machine lubricant, demand for the happy by-product swelled.

But light from another source threatened to do in candles altogether. Each year, gaslight further eroded the income that candles brought in. Resolve, in every other respect a man of progress, refused to let the enemy into his own home. But the end of candle profit, however distant, was inevitable. The books predicted this unhappy end. Unless some gain could be extracted from the same costs, the blessings of the Clare works would begin to contract.

We need to increase production, Resolve told Samuel. We must implement a new round of stretch-outs.

Samuel shook his head. A stretch-out would not go down with labor. Neither would a fresh round of speedups. Work had sped up and stretched out to its outermost limits. The workers had taken to singing ironic choruses at the dinner ring-out. The most popular tune aired often enough times to lodge in Samuel's conscience:

For Liberty our Fathers fought,
Which with their blood, they dearly bought,
The Fact'ry system sets at naught.
A slave at morn, a slave at eve . . .

At which point, the youngest candle girls trilled their way up into an undeniably thrilling descant.

Worst, the denizens of the boiling floor, encouraged by the Massachusetts Supreme Court's decision in *Commonwealth* v. *Hunt,* were organizing. They had begun to make collective noise about a ten-hour day. To Resolve's astonishment, the law no longer let their very employers shut such movements down. Chief Justice Lemuel Shaw's majority opinion announced that labor societies were no longer to be considered criminal conspiracies. The court declared trade unions, closed shops, and even strikes to be as salubrious as any market auction—in fact, free competition by another name.

Samuel spelled it out for his brother. Any further attempt to force labor into greater profitability would ruin them. The Clares needed a breakthrough: the holy grail that Ben had been laboring on for so long.

Only the recovery of glycerin held out the hope of countering candles' sagging returns. After saponification with soda ash, soap simply waltzed away, abandoning glycerin in crude water solution at the bottom of the vat. The Clare brothers, like their Boston competitors, simply ran the dregs into the gutter, flushing them away as cheaply as they could. Meanwhile, imported English glycerin, a golden heal-all, fetched prices as high as two dollars the pound.

Salvation depended upon converting that slag into the much-sought-after salve hiding inside it. From kettle piss to medical emollient: thus the task confronting modern chemistry, the age's enchanter. Ben devoted himself to the problem, sneaking away only to tend to his beloved namesake, the contraband South Sea plant now kept alive only through virtue of Cambridge hothouses.

Ben's alchemy, when it came, took a Jewitt autoclave to bring it to life. Hermit botanist and misanthrope tinkerer worked out the details in a series of lengthy notes to each other. Remarkably, specification and prototype drifted close enough to each other for Ennis to make the thing work. Not well, at first. But gradual refinements in the process at last turned their factory's sewer effluent into cash.

Soon the Clares were making glycerin at half the cost of British imports. As the price of the elixir fell, its uses multiplied. At the right price, all manner of other manufacturers lined up to place orders: inkers, decanters of boot black, papermakers, printers. Word spread of the Clare grubstake, and entrepreneurs from far and wide descended on the claim.

The Panic of '57 blasted their prosperity as a coolie blasts rock. The distant Ohio Life Insurance and Trust Company failed, and began pulling the entire fabric of overbuilt, overextended American commerce down with it. The nation's business ran to the brink of disintegration. Employment vanished again, and money along with it.

Soap and candles were somewhat less recession-proof than firearms. Resolve, drowning in overproduction, hoped to pull the company through hard times by laying off much of the workforce. They could weather the stagnation, drain inventory, hope for an improvement in national well-being, and rehire later, after wages collapsed.

But hard times brought a harder recovery. In the midst of depression, a certain Richard Tilghman, chemist from Philadelphia, notified Clare's Sons of Roxbury, Massachusetts, of his intention to sue them for patent infringement. The notification referred to papers filed with the U.S. government, blueprints of a process not identical to Ben's and Jewitt's autoclave but so close a progenitor as to produce an ironclad case.

Pleading ignorance would not protect the Clares. The law was the law, built to settle the frontier, protect cleverness's property, provide incentive for gain, and compound the power of capital. And toward that end, the law would gladly shut down all manner of soap manufacturers, whatever their size.

The Clares settled with Tilghman before the suit reached a court. But settlement cost them dearly, both in license fees and in retroactive penalties.

Benjamin had thought himself on the verge of paying off his debt to family and business. He dreamed only of escaping the chemistry of fats and returning, at long last, to his beloved botany. He had imagined his indenture to be almost over. And now it was set back decades.

For a time, he considered killing himself. But he soon realized how little fiscal recompense his brothers could extract from such an act. Instead, he resorted to a move that was, for him, far harder. Far more a sacrifice.

He approached his brother Samuel one day, in the wooden supervisor's office above the cooking-vat floor. Samuel, the one who would force their brother Resolve to return an overcharged dollar on a billing of one hundred. Samuel, the one who refused to follow the common practice of underweighing, however widespread. Samuel the good, who still thought of earthly business as preparation for the business of eternity.

And Benjamin laid down upon his brother's desk a packet of thick, succulent leaves. Each oozed a viscous milkiness from the slit where it had been severed from its roots. And he signed over the first, native-born North American crop of *Utilis clarea*.

The Red Man never worried about his skin, Benjamin announced. *Why should you?*

———

"Your husband seems to be threatening to sue me," Dr. Jenkins says, when Laura checks back into Mercy for her first round of chemotherapy. Two parts embarrassed and one amused. Or maybe the other way around. It's hard to say, with so professional a caregiver.

"Not my husband," Laura apologizes. Just some creep I used to be married to.

The surgeon has dropped in just to well-wish. Laura's not really her beat anymore. The ball, Laura's cancer, is in Dr. Archer's court now. Mercy's oncologist has come back from retirement after his young replacement suffered a nervous breakdown and put himself indefinitely out to pasture.

Everything about the returned retiree gives Laura the heebie-jeebies. Dr. Jenkins, at least, provides a little color. The changing plumage. One day surgical scrubs; the next, thigh-length mauve.

Laura's own fashion statement today consists of her shortest hair since the home Toni days. Ease the transition, make the change seem semi-deliberate. It was time to lose her locks anyway. She wore them five years longer than she should have. She always disliked the rule that says older women can't wear long hair. But they shouldn't.

Don hates her new look. That, at least, is some small compensation. "It's not you, Laura. It makes you look . . . severe." By severe, he meant lesbian. Feminist. *Just you wait, babe.*

"I didn't see a reason to take the lymph nodes," Dr. Jenkins says. "You'd lost a good deal of blood already."

"The man is a little excitable. Don't pay him any attention."

"People don't always know how to help," the doctor suggests.

"People don't know anything."

He'll never sue you, she wants to assure the doctor. Ask you out, maybe. But he'll never sue you. It's the woman's perfume, Laura figures. That faint bouquet of carbolic acid. The Spanish fly of the industrialized nations.

Hospitals everywhere: that same aroma. More distinctive than a Crabtree & Evelyn's. Does everything medicinal have only one available whiff? Vitamins, Band-Aids, antibiotics, prosthetic limbs. Obstetrician-gynecologists. Heady, solvent smell of the safely disinfected. Death Beater Number 5. *Kinda new, kinda now.*

The perfume of this building, of the nurses' carts, the packed supply rooms, takes her back to her last serious hospital stay. Tim's birth. The hospital in Peoria. Same as this one. Same as any of them. Tim, so early, so tiny, so purple. Dead on arrival, save for those machines.

And for five months she and Don didn't know what their baby's face looked like without a nosegay of tubes strapped to it. But they knew how the little thing smelled. They could smell him at night, back at home, the two of them spent and exhausted, the smell still on their helpless hands, staining the sheets of their own ignorant bed.

He smelled like a hospital. Like they might lose him at any minute to this health scent. This chemical antiseptic: the stink of medicine and meters. The little guy smelled like he'd been swabbed in some formaldehyde, a bath to put him beyond all earthly corruption. In her mind, that smell bumps up against the aroma of boeuf bourguignonne. She and Don at that ruinously fancy French restaurant, one meal like a month's worth of groceries, swearing to each other the most serious vow that life allowed. How they would see that tiny purple thing through graduation from college. How they would love each other and support each other as long as it took, and bail each other out for as long as there was bailing.

Dr. Jenkins moves on to her real rounds. Laura lies back in her chair-bed, in a room with half a dozen others in her same boat. A ring of people lie attached to drips, a wayside filling station. The room is large and bright and flowery, freshly stamped, like one of those recently airdropped tract homes.

The chair-beds don't exactly face each other. Two have already changed occupants—booths in a short-order restaurant—during the time she waits to get hooked up. A room full of other poor cancerous souls. Tomorrow, another group just like them.

Laura checks in to the circle for a longer stay. The same amount of chemicals, only dribbled through her system at a quarter of the usual rate. They give her this much choice. Some patients seem to experience less nausea if the poisons are spread out a little. The trade-off sounds fair. It's not as if she's losing any quality work time, after all. And this way, with luck, she'll get the retching over with before the kids have to see her.

She lies back, sloshing inside. Cisplatin tends to hammer the kidneys, so for the last twelve hours she's been gulping water until she feels like a fifty-gallon fish tank.

Dr. Archer breezes through while the onco nurses are prepping Laura. He greets the other patients—veterans and rookies—with the cheer of someone who in his heart's heart is still retired. Invulnerable. Only a matter of time before the hospital makes the replacement hire.

"Mrs. Bodey." The oncologist beams. He scans her chart and reviews all the indicated dosages. "You have someone to pick you up and take you home when you're done?"

"Yes, Doctor."

"Can you believe those clowns in Congress?" Dr. Archer looks up quickly, to see if she can. If she can believe the clowns.

Maybe it's a trick question. She can't wrap her head around it. She can't quite say anything.

"They think they're *protecting* us." He returns to studying her chart.

Health care, she wonders? But no. He's just relaxing her. Making polite conversation. Chatting over the eternal budget impasse. Partisan politics. What kind of world do we want? Who do we want to win the big game?

"I suppose they want what's best." Dr. Archer sighs. "That's the heartbreaking thing. If they'd just get the hell out of everybody's way and let people get ahead with their lives. Let us all do what we do best."

She smiles as warmly as she can. She shrugs at him. Those nutty legislators. What are you going to do with them?

"You think our noble government protectors would have let electricity on the market if they'd been around to take care of us? Cars?"

"No?" Laura ventures.

"Damn straight, no. Too dangerous! We'd still be living in fail-safe lean-tos. Good old safe holes in the rock, if our lawmakers had their way."

Dr. Archer signs off on her clipboard and hangs it back on the foot of her bed. He inspects her PICC line. A narrow plastic straw now runs inside her, a phloem tube into her wrist and up her arm, coming to rest somewhere south of her collarbone. Snaking toward her heart.

"Sweetheart, we're going to start you off with dexamethasone, 20 mg. It's a steroid. Anti-inflammatory. Good stuff. Throws a damper on the worst effects."

Effects? Like that little booklet, *Chemotherapy and You.* You may find yourself not wanting to eat. Your ears may ring or your fingers may feel slightly numb. Everybody bracing the patient for the worst, all the while cueing her to make the worst even worse.

The dexamethasone starts leaking into her at two-thirty in the afternoon. It dribbles for an hour and a half. She lies back with two folders, Properties and Clients, open across her lap. By 4 p.m. she's reviewed maybe three entries. Made some checkmarks that will mean nothing to her tomorrow.

At four, Tracy, the supercompetent onco nurse, comes to change her bag.

"This is Benadryl, 50 mg. It's an antihistamine and an anti-emetic."

"What does that mean?" Laura likes Tracy. She's like Ellen, only old enough to have outgrown the attitude.

Tracy grunts. "That means the second course is supposed to keep you from throwing up the third course."

"Terrific. Wish me luck."

"Oh, you'll do fine, Mrs. B."

Sixty seconds after the first drop of fluid hits her blood, she feels how right Tracy is. She's going to be fine, and more than fine. Everything is going to turn out like magic, only better.

The potion baptizes her with a wave of well-being. The front edge of that liquid blessing flows into her, intact. Its chill rushes past each of her body's way stations. She lets herself rise, a blissful thermometer, the silvery glow of mercury coursing through her, up into her neck and through her throat, splashing across her head and out her ears. She gives herself to the strange wash now delighting, now calming her cells.

And her cells respond like succulents after a rain. This must be what heroin is like. A perfect, wonderful, absurd feeling, beyond description. Of course people want to stay here, bathing, forever and ever. "Hooked" isn't right, isn't fair. Not for such peace. A drowsy syrup of sleep frees her from anxiety she didn't even know was hers.

Alan, Tracy's second-shift copilot, slaps on a pack of Zantac, 50 mg. Laura looks up for an ID. But it's not a big deal. Whatever they do is right. From some distance away, across the air's chasm, she hears Alan say that it's an anti-ulcerative. To coat her stomach and soften the chemo's landing.

Gladness takes her up through 4:30 p.m.: the start of the taxol, 200 mg in 1,500 cc of saline. Somebody—Tracy or Alan—tells her the thing about the tree bark again. How can tree bark hurt you? Tree bark is 100 percent natural. The Native Americans used to make all sorts of things out of tree bark. Canoes and houses. Mighty medicines. The completely natural toxin is set to drip into her for the next twenty-four hours.

She calls the kids. Everybody's fine, but she has to get off the phone because Ellen's expecting a call. She'd like to call Ken, but of course she can't. Nor, apparently, can he call her.

By 7 p.m., bliss is gone.

She sleeps maybe a total of forty-five minutes that night. For one, they keep waking her up, just to see if she *will*. For another, the early-warning beeper on the IV pump keeps going off every time she flexes her fingers. She shifts her arm, and it's an emergency. After the millionth beep, she starts talking to it. "Shut up. Oh, shut up." But it won't shut up, and the nurses can't make it any less sensitive.

A day dripped out in microseconds outlasts the idea of time. She sits with her two folders across her lap, as the world runs its whole arc from light to dark and back to reconstituted light. Weird ideas come to her at three or four in the morning. There is no history. Everything already is. Humanity is a child locked by accident in a library, reading its way through the permanent collection, looking for a way out.

This is no time for sleeping or eating or reading. No time for plans. She gives the day over to breathing. She needs all her powers of concentration. A day of doing nothing at all, of simply keeping the tedium from killing her. Nazis are loose in her blood's lowlands. She must break the dikes and flood out their armies.

Then four-thirty again. The next day, whatever "the next day" means. Her system gets a flushing: pure saline for five hours. Like the stuff her mother used to throw into the wash machine after several loads, to keep the works from clogging up.

Someone calls. Some man. She doesn't take it.

At nine-thirty that night—which night?—they hook her up with Zofran plus a dexamethasone chaser. She's not catching dosages anymore. Zofran to keep the nausea at bay. What took you so long? Medical research, working on cutting-edge solutions to the horse/barn door problem. All these meds—discovered, researched, tested, refined, combined, advancing in perfect parade formation, from hospitals everywhere. Some woman in Flagstaff, Arizona, roughly her age and weight, her same ambiguous staging, gets this exact cocktail tonight, administered with like expertise by her very own teamlet of onco nurses.

The ingredients multiply without limit, most of them less than a month and a half old. How we live, now: a new set of doses every day. From experiment to established practice, even before the first round of guinea pigs can sicken or get better. This huge practice, this sacrament, millions of interlocking decisions implemented by tens of thousands of orderlies, each doing his expected turns. An anthill beyond anyone's ability to manage.

"What's next?" she asks at 10 p.m. Square-jawed, but still game.

"Cisplatin, 120 mg, plus mannitol, 37.5 mg, for about six hours." Alan is on shift again. Somehow, she's missed Tracy's shift all together.

"For?"

But who can say what for? Thiamine for metabolism. Rosemary for remembrance. Doan's little liver pills, for whatever ails you. Just so long as the number of cures, however narrowly, stays ahead of the number of ailments. And always water, more water, keeping the metals off her kidneys until she floats queasily on her own insides.

Cisplatin, she remembers. The killer heavy metal. Platinum, like her spent wedding ring. The kind of stuff they'd sue you for letting within ten miles of the village water supply. But here they've worked her up a private hip flask. She cannot even think about how much the drink costs per sip. Thank God for insurance. Anyone who denies modern progress has never watched a parent die from inability to pay for treatment.

Karen, the graveyard nurse, gets her up at 3:30 a.m. Rather, the tube alarm gets Laura up, and Laura alerts Karen. Time for another saline, this one rich with assorted nutrients and electrolytes. Set to last eight hours, roughly what sleep used to run, back when Laura used to sleep.

On the third day, she wakes to another Zofran-dexamethasone combo. Tracy's back. "Haven't we done this one already?" Laura asks her.

Tracy rolls her eyes in sympathy. "Yup."

"Buy two, get one free?"

Tracy laughs. "Almost done, Mrs. B. You're in the homestretch now."

By noon the third day, she can almost imagine the alien idea: *home*. As unceremonious as any finish line she's ever crossed. 'Bye. On your way with you. One down, five to go.

They try to make her eat before she leaves. But the smell of food fills her with a nausea so severe that her body overrules everyone's best intentions. Her body screams one thing while Tracy insists another. Laura gets through lunch only by wadding up half the entree and stashing it in her purse for later disposal. As if she's a little child again, only now blessed with a handbag.

No one really knows their real body. Hers has turned electric, buzzed, frizzy. Her internal organs go some horrid shade of Naugahyde. No one knows what food really smells like. Well-being is nothing but an impostor, a beautiful girl who turns into a hag at neap tide when the spell breaks and reason at last sees through her.

Don picks her up out front. Avoiding Dr. Jenkins, most likely. "How did things go?" he manages to ask. But he looks away when she answers. As if he'd prefer the short version. "Do you need to hydrate? Should I stop for some water?"

"You do and I'll scream. I feel like a bloody Perrier factory."

"Ellen's been suspended," he announces.

"Ellen *what*?"

"Your daughter's won a three-day vacation from school."

"I know what the word *means*, Don." Now that she remembers it. "When did this happen?"

"Yesterday afternoon."

"Nobody told me?"

"You had other things to worry about."

"What did she do?"

"Brawling. She and a pretty classmate of hers. Fists. Teacher dragged the two of them down to the principal. Neither would say what was going on. Some kind of silent honor pact. The principal threatened to throw them both out. Finally Ellen admitted to starting things. She says . . . she says that she asked the girl how many viscoses died to make her blouse."

"Don! How can you laugh? It's horrible."

"I'm not laughing."

"How can you even grin?"

"I'm not grinning."

"Suspension?"

"Seems this was her third offense this week."

They coordinate parental responses. Each household agrees not to undercut the discipline of the other.

Ellen greets her at home, one part contrite and two stubborn.

"Honey. You picked on a girl because she's poor?"

"Camille Wexner is hardly poor, Mom. Her father's some project manager with Clare. Probably makes twice what—"

"You picked on her for her clothes?"

"Oh my God. Mom. The girl is, like, constantly in my face. She's a cretin."

Cretin? So many words have gone by Laura in her life. She wonders how she has learned any one of them.

She makes an early New Year's resolution. Look things up. She starts that night. The nausea sets in. She gets acquainted with her toilet bowl, up close. She learns the smell of the blue crystals she uses to erase the smell of her insides.

She cannot eat. Sleeping is ludicrous. Work is out of the question. She wonders how she has ever done it, even when healthy. How she ever thought she could keep at it, through what's to come.

But she can look up things. Some fraction of those petty bafflements that have victimized her all these years. She can search for them on the computer, that reference CD she got for Tim, the one he refuses to touch.

Taxol: not found. Cisplatin: not found. Cretin: A person suffering from congenital myxedema. An idiot. From the French word for Christian. Meant "poor soul" once, in another world.

BREATHING EASY

This year, Melissa blew out all her candles. In one breath. By herself. Last year, just humming along while the other kids sang *Happy Birthday* left her gasping for air. Until Respulin appeared among the rest of her life's presents, each new candle taxed her lungs to the breaking point. She could not run, sing, shout, or even jump a rope. She lived in constant fear. A spring day felt like being buried alive.

Melissa turned nine today. Maybe she still can't spell oral leukotriene D_4 receptor antagonist. But she does know how to spell Happiness.

The Biological Materials Group
CLARE MATERIAL SOLUTIONS

The Red Man never worried about his skin. For that matter, the Red Man had very few modern anxieties. He lived in a state of noble simplicity and rapport with the world about him. His native insight penetrated into Nature's deepest intricacies, giving him true knowledge, however unscientific.

The Indian lived in harmony with the measureless tangles of life. Men of industry, crowded into their cities, celebrated the depths of his natural communion. Guided by Nature's light, the Indian walked noiselessly upon the ground and, ear to that same earth, listened across unthinkable distances. He could pull fish from the streams with his hands. He could sense a bear before its appearance. He could stalk and snare the most skittish deer.

Whites thrust into this wildness had survived as well. More than survived: they had subdued the earth to the extent of their reaches, as their Book instructed them. But white cultivation simplified much that otherwise eluded their subtlest study. In pruning back the forests of this immeasurable and wild place, white husbandry had lost some ancient insight, an older lore.

All this Benjamin discussed with his brother Samuel. They quoted to each other the sage of Concord's advice to the Young American. This land, too, was as old as the Flood. "Here stars, here woods, here hills, here animals." But here, too, were vast tendencies concurring of a new order.

Natural scientists, God's spies, had changed the rules of life. The hand of industry was at last succeeding in turning stones into bread. In every quarter, labor and plan now outpaced easy, languorous culling. The simple parasitic relation of savvy native to Nature had been routed, force-marched into the Territories. The Red Man was no more.

For all that the Indian knew, for as little as he worried, he had never once contemplated the collapse of his world in the face of his fellow humans, delivered from Nature's chains. Never in a thousand years could he have comprehended the amalgamated age, the age that Emerson extolled:

> The locomotive and the steamboat, like enormous shuttles, shoot every day across the thousand various threads of national descent and employment, and bind them fast in one web, an hourly assimilation goes forward, and there is no danger that local peculiarities and hostilities should be preserved.

Yet the White Man, in this all-promising age, now mourned the passing of the Indian's Arcadia. The fiercest way forward produced the hardest look back. The cheaper the future, the dearer the past. One had only to consider the flurry of communal experiments within the Clares' own Commonwealth. A rash of utopias bore witness not to final deliverance but to widespread disenchantment, stubborn refusal of man's manufactured sorcery.

The expansion of human affairs offered abundance on a scale never before imaginable. And yet, Benjamin submitted to Samuel, not everyone was ready for the cost of abundance. Merely imagining all this bounty did some hidden injury to the children of promise.

Where the past commanded a firmer price than the future, the future looked backward for its newest markets. Contrition made for a booming business. The nation that footed the $30 million bill for Jesup and Taylor's extermination of the Sac and Fox and Seminole now bought Catlin's engravings at limited-edition prices.

Samuel ran Ben's idea past the more market-savvy Resolve. In the whiff of temporal homesickness hidden in *Utilis clarea,* even Resolve could smell opportunity. The scent called him back across time's sea-lanes to the old family adage: profit equaled uncertainty times distance. The farther one hauled a thing, the more one could make from it. Out of the depths of the past, Clare might haul a new gravy run. The Red Man never worried about his skin. Why should we?

In his mind, Resolve tested out the full beauty hidden in Ben's offer. The age of steam produced certain unprecedented shocks to the skin unknown to earlier ways and races. Live as the natives once did, and those shocks might disappear. Unnatural skin needed a natural cure, a cure whose formulas machine progress had somehow mislaid.

Resolve Clare found the idea truly majestic: they could solve the needs of progress by selling the very condition that the need remedied. Resolve pondered this twist while turning over his younger brother's tuberous gift. The underpinning philosophy seemed sound. But finally, philosophy was nothing but the hound of business. Soon enough, someone would need to take the cur out for a brisk run.

Samuel and Resolve studied Benjamin's *Utilis* notebook. The two pored over the pages of careful observations describing the plant's peculiarities. Together, all three brothers reproduced the series of chopping, burning, leaching, boiling, filtering, and drying that released from the plant a pungent powder midway between viridian and chartreuse. This form, unknown to its native island cultivators, proved, in Benjamin's estimation, the herb's most manageable concentrate.

The extract tasted of burnt pine nut—pleasant on the tongue, with a distant after-hint of bitterness. Benjamin, having ingested minute quantities for years, reported some melioration of both gastritis and gout. The powder spumed when moist, like bicarbonate upon contact with acid. Plain water, however, did not easily wet it. The paste form was most definitely styptic. Applied powder preserved the freshness of butchered meat by as much as a day. A coating of dried froth cured a lesion on the back of Resolve's hand in a little over half a week.

Paste, powder, or recalcitrant solution, *Utilis* wore the hue of strong medicine. It looked restorative. It *felt* restorative. It smelled like the liniment that the angels applied in God's own sickroom.

The substance could have packed a delayed punch more poisonous than henbane. But no bureau, no business police existed to prevent the Clares from discovering that toxicity *in vivo*. They set to work retooling their soap works to make a product that would brook no substitutes. Once again, they scrapped perfectly good machinery while it was still profitable, to build new equipment on no more than hope.

Ennis tried several abortive methods to get the substance to adhere to a finished product. The *Utilis* admixture remained insoluble during the boiling process, separating out with the spent lye. When Ennis at last got the extract to survive until strong change, the stuff failed to survive pitching and settling, coming out with the nigre. Cut directly into the finished neat, it clotted most unpleasantly.

The milling process for the fancy Clare toilet soap supplied the answer. Ennis built a planing table where workmen whittled white soap into thin shavings. These shavings went into a rank of casks made from rum puncheons with their heads removed. Ennis fitted out these casks with galvanized iron pans luted to steampipes: the perfect second-cooking apparatus.

Here the soap was carefully remelted and recondensed. Now the precise amounts of additive could be spooned in by a giant spatula, crutched continuously, and incorporated into a homogenous mixture.

Cooled, cut, and trimmed into rounded oblongs, the cakes went into a drying room until cold, firm, and smooth to the touch. Last came the crucial step: one by one, feeders fed the raw oblongs into an ingenious, foot-powered mechanical stamper. All day long, pressers slammed down the pedals, snapping back the lever that sprang the soap free of its imprint. And all day long, from out of the jaws of the mold, fell glistening, aromatic cakes, each one perfectly incised with the profile of a noble Brave.

———

She weathers the worst stretch of retching. Her energy comes back. She stops vomiting when there is no poison left to vomit. The Compazine begins to kick in, about the time the nausea would have gone away on its own. By the week before she has to go in again, Laura almost remembers how she felt before she went in the first time.

The calendar shrinks to its barest rituals. She forces herself through the reflex routines, the searches and seizures so usual that she's doing them already before she wakes. She checks the day's tasks off mentally as she hits the forest-green shag. She felt-pens her stations to the washable whiteboard Super-Glued to the refrigerator. Nothing must change.

Her life. *Her life*, Laura keeps telling herself. But the thing feels like nothing she's ever visited. She's back in some alien England, after years shipwrecked on a coral shoal that shows up on no one's map. She's perched on her own shoulder, watching her puppet body jerk through the checkpoints at her hours' borders, squaring off against her pocket diary's To Do list.

Game, Goodies, Saturday's entry taunts her. She stares at the words, clueless in the face of the cryptically familiar. Something obvious. It must be some weekly rendezvous, something she does unconsciously, by force of habit.

She does not remember until Don calls her. "You need a lift?" That tone in his voice: Do not operate heavy machinery under the influence of Cancer.

"You . . . uh . . . when . . . ?" she bluffs.

"Laura. Tim's indoor soccer team. The one I've been coaching for the last four Saturdays running?"

Impossible. Impossible that it's been four weeks. Impossible that she's forgotten.

Blame it on the chemo. One of her chemicals, messing with her memory. She's studied the list of side effects. From ringing in the ears to renal failure. *Neurotoxin:* surely that can't be good. And then there's all the meds she's taking to counter the original meds' side effects.

And she's only just started. Only ingested the first little bit. True, she's had other things on her mind than indoor soccer. But she's never forgotten anything the kids do. Laura Bodey: the person who remembers for everyone.

This is her week to bring the goodies for Tim's team, and she forgot. Forgot to make anything. Forgot the team. She makes herself swing out to the Price Warehouse. Volume-packaged everything. Blackberry pie six-packs. Footlockers full of ravioli. She gets the pre-catered crudité platter with the multiple dip wells in the middle to placate the soccer parents. And for the boy players, she grabs the 144-count Candied Fruit Wedge Collection.

She gets to the gym just after things have started. As soon as she unpacks the goods, she sees the extent of her mistake. She's broken the unwritten rule. Bought, rather than whipped up from scratch. Worse: everyone knows why.

Tori Gwain, mother of the relentless Gwain twins, consoles her. She dips a celery stick in a well, miming wide enjoyment. "Mm, mm. Good, Laura." The exact sound as that old soup commercial.

"Yeah, real good," two or three others echo. "Real tasty."

They know exactly where she bought the stuff and how much she paid for it. They know it was a last-minute panic correction. They're all careful not to berate her or make her feel bad in any way. She sits in the stands, under her knockoff Hermès scarf, surrounded by moms in jogging suits who appraise her headgear and say nothing.

She fakes eating a carrot, but gags on the smell. The key is to not let anyone see. She settles in to watch her Timmy. For most of the first half, he chuffs downfield, alternately running and sulking. He stops often, first to tuck in his T-shirt, then to untuck it. He seems to be avoiding the ball. Staying out of trouble, away from the action. The ball sputters to him by accident. He passes it off quickly.

And he so loved sports, once. Before he had to play them. Used to draw up those fantasy teams. The Rocky Mountain Marmosets. The Louisville Ring-tailed Lemurs. Whole leagues, not a Spartan, Trojan, Warrior, or Bomber to be seen. So gentle, for a boy. The bug-torturing didn't start until later. After they started pushing him around at school. After she and Don hit the skids.

He used to litter the house with drawings. Stacks of them, everywhere. He gave them away as presents—to her, to strangers, to the mailman. Maps of the ballparks, drawings of famous players, mascot portraits. Great stop-action moments from team history. Detailed uniforms. The Ring-tails: alternating white and black stacked bands, like a prison outfit gone jaunty.

And those continual streams, half play-by-play, half silly kid's stand-up comedy. "The Lemurs are really up a tree now. Time to show those opposable thumbs. Time to step up to the plate and defend the name of Primate." Calling whole imaginary games, down to the last strike. But only if he thought no one could hear him. She'd have to slink off to the basement and stand with her ear to the laundry chute, eavesdropping shamelessly on the flesh of her flesh.

The Lemurs are all gone. He's left them to that universal trash bin of extinct species. Consigned to the Dead-Ball Era, that place where Don consigned the marriage, with his good-sport shrug, on the day their franchise quit town.

Her Tim plays team sports now because his father makes him. Today's match pits Caldwell Glass versus the Park Mall Medicine Tent. Every team has its own patron. Next Millennium supports one, too. Can't cost much. A dozen jerseys, and a pizza party at the end of the season. Sponsor a future client: Lacewood's next generation. Foster fond memories. Be a team player. Each boy a tax write-off for some local retailer. Keeps big government out of amateur sport. Cheap at the price. Especially if the team's a winner.

Caldwell Glass is not a winner. Not today. Not since Don and Tim have joined. Caldwell Glass has about as much chance of winning any of its games as Laura has of winning the Publishers Clearing House. Mr. Caldwell's probably thinking about suing to retrieve his investment.

It's Don. He wants them to win so bad. The boys can smell the need to win oozing out of the man's pores. It spooks them. They're hearing footsteps for next week's game even before this week's is over. Don already berating them, lashing them with sarcasm two practices and an exhibition game into the season.

She almost pities the man. On the one hand, he's got all the other dads riding him to drive the team harder. On the other, he has the team totally freaked, each boy pointing fingers at every other. Even worse than the usual Little League lesson in community spirit.

It wouldn't be so awful, except for poor Tim getting caught in the middle of it. Forever bearing the brunt. All sides of indoor soccer target him: everybody's enemy. The boys all hate him because he's the coach's son. And the father hates him for refusing to be Dad's little henchman.

Just watching him run around on the court for an hour is an exercise in torture. Just appearing in public, just flexing in front of the other boys is a humiliation Tim despairs of outliving.

And he did so love running around, once. Kicking that yellow plastic ball in the backyard with Goldie chasing at his heels. Tossing the pigskin with Don, the horsehide, whatever. She'd have to shag both of them out of the house before they broke the last intact lamp. She thought they'd never grow up, either of them. Boys.

Now both father and son detest the whole idea of sport. The hatred of a betrayed lover, obvious in every muscle flinch. But both go dutifully through the motions rather than shame each other in public. Don's hoping to win by some fluke. Win the game, win over his boy, win the team's love. Take them all out for celebratory root beer floats. Tim's only desire in this world is to go home, get on the computer, and spend the next two days blasting the hell out of anything that moves.

"Hey, Bodey," Coach yells from the sidelines. Careful not to show any favoritism. Can't call everyone by their last names except his own son. "Bodey! You deaf? Get the lead out. You call that running?" The other parents chime in. Don's tongue-lash of his own boy winds them all up, like a reprimand by the boss to pick up production.

Kay Huber calls to her son. "Kyle: come eat the rest of this PowerBar. I don't want you on that court on an empty stomach." Stunted Kyle wavers. He wants to comply, but can't quit in mid-drive. He hesitates toward the stands, a stutter step. Then he breaks downfield, trying to pretend he doesn't hear her.

Kay starts to shriek. "Kyle. *Kyle!*" Over the top, even by soccer-mom standards. The cut-short tone of medical emergency. At that decibel, not even Don countermands her. The poor little boy covers his crotch and comes to a full stop. He trots over, head bowed, a cow submitting to the stockyards.

"I don't want you running around out there depleted," Kay scolds, betrayed. She makes him swill the banana-flavored bar down with Spor-teen, the choice of more multimillion-dollar contracts than any other leading teen sport electrolyte replenisher. Sends him back out, where his shorthanded team berates him for the goal scored in his absence.

Whatever aggression these boys inflict on one another they learned in their parents' playbook. Maniacs of nurturing, giving their kids a leg up, whatever the cost. The best-off are the worst offenders. Pushing at every step, staying ahead, from private school to pre-med. Laura has done it herself, wherever she can get away with it.

All these dads, yelling for the full-body check, as if their child competitor might one day make a living as a pro, if he just hangs tough. *Indoor soccer,* for God's sake. By the time you start talking about the money sports, the parents are rabid. Tim's friend, Gordy Johnson: his parents actually redshirting him. Taking him out of school for a year, just so he'd dominate varsity. Probably dosed him with bovine growth hormone. Laced his beefalo with steroids.

Standings mad, the entire country. That's why Ellen's the way she is. A girl too smart for the public silliness. Two summers ago, when her body hit her all at once, she took up running. Just wanted to jog, long-distance, for hours at a shot. Run until all Lacewood dissolved into fields. Run until she disappeared into blank, rolling agribusiness.

"Why don't you go out for the team?" Laura tried. Thinking that might turn the trick. Fix things.

Stupid. The team wasn't the fix. The team was the problem.

"I'm not good enough" was all the girl ever said.

Laura made her come today. Last thing in the world Ellen wants to admit to now, her family. What's left of her family. Big Sister came, but only under much-declared duress. Political prisoner. Riding Tim the whole time. "Okay, Slim. Today's your big chance. Don't blow it, Slim. We're all counting on you."

She called Camille Wexner to come meet her here. Camille—her high-school brawling buddy. The two of them sit at the foot of the grandstand, now beside it, now vanished, now underneath it. Giggling uncontrollably, elbows out, pressing their palms together in manic calisthenics, shouting so everyone can hear: "We must! We must! We must develop the bust!"

Laura wants to shush the act, but doesn't. She can't very well force the girl to come, then force her to enjoy being here. She's having a little trouble on that score herself, at the moment. For that matter, if Tim were choosing, he'd probably beg them all to go home right about now.

If there is a master plan, the Caldwell Glass Gladiators fail to execute it. The enemy scores again while Tim, on defense, is fiddling with the little Velcro strips on his shoes. She wants to tell the ref. The ump. Whatever he is. Unfair. Take-backs. But what difference would it make at this point? No more than the difference between humiliation and mere disgrace.

Every win has somebody's loss pegged to it. Someone has to go down for anyone else to rise. How can any culture be so nuts about any pleasure that depends on someone else's misery? Yet when a Caldwell player gets free by some fluke and almost makes a goal by accident, she's right there, springing to her feet, screaming for the score.

When the game ends, she sneaks a glance at Tim's father. Don is too mad even to think about getting angry. He's on the sidelines, doing the good-sport thing. He sets his jaw in cheerful acceptance, the jaw he's studied in countless pro coach close-ups. The grim, grinning jaw you have to look at three or four times every weekend. He walks across the gym to shake the enemy coach's hand. Laughs, shrugs. Threatens a rematch.

Then he walks over to where Laura is throwing out the four feet of Styrofoam and the stale crudités that no soccer parent or kid would touch.

"Looking good, hon." Pure phys. ed.

"You too, Don. Sorry about the, uh, game."

"Ach." He waves his hand. "There's always next time."

The prospect is too painful to consider. Tim slinks back from the locker room, his hundred-dollar indoor soccer shoes replaced by hundred-dollar cross-training shoes. Ellen and Camille stop giggling. They sit, mock-lady-like, until he passes. Then they hum the official theme song of the Olympics.

"Fuck off," Tim snarls.

"Hey. Hey!" Don grabs him by the shoulder.

Tim struggles to break the grip. He stops when Don escalates, not wanting a scene in front of the guys he still thinks of, somehow, as his buddies.

"Remember what we talked about?"

Tim sneers.

"I said, remember?"

"I remember."

"Okay." The grip turns into an awkward pat that slides off Tim's moving back. "Good man."

Don takes Laura aside as the kids head for the car. He has fallen into that confident, confidential mode. Protective. Still shooting for Don Shula. Laura can't deal with it. Whatever it is.

"We need to talk, hon."

"Not 'hon,' Don."

"We need to talk, Laura. About our daughter." As if there were anything else.

"What? What about her? She's back in good graces at school. You can see how she was with Camille today. It's all blown over."

"Laura. She's getting wild."

"Don. She was born wild."

"Not like this. She's up to something."

Laura doesn't even want to consider the possibilities. "What do you want me to do, Don? Confront her? 'Ellen? Are you getting mixed up in things you don't want me to know about?' "

"I don't know what I want you to do. Maybe nothing. I'm just saying."

"You're always just saying." Saying *talk*. Saying *us*. Saying *our*.

"Maybe we could sit down for five minutes sometime? When neither of us is running?"

She fishes in her purse for her keys. The large yellow plastic sunflower key chain reading *Ackerman Insurance. The one-stop shop for all your insurance needs.* She waits until he's looking at her.

"You think we're going to get back together, don't you? Just because I'm sick?"

"Laura. I don't think anything."

"No. You don't. That's your problem, Don. That's always been your problem."

He smiles. Thick wax death mask smile. "Nice to see that illness has worked such wonders for your disposition."

He turns and walks away across the empty court. The shoulders hunch as he crosses the gym. The same hunch as Tim's, evading the ball. Genetic. Like the floppy forelock. Like those gray eyes. Their criminal bewilderment.

He walks in time-lapse. Each step turns the boy back into the father. The jaunty twenty-three-year-old she fell for and married cracks open and sets free this brittle man. She sees in the walk how much she has devastated him. Cut the legs out from under him, these ten years and longer, and she must call out. Kind, mean, wrong, right. Anything but this killing silence that she specializes in.

" 'Bye, Coach," she mumbles to the coiled back. Loud enough to hear. But he does not turn around. Does not even raise his spine.

She catches up to the kids. Herds them into the car. Tim's still in a rage. Ellen is still all giggles.

Don's right. She's bitched at him forever. But he pushes for it. His way or the wrong way. Can't even disagree with the man without his faulting her. She never saw things fast enough. Never took appropriate action. Any woman would be an emotional mess, living with that. Would have had to jump ship or die a cripple.

Tim shimmies into the backseat, his lip quivering. Always the backseat, chauffeured, even when it's just her and him. Ellen's manic. She bounces on the seat next to him, miming an obnoxious pompom.

"Gimme a 'G.' Gimme an 'L.' Gimme an 'Ass.' What does it spell? The Glass Gladiators. Shattered again." Fake twink voice, the detested group that wouldn't have her. "That's all right, that's okay, we'll try again some other day."

Too obvious a provocation. Or Tim is too enraged to counter. Ellen insists, pushing things past the break point. "The Glass Gladiators. I mean, really. Like, what pea brain . . . ? Who in their right—"

"Ellen."

"No really, Mom. I'm like: what zero could possibly have come up with—"

"Ellen. I said that's enough."

"You didn't really say, 'That's enough,' per se . . ."

Too smart for her own good. Tim has the right idea. Ignore her. Let her knock herself out.

"Okay, you two. Where are we having lunch?"

"Ooh. Mom's splurging. You should lose games more often, Slimmy."

Tim just says, "Feed Bar Buffet."

"Totally polyester," Ellen jeers. But she wants to go there, too. She likes the endlessness. The free returns. The pick and choose.

Tim likes it because he is in a stage where he will eat only things that are either brown or white. Laura likes it because it's only $3.99 for teens, and it sometimes holds them for as long as two hours before they get hungry again.

Over a flowing crater lake of mashed potato and gravy, Tim croaks, "Mom?"

That small voice. She would give it anything it asks. Because it always sounds as if it's asking its last.

"Mom? Can I have a beeper?"

"Can you *what*?"

"A beeper. A pager. It's this device that, if somebody—"

"I know what a beeper is, Timmy. Why in the world would you want one?"

"They're cool."

"Only businesspeople use beepers. And doctors."

"All my friends have them."

"All his friends *are* businesspeople," Ellen intones.

"His friends? *Tim's* friends? What's that supposed to mean?"

But Ellen drops into her routine of ominous, suppressed giggling.

"Your friends have *beepers*? Whatever do they do with them?"

"You know. Like, answer them. Say somebody wants to get in touch with you when you're not at a phone. Like at school."

"Who would want to get in touch with you who isn't in school with you?"

"Mom." Don't be stupid. "That's not the point."

"What's the point?" At this stage in life, she cannot understand why anyone would want anyone else to be able to get in touch with him.

"The point is: what if I bought one with my own money?"

"Do you know what those things cost per month?"

Wrong step. The minute she starts arguing price, she's already lost.

When they get home, the answering machine is flashing an LED 7. On Saturday. Two follow-ups on a Sloan Street duplex, a computer-generated reminder of a doctor's appointment, a furtive, coded message from Ken that fools neither kid, two solicitations for cash from humans and one from another computer, which patiently plays music while waiting for someone to press a Touch-Tone button on the other end. Waits until the tape runs out.

When she showers that night, Laura looks down to see a patch of hair the size of Tim's dead gerbil nestling in the drain. She jumps in fright, slips off balance, and cracks her elbow on the sink going down. She sits on the side of the tub, nursing her pain, crying as softly as she can, so neither child can hear her.

B-32CT: **Boys' 100% Cotton T-shirts.** Short-sleeve, taped neck and drop shoulder for perfect fit. Durable, reinforced seams. Made in USA. Everyday Low Price: 2 for $7.

B-34SJ: **Boys' Cotton Sport Tees.** Short-sleeve. Teal and emerald. Front reads: Fear Is For the Other Guy.™ On back, the famous logo. Sizes S–XL. Everyday Low Price: $14.95 . . .

She misses the following weekend's match. She misses Don's rebuilding pep talk. Misses the meager but miracle victory. Misses Tim's one goal of this or any season, all because she has to check back into Mercy, for her own Round Two.

Dr. Archer greets her happily. Her oncologist seems glad for the chance to check her vitals and talk more politics. Cancer patients: the perfect audience. "Those Bosanians, they've been slaughtering themselves for over four hundred years. They want to. It's not our problem. We should let them do what they please."

"You might be right," Laura says, keen to stay on Dr. Archer's good side.

"The problem with those people is that they have to live in Bosania. You know how lucky you are? Everyone wants to live in the States. Look at my Indian interns. They come here to do their medical training. Of course they don't want to go back home afterward. Would you?"

"No, Doctor."

"Damn straight."

"Doctor? Will this treatment be the same as the first one?"

"Well, the effects are cumulative," Dr. Archer points out.

"Cumulative?"

"We can't kill this thing off all at once. We have to sneak up on it."

By now Laura knows that the oncology nurses will do all the work. They welcome her back like old friends.

Tracy, opening a tap in her arm, asks, "Do you think I should go blond for a while?"

Laura inspects Tracy's mouse-brown pixie. "Go for it, Trace. Do you think I should shave?"

Tracy's expert fingers run through Laura's shag. "I'll tell you what. It's going to get patchy real quick."

"Real quick." Laura laughs.

Alan, on the second shift, seems a bit down. "You doing okay?" she asks.

He grimaces. "Spat with the mate."

"Oh? What does she do?"

"He's a junior faculty member at Sawgak."

"No kidding," she starts to babble. "My husband's in Development there. Ex-husband, I guess I should say. Since he's my . . . ex."

"I don't mind all his other guys," Alan claims. "It's just a novelty. They don't mean anything to him. He's a lot younger than I am. Young gay profs are expected to lay pretty much everything that moves these days. But he's being incredibly stupid. On theoretical grounds. Says he doesn't think a virus should run our lives."

She thanks Alan silently for letting her pass. "What should?" she asks.

"You know something?" Alan rolls the irony around on his tongue. "He doesn't say."

"Tell your friend that a good third of the people I find new houses for, six months later, wish they'd never moved."

"I'll tell him that, Mrs. Bodey."

The effects are cumulative. While the heavy metal toxins scour her veins this second time, she finds herself humming, "Rinso *White*, Rinso *White*,

Happy little washday song!" Something ancient of her dad's. He'd never let anything but Lever Brothers products into the house. Swan, Spry, Lux, Rinso White. All those cardboard samples piled up on the car seat, back when he was still on the road, before his promotion to Chicago regional manager. If Dad returned to earth and saw what she keeps under the sink these days, he'd have a second heart attack and go right back.

Once again, the IV is cranked to screech every time the line gets blocked, namely, every time she moves her arm. Don shows up when she is just starting the taxol, even though she told him not to come. She's still a little high from the disguising rush, the thing she's been waiting for. Every bit as delicious as the first time.

"Don *Bodey*," she identifies him, cheerily. Happy little washday song.

"I chased down that Dr. Jenkins. Seeing as I was here."

"I bet you did."

"I made her tell me how you could have cystadenocarcinoma if your CA-125 level was so low?"

"Don. I've got cancer. There's a big tumor sitting in the freezer here, and a couple little cutlets in somebody's icebox out in Indianapolis."

"Oh, I'm not denying the lab reports."

"What *are* you doing? Flirting with her or suing her? Don't badger the poor woman, Don. She's only doing her job."

"You see, the literature actually explains it. I was reading the article wrong. They don't test for low or high at all. They test for whether the serum is rising or falling. They didn't bother to determine your baseline, is all."

"I've arranged a ride back," she tells him. If Ken can get away without trouble.

"Cancel it." Don grins.

When he leaves, the heavyset woman in the next bed leans over and confides, "Your husband's a gregacious kind of guy, isn't he?"

"Hopeless," Laura concedes. "Completely hopeless. The fastest talker in the world. He used to talk my kids out of burping, when they were infants."

"That's nothing, honey. I just had our fifth last year. And my husband still tries to use the a.m. diapers at four in the afternoon."

"Don't I know," Laura says. "What are you in for?"

The woman groans, but not at Laura. The long sigh, low on octane, rattles into a laugh by exhale's end. "Two to ten for sassing off. Hoping to get a reduction for good behavior."

Her name is Ruthie Tapelewsky. She lives in a ranch on South Sutton. "Houses?" Ruthie shouts when Laura tells her. "You sell houses? Ain't that a kick. Nice work if you can get it. I'm in Building and Maintenance. You hawk 'em, we caulk 'em."

Laura looks up at the Damoclean drip hanging above her neighbor's head. What intricate tubes tie the two of them together. What hopeless husbands. What precarious cocktails we all are.

———

From the start, Clare's Native Balm had its share of competing secret healing extracts. Native remedies greased prosperity as much as did any machine oil. Companies everywhere sought their own brown font of patent elixir: Kickapoo Kidney Cure. Choctaw Chew. Wright's Indian Vegetable Pills (Philadelphia, 1844), "opening all the natural drains—a general Jail Delivery, as it were, by which all impurity is driven from every part of the body." Each cure was as pure as Nature herself.

In 1846, in Utica, New York, Theron T. Pond, together with an "Oneida Indian medicine man," turned witch hazel into a white cold cream with preternatural abilities. But Pond's was but one of the Native Balm rivals that Resolve Clare lost sleep over.

In an age when life was still local, soapmakers up and down the seaboard copied the Brave. Even the British tried to steal his silhouette. They matched the soap's iodine color, but they could not quite reproduce its brackish, medicinal smell. The foreign imitation sold healthily enough in the British Isles and on the Continent. But few in North America were so foolish as to believe anything that the British claimed to know about Indians.

All the British knew was how to undersell. And this they knew cold, on account of their advanced alkali industry. America suffered from a superabundance of potash: lyes leached from wood ash, burnt seaweed, waste wool—all the hydroxides and carbonates that littered the American woodlands the way buffalo littered the endless plains. Lacking this natural blessing, English soap- and candlemakers were thrown back upon ingenuity. After the Frenchman Leblanc stumbled upon a formula for making soda out of table salt, Albion leaped upon the process and engineered it into functional reality:

$$2NaCl + H_2SO_4 = Na_2SO_4 + 2HCl$$
$$Na_2SO_4 + 2C = Na_2S + 2CO_2$$
$$Na_2S + CaCO_3 = CaS + Na_2CO_3$$

The symbols traipsed across the page, as cryptic as the skittering beetle code in that story by Mr. Poe from the *Philadelphia Dollar Weekly*. The first equation was a cotillion, a quadrille of decoupling and recoupling. Na and Cl parted amicably, grabbing the split partners of 2H and SO_4 to forge new squares while still balancing beautifully across the equal sign. The second spun a sprightly Roger de Coverley, the terpsichorean set-and-a-half breaking down longways in the winding hey, SO_4 cracking into two new dancers of its own right, with never a leg being gained or lost.

The third equation spun to another dos-à-dos, still balanced, yet changing everything. This time, the recombining partners found, in their new mates, a net increment of worth left behind in the retort. The human hand led matter into a more beneficial state, leaving Britain with a booming trade and bringing to the world hitherto unimaginable riches.

For half a century, these three equations *were* the international chemical industry. Salt and sulfuric acid in; calcium sulfide and all-useful alkaline soda out. A wave of the invisible hand turned the commonplace into the invaluable. The scientific age at last stabilized the old fairy story. Man now spun worth from worthlessness, gold from dross.

What was good for the supplier was good for the purchaser. Plentiful and consistent alkali passed down the chain of consumption, enriching all intermediaries. It made for a better and cheaper soap, the whole world gaining.

The Clares applauded the alkali process's transforming dance. Yet they did not fancy anyone else's distant empire calling the tune. Native Balm at last gave them the first hint of how to beat the industrious British at their own game. The brown and aromatic herbal soap with its secret healing extract might make of that chemical quadrille a brisk New England square dance. Might turn that sprightly Roger de Coverley into raucous Virginia reel.

Native Balm soap with secret extract of Healing Root
will cure several cutaneous and dermal disorders,
including, but not limited to, pimples, Salt Rheum,
freckling and discoloration, Etc.
It will remove Tetter, heal ruptures and boils,
firm the muscle, and prevent many further diseases
of the skin as well as graver bodily illnesses.

Native Balm is a Consummate, and unequaled,
fully warranted article for washing and cleaning,
and for the overall promotion of the Body's
Health.

———

Native Balm Soap with extract of Healing Root spread by word of mouth. Its fame traveled infinitely slower than Morse's idle theological banter spread down the copper wires. Yet over time, regional salesmen refused to leave the Hub without ample stocks.

Within the decade, general stores as far away as Ohio began to ask their jobbers for the bar with the Indian head on it. The Brave eventually made cameo appearances in jingle and joke. If, as the slogans soon put it, soap was the measure of civilization, Native Balm, in its peak years, became the measure of soap.

The factory system's best trick lay in releasing nature's secret of simple beneficence. Nowhere did any promotional matter claim that this bygone savage knew the first thing about soap's existence. Imagination and the health movement supplied that suggestion. The Indian never worried about his complexion. It was up to the savvy purchaser to recover that state of worry-free grace.

Ordinary soaps, especially the homemade, merely cleaned your skin. Native Balm not only removed those same harmful oils and impurities from the integument. With its herbal extract it also restored chemical balances that modern living forfeited, correcting and returning the skin to its state of initial purity.

In time, its appeal cut across social strata, from Astor to ash tender. Taverners lathered it on. Scions summering at Sulphur Springs compared cosmetic results. The noble Indian profile stamped on each otherwise plain bar proclaimed, even to the illiterate, the revival of powerful, primitive arts.

Native Balm Soap entered the homes of the poor as well as the middle class. Patent medicine at a factory price, home remedy in a box: it crossed over the line dividing these two worlds, selling each side its own desires. In a world that washed up with death, soap was the chief weapon against disease and fever. And Native Balm spared lives while saving pennies. It appealed to the freed Negro and even made inroads into the desperate immigrant nests of Boston's North End and New York's Five Points.

It fought William Colgate and Son down the seaboard. It worked its way out west, as far as Chicago, where trade with the Sac, Fox, and Natchez had recently been forever wiped out. There it competed with some success against the brothers-in-law Procter and Gamble, whose Mottled German and Oleine had good head starts. Peddlers purchased lots on their way out to work the Indian Territory.

The national dance craze boosted use, as did the rise of photography. No one wanted skin they had to worry about. The steady accumulation of personal wealth only fed the national dream of one day spending oneself free of prosperity.

As much as they sold soap, the Clares also sold dependability, which is to say trust by its married name. Buying no longer involved a gamble. Any bar stamped with the Brave was in every way indistinguishable from any other.

Native Balm Soap grossed $40,000 in its first full year of sales. In the years thereafter, the company grew almost as fast as the country itself. As candles disappeared, various native unguents took their place. "How are you off for soap?" went the era's favorite sass. To those in the business, the link between cleanser and cash—the whole idea of "cleaning up"—was never less than literal.

The Red Man worked a change on all the lives that had brought him into being. The Clare factory swelled to a hundred workers, then another hundred. Jewitt retired at fifty, to a heaven of novels. Later, in his waning years, he produced a book of his own, about a dynasty of insidious Boston Brahmin manufacturers. The book sold well, though not as well as Native Balm.

Ennis, promoted to operations manager, amassed enough capital to build his wife a small mausoleum. A monument paid for by cleanliness, hygiene that might have saved her life, as it now saved so many others. Ben Clare now tended to his beloved Cambridge greenhouses with his brothers' blessings. His life neaped and ebbed to the hushed surf of a solitude bought by soap.

The Red Man never worried about cash, Resolve told his small band of employees. Why should you? The 1860 edition of *Biography of the Wealthiest Men of Boston* listed all the Clares. But Resolve was the wealthiest of the three. He stood in every way at the height of his powers. He was fixed for soap forever.

His own father had brought his family to the colonies on a pallet of Wedgwood plates. Jephthah Clare's world had vanished in steam, slaughtered like kine straying across time's thundering tracks. But Resolve had ported the Clare capital over into new worlds, widening that wealth beyond imagining. His own daughter had even risen to the gentility of published poetry, albeit a volume secretly subsidized by the company coffers.

By all measures, business left him with nothing left to do.

Samuel was too aged and benign to be of much more use. Ben had paid his dues; the soap works had gotten more out of the chemist than anyone ever expected. But Peter, Douglas, William—the next generation—would in time mind the store, sell the soap, tend the production runs. And after them: other Clare fathers, other Clare sons.

A businessman must know his every purpose. He must know every detail, must keep all his goals well defined, while still keeping the shape of ultimate arrival somewhat obscure. Resolve's mistake was in letting himself arrive.

Resolve Clare died six weeks after Beauregard bombarded Fort Sumter. The death certificate indicated natural causes. But he died, in fact, of fulfillment.

———

She follows the week of the treatment with a week of vomiting, a week of debilitating nausea, and a week of mere massive fatigue, during which her chief illness consists of knowing that next week is treatment week again.

"It's just like the ancient past," Tim decides, "when everybody was sick all the time?" The first little glint of analog interest in his eyes she has seen for months. "I had to do this report, for science? Man, you wouldn't believe what those olden guys used to do for medicine. The barber used to be the surgeon? And he'd cut you up with razors, to let your blood out. Or they'd stick leeches all over you. Or they'd make you eat little bits of mercury, even though—"

"Sweetie. Sweetheart. You like science?"

"Guess so."

"Better than poetry?" she teases.

"Beats the sulfite out of poetry."

"How's come?" Like he used to say for everything, until he was ten. How's come you do that? How's come that happened?

"Cooler stuff. You can do things with it."

Medieval: he's right. Bloodletting and mercury. Sometimes when she wakes, for several seconds, she cannot say whose life she has been spirited into. She lies fetal, crumpled into the no-crumple comforter, all stick and corn silk, one of those burial mound mummies that so spooked her on grade-school field trips, before they closed the mounds forever.

Often she lies awake through the entire night. When she does somehow drift off, she sometimes dreams ravishing music. So much richer than any music she has ever heard that it wakes her up in fright.

She suffers the drive-by assaults of friends and acquaintances, people who would never drop in were she not sick, but who refuse to say the word when they do visit. Get together, to ignore the rhino at the table.

Grace Wambaugh, a colleague at the office who never speaks to her, shows up with a case full of herbal remedies. "This one's ginkgo biloba, from the tree. It'll repair your brain-blood flow. For any memory or absentmindedness. The ginger can help with nausea. Here's some echinacea, to boost your immunity system. You could probably use a little boosting about now. This one is called ephedra, although you may know it as mahuang or epitonin. It'll get your energy levels back up."

"You take these," Grace tells her, tumbling a small mountain of plastic sample containers onto Laura's coffee table. "My gift. If you need any more, you just call me, anytime. And maybe someday you'll do the same for folks who you know who, you know, aren't feeling too well."

"This is awfully kind of you, Grace," Laura says. It touches her, this cold woman, coming to bring her these cures. All plants: the gardener in her has always believed in the health value of green things. And even if these remedies come closer to patent medicine than to nature, this stranger's concern works its own medicine.

"Thank you, Grace. I'm . . . I really appreciate this."

Only after the visit, when Laura looks over the material that Grace has left behind with the bottles, does she realize. It's an Amway scheme.

The jewel-like gel caplets stink like rotting squirrel meat. Before chemo, she never knew how weird the world smells. Never suspected that a crust of white bread really tastes like chrome. Until getting sick, she took edible things at face value. Now they gang up, show her what's under the hood. Just like that old film. The Scent of Dorian Gray. The thing may look like a firm, fresh, golden banana. But just underneath the slick disguise, it's worms smeared on wet concrete.

This universal left shift of aroma makes it harder and harder to drag herself down to breakfast. She knows she's in trouble when even Ellen starts beating her to the kitchen in the mornings. Ellen's in the breakfast nook when Laura comes down after her first night of valerian-supplement-assisted insomnia. On a Sunday morning. After a Saturday night. It must be close to noon. Ellen, crouched over a cereal box. Proof that the age of print is not yet dead.

"Good morrow, Mama-san. Hey, Mom? I gotta read you something. Did you know that modern, industrial-era grains have been weakened and degraded by mass agricultural practices? I'm not kidding. Listen to this. It says right here. Monocrop inbreeding. 'Only archaic grains like spelt and quinoa give you . . .' "

Her daughter's idea of a peace offering. Mom, Mom, Mom. Look at me. Play with me. Don't you dare pull anything. Continuous performance, not daring to stop for a second.

"Not awake yet, Ellie." Not asleep yet from yesterday, actually.

"All is forgiven, Mother Unit." Cyborg drone, now. "We will assist you in achieving consciousness." Ellen swings behind Laura's chair and begins to knead the mother unit's shoulders. In her previous life, Laura would have lapped up this touch. Now it just hurts, although she says nothing.

From can't-stand-to-be-in-the-same-county to this constant touching and banter. An abrupt one-eighty, in just about as many hours. It's the hair loss that did it. The patch at the crown of her head. The little, pink, cured-pork rind of Mother's bared scalp brings it home to Ellen: this is really happening.

Shifting, wincing, Laura suffers the raw press of her daughter's hands willing her softer. At the same time, she tries to sort through the pile of yesterday's junk mail and catalogs. All she gets anymore. She's even started to get junk E-mail.

"Mom, Mom. Don't throw that out. Didn't you read what it says? 'This may be your last issue of our free catalog, if you don't order.' "

"Ellie."

"And then again, it may not. Ooh, look! Little fake security systems. Just stick this remarkably lame-looking plastic template to the side of your house, and it might trick a blind, reality-challenged burglar into thinking that your house is protected by alarms."

"Providing he's not on the same national advertising mass-mailing lists as you are."

"Shrewd mom. Savvy mom. Don't let them catch you napping."

"I wish they *could* catch me napping."

Ellen leans around, face in her face. "Trouble again last night? Did you try eating that lady's herbs?"

"I ate the one for sleep problems. Maybe I should eat the 'Carnal Appetite Booster.' "

"She gave you that? Lemme see."

"Absolutely not."

Laura looks over the flier ads while Ellen grows newly entranced with hammering her clavicle. She catalog-shops for the new sofa she ordered last week, just to see how much better she might have done somewhere else. She tries to concentrate, to cull the good deals from the good copy.

"Remind me again," she asks her daughter. "Which is stronger: Mega, Super, or Ultra?"

"Mom! Get real. Which do you *think*?"

She doesn't know what to think. Thinking is increasingly beyond her. She studies the stack of no-risk offers. She imagines a house full of complimentary magazine issues. Like her bookshelf when she was growing up, all the fifty-nine-cent Aardvark to Azimuth volumes her mother never followed up on. If she'd only gone to a college where she could have specialized in the early part of the alphabet. If she'd only gotten a disease that started with "A."

Free, Mrs. Laur A. Bodey. No obligation. If you aren't satisfied, just mark "cancel" across the invoice and this free issue is yours to keep. As far as she can see, the only catch is the minor humiliation of having to punch out the little sticker and put it in the premarked circle. But even that is part of the sell. Back in real estate school, they taught her that people actually like to get involved. Like to insert the irrelevant tab in the unnecessary slot. Makes you feel that you're doing something to earn the prize.

She wonders if it's immoral to take one of these offers, knowing full well that you have no intention of subscribing. But no; that's the deal. That's the promotion. They're betting you'll change your mind, or that you'll forget and pay the invoice by accident. They're so sure it's ad money well spent that they sell their mailing lists to one another, even after you've stiffed them. Or maybe they sell your name *because* you stiffed them, to stiff the other outfits they're selling the mailing lists to.

But then, how is it that she gets second offers from the same place? Hit me again. Of course, they're all set to cheat her back. They lose her cancellations, keep sending her issues. She's canceled this *Amateur Gardening* three or four times—by print, fax, and 1-800 order line—and still keeps getting copies. Like they think that one day she'll throw in the towel and put her savings back into circulation. Share the wealth. Better for everyone.

She has a look at the latest issue: another cover story on the composting controversy. She tries to follow the feature article, threading its way down the page between ads like a column of cavalry down an ambush-studded defile.

With some effort, she gets to her feet. She moves across the kitchen, absently pursuing her belated health diet. High fiber. Antioxidants. Better late than never.

"I thought you weren't supposed to have coffee," Ellen rags her.

"I can have coffee."

"I thought you weren't supposed to have any coffee until after you were done with all that medicine crap."

"I can have a cup of coffee, Ellen."

Her daughter storms out of the kitchen in a huff. The clowny nonaggression, the pact against hair loss follow behind her.

Laura decides to spend Sunday the way the day was meant to be spent. She will go sink her feet in the season's last mud. She can bend over now without busting a gut. The garden is a nightmare of neglect. Her plants have forgotten that a hand ever tended them.

But the lightest workout winds her. She goes around back and gets a lawn chair. She winnows for a while, then sits for a while. Soon she is sitting more than she is winnowing. Then she winnows while sitting down.

For her entire adult life, she has needed to somehow reduce the number of weeds in the universe. Not that the war against noxious plants could ever be won, or even that anyone would want to win it, really. Only, on her small parcel of ground, she needs to tilt the scales slightly toward sweeter growth . . .

But today she reaches the point where she can no longer tell plant from weed. And even if she could, she wouldn't be able to wedge the trowel in between them. She sits in the green-and-white shredded-PVC-weave deck chair, her eyes tearing at the planting plan that has gotten away from her.

She will take everything in, in one go. Up by the roots. Even the stuff that has two or three good weeks left. Rather spade it all over into black than this. This uncultivated, silkweed chaos. And she would, too, except that now she might put her full weight to the spade and still not succeed in sinking the iron lip.

She closes her eyes and tries to collect herself. To remember the voice on those cancer tapes, from the back racks at the Show Stopper rental warehouse. Tries to summon up the waterfally earth music, perform all the visualization tricks she's training in. She can almost hear the narrator, whom she imagines looking like one of those beautiful Sheen guys, repeating the litany: "Surround the tumor in a solid, silver casing, and just throw it away . . ."

She needs to remember that trick she never mastered, back when she played the oboe. The impossible trick of circular breathing—already drawing the next inhale, even while having the last one siphoned out of you.

She is trying to do just that, trying to remember how to breathe, when Ellen rouses her. Her daughter stands blocking the few, wobbly rays of sun. She holds out in front of her two flaps of newspaper, like a boy holding up the wings of a dazed bat whose defective sonar mistook the garage for Carlsbad Caverns.

The *Post-Chronicle*? Ellen? Her Ellen?

"Mom?" Tentative, low. Like it's not archaic grains this time. Like it's not the mother unit but just this winded woman in a lawn chair. "Mom? Did you see this?"

It's a half-page piece, on page A10. "**EPA LISTS LOCAL EMISSIONS.** Annual Toxic Release Inventory Details Area's Plants." The sort of piece the *P-C* uses to fill out the Sirens page on a slow day: half obscure federal data, half personal anecdote. " 'I've stopped hanging my clothes out on the line,' says Viola Johns, who lives across the interstate from the Clare Quikpak facility. 'Look at my front stoop. I have to sweep it twice a day.' "

Laura skims the copy, glances at the sidebar charts. She looks up at her teenager, puzzled.

"Here," Ellen says. "Ri-ight here." Counties ranked by toxic discharge. Lacewood, Sawgak, Vermilion, Champaign, Iroquois. Area's top carcinogenic chemical emissions. Benzene, formaldehyde, dichlorodifluoromethane, epichlorohydrin . . .

Laura looks up again at her daughter, disoriented. "You read the paper?" Neither cruelty nor the usual parental goad. Surprise. Pleasure, really. Like she doesn't have to worry about Ellen as much as she thought.

"Mother! You never give me credit for anything." Ellen stamps on the ground, but small. Insistent.

"Oh," Laura says, the penny dropping. "You think . . . ? Oh, sweetie. Mine's not like that. Dr. Jenkins said they don't know what causes ovarian. It's probably genetic. That means—"

"You think I'm stupid, don't you?" Ellen stares, eyes welling. She turns and breaks for the house.

"Ellie!" Laura calls. "Sweetheart, stop."

But Laura's sweetheart doesn't stop. She hits the back porch and keeps going. She leaves her mother alone, flapping the pages of the ridiculous local paper, the one that cannot spell "trichloroethylene" the same way twice. Leaves her gazing at the chart labeled: "Total toxic emissions from local plants." "Viola Johns says she would 'probably move' if she knew the facility put out cancer-causing chemicals."

———

GOOD BUSINESS MAKES GOOD NEIGHBORS

In the quiet, meandering Sawgak Valley in rural Illinois, the people love the land they work so fiercely. The days are long, and the harvest never certain. Frills are few and luxuries saved for holidays. But faith and effort combine to keep the region as fortunate as any place where you might hang out your shingle.

If you live in Texas or California or New York and you've heard about the Sawgak or its most prosperous town, Lacewood, most likely we're to blame. Because of what we do in Lacewood, people the world over eat better, live longer, and enjoy healthier lives.

Yet even though three out of every five jobs in this county depend on us, we're still a relative newcomer to the area. We've only been living here for a little over a century. We know what the real old-timers expect of us, and what we need to do if we want to belong.

So we pitch in. Our volunteer agreements keep the fire and police departments on the alert. We sponsor rescue and emergency efforts and train county crews in the handling of hazardous wastes. Our environmental fund has left the Sawgak more beautiful and cleaner by every measure than it was ten years ago. We support the work of local youth clubs and recently funded the conversion of many of the town's public buildings, making them more accessible to people with disabilities.

When the twisters hit in '91, we turned our Conference Center into a relief station for over two hundred people. Every year we host the annual corn boil, sponsor the youth symphony orchestra, and kick off a 15K race, just for the health of it. (If you're still getting in shape, you can tone up with our 5K walk.) Our Fourth of July float has won a trophy in eight of the last ten parades. And when Central High School's llama was pining with loneliness, we bought Lacewood's beloved mascot a mate.

Clare has more than twenty production facilities on every major landmass but the icy ones. We market our products in 83 countries to half a billion consumers. As corporate bodies go, ours has grown beyond belief in this short century. But however big a body gets, there's still no place like home.

Clare: Small Wonders

———

Resolve and the American Republic died at the same time. But as with the old national federation, Resolve's shares stayed in the family. Julia took charge of them, in trust for the children. Her husband's death left the expansion-minded journalist in partnership with her brother-in-law, who was still waiting for the heavenly pruning of earthly enterprise. The match between Julia and Samuel was never any contest.

Julia wrote an open letter to Samuel, Ennis, Benjamin, and the firm's bankers:

I trust that you will have the prescience to see, in the outbreak of this Conflict, the opportunity that our manufactories might enjoy, not only in determining the ultimate outcome, but in enlarging the scope and the force of their own activities.

The long-delayed devastation of a nation was, for industry, no more than confirmation of the inevitable. The agrarian idyll, already the stuff of hand-colored Currier and Ives nostalgia, elected for self-immolation. It chose to go out in a rich, harvest bonfire. The outcome of secession was already a foregone conclusion. Northern mills would whup landed gentry's tanned ass, with draft-rioting immigrants and striking labor thrown in for good measure.

As far as business made out, war was less crisis than its antidote. The Clares saw disaster's chance. Lard and cleanliness were the only suitable exchange for a society in cataclysm.

War required deliveries of all these commodities on a scale made possible only by the machine. If the turbine rendered war inescapable, war alone afforded the turbine its lucrative culmination. McCormick raised the reaper to apotheosis, and Gatling fit mass production to its ultimate use. The Clares, with the luck that always accompanies an accommodating business, stood by, ready with straw to stable the Four Horsemen's mounts when those steeds blasted through town.

At the moment that McDowell and the Union troops fled down the Warrenton Turnpike from their thrashing at Manassas, the Clares reeled as well, from their own initial skirmishes. For a decade, they had struggled with perpetual overproduction. They could make commodities faster than innocent consumers could need them. Yet the Clares had no solution for overproduction but to cut costs and become more efficient.

Overstock reached its peak just before Resolve's death and the outbreak of hostilities. The teenaged Douglas Clare made an ill-advised sales trip to Charleston, attempting to open up a market that everyone else knew was about to drop off the face of the sales map. On the wharves behind the old Customs House, about to return home empty-handed, he came across a merchant deep in the throes of history's panic.

Douglas smelled on the man the absolute terror of things to come. If Douglas was guilty of believing that such a robust country would never go to war over so irrelevant an issue as human bondage, the West Ashley merchant suffered from the certainty that Armageddon was no more than an hour away.

The man had an entire fleetload of rosin, and young Douglas somehow detected that the merchant had already written it off. By the end of the afternoon, Douglas had the man down to a dollar a barrel.

His father had given the boy no license to purchase anything. Douglas's task was to discharge inventory, not to build it up. His extravagant shopping spree required half the drays of Fort Point to deliver to Roxbury, and the firm had to rent two more nearby lots just to store the rosin mountain. However cheap the per-barrel price, the bargain, in toto, threatened Clare's Sons and Grandsons with ruin.

Furious, Samuel ordered his son back into the exile of factory shoveling. Stolid Julia began to direct the decimation of the plant's workforce. But at that very moment, vanishing agrarianism took up arms against the industrial aggressor, and the angel of Fort Sumter came down to save all Clare's generations.

Within weeks, rosin shot up to three dollars a barrel. Samuel, breathing again, ordered the whole lot sold at a 300 percent profit. But his prodigy son, emboldened, stayed the old man's hand. Rosin rose again, doubling and then redoubling. It climbed as high as fifteen dollars. And soon enough, for long stretches, it was not to be had at all.

Young Douglas saw that they could gain far more by keeping the congealed sap out of circulation than they could by trading. And when the Union—what was left of it—came through town waving its thousand-box orders for field-army rosin soap, the Clares were the only businessmen in the area who could even think of filling the bill.

Overnight, the Clare soap works landed the largest, steadiest, and most demanding customer of its thirty-year existence. And just as quickly, Julia marshaled the home operations.

The Union armies needed soap more than they needed a few extra carbine targets. So anyone with Clare work papers won immediate draft exemption. But Ennis fell in the Union cause, sacrificed to the needs of the country that had done so well by him. In the wartime speedup an accidental kettle spill scalded him across nine tenths of his body. He lay for three days, raving and screaming, before giving up the industrious ghost.

Ennis's death nearly tempted Jewitt back to the firm, out of the spite that covers for grief. But Julia, ascendant, took the chance to hire on a new knot of machinists, ones young enough to understand that nothing in this broken country would ever take place on the old scale again.

On the road from Manassas to Appomattox, industry learned its marching formations. The war forced manufacture into ever-wider markets, over whose birth the delicate midwife of carnage hovered. *I trust,* Julia beseeched her partners. *I trust you have the prescience to see that this hour will belong to those who can meet its shipments.*

With a million men in the field, the North needed the Clare stamp of Full Weight. Even the wooden boxes that bore this processed fat were worth their weight in silver. Crates stamped with the Clare mark served as the most opulent furniture these million Union men in their four-year wilderness encampments would enjoy. Clare kept them clean and gave them a place to sit. It won the firm a following that lasted another two generations.

The system of anticipatory supplying that once made it possible to fill the largest orders broke down under fire. Disturbance disrupted distribution, production outran stockpiles, and orders outran production. Douglas rose quickly from rosin shoveler to emergency manager. He began to staff the factory with continuous shifts. Finally he and his Aunt Julia informed Samuel that, for the first time, Clare workers would boil and press and cut and package on the Sabbath. The news almost broke the old man. But he did not resign from the firm.

Clare began the war a generic good and ended it a handful of brand names. At the same time, somewhere between the mortars and the ironclads, Clare's Sons became Clare.

The company continued to market Native Balm for civilian consumption. Gatling's apotheosis—the victory of mills over fields—produced its own futile consumer backlash. Those who glimpsed the world beyond this strife's horizon turned for comfort to all manner of belated herbal cures. For what has any customer ever wanted but to purchase time's defeat and raise yesterday's dead?

The Cambridge greenhouses groaned under the demand for magic plant. The only fields in North America where *Utilis* might grow now belonged to a breakaway nation. At first, Ben Clare tried to substitute willow bark or spurge or echinacea—some genuine Indian catholicon—for the South Sea impostor. But jobbers resisted taking on this Improved Native Balm in any quantity. They feared the public would reject the thin wartime substitute and insist on the genuine article. More than ever, disaster demanded its heal-all.

For four years, the price of Native Balm inflated absurdly. True, Clare's own costs also ballooned. Company supply was a worse shambles than the Union's. The Confederates sank their every fifth seaborne shipment, and the calculating British threatened to cut off soda ash entirely. By laws older than speech, a bar of Native Balm rose from seven and a quarter cents to well over fifteen.

Price measured how costly it was to extract soap from its opposite. Human need sank its shaft into the surrounding chaos and called every hunk of ore it hauled to the surface precious. The harder to mine, the more the thing was worth. When the warm-ups ended and the full-fledged program of apocalypse at last arrived, collapse itself would doubtless prove the greatest value-added reseller that civilization could hope for.

Julia understood these politics of price and appraisal. What was more, the timely arrival of Douglas on the scene further absolved Benjamin from having to wrestle with the market's equations. The first year of hostilities found Ben in a condition approaching happiness. Ad hoc and ex nihilo, he built one of the first commercial research labs in the country.

He recruited a team of technical assistants: orphan girls raised at a charity seminary school that Ben funded out of pure philanthropy. The school now yielded him a staff of eager and competent researchers. For as the president of Amherst College had once confided in writing:

> If a girl be accustomed to sound domestic practice, she would be more than well suited for the lab.

Assisted by his crew of orphan titraters, Ben tinkered, building his understanding of material processes and taking a child's delight in the pure problems of chemistry. He no longer answered to the firm. No subject struck him as more tedious than taming the market. But teaching the earth's very elements to jump through hoops: *that* seemed a dignified pursuit.

The firm gave him license to explore at will. Ben had long since earned his keep. Clare could get nothing more out of the man anyway. His family wrote off the aging bachelor scientist as used up. Amortized. Depreciated.

Yet Ben pursued a goal more practical than business itself. The wayward naturalist now fixed upon the dream of a use even greater than Use. He sought a converting kettle bigger than any the firm had ever dabbled in. His research chased the end of all chemistry: a soap works as wide as deliverance.

His brother's death focused Ben's mind on the task. Just as a body dies away from the lock of its own locale and rejoins its earthly parent, so might the host of common and unprofitable elements be made to reconstitute themselves inside the engine of chemistry. If one could turn salt and sulfuric acid into all the colors of the industrial rainbow, might one not turn the very acrid wastes of nature into a park fit for future habitation?

Human progress had already taken a considerable toll. The very gas lamps that lifted the pall of night also issued a rising tide of coal tar treacle that threatened to drown the nation in advancement's sewage. One might well have begun to doubt that the pall of night was meant to be lifted. Ingenuity threatened to choke on its own by-products before it led even the most willing to the promised land.

But suppose, Ben reasoned, that the fault lay not in our desires but in our infant chemistry. Coal tar waste need not be the end of light's line. Ben steeped himself in the work of Mansfield, who described the wonders hiding in that slag. Who knew what chemistry might emancipate from the fecal paste? Just as the manumission of our slave class required terrible, swift slaughter, so might humanity as a whole have to pass through a darker valley before ingenuity freed it from material bondage.

Mutable substance had no final shape. Homologies, like-shaped compounds, tumbled one from the other through perpetual combustive laddering. As grain itself sprang from converted dirt, so might precious goods rise up from chemical castoffs. Once free of its neolithic age, chemistry might work upon humanity a slow and undeserved deliverance.

Of coal tar's unlikely children, phenol most intrigued Benjamin. Poison in concentration, it turned to disinfectant when diluted. It dampened the stench of sewage and cleaned what no soap could. Benjamin threw himself into phenol's chemistry. He wrote copious notes about solvents stronger and more hygienic than the ones they now peddled. A soap brought to life by the cunning reconfiguration of coal tar.

Ben dreamed of a land purged of disease. He ceaselessly applied his intellect to locating the remedies for a wounded world. Filth and putrefaction were no more than powerful spurs to keep him on the scent.

He read the reports from France and England. He watched as research confirmed, at its own careful pace, Dr. Holmes's speculations about a final victory over infection. Phenol acted by killing the microscopic cellular agents responsible for corruption. How much misery might be averted by bringing civilization's struggle to these smallest gauges! Surgery, released from the threat of infection, could free the body from those ills that kept it forever battered down to its lowest level.

Holmes further awakened in Benjamin an interest in what the doctor christened "anaesthetic." Morton had demonstrated ether's deadening godsend during surgery at Massachusetts General, down and across the Charles from Benjamin's laboratory. The war now served as this miracle's great proving ground. The deliverance of the race was indeed close at hand.

Ben stood as on a hill, above Jordan's banks, looking out upon mankind's constant campaign against contamination and pain. Since the beginning, that fight had remained deadlocked. Now the scales had shifted; life might win. Possibility exploded in Ben's imagination. Clean at least, and released from pain, humanity could rise and expand to fill the day. No deeds would be denied the race. From such a dock, man might undertake the furthest voyage.

By God's grace, Morton lost exclusive patent rights to ether. Priority disputes with two other researchers left the dentist without enforceable claim. The way cleared, various companies, the naval Dr. Squibb's among them, raced to perfect industrial processes for redeeming humanity at an affordable price.

Liebig's pioneering discoveries opened competing paths to Lethe. Wells's laughing gas, Guthrie's chloroform: anaesthetic erupted in a single breath. The meager government subsidy of the soap business paled before these stakes. For the nation had no greater interest than the conquest of pain.

Benjamin set his sights on this final prize. He commenced the search for further answers to suffering, better solutions than chloric ether or nitrous oxide. Superior compounds surely existed: more robust, more expedient, safer soporifics that exacted lighter tolls upon the taker.

Ben's search sketched a formal beauty beyond his power to describe. Alcohol and ether shared a common heritage. Each roughly resembled the other, with only the fruit of their functional groups substituted. Other substances perchance existed that could extend this series of benefice and lift the body past all obstacles. Somewhere down that series lay salvation's aqua vitae.

The thrill of the chase kept Benjamin working through long nights. He waxed inexhaustible with the sweet prospect. He tested in arduous cycles. For want of adequate assays, he held his derivatives up to his nose or tasted them with a volunteer finger. He noted the effects of his chemical trials on his own body, the only research subject that returned reliable data.

Benjamin entered the most intense period of work in his life, beyond college, beyond the sea, beyond the harshest shifts of industry. The effort exhausted him. Yet never had he been so awake, so certain of his physical stamina. When his compounds disoriented him, he rebounded quickly from their noxious impact. When other tests produced in him lost memories or unimaginable euphorias, he jotted down their effects in his notes and pressed on. Hazard to his own body was a trifling price to pay for freeing the human race from its bodily ransom.

He needed more studies. Studies to ascertain proper doses. Studies to determine levels of purity and mixture. He circled back assiduously to the most promising substances and their derivatives. For some months, he kept meticulous notes of the scrutinized compounds, their precise synthesis, the frequency and quantity of ingested doses, and rigorous descriptions of their physiological effects.

After a time, these notes became more perfunctory. His hand grew more hurried, harder to comprehend upon review. Finally, Ben's notes stopped altogether.

It fell to Samuel to find his brother. Worried by a long lapse in communication excessive even for Benjamin, Samuel made the trip out to Cambridge, to his brother's combined residence and experimental laboratory. At the door, meeting no response to his entreaties, he broke in.

In the shock of entry, Samuel thought some denizen of the underclass had murdered Benjamin for the warmth of this decaying shelter. But the lethargic, speech-impaired man with the red-veined eyes cowering from invisible sprites in the air was his youngest brother.

Samuel searched Benjamin's notebooks for an account. But science's records came to a halt, silent and complicit, long before tendering any explanation. Even as they descended to illegible burlesque, the notebooks stuck to their one investigation: what might the species become, once sprung from its waking nightmare of infection and pain? Here was the twitching shape of that freedom, sunk into a crepuscular night known only to itself.

The family spared no expense in Benjamin's rehabilitation. At the height of wartime, they hired a private nurse to attend, feed, and restrain him at all hours. They laid in stocks of ruinously expensive blood purifiers and nerve tonics. What accident had induced, application might yet remedy.

But Benjamin refused to be cured. The man whom his family sought to bring back had vanished. Twice, for periods of two weeks, he recovered a decorum whose sole aim was relapse. Twice he repeated the willful humiliation of his family. Health now was only a trick he employed in their deceit, a parody of cleanliness that let him sneak past their benevolent guard and return to his sickness.

Samuel and Julia pleaded and reasoned with Benjamin. But Ben had landed well beyond reason. For reason was itself but a latecomer, an upstart Tudor needing all the propaganda of a Shakespeare to legitimate its autocracy. Deep inside the human lay an animal, a brute nostalgia that wanted only to take the bit in its teeth and be free to run.

There was something in the human that wanted, above all things, to be a plant. To return to its vegetable origin. And once the body tasted that return, no earthly kindness could deflect its further hunger.

Samuel removed Benjamin from all association with the company. He repurchased Ben's shares in the firm, at a price that only someone indifferent to and desperate for cash would have agreed upon. And for the good of Benjamin's immortal soul, Samuel deprived his erstwhile brother of all other fluid assets.

The company saved what could be salvaged from the notebooks. The best of Benjamin's chemistry laid out efficiencies that might redeem his otherwise senseless sacrifice. Bankrolled by federal subsidy and backed by the research of an addict, Clare eventually entered the growing market for disinfectants and anaesthetics.

The sole remaining problem in applied chemistry now facing Benjamin took on a different shading. His means and will evaporated more or less in tandem. He lived only to lose lucidity, for, lucid, he had lost the point of living.

In those hours when he was not beyond power of thought, he thought only of how to commit a discreet suicide, one that didn't seem self-murder. He wished only to avoid further hurting the firm's reputation, which he had already damaged. He stood outside in high places during electrical storms. He waded into the Fens, seeking cholera or the bite of a rabid rat.

He had died once already. He had taken the scent of scentlessness into his nostrils, out on the pack ice at earth's end. He had already worn perfect white, that bleach past all manufacture. He could die a second time, almost without giving it a second thought.

The tune of his chemical reverie was a shape-note tune. He hummed that bit of sacred harp hymnody to himself at all hours, long after he could hear himself humming. No chilling winds or poisonous breath could reach that shore. Sickness, sorrow, pain, and death would rule no more.

His family reclaimed Benjamin's corpse from where it settled, in an immigrants' alley off the North End. They interred it at Mount Auburn, next to his older brother Resolve, in a private ceremony in early April 1865, three evenings before President Lincoln ordered the White House band to strike up that fine and lively tune "Dixie."

———

"Hey, lady," a voice calls out as Laura enters the chemo room for the third Chinese drip torture.

Ruthie Tapelewsky, staked out in her old corner, waves Laura over as if the two of them have just met for a lunch date. "This here's one happening place, hey? Where the elite meet."

"Like I never left," Laura says, dazed. "Like the month between treatments just fell out of my pocket and vanished into the sofa cushions."

"I hear you," Ruthie says. "Wanna form a Fifteenth of the Month Club?"

"Tell you what," Laura tells her. "When it's over? When it's all over? We'll have a Sweet Sixteenth. Every goddamn month, if you want to."

Ruthie chuckles hard. "You're on, doll. Hey! You're halfway, this time, aren't you?"

The woman remembers. Keeps track of a stranger's numbers. Laura hasn't been able to keep track of the days of the week.

"Well, I'll be halfway a month from now. When I'm *done* with this one. How about you, Ruthie? I'm sorry, I can't remember how many you have left."

"Me? Oh, I got a couple left."

The big woman grins at her. Couple. A couple.

"Waiter's coming," Ruthie says, pointing across the room at Alan, the approaching chemo nurse. "Make sure to ask for a clean straw."

Alan straps Laura in and gets her started. All the while, Ruthie keeps up a running monologue. "Don't let him fondle your catheter, doll. Ask him to give you the good stuff."

Laura has forgotten the distraction of talk. Forgotten that another person might even be a pleasure. "Nice scarf, Ruthie," she says, settling in for the long haul.

"Thanks, honey. You too. But you know: I think you ought to go wild. You'd look real good in one of them blood-red wigs. Something in black and purple, maybe."

"I've tried all sorts of creative hats. My daughter won't let me wear them out of the house. I'm thinking about just going around bald. Save a lot of energy."

"You should! You should, Laur. Whose business is it but yours? Most people just want to sweep us under the rug. Hey. I made a funny." She laughs like a blancmange on an airplane cart. "Not that the rugs they sweep us under fool anybody. I think the third word my youngest one learned how to say was 'wig.'"

Laura lies back and takes the venom into her. Ruthie entertains her with tales of the Tapelewsky offspring. They tumble in and out of her account like bands of roving pickpockets and street buskers. Her eldest, a tenth grader, candy-stripes at the nursing home, where she has been named as major beneficiary in the wills of half a dozen eighty-year-old men.

"She kind of developed early," Ruthie apologizes. "They all do, these days. I think it's the stuff they put in the breakfast cereal."

Her second child was just fingered in some kind of scheme to distribute tens of thousands of dollars of application software to Pakistan and China over the Internet.

"God," Laura says. "Don't let him meet my boy."

"I mean, where do they learn these things? My little Elliot, the international software pirate. Come to find out, he didn't see anything wrong with the operation. Even after the FBI came by and gave us that little wake-up visit at three in the morning. He didn't see the harm in making an extra twenty bucks a week while helping these Third World countries develop."

That gets Laura laughing, too, which sets off her IV alarm. The alarm summons Alan. "Now, will you two ladies behave, or am I going to have to dope you?"

But Ruthie is already well into the saga of the terrible twins, who have worked every angle of identity-kiting that their interchangeability allows. And finally—for now, anyway—there's the one-year-old, the one who gets on her case for wearing a wig.

Laura has seen this woman somewhere before. Something about her feels incredibly familiar. Reassuring, too. Like nobody's going to come to any lasting harm while Ruthie is around to keep them entertained. Ruthie, against whose snort and chortle the latest in organized madness slinks away embarrassed.

It nags at Laura: Where has she met this person? How does she know her? Then the penny drops: a childhood friend, an ancient comfort. The old woman who lived in a shoe.

"How's that hopeless husband of yours?" Ruthie asks. "You teach him when to use which diapers yet?"

"No, Ruthie," Laura squeezes out, between giggles. "That's *your* husband."

"Oh. Come to think of it, you're right. I get your husband and my husband confused."

Laura would wet herself, if this weren't a hospital. "He's not my husband, Ruthie."

"Don't I wish," Ruthie says.

They watch afternoon TV, Laura in a growing fog of nausea, Ruthie sassing back at the angst-ridden soap actresses and the airhead talk show hosts.

"Problem Shoppers. Now there's a support group whose fax number I need. Teens Who Kill for Clothing. What do you say we skip this one?" To the various sales pitches whose stories interrupt these stories, Ruthie blows assorted raspberries. "Yeah. Right. Like I've got time for a lifestyle." Or: "It's just a damn car, lady. Stop jerking off on the fender."

Ruthie winds up her treatment just as Laura's own chemo starts to slam her. "Ride it out, kiddo. Don't let them catch you dragging."

"Don't leave me yet, Ruthie. I need you."

"Oh, honey. I'll be back soon enough," the woman groans. Somewhere along the line, the groan becomes another quaking blancmange without Laura seeing it change.

And she's left alone. With each go-round, her body's revolt starts sooner, digs in deeper, and departs with more elaborated viciousness. The biohazards are building up in her bloodstream. Or maybe she's just getting conditioned to puke whenever she sees a plastic tube.

But it can't all be conditioning. Because the bad stuff gets worse while the good stuff gets weaker. She can't understand why the Benadryl hardly works at all this time, even though she knows exactly what she was waiting for.

Dr. Archer makes his rounds as she is nearing the end of the taxol. "Thank God for the home team, huh?" he asks her.

She pushes herself through the cork wall to answer him. "Home . . . ?"

"The home team! Our local gravy train." He clinks the inverted bottle with his fingernail: municipal champagne. No sooner does he tap the empty jar than Alan comes by to change it for the next wash. Dr. Archer gazes at the laboring nurse, but says nothing.

"What do you mean?" Laura asks. She looks at Alan for help. Alan keeps working. "What gravy train? Where?"

"Tell me life's not strange," the semiretired oncologist says, by way of explanation. "Stuff's brought to you by the same folks who took the fat out of deep-fat frying."

"Clare makes this?"

"No. That would be Bristol-Myers Squibb. NoDoz, Ban, and a few cancer and AIDS gold mines. But Clare sells them cheap materials."

"I thought the stuff was made with tree bark." She looks at Alan. "You told me it was tree bark." Alan just shrugs.

"It used to be," Archer says. "Now they use artificial tree bark. Used to take six mature hundred-year-old Pacific yews to treat you. Pretty expensive, when you figure yew trees can only be harvested by clear-cutting. The problem was, cutting the trees was triggering some local extinction event."

"An owl," Alan inserts.

"Right. Some kind of spotty owl. Now me, call me irresponsible, but I'm one of those Humans First folk. I say, if somebody needs the trees to get well, to hell with the owl."

"What about the trees?" Alan asks. "No offense, Mrs. B."

She waves him off. "Of course not."

"What do you mean?" Dr. Archer spits.

"I mean, a lot of people might have said to hell with the yews, a year before they discovered taxol in the bark. And besides: six hundred years of tree for every sixty years of human being? As the song says, something's gotta give."

"Well, young man, that's exactly where science comes in. One of our home-team chemists has figured out how to make, in a test tube, what used to cost an arm and a leg and half a dozen yew trunks. The molecule that does all the good work is so complex that synthesizing an imitation was supposed to have taken years. But so many people were willing to pay so much for it that science has produced a substitute in record time."

Alan waves his hand. "Whatever you say, Doctor."

"If you just get out of people's way, they'll figure out how to make what people need." The oncologist strolls on down the gauntlet of patients, still shaking his head at the simplicity of the lesson that humanity stubbornly refuses to see.

"Ask him about the pill form of your anti-nausea drip," Alan tells Laura. "A weekend dose would run you a couple hundred dollars. Managed care won't let the doctors prescribe it unless the patient is ready to croak."

"You mean they have a better thing than they're giving me? Something that *works*?"

"Well, the one that works is always too expensive to use."

"I need that one," Laura says.

"I can imagine, Mrs. B."

But he can't. Can't begin to imagine. If he could imagine, he'd say something useful.

She starts planning in her head. An all-out bake sale. How many Kahlúa Nut Bars would she have to sell, to make enough to pay the difference, to buy herself deliverance from this month's agony?

"Yeah," Alan is saying. "A lot of people out there, figuring out how to make what we need. They say Philip Morris has thousands of acres in North Carolina, just ready to go to pot the minute the FDA blesses it as a chemo palliative. Pretty ironic, given what the fields grow now."

"Marijuana, you mean? Weed makes you . . . ?"

"Well . . . sure. It works for some people. Does that . . . ? Is that interesting?"

"No, no," Laura says, wildly interested. Anything. Anything that might keep her from heaving again.

"Tell him you're dying," he suggests. "Say you won't be able to make it through the week, otherwise. Tell him you'll throw up on his alligator shoes if he doesn't get you some decent pills."

––––

LIFE AFTER CHEMISTRY

No, there's nothing wrong with this picture. There's nothing wrong with your magazine or its printers either. We just thought you'd like to see what life would look like without those life-threatening chemical processes you read so much about these days.

The thing is, all those exposés that you read are printed in high-quality inks on treated paper. Illustrated with four-color photochemically separated pictures. You flip through them lying on your no-stain couch in your favorite freshly laundered robe while sipping a diet lemon-lime . . .

We could go on forever, but you get the picture. And a good, clear picture, too. Life without chemistry would look a lot like no life at all.

Civilization has had growing pains, to be sure. It always will. That's no reason to throw in the no-iron, synthetic-fiber towel. We just need to choose what kind of world we want to live in, and then build that place.

And to do that, whatever our dream world looks like, we'll need the right building blocks.

Less knowledge is not the answer. Better knowledge is. Chemical processes are not the problem. They're the rules of the game.

It's elementary: your life is chemistry.

So is ours.

The Industrial Processes Group
CLARE MATERIAL SOLUTIONS

––––

War's end left but one merchant's son, but one founding brother. Samuel had lived to see the glory of the machine. Northern industry was victorious. It bought victory with cigarette and whiskey taxes and mass production of ironclads and repeating rifles.

But the industrial future demanded payment on delivery: $4 billion dollars in current assets and a million and a half casualties. Everyone was dead, from the President on down to that fool of an Irish kettle man. Only Samuel remained, the oldest brother, the archaic one. Industry had spared the one Clare who had never understood the purpose of industry in the first place.

Samuel's wonder at the speed and ubiquity of destruction wrung all manufacturing from his heart. The world's end had come after all, invisible, secret, snickering, some time after that promised night when he had stood waiting for it. It came one night in late 1865, when he surveyed the factory floor and saw in it only a quatrain of human folly carved in limestone and capped by a winged skull.

One might better have given the world away and become a mendicant. Once more, Samuel elected to hang all worldly goods. For the making of goods had grown beyond his comprehension. And so the last of J. Clare's Sons withdrew from the arena he had helped to usher in.

As Samuel shrank from the business, those who still knew the point of progress stepped in. Led by young Douglas, the firm carpetbagged into the beaten South. By extending liberal credit to impoverished distributors, Douglas and his remote agents began to sell as far south as decimated Georgia, a step before Clare's New England rivals followed them down.

Toward this end, Julia courted the Southern woman. In the humbled returnees, Julia imagined the perfect market for an edible lard that Clare now rendered in abundance. With a welcome product and irresistible terms, Julia initiated the sale of Clare Cooking Curd to thousands of women who, two years earlier, would have greased their pans with any Clare employee within gunshot.

Thus the company secured a foothold on the soil of their prostrate adversaries. Time and trade would revive the region. Wealth would return, like a forest after a fire. And Clare would be there, exchanging its lard for Dixie's returning crop, under the seal of the new Union.

Clare's wartime government contracts had squeezed honey from the stone of national catastrophe. Southward postwar expansion helped to offset the loss of those standing orders. But prosperity alone would not ensure the company's continued existence. War's meteor, the wrecking ball of progress, brought home to all survivors the need to reorganize. Samuel, senior partner, was already a shade, even now cutting closeout deals with death. The time had come to pass the torch. The second generation stood by, ready and eager. All it needed was a code of succession.

After prolonged debate, Julia at last forced her brother-in-law to concede to the inevitable. The operation had grown too large, profit had gone too wayward for any other solution. A few men no longer sufficed to run the kettles and handle the sales. Business now far outstripped the single life's span. Continued competition required a new kind of charter. Survival offered Clare no alternative but incorporation.

To Samuel, the very word smacked of failure. Incorporating would betray all that he and his brothers had worked these three decades to assemble. Back when the merchant Clares still wrinkled their noses at the stink of manufacturing, incorporation evoked universal hostility and suspicion. Governor Morton, in his 1840 Inaugural, had stared down his legislators and thundered:

> One of the vices of the present age, stimulated by extravagance, and a thirst to acquire property without earning it, is a desire to transact ordinary business by means of charters of incorporation.

The Whiggish *Boston Courier* voiced similar doubts. Easy licensing would create a rush into incorporation akin to the California gold rush, with even less attendant gain in real national wealth. Corporate franchises played fast and loose, a kind of cheating that nobody cottoned to, least of all the American capitalist. Such a social experiment spreading throughout the business community seemed a gamble that few felt the need to take.

If an owner couldn't manage his own firm without special privileges, he had no right to stay in business. At first the law permitted incorporation only for public utilities or those endeavors in the public interest that required large amounts of capital, huge workforces, or special legislative protection to run at all.

But since the soap works' founding, law had loosened and the populace had warmed slightly to the idea. The giant manufacturing companies that ran Lowell clothed the whole seaboard. As gins worked cotton's boll, so the corporation combed out the world's most valued fibers and wove them solid. The city of million-spindled mills outstripped the hand of man as much as man outstripped the animals. When risks were distributed and liability defrayed, what might collective humanity not accomplish?

The shattering bounty that steam-driven factories stamped out required an institution to house it. Civilization had stumbled upon that institution, one that might take it anywhere at all. The race had learned how to build a combine to do the endless bidding of existence. And the work of this compound organism outstripped the sum of its cells. Enterprise's long-evolving body now assembled goods beyond any private life's power to manufacture.

Incorporation promised to do for its hundreds of discrete, laboring constituents what the kettle did to alkali and fatty acids. The societal manufactory had hit upon a way to enact a similar conversion. Only now, as the late Ennis once put it, the kettle was "bigged up" to life-size and larger. Human lye, passed over these corporate coils, suffered its own strong change, leaving behind the thick, soapy foam of value.

Increasingly, the limits on incorporation began to seem like mind-forged manacles on the legs of a freed slave. The state did not ask its grain to apply for a special bumper harvest license. The best the state could do to ensure its people's deliverance was to get out of the way and let the genie do its bidding.

By the outbreak of war, Massachusetts allowed any firm of a certain level of capital to self-incorporate. Incorporation grew easier than petitioning for a formal charter. And it bestowed more protection, while requiring even less disclosure.

All the arguments for Clare's transformation were on Julia's side. She pressed the case with a zeal she'd hitherto reserved for the repair of the Atlantic cable. Yes, the firm would have to answer to a board of directors. But vitiation by democracy would cost them little, Julia insisted. They would still hold all the stock in private, and they could pack the board so that any outsider would have compliance forced upon him. Clare had nothing to lose but its paper sovereignty and its family pride.

Against this loss, she stressed the gains of limited liability. Incorporated, Clare could push its business into regions previously too expensive, exhausting, or risky to consider. Already, complaints in Roxbury forced Clare to consider relocating the plants farther afield. Sales stretched to several states. The company experimented with growing *Utilis* in open fields, far to the sultry south. They bought alkali from England, sperm oil from the antipodes, and scrap livestock fat from any slaughterer between Boston and Canada. In short, they now did business in enough places to mandate simplified protections under the law.

Still, to Samuel, incorporating felt like hocking the prize brooch from out of the heirloom strongbox. Already past the age that the Bible assigns to a full life, the old man took his hardest decision since forsaking the import trade. He started across this Potomac, well-nigh uncrossable. But neither could he turn back, for the angel of advancement stood behind him on the deserted bank, beating a tailwind with its wings.

The very idea of incorporation opposed all the business virtues he had ever stood for. Had he held out for the stamp of Real Weight, only to give in to this? And yet: an incorporation could live forever. It carried on beyond the span of any owner's life. It passed itself down through the generations of those assembled thousands who would, in time, work its engines. Its dynasties surpassed the longest family.

That vision of continuance clinched Samuel's choice. For the end of business was to outlast the needs it satisfied.

The laws of private incorporation required precious little. The incorporators had to name a president and a treasurer. Samuel kept the first title and gave the second to Resolve's oldest boy, Peter, a queer young man with a frightening head for numbers. Julia packed the minuscule board of directors with two business affiliates, two cousins, and the family's banker. Anthony Jewitt, hauled from retirement to stuff the board, could rarely be troubled to come to meetings. He and his machines had always let the Clares do exactly as they needed.

The officers and board had to file a certificate declaring their own names and residences, the amount and par value of capital stock, and the shares owned by each member. Julia dealt out the shares to preserve the family's old split of ownership. The certificate also had to specify the new venture's official name. After much agonizing, J. Clare's Sons became the Clare Soap and Chemical Company.

The Joint Stock Act required the officers and board to publish this data in a public newspaper, like wedding banns, for all to read or forever hold their peace. The certificate also had to declare the purpose of the incorporating enterprise. Here, too, the law had grown more liberal, allowing much broader ranges of activity. Once upon a time, a company chartered to spin silk could not also make muslin. But now the law let Clare declare its purpose to be "pursuing the art and manufacturing of soap, candles, lard, and all things thereto belonging, as well as the distillation by boiling and chemical processes of such products related to that trade as are fit for public consumption."

In short, a charter so wide even a room-sized kettle could not fill it.

They put Stoughton, the lawyer, whom they once consulted no more than a few times a year, on permanent retainer. They formalized relations with a State Street financial house. Howe and Howe hid its accumulation of railroad debt behind a row of Corinthian columns mocked up to look like the Maison Carrée in Nîmes. Boston now specialized in such compensations: churches that looked like banks and banks that looked like Roman temples. Howe and Howe put its seal to a move as prescient as it was inevitable.

Clare filed for incorporation with the Secretary of the Commonwealth of Massachusetts in 1867. The paperwork done, Samuel gathered the clan and as many people as then worked for them. He gave the lot an hour's party, with pay. After, he cleared his phlegmy throat above the din to speak.

He spoke of his father, Jephthah, of his tireless brother Resolve and the devastated Irish widower they had befriended. He spoke of baby Ben's magic *Utilis* root, brought back from the far side of the globe, the seed for this ever-spreading Native Balm.

He spoke of the larger plant, the factory that housed them all. Business, he declared, of rights ought to be our ancestral home, stately and permanent, upon whose paneled halls hung the portraits of all those whose hands had raised the beams and sped the plow.

These words made plain to anyone who had ears to hear: Samuel was failing. The last son of Jephthah Clare had lived long enough to preside over his obsolescence. His life, what was left of it, hereafter would consist of vetting strangers to run what he had once run with his own hands.

Samuel's public vanishing act doddered on, his speech peeking into various shambles like an official inspector of war damages. The very irrelevance of his words laid bare the commercial paradox. For he spoke on behalf of their mass, solitary successor. The law now declared the Clare Soap and Chemical Company one composite body: a single, whole, and statutorily enabled person. Rambling on, Samuel reached back to quote Chief Justice John Marshall, whose death had long ago cracked the Liberty Bell. He sounded the classic definition that Marshall gave in *Dartmouth College* v. *Woodward*, a half century before:

> A corporation is an artificial being, invisible, intangible, and existing only in contemplation of law.

By this point in Samuel's oration, most of his day laborers had slipped quietly back to work. Those who remained, whether out of amusement, sloth, or sentiment, heard their president invoke the beast that gave them all eternal life. They heard him speak of an aggregate giant, one that summed the capital and labor of untold Lilliputians into a vast, limbered Leviathan. Those who remained to the bitter end saw the old man's wife and sister-in-law lead him mercifully from the rostrum in mid–coughing fit.

For a while after incorporation, business remained business. And for some time, despite its newly granted privileges, Clare remained just a company. The American vat as yet lacked one essential precursor, one secret additive that would corner the market for incorporation. Time and Clare required one more catalyst to render life's waste fat and solidify it, stainless and inexorable.

A little power politics and some sleight of hand produced this catalyst just as Clare took up its corporate destiny. The Fourteenth Amendment came into the world to serve as Reconstruction's conscience. It cast a protective net of unabridged citizenship over the freed slave. Commerce and cash were the furthest things from its framers' minds. But such pure acts of idealism never know their practical ends.

The linkup lay a few more years in coming. But who could gainsay the logic? If the Fifth and Fourteenth Amendments combined to extend due process to all individuals, and if the incorporated business had become a single person under the law, then the Clare Soap and Chemical Company now enjoyed all the legal protections afforded any individual by the spirit of the Constitution.

And for the actions of that protected person, for its debts and indiscretions, no single shareholder could be held liable. Each part of the invention shone out, innocent and beautiful. But the whole, like some surprising mathematical proof that twists its modest axioms into a stunning QED, ended up providing just that slight boost needed to propel the Roxbury soap works—and with it, all world history—into its final, irreversible form.

Such was all the nod needed to turn a handful of harmless beans into a beanstalk that, in time, outgrew the world's terrarium. The limited-liability corporation: the last noble experiment, loosing an unknowable outcome upon its beneficiaries. Its success outstripped all rational prediction until, gross for gross, it became mankind's sole remaining endeavor.

It would fall to Douglas Clare, Samuel's son, to be the first head of the company with enough leisure time to read. Years after Clare filed the papers, Douglas came across a definition for the thing in Bierce's *Devil's Dictionary*:

> Corporation: An ingenious device for obtaining individual profit without individual responsibility.

Douglas Clare could do no more than scratch his head at this attempt at humor. He might have found the explication clever, funny, perhaps even diabolical, if it weren't the absolute letter of the law.

YOU KNOW OUR NAME
(LOOK UP OUR NUMBERS)

Be a part of a life that's already an integral part of yours.

A copy of Clare's Form 10-K Annual Report as filed with the Securities and Exchange Commission is available upon request, without charge, after

March 31 by writing Clare International, Stockholder and Investor Relations, One Clare Plaza, Boston, MA 02109.

INDEPENDENT AUDITORS: EARL AND ANDERS, NEW YORK

———

Don sends her the same *Post-Chronicle* article that so upset Ellen. The one about the benzene and formaldehyde, laid out in all the little tables. He faxes it to her at work, without even the decency of a cover letter to hide it in the fax machine tray. Just: "FYI. No comment necessary, D." penned in the upper left corner.

Ellen must have put him up to it. The two of them, making each other jumpier than guard dogs at an open house. What in the world does he expect her to do with it? No action necessary, she assumes. FYI only.

She never could figure the man out. How the world owed him a perpetual explanation. How everything had a secret angle, waiting to be figured. Even when they were first dating: always a back alley somewhere that the other seventy thousand concert fans hadn't discovered yet. Some cut-rate package deal that only the inner circle knew about, if one just nosed around a little.

She might have been able to live with that. But nosing around by himself was never enough for Don. No: he always needed to enlist her in the eternal search for that missing bit of information. Made her tune in the radio at the smallest nearby siren. Made her phone the kids' school when the nearest flurries were just specks of Iowa dandruff on tomorrow's weather map. Just to involve her, somehow.

The man could not take out a magazine subscription without running a character reference check on the entire masthead. He never let her charge things, even if she paid the balance off as soon as the statement came in. "It's not the cash, Lo. Every time you order anything, you're giving every stranger with a database a thousand more conclusions to draw about you."

And everybody else's database always had some unseen edge over his. Professionals brought out the absolute worst in him. The inside traders, the ones who ran the racket. When Tim was in that respirator for so long, gasping for life, Don spent days just trying to get the doctors to admit all the things they weren't telling. "That's our job. That's the patient's *job*." And the doctors' job was to maintain their edge by keeping us in ignorance.

Back when they were married, Don couldn't even pay the phone bill without second-guessing the entire cartel, from Bell Labs down to the guy who climbed the pole. Always *figuring* people. The mortgage officer, the clerk at the video store, the paper boy. That's what made him so good at his own job. His way of making people think they're cleverer than they are. That they're holding more cards, closer to the vest.

He only got worse as he moved up in the world. Every promotion left him more of an old maid. Director of Development had that many more angles to second-guess than Associate. He had to make the appropriate second-car statement. He had to pick the right investment for their retirement account. He once spent half of January researching the perfect summer camps for the kids.

It drove her nuts, finally. After a decade, she got tired of trying to get him to take the world at face value. He wore her down. She started imitating him, unconsciously. Asking the woman at the post office if there weren't some better way to send things. Getting a second opinion after the termite guy gave the house a clean bill of health.

Such a relief, finally, breaking free. Like getting out of those old size-10 suits after a size-14 day. Like having that nose tube pulled out of her gut, only bigger. The freedom to breathe, to be ignorant of the worldwide conspiracy, to fuck up sometimes, to say "fuck up."

While all the blood was being spilled, she swore she'd never do it again. Never get involved. A person would have to be sick. It dies hard, the habit of a man. Worse than quitting smoking. And Ken seemed almost perfect: invisible, low-maintenance, like one of those renewable, twenty-ride monthly passes for the commuter bus. He'd watch any film in the world. He didn't care whose name was on the six-pack. And he never made her call the radio stations about anything. Never.

Best of all, he was never underfoot. A lot like eating out: you got to have the roast beef while somebody else did the dishes. Of course, there was that part about having to drive for an hour just to find a safe restaurant. But then, if it weren't for Ken, she would never have gotten out so much.

They sit in the Round-Up Steak House, Peoria. Ken wanted the view of the river, but he didn't want to wait the twenty minutes for a window table. Not a waiting kind of man, Ken. They sit in the back room, filled with bronze statues of bucking broncos and wall tapestries of the Marlboro Man.

His eyes wander around the room, as they always do. Appraising the situation. Planning the quick exit. He glances at her plate and frowns. "Honey, you aren't eating very much."

"I'm sorry."

"You want something else? You want the Surf Special?"

She tries to remember the last time she saw the surf. The last time she was anywhere near the ocean. Not since that abysmal vacation to Nags Head when the kids were little.

"It's fresh," he insists.

"Ken. Fresh shrimp? Peoria?"

"Sure. They fly them in by the ton, every day. Okay, they're packed on ice. But they never actually freeze."

And St. Louis, she wonders. Lawrence, Kansas? Denver? Bozeman? How can there possibly be enough Surf Specials to go around?

"Honey?"

"Sorry. I'm back!" She grins as wide as she can.

"*Laura*. Would you like something else to eat?"

She can tell he's getting angry by how polite he's becoming.

"That's all right. I'll just pick at this for a while."

"Picking is not eating."

How to tell him that the steak tastes like that yellow scum that builds up on the inside of the toilet tank?

"Ken. I've got cancer. I have three months' worth of heavy metals in me."

"Okay. Should we talk about something else?" And he smiles at her. What he loves most about her is her offbeat sense of humor.

"Sure. Why not? Something else. That would be great."

"Work?" he asks, pouring on the irony like A.1. sauce.

"Yeah! Tell me again. What is it that you do for a living, buster?"

"Nothing that polite people would want to talk about at dinner." He looks away, toward the room with the window tables.

She's wounded him. And it won't be right until she sucks up and apologizes. As usual, she cannot really pinpoint what she did wrong. All men, every last one: no matter how casual they seem. No matter how mature, how much money they make, how secure. No matter what, they need you to eat what they've killed and brought you.

He'll sulk now, for as long as it takes for her to apologize. Which, at the moment, is fine by her. They sit in silence. Actually, nothing so nice as silence. The ever-present audio system supplies them a sound track. The equipment is out of sight, back in the kitchen with all the illegal Latino cooks. Some kind of multi-CD changer, set to shuffle tracks from seven different disks at random. Now that she listens, she hears it go from some kind of plunky Bach thing to sixties psychedelic, followed by Billie Holiday singing "Strange Fruit," followed by another movement of that Bach. Schizophrenia, raised to an art form.

Ken sees her listening. "Something for everyone," he scoffs.

She studies him, trying to remember what the assets were. All the assets have fled somewhere offshore.

"So what the hell's eating you?" he says, when they are back in the car.

"What? You couldn't ask me that in the restaurant?"

"I *could* have. But I'd just as soon not air my linen in public, if it's all the same to you."

"Ken. You and I don't *go* out in public. We just skulk around Peoria."

"So you would have eaten the damn steak if I took you somewhere in Lacewood. Is that what you're saying?"

"And you and I don't even have any dirty linen. We just have Handi Wipes."

She hears the pathetic jab dribble out of her mouth. She hates herself for saying anything. She doesn't even know why she's angry. She wouldn't want linen with this man, even if he were buying. The last thing in the world she wants is more of someone else's wash.

This is their private fight, their quiet, familiar combat. The one they've been having since the beginning. They know this war. They do it by heart, even when happy, even at peace with each other. They go through its motions while whistling cheerfully and shoving all the corpses under the rug. But she has no idea what the power struggle is over, what either of them hopes to win.

It does not even feel raw to her, anymore. Just these ancient scabs, bloodless festerings that they've calked over with realism and styptic pencil. The most civil of aggression, so domesticated that they might as well be married. I don't want to pull, but I hate you pushing. You don't have to be in this with both feet; you just have to be in deeper than I.

"I thought we agreed on this," Ken starts.

And Laura begins to will him into the lamp poles by the side of the interstate. How did they get from perfect to this? They started out with all the convenience of companionship and none of the responsibility. Now, for months, ever since she's been sick, the man has felt like all the responsibility with none of the convenience.

"Do you want me to leave Julie? Because . . . Because we've talked about that, Laura. You know that I . . ."

"No, Ken. I don't want you to leave Julie." The first time Laura has spoken the name since her operation. Julie. Perfect name for a small, high-strung, soap-opera brunette.

"What do you want, then?"

She breathes from her stomach, as the self-cure tapes tell her to. "I want you to leave me."

He turns steely. His hands look like driving gloves, on the wheel. Of course it had to come to this. She should have known not to implicate herself, even casually. Never get involved with a man who uses a Relax-Or car seat and lashes rubber grips around his steering wheel.

They go three No Passing zones in silence. Or not silence. Nothing is ever silence anymore. It's a radio call-in show, deciding what's best for America. Trickle down: always trickle down. Apparently, most people with phones still believe that when the water in the harbor rises, all the boats go up.

"Honey," he says, talking right over the caller who's pushing for medical savings accounts. "Honey, you're right. You have to forgive me. It's just . . . I can't . . . You know, that awful medication . . ."

It wrecks her, his even trying to name her illness. She did not imagine him capable. To want her so much that he's willing to talk about it. She has not realized how much the threat must poison him, too. She feels awkwardly for his hand on the wheel.

"Oh, Ken. It won't last forever. Only three more doses." She wants only to reassure him: I won't puke forever. I'll get my strength back. My hair. My color. My self.

He shoots her a confused look. And before he can grasp the mix-up, before he can recover, she sees the error register in his eyes. He doesn't mean her taxol. He means his flurazepam.

"Oh," she says. "Oh."

Another caller pushes for privatization of the Marine Corps.

"Laura. I didn't mean . . ."

"I know what you meant, Ken."

She never had him anyway. You can't miss what you never really had.

After a long time, they see the Lacewood smokestacks. He rushes his words, as if he has to get them out before they hit the edge of town.

"I need you, Laura."

Need? Like that's the deciding factor. Like *need* would clinch it for her. Some inarguable staple.

She's not even numb. It's just over. Last week's lottery ticket. She can't even remember why they were going out for dinner. She looks at him. Like looking at all the funky hairstyles in her high-school yearbook. Is that how we looked, once? It's as easy to be kind to him as it is to the mailman.

"Ken. This isn't how two people are supposed to be."

"Maybe we should try again. From the beginning."

She wants to smother him again. "What beginning?"

"Look. Why don't we just forget all this, and . . . Why don't we just enjoy each other?"

"I've got too much else on my plate to enjoy you, at the moment."

"I know, honey. I . . . do you want me to leave Julie? Because . . ."

"Ken. Look. I can deal with cancer, or I can deal with you. But I can't deal with both."

Something plays across his face. Not distress. The conventions of distress. Distress's opposite. All these wretched days, she has put off the inevitable break, sure it would devastate him. And he's relieved. Exonerated. Off the cancerous hook.

He inhales, starting to reason with her again. Going through the motions. Her one, crimped eyebrow silences him.

"Stop here," she orders. "I'm getting out."

"Honey, don't be crazy."

"Stop the fucking car."

It takes her as long to walk the last miles in as it took them to drive to Peoria. The air is cool. Mist tattoos her face with tiny needles. She feels like a little girl.

She walks home, wondrous in the dark. She has never seen the town on foot. Never realized how many people live here. Never imagined what the place looks like at eye level. She gets turned around, lost. Lost in her own neighborhood, six streets over from the one where she lives.

———

For three decades, the firm had shot up like a backwoods boy fed on bear meat. Each return on investment financed new rounds of growth. Clare Soap was now too large for any one Clare to conduct. But by assembling into a single body under the law, that body of men could learn to conduct itself. And so, while the century began to experiment with laissez-faire, Clare began to experiment with management by chartered structure.

Size bore no delight for Samuel. He watched the teams of anonymous labor, transient and unreliable, blow through his swelling assembly plant. He yearned for the days when he knew all his employees' names by heart. Now he no longer even recognized the men by sight. He lost himself in the thundering thicket of steam-powered shafts and belts. The hulking machinery, custom-built at great expense, breaking down more often than it ran, utterly bewildered him.

He stood baffled before the maze of diverse retailers required to sell into the opening continent, the same continent that Mr. Jefferson once predicted would take a thousand years to settle. He could no longer tell his reliable distributors from the hopelessly inefficient ones. Suppliers changed orders on him without his noticing. Carrying expenses cropped up without cause or occasion.

Chemistry confused him most of all. Samuel knew only that the chemist would soon do to the manufacturer what he and his fellow manufacturers once did to the sedentary trader. The future belonged to the man who could turn sulfur into bleaches, tar into dyes, and salt water into libation.

Fortunately, Clare Soap's president did not need to trouble himself with labor or retail or equipment or science. Such was the glory of governance by chain of command. The incorporated firm matured to where each business task now fell to someone with some skill in the matter. For almost every concern, a son or nephew or clever foreman. The grooves and tongues of the second generation meshed like the gears of a most marvelous machine.

Samuel left to his remarkable sister-in-law all monetary concerns. And Julia, with her fiscal skill, kept the corporate open boat from smashing up on the shoals of a prolonged postwar depression. She could not, of course, be an officer of the firm in anything like public fact. J. H. Clare had long since been unmasked as a woman. Men of business would not knowingly deal with such a creature. But Peter Clare, the nominal treasurer, knew enough about cash to act tacitly on his mother's instructions.

Clare passed out of the fiduciary age still a family business. But Julia brought it into the monetary age a true company. She edged operations onto a cash basis. She greatly curtailed the drain of suppliers' credit. She steered the business clear of those ever-deeper spirals of murderously expensive borrowing that claimed so many of its competitors.

In these actions, too, Julia beat her favorite political drums. Commerce aimed at manipulating nature on a truly grand scale. For that, it had to put an end to such travesties as sixty-day payments. Debt handcuffed development and held capital hostage to indigence. Inventory had to return hard coin, if anything was to be left over to stoke the next boiler run. The destiny of American business required fiscal terms fast enough to match it.

Lotus-eaters in the lazy plantation latitudes might get away with trafficking in a papier-mâché profitability. Such storybook climes could cleave to the pace of nostalgia as if there were no competition, no tomorrow. But in the North, in the land of turbine and loom, only cash would carry the day.

Julia grasped the radical rearrangement that the coming era required. And her monetary reorganization of the firm opportunely coincided with Clare's chemical expansion. The same inspiration piloted both. For in Julia's self-making mind, cash was a kind of chemical conversion, and chemistry, highest finance. Rub two coins together. Boil two reticent compounds. The turn of these ceaseless turbines transmuted coal grit into the heat of heaven.

Clare's finished soap had always exceeded the worth of its sources. Everything that lived and breathed depended on that same slender edge. The noblest business on earth would have expired without the slight profit residing in conversion. One could not, Julia often tutored her son Peter, long survive by feeding expensive soap to a machine that took it apart into cheap alkali and fatty oils. At each repeat of the seminal lesson, the sickly child would nod profoundly.

Yet mother and son both distrusted extreme profit. Too fat a margin meant something was wrong. Today's excess spelled tomorrow's liability. Profit bred complacency, and complacency bred the death of endeavor. Advantage existed only to be reinvested.

For a long time, profit seemed to lie in boosting the finished product's value while holding the cost of raw materials to a minimum. In keeping this gap of gain as wide as possible, Clare naturally sought out the cheapest and best alkali available. But the sheer plenitude and quality of British soda so oiled the soap cycle that it blocked fabrication's next leap, a leap already made on the other side of the ocean.

Common wisdom had it that you don't fix what ain't broke. And yet, Julia argued, by the time the thundering thing is broke, no doctor exists who can put it right again. It became the woman theorist's favorite litany: Clare needed to shed the plum of near-term profit in order to reach for a vaster fruit.

Even back when Clare's self-bootstrapping soap works ran on natural potash, it already depended on countless other linked operations. Like those chained catalogs of biblical begats, Clare subsisted on the industry of innumerable ancestors. Its glass, nails, paper, wire, its stoves and boilers, the clocks and bells that regulated the workers' shifts—the entire Clare factory had been constructed in a score of other so-constructed factories, sprouting up everywhere across the face of the land. Saugus supplied the compressors and pipes needed to build each new harrower. A firm in Lynn sold Saugus the tools it needed to machine its parts. This outfit got its iron from the Bridgewater hoop works and the Norwich rolling mill, which got their coal from the anthracite fields in Pennsylvania, transported by the Lehigh canal company and Reading railroad and New York chartered steamers.

And by the beauty of this closed loop, three of every dozen and a half of those precursor miners, shippers, and forge laborers now worried no more about their skin than the average Red Man. Clare had long since converted the home soapmaking competition into its best customers. Along the way, it also made devoted clients of its own providers.

But the circle of wealth called out for more linkups, more loop-backs within loop-backs before the *perpetuum mobile* would run its course. All parts of the process had to be broken up and reconstituted, brought under the umbrella of making and management if manufacture were to pay for itself. To become true master of its own materials, to take charge of all the directions toward which the raw world might be sent, Clare, too, had to take its supplies, as much as possible, in-house. It would need to make its own synthetic alkali.

Julia and Peter pitched this case to Douglas. Together, they convened the board. The real purpose of business, Julia assured the assembled directors, lay not in getting but in spending. In the struggle for survival, the company had to pitch itself against a concern greater than its local competitors, greater than the soap castles of New York and Philadelphia, greater, even, than the mighty British. Clare Soap existed to level and bring low no lesser enemies than dependency and privation.

For the bemused businessmen, Julia traced out a kind of industrial allegory. She related a vision she had had on the factory floor, while watching the kettles split out products according to the levels each sank to in the agitated parfait. What if this whole tuned process, this entire ensemble generating its steady stock of Native Balm, were but one linked input feeding a far deeper churn?

Soap was but small potatoes. No more than the tiniest wart. No: a wart's wart on the back of an amphibian just now rising from its quiet pond to take to the dry lands of this empty continent.

Think big, Julia implored them. Every manufacturing system that Clare had yet assembled resembled those smudges in an eye-fooling painting: the crowds on a middle promontory that, to the observer who takes two giant steps backward, suddenly reveal themselves to be but bristles in the nostril of a behemoth.

Throughout Julia's delivery, Douglas shook his head. After she finished, he noted that no one had ever accused J. H. Clare of lacking ambition. His aunt's vision would have appalled the young man had not something in its scale thrilled him. He perked up at the suggestion of interlocking processes, whole rings of marketable substances he might be able to vend.

Nevertheless, Douglas did not see the business sense in her vision. Clare made soap. Its soap sold. Nobody in his right mind abandoned the farm while the crops were still profitable. Granted, the years had gone tight. Yes, another depression pinned the country to the ground and picked at it like a turkey buzzard. But another boom would come along soon, to answer that bust. Another always did. Clare needed only to concentrate on what it did best. Mind the pennies, and let the dollars mind themselves.

It took Peter's appeal to the memory of their Uncle Benjamin to bring Douglas around. The sickly cousin, who rarely came out in public, spoke of Ben's untapped legacy, the coal tar work, the copious notebooks filled with the chemistry of anaesthesia. Peter invoked the orphan seminary-school students, their late uncle's lab assistants. Without Ben Clare's scientific ramblings, there would be no *Utilis*, no Native Balm Soap, no Clare. What would it cost Clare now, to continue that research?

Some negotiation passed before even Peter understood the shape of his proposal. At last, he hatched the unprecedented idea of an industrial lab. The cousins hammered out an agreement on what the lab would look like, how they would run it, where to enter it into the books. They settled on a shape somewhere between Peter's idealist philanthropy and Douglas's hunger for new products.

Although she really wanted new factories, Julia latched upon this compromise. Here was the first step toward a business worthy of the name. The board approved the new industrial lab, and Samuel attached his signature to it, without even bothering to read the charter.

In photos, the lab appeared as little more than a dingy, narrow stockroom fitted with beakers and basins. It occupied a back corner of the new Walpole plant, completed shortly before the first train ran from one American ocean to the other. Walpole produced twice the soap of all the Roxbury operations put together. It was a self-contained village, with candle factory; alkali, boiler, sal, soap, and still houses; cooperage and carpenter shops; stables, sheds, and warehouses for a dozen different commodities. A vast building four stories high housed the huge kettles designed expressly for it. Erected over its own private rail siding, the modern plant saved the firm an easy $50,000 a year in transport costs alone.

The Walpole plant molded and packed almost a hundred thousand bars of Native Balm every working day. And in its cramped research quarters, Walpole chemists developed products that in time proved more valuable than any then being made.

The man who ran the Walpole lab had come to Clare as one of Ennis's first "college kettle boys." He stayed on to master every aspect of the practical chemistry of fats and oils. While still a young man, James Neeland had impressed Ennis by producing a larger laundry bar to supplement the original washing-up soap. Neeland had also been in on developing the hard-milled and vegetable soap formulas.

But Neeland owed his major advance to happy accident. A bitter worker tried to sabotage a run of Native Balm by spiking the pitching brine rinse with the slightly acidic coil wash. No one caught the batch until it came out of the crutchers. The foreman wanted to throw out the entire lot.

The foreman called Neeland in to inspect the botched job. Fearing the Queen Bee's notorious thrift, he ordered the batch to be poured, set, and crated for shipping. Some weeks afterward, the distributors began asking for that wonderful hair soap, the one that left less oily residue and did not require a vinegar or lemon after-rinse. No one in the front office had any idea what was meant until Neeland stepped forward to describe his experiment. As a reward, the Clares gave Neeland charge of one of the country's first industrial labs.

Neeland refined a glycerin recovery process that Clare did not need to license. The savings allowed him to turn his crude refuse into an emollient that undercut everyone on the market. When the factories began swimming in glycerin, Neeland tinkered with turning it to further ends. In time, Clare would make millions on the former waste, using it in everything from lipstick to explosives.

A more efficient recovery of Glauber's salt from spent lye let Neeland close yet another internal production loop. Just as coal miners bought the very soap whose manufacture their digging helped fuel, so Neeland's chemical recirculation fed upon itself, like a stove that ran off its own ashes.

The chemist, when he dreamed, dreamed of turning the refuse from every transmuting process back into the supply path of another. In his ultimate heaven—nothing so mundane as God's—all growth lived off some other's compost, like a gentleman farmer's estate, or a balanced aquarium.

Neeland cast his eye across the ocean, to England, where chemists rolled a giant hoop around a regenerating hub, a wheel outputting its own inputs, its rim spinning off tangent substances, each the potential feed for whole new industries, each new industry a feed for the next. Neeland made a chart of the great wheel and hung it upon his laboratory wall, for all his assistants to study.

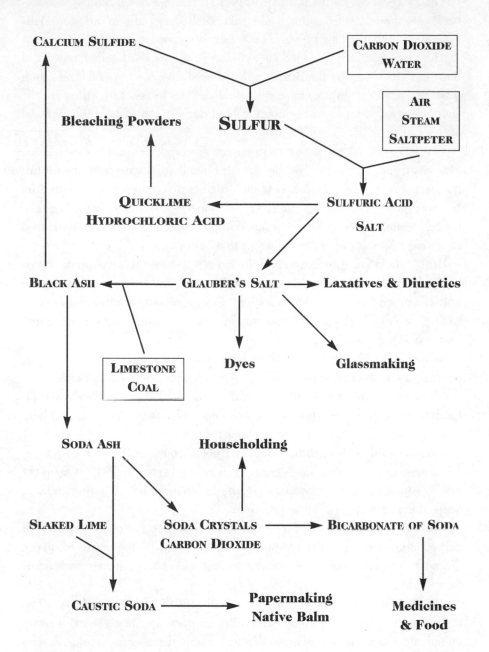

The synthesis of artificial alkali turned all manner of wasted by-products back into the vat. Only sulfur could yoke such fiery bulls to the plow: Vulcan's seed corn, the best measure of a country's economic might.

The British had long seemed past challenge at this alkali game, a game of their own devising. But the British now suffered from the law of the retarding lead, where the innovator, having worked out the kinks, gets killed by the successor pack who improve upon the lead dog's tricks without the expense of discovery.

The late starter had certain advantages, Neeland lectured his assistants. The great intersecting arcs of the British chemical industry were beautiful: the century's crowning ballet. Leblanc's artificial soda process showered its bounty upon all people in the form of paper, glass, soap, baked goods, bleaches, medicines, and dyes. It made luxuries commonplace and delivered new necessities at exactly the moment that history needed them.

But Neeland's chart failed to include every substance that the process produced. Decades of live experiment upon British alkali towns now showed the Leblanc process to be cruelly inefficient. For every unit of sulfur that created wealth, two units rained back down upon wealth's beneficiaries as crippling soot and sulfurous drizzle.

Somewhere, Neeland's chart had to harbor undiscovered branches, cleaner, more efficient arrows curling from sulfur to soda and back. Already the Belgian Solvay had invented a carbonating tower that made soda ash for half the price with a fraction of the poisonous discharge. Who knew where ingenuity might yet take the venturesome?

The self-sufficient machine would not come about in Neeland's lifetime. His sons—even his sons' sons—would pass away before the perfect hoop got rolling. But until that day, work in Neeland's lab crept on, accreting cheaper soaps, cleaner methods, better products.

Neeland closed in on the long-term goal by successive refinement. Profit gained along one of the arrowed paths supplied him with the means to survey the next. And the more links Neeland's crew added, the cheaper each addition would be.

The Walpole lab experimented with small runs of bleaches and dyes. The nearby, failing Wamesit Rapids cloth mills snapped up Clare's stock of ready chemicals. For a time, Clare made Wamesit competitive again. Neeland's men cracked engineering challenges as well as chemical ones. They built enormous, watertight lead chambers for the soap baths. They toyed with the cold process and with saponification under pressure.

Each increase in laboratory know-how led Clare Soap closer to that businessman's grail of relative advantage: selling more for less. Five years after starting this first industrial research program, Clare made ten cakes of Native Balm for what it had once cost to make seven. The savings paid for new equipment, and new machines bought new economies of scale.

At the end of the day, or at least by the end of that adventurous morning, Clare produced a soap cheap enough to sell back to England, the mother country of all soap products. Colonial revenge—mercantilism getting its own back—had been Samuel's chief incentive to hold out into old age. The last pleasure that business offered the old man was to sell back to his ancient supplier all those obligations that had so long held him hostage.

The first shipment put in at Liverpool; a British customs agent instantly intercepted it. Certain that the shipper was undervaluing the stock in order to evade paying the lawful duty, the agent exercised the Crown's prerogative and bought the entire lot, at the suspicious declared price, even before the soap could be offloaded from the ship.

Gleeful, Clare's new order-handlers packed off another cargo at the same price. This time, the British customs officials smelled a dumping racket. No doubt the upstart Americans meant to sell this Native Balm below cost, in order to force an entry into British markets. Once again, Inspection bought up the entire shipment right there on the docks, to punish the company with pointless mounting losses.

Clare redoubled its shipment, delighted to shoot the fish so long as someone else kept stocking the barrel. At this point, the bewildered British concluded that if they had not yet wiped out this manufacturer, then the parvenu's price must in fact be yielding an honest profit. This time, customs let the soap through to market, where it sold well, although never again quite so briskly.

The chemistry that issued from Neeland's lab altered every aspect of Clare's soapmaking but one. The magic additive—the truculent vegetable, remarkable *Utilis*—remained beyond synthesis. Although only trace amounts of crushed root sufficed to bestow Native Balm's fabled properties upon a large run of neat soap, supply no longer kept pace with the volume that the factories could now deliver. Clare remained bottlenecked by the tiny stores of tropical plant it could cultivate.

Douglas commissioned Neeland to develop a workable substitute. The labs tried wheat grass, agave, and other promising chemical matter. But any alteration in the recipe produced unacceptable changes in the finished product. The same agrarian nostalgia that pushed the brand to national prominence now prevented its wholesale adoption of rational production methods.

And yet that same recalcitrant vegetable nature now made Native Balm the perfect cure for the country's growing ablutomania, a cleanliness craze Clare had helped to cause. Native Balm embodied all the natural wisdom lost to the onslaught of modern industrial chemistry, while each package remained immaculate, milled, dependable.

On the strength of the discoveries that trickled out of Walpole's scientific back room, Clare parlayed Native Balm into a dozen new products. Clare now shipped as much soap into the once-wastes between Ohio and Missouri as it had shipped in New England prior to the war. It began to toy with the idea of national advertising. The notion no longer seemed absurd. In fact, the Chicago meat-packer needed Native Balm perhaps even more than did the Boston Brahmin.

The company's earliest printed proclamations read like revival meeting transcripts. Sermons in a circus of typefaces framed earnest copperplate engravings depicting some languorous Allegory enjoining the benefits of proper sanitation. A person needed a good five minutes to read the full text. And when finished, he still could not be sure just what was for sale: whether Native Balm, Healing Root Extract, the abstract idea of soap, or simply "Trade, that plant that grows wherever peace and labor water it."

As Thomas J. Barrat of Pears fame so cleanly put it: "Any fool can make soap. It takes a clever man to sell it."

———

A series of posters all bear the same look: sepia and gilt-edged, a vanished world somewhat naïve but wholly right-hearted. Each one is an irised page torn from some family scrapbook. One snippet of old advertisement ends: **Highest Prices Paid for Tallow.** *A slightly crinkled photo shows a man in thick mustache and blacksmith's apron in front of a complex nest of pipes labeled "Recovery Unit." A fragment of paper label promises:* **Save and send us 10 Native Balm Wrappers, and we will mail you a beautiful reproduction of this artwork, postage paid.**

The series appear on billboards, in magazines, and in fifteen-second spots. Each entry bears the same captioned refrain:
"We recycled before the word even existed."

———

J ane Lauter wins the agents' Florida trip this year. Laura doesn't come close. Even Phyllis Gant beats out Laura's total—Phyllis, who tries to show prefabs to college professors and palatial golf course spreads to assembly-line workers.

Not that Laura has any great desire to go back to Orlando. She hated it last year, when she won by a mile, although Tim did dote on Epcot and Ellen didn't seem to mind strutting around the pool in a string bikini. But Laura came back home from the all-expenses-paid vacation a total basket case, jittery with entertainment, mouthing that old joke: Second prize, *two* weeks.

Even if she'd won this year, what good would it have done? She would have just thrown up all over the Small World ride. But it's the principle. Laura's as good an agent as Millennium has had for a long time. She has grown to be as productive as anyone, as far as the house part goes. And she's better with more kinds of people than anyone in the office. They toss her all the problem cases, the people going into retirement homes who don't really want to sell, the young, childless couples who like to look at houses on Sundays as a hobby. And she does as much business with the castoffs as some agents do with the plums.

She has to be good. It's not just a second income for her. She's not just paying taxes on her husband's take-home so that the family can afford that matching fleet of Jet Skis. She's supporting two kids, shouldering her half of their upkeep.

At the same time, it's more than just making a living. Orlando can go down in a killer-whale synchronized feeding frenzy for all she cares. But she needs something from this job, some small corner, some recovered scrap of her life that she has made, that she excels at, that's hers. She *likes* the stupid little maroon Millennium jacket that clashes with everything. She looks good in it. She got to the Million Dollar Movers Club faster than any Lacewood agent ever. She's been there the last three years running. Until this year.

Yes, she has missed some days. But fewer with each round of chemo, despite Dr. Archer's warnings about cumulative results. This last time out, just three full days and a couple of afternoons. And even on those, she's tried to work at home some, on the computer. Her energy flags, and she moves a little slower at everything. But she shows properties almost as often as she did before getting sick.

It's just that she doesn't seem to do as well per showing as she used to.

Grace Wambaugh, who talks to her more now, since coming by to sell her herbal remedies, tells her, "You ought to be proud. Going through all that, and still managing to turn a little profit for the company."

Grace. She probably doesn't mean to be insulting. Or at least not noticeably rude. Besides, she's right: there's a lot to feel good about. But all Laura can feel is a vague anxiety. A pit in her surgically evacuated viscera at having missed her quota.

In part, it's a money thing. Totally irrational, of course. She's still making enough to cover most everything. Her credit cards have lots of carrying room, and there's more than enough in the savings to tide the three of them over until she's back to full strength. And even if they have to tighten their belts a little, even if they have to make adjustments . . . It wouldn't kill the kids to go without a new concert ticket or CD-ROM every other week.

The thing that terrifies her is having to go to Don. To tell him she's having money trouble. The last time she had to do that, the man gloated for weeks. Acted like it proved everything he ever said about her. Like it vindicated his entire life, confirmed every prediction he made about their splitting up. Like a jury just acquitted him on overwhelming evidence. She couldn't bear it.

She could still wait tables. The chemo hasn't done anything much to her legs yet. She'd rather moonlight at McDonald's than ask Don for more money. She'd rather get back with Ken. But at this point, she'd rather die than get back with Ken.

Business will pick up. She just has to ride things out. Try to pick up the pace, whenever she can. Keep everything managed. Try to look as good as she can. She drinks those cans of Ensure so she doesn't seem totally gaunt and wasted. She boosts her arsenal of headgear, trying to find some turban that won't look totally ridiculous with a two-piece suit. She even goes with a tawny wig, one that fits her without making her face seem like a plastic taxidermist's inset.

In the mirror, she hikes up the edges of nausea's mouth. Yanks at her cheek muscles, like trying to ring the bell at the state fair. She can almost make it as high as pleasant bewilderment. About that cancerous color she can do nothing. That slight sulfurous tint, like a bad black-and-blue mark three weeks after impact.

Her client list seems as full as ever. The pool of houses is not especially great for this time of year, but prices are livable. She would blame some downturn, some break in the cycle, except that everyone else seems to be doing fine. Grace is all over her listings. Phyllis polishes off that funky Victorian on Main that Laura piddled around with for weeks.

Her boss asks her to lunch. Wouldn't have set off any alarms if he hadn't made reservations at Fallcreek. Lindsey never eats at Fallcreek unless it's bad news or a big account. These days, Laura doesn't qualify as the latter.

"It's just lunch," he tells her, on the drive over. "You didn't have to dress up."

"Lindsey! This is my work suit. This is what I always wear."

"Is it? Oh, listen. I love this song."

Laura listens. It's easier than talking. The song is some throbbing bass thing that Ellen might get off on. Lindsey ought to be listening to light classics. He's forty-four if he's a day. The song is sung by a girl who sounds as if she's eight years old and addicted to heroin.

"What do you like about it?" she asks.

Lindsey looks at her sidelong and laughs. "Are you kidding?"

At the restaurant, the hostess tells them there will be a ten-minute wait.

"We have reservations," Lindsey tells the woman.

"I know. We have you right at the top of the list."

"What's a reservation?" Lindsey demands. "I mean, what does that word mean, 'reservation'?"

The hostess is frantic with calm. "You can sit at the bar and order drinks if you like. We'll call you when we have your table cleared, sir."

Lindsey looks at Laura: Can you believe this?

"I know," Laura says. "It's okay."

They sit in the packed bar, Lindsey complaining about the house red, and Laura nursing a seltzer. "Would you like to take a little break?" he proposes, apropos of nothing.

"Break?" she asks.

"Sure. Go play. Someplace warm."

"I've got kids, Lindsey."

"Bring 'em. Relax somewhere. Vacation. Get better."

"I've got a closing on Thursday and two inspections next week."

"Oh, finish whatever you're winding up."

"And all the other stuff I'm in the middle of?"

"I've spoken to the girls. They're ready to help."

She tries to slow things down. Worse than she thought. She can't seem to think fast enough. "You want me to stop working?"

"Just for a while. I'm not saying you shouldn't come back later. When you feel like it."

"I feel like it now, Lindsey."

"I don't think that people, people . . . who are dealing with what you are dealing with should have to try to sell houses on top of it."

"Bald people, you mean?"

He looks away. Out the window. There is no window. "A lot of people have been upset, Laura. Upset for you, of course."

"People? What people? You mean the other agents?"

"I mean people. The people we work with. The people we work *for*."

"Clients?" A hand rises up to worry her mouth. "Has anyone said anything?"

He smiles at her. He moves to put his hand on her shoulder, but she wills him not to.

"I'm still making money. Aren't I still making money? Lindsey?"

"You are . . . making some money."

"Not enough. Not enough? Lindsey, how much . . . ?"

Lindsey nurses the house red, which has all of a sudden improved in quality. "It's a per-broker averages thing. We need to be more competitive. Millennium is about to convert from a partnership to a . . ."

She begins to cry. Then harder, because of how stupid it is, to cry here, the very place he brought her so that she wouldn't be able to cry.

"I wear these scarves. I'm spending a fortune on the damn scarves."

She can't control herself. She sits there sobbing, proving Lindsey's point. Women exist on this earth just to prove men's points. She only hopes it's killing him, to be stared at in public.

"Go ahead," he tells her. "Cry. It's good for you. Not healthy to keep all that bottled up."

She goes flinty. She will not do anything that this man thinks is good for her.

"Just a little sick leave, Laura. Of course we'll hold your job for you. For when you come back. When you're better."

"What am I supposed to do for cash?"

"We can get you a little cash. For starters."

They get their table, at last. After it's no longer necessary. After all their business has been transacted.

"Have whatever you want," Lindsey encourages her. "It's on Millennium."

She has the garden salad. Picks at it and wonders what garden these leaves could possibly have come out of, looking like that, at this time of year.

The beautiful Fallcreek dining rooms occupy one of Clare International's original Lacewood offices. (Back then they were still just Clare Soap. In the case next to our brass NCR cash register from the turn of the century, note the "half box" of Clare Candles: "Still only a dollar!")

Our double-height hammer-beam ceilings were specially built to accommodate the firm's old-style wall-mounted mahogany filing shelves, a section of which are still visible on the north wall. The print of the McCormick harvester over the fireplace, ca. 1850, hung in the offices of Douglas Clare, Sr. The tintype of the World's Columbian Exposition (Chicago, 1893) shows the "Manufactures and Liberal Arts" building, where Clare Soap exhibited. The stained glass in the alcove to the southeast is from the original factory chapel, torn down in the 1930s, when the company moved to its present location . . .

We want your meal here at Fallcreek to be the best that dining has to offer. Please do not hesitate to ask for anything. For fun, casual dining, visit our other location, The Old Mill Race, *on West Gifford, by Northlake Mall.*

Neeland's laboratory tinkered away at all the processes that a manufacturer could wish to perfect. Turning soda and animal waste to balm. Sulfur and soda to bright bleaches and colors. Gaslight waste to fertilizer. Medicaments from bicarbonate and lime.

Chemistry arose from its own saved seed. The surplus of each harvest left the furrow a little longer for the next year. Industrial science raised up the race of man, lifting it to the heights of the tallest brick smokestack for a look around.

All things chemical came from some other chemical thing. Man might learn to become matter's investment banker. Our task on this earth was to discover the paths available to the recombining elements, and clear them. Hack back the undergrowth and free the trapped expedition.

Eventually, Neeland's string of successes in the lab landed him an unwelcome promotion. The Clares ultimately begged him to manage, first the new "chemical detersive" line, then all of Walpole's soap products, then the entire plant itself. For a long time, Neeland chafed under the yoke of this responsibility. At first, he detested presiding over laboring men. But after a while, he discovered how much the human personality resembled caustic compounds. One could produce the most unexpected properties from the most unlikely substances, given the right admixtures. Once Neeland came to see each person he managed in terms of his reactive potentials, he rose to the occasion with laconic skill.

Neeland made from chemistry a business that resembled it. People wanted the substances that Clare released and the compounds it assembled. The public bought this breeding mare's continuous foals. And as clients lined up to purchase their needed nostrums, the flow of incoming cash financed further feats. Buyer and seller enriched each other, enlarging the loop of leg-ups that linked them. Wealth made it easier to make more of the same.

Clare's warehouses and factories, twenty separate buildings in all, stretched from Boston to Harrisburg. They, too, fed off one another. After each national panic or recession—in '37, '43, '57, '60, '65—sales always managed to rebound somehow. Business changed to meet the upheavals that business instigated. Those oil presses and kettles and tanks, the drying racks and coloring pens combined to answer any question that human need threw at them.

Hoary Samuel saw no reason why the corporation—no longer his to control—could not go on self-propagating forever. Soap had caught on in prospering America, more than anyone could have predicted. The clients could be counted on to generate a steady demand. Each year brought increases in efficiency. Supplies grew cheaper. Distribution deepened into old soils, while putting off shoots to start new colonies. Competition shook out smaller firms, while latecomers could not hope to win a foothold in ground so densely planted.

Samuel toured Neeland's labs, shaking his head. He tried to follow his enterprise as it expanded into unlikely cousin substances. Fertilizers, dyes, finishes: some new elixir, this time next year.

Not every part of this diversifying font turned a profit. Even the old mainstay, Native Balm, had its unprofitable quarters. The world's work lay still all before them. Simple selling remained an eternal challenge. Commerce had yet to surrender herself past the first hint of consent. And yet for Samuel, life had forever lost its first flush of innovation. Success was a done deal. Already the glow of consummation shone its managed beam as far down the pike as Samuel cared to cast his eye.

The game was as good as solved.

Samuel had never lacked for either courage or hunger. He leaped from merchant to manufacturer without a backward glance. He watched as war turned manufacturing from a living means to the meaning for living. He marched down that war's sunken road to his own destiny. He pursued the routed past with the victor's whoop at things to come.

But through all these changes, Samuel remained a son of his childhood. Though he brought the old agrarian era to an end, he could not escape it. He needed to know what happened next. He had built his whole life toward *out-*

come. And the moment that outcome settled into the routine of well-tuned pistons, life's engine gave in.

The man who helped found the company had never desired to run it. Wealthy beyond wonder, he'd never wanted money. All Samuel ever wanted to do was to change the rules of material existence. To cleanse the multitudes and complete the journey of days.

He had lived long enough to see the constitutional amendment preventing any law that would abridge the privileges and immunities of Clare, Incorporated, that legally created person. Such a law guaranteed the immortality dreamed of by the poets and prophets. Beyond seeing due process granted to a collective activity, anything else poor Sam Clare might live to witness seemed irrelevant.

The invention of the corporation killed Samuel's dream of progress by completing it. There was nothing left for the experiment but its success. Sometimes in Temple Place, closing his eyes, Samuel could almost see that far shore where things would come to their necessary end.

As for his own life, Samuel no longer feared what must soon happen to him. It seemed to him that nothing significant could possibly change with death. Death changed a man no more than the alkali process did sulfur. Spent inheritance somehow flowed back into the hopper, scrap to be recovered. Commerce promoted those who passed away to the supreme silent partners: his father, his brothers, Ennis, all the bygone soapmakers whose recipes Ennis had gleaned. In that company of spirits, Samuel would preside over future board meetings from beyond the grave, like Bentham's watchful skeleton perched in its glass display case.

And in the measure of earthly time left to him, Clare's president had simply to stay out from beneath the wheels of change. He tinkered with designs for the company letterhead. He toyed with endowments to the school that Benjamin once subsidized. On occasion, he even wrote letters to irate customers.

His family humored him in the exercise of that office. He was their company's ceremonial diplomat. Composite bodies might still need a titular head. Yet from Samuel's vantage, a corporation president had precious little to say about the firm's development. A bad one could no doubt undo half a century's advancement and dissolve rock-solid earnings like soap in water. But a good one could do no better than unleash the collective enterprise. The best ones no doubt came to believe that the will of that collective was their own will.

If ever a chief executive tested the idea of his own necessity, it was Clare's first chief executive. The man had never fully recovered from his renunciation of worldly business. Office recalled Samuel to the realities of revenue and cost. Even the largely honorary title forced him to grapple with how enormously the sphere of business had compounded in two decades.

The aged and bewildered Dorcas did not protest her husband's brief comeback. Her patient, weekly wait for the Rapture once again found much cause to accelerate its expectation. The President's death, the San Francisco quake, the golden spike completing the continent-spanning railroad: all signs agreed. The world was once again about to end soon. And soon enough, Dorcas's world did.

Throughout Samuel's blundering tenure, Julia Hazelwood continued to run the company from the wings. She never remarried, nor did she ever give the possibility a thought. She needed no warm body other than the corporate one.

Julia's passion for politics slid easily into a passion for rational management. Her knowledge of business settled out in the kettle of experience. She harbored no material ambitions aside from those she nursed for the ghostly and disembodied Peter, her firstborn boy. She neglected her other children, tending to the welfare of her youngest, William, only as a worst-case insurance policy.

Immediately after the war, the company might almost have run itself. Ether and the federal government had seen fats through their lean years. Peace returned Clare to its faithful consumers, without forcing it to abandon its new industrial markets. The soldiers who'd slept upon those factory-made packing crates emblazoned with Clare's new emblem stayed loyal to that lucky Indian head long after the last army field hospital vanished.

But as that logo grew in repute, it began to spring up on crates that had never been near a Clare factory. ***WARNING!*** a hail of grocer trade sheets proclaimed:

> *Diverse and unscrupulous counterfeit manufacturers are attempting to pass off their goods as Clare commodities. They are not! These mimics do not sell Balm, but rather mere soap. Demand only the genuine Clare Quality, and be careful that you receive it. Accept no imitations.*

Counterfeiters at last forced the firm to register its noble Brave with the U.S. Patent Office. Within a year, Clare pressed its first trade infringement suit. After a time, Peter and Douglas almost began to welcome the chance for legal action, if only for the cheap publicity that such prosecution provided.

Native Balm seemed set to resume its climb toward wider recognition. Sales outpaced the surge in national population. The nation's appetite for native remedies soared after the government sent General Sheridan to the territories to improve the Indians.

Native Balm Bitter Tonic appeared, over Neeland's scientific objections. The tonic cured a bewildering array of ailments including headache, neuralgia, women's difficulties, and certain forms of abdominal distress. On the label, two inked men discussed the lay of the land:

"Why not take Native Balm Bitter Tonic?"
"I shall, for Unneeded Suffering is a thing of the past."

The age's cadence fell to the bold. Operations seemed likely to grow beyond even Julia's predictions. The speed and structure of American life had altered under its own heat and pressure.

Capital's long-predicted lift-off was at hand. From the Grant Administration on down to the speculating bootblack, the country swam in cheap credit and even cheaper debit. Money made money, simply by spending itself. Seed plus feed now easily exceeded need. Who could number the millions that the future might sprout?

The moment soon produced the men equal to it. Gould and Fisk discreetly asked the government to let them corner the nation's gold market. After all, the law of the land had always been there in the past, eager to grease the freest of enterprising wheels.

But this time, inexplicably, government declined the invitation. The federals opened the national tap, washing Wall Street down with a flowing river of gold. Grant thwarted the robber barons' gold plot, but at the cost of Black Friday. Overnight, the glory train derailed into material reality's steepest defile.

The public briefly saw the light: if gold was now worth so little, how much could worth itself be worth? Credit dried up overnight. Savings vanished. Sales contracted. Businesses defaulted, pulling apart the shoddy blanket of interlocking debt. Just as quickly as it had embraced prosperity, the nation pulled frenzy tightly around its shoulders and entered the sixteenth national depression since Independence.

Even in the soap trade, receipts fell off sharply when growth's bills came due. A deep contraction of all commerce reduced orders for Clare products. Crates stamped with the law-protected Indian stacked up in expensive warehouses. Shift foremen reported hearing the workers' stomachs conversing above the ravenous factory steam.

Clare had weathered depressions in the past. But in the past, the merchant inventors had always found some new means of turning trade. Now trade was left without any new trick to turn. Candles were dying fast, killed off by gas. Soap was reverting to superfluity.

Profits fell from a monthly high of $39,000 at the beginning of 1870 to losses by September. The board voted to cut prices on soap four times in as many meetings. Douglas slashed the traveling sales force from five to two. The few-thousand-dollar budget for printing and promoting vanished, an unaffordable irrelevance.

In three massive contractions, the labor force shrank from five hundred to little more than three hundred. Plant salaries fell from twelve dollars a week to nine, and then eight. Those who held on to their jobs felt lucky to have them at any price. Elsewhere, the situation was even worse.

Two regional wholesalers offered to buy significant shipments of soap stamped with their own names. Clare, lathered but unbowed, proudly refused that sore temptation.

By '73, a new panic—or just the latest low point in a four-year extended depression—triggered another round of defaults. Creditors, like an embrace-crazed Pentecostal congregation, suffered their neighbor's squeeze and passed it along. People from Boston to Chicago began to sing "Good Night! Good Night, Beloved!" with all the gusto they'd recently given that now-lamented toast to the man on the flying trapeze.

Clare, drained by collateral-secured obligations, threatened to dry up and blow away. Promise had peaked and passed, like some silver-mining boom-town hitting vein's end. The Spirit of Prosperity Yet to Come now seemed a vaster, less plausible hoax than the Cardiff Giant.

The Clare Soap and Chemical Company might well have gone the way of the overwhelming majority of human enterprises in any given year. In the end, the only thing that stood between soap and its damnation was the boy genius Peter, the Saint of Hygiene.

———

She sits at the empty table, wrapped in the smell of fish sticks. At least, the box said fish. Full of her own chemical preservatives, Laura would have a hard time of it if blindfolded and put to the scratch-'n'-sniff test. The smell is, indeed, deeply familiar, but it is not perch or turbot. Miscued, she takes a minute to name it. But once she places the aroma, it's unmistakable: chipboard glazed with nail polish remover.

She started out wanting to make her goulash. The one that Don liked to call the "ragoodest meal on earth." But the kids haven't touched it the last three times she made it. They're into cleaner, more geometric foods: the stick, the cube, the wedge. Keep the green stuff off on the side of the plate, where it can't complicate anything.

For the first time since Ellen and Tim were little, she finally has all this time on her hands. Time when she might at last cook all the things for them she never has time to cook. But all they'll eat is timesaving stuff. There's nothing left to do but heat and eat.

All she's supposed to do with the damn fish sticks is leave them alone. Let them sit on the cookie sheet until golden brown. But she can't resist turning them over every two minutes, some manual intervention. Responsibility. The radio plays in the kitchen: background tunes for fish-stick-flipping. A woman wails a C and W song about caller ID machines. After the first go-round, the refrain has Laura humming along. "I'll always pick up for you."

As if on cue, the phone rings. Don or Ken, probably, listening to the same C and W station. She doesn't want to talk to either of them. When she answers, she's more angry than she means to be.

In fact it's Ellen. "Hey, Momish. Can I stay and eat over at Camille's?"

"I've already started dinner for you guys, sweet."

"Well, Mom? To tell you the truth? We've already finished eating over here."

At least Tim shows. One for two. Mealtime conversation isn't much, but he does seem to enjoy the meal's Euclidian perfection. She even gets him to sit down, weight off both legs.

The phone rings again.

"Mrs. Bodey? This is the Lacewood Police Support."

She hears the word "police" and instantly thinks: *Ellen*. She's been expecting this call for weeks.

"Mrs. Bodey, we're wondering if you would like to send a child to the circus?"

She tries to regroup. She looks at the clock: dead on the dinner hour. Of course it couldn't have been a real call. Real people don't call between 5:30 and 7:00 p.m. Those are the ninety minutes reserved for the telemarketers.

"I'm sorry," she says. "I don't give out money over the phone."

"Mrs. Bodey, we're talking about an underprivileged child who isn't going to see the circus otherwise. And the money for the ticket goes toward supporting the police who protect you every day. I'm not saying you won't get that same level of protection if you don't help us out. But your contribution does good work two ways."

"I'm sorry," she says. "Thank you. I'm sorry." She cannot lower the receiver to the hook until she hears the click at the other end.

She feels guilty after she hangs up. Bad. She doesn't blame the police. There's no other way, really. Everything costs money, even doing good. Especially doing good. How else are you going to compete in this marketplace? The money has to come from somewhere. And that means private people. Nobody wants the government telling you what charities to support. And the only time you can catch the private person at home anymore is dinner. When that, too, vanishes, she figures they'll start paging people at restaurants.

Tim slips away to his room during the call, all chance of talking to him lost. She clears the table, rinses and scrapes the dishes, sticks them in the machine. Why is rinsing and scraping any easier than washing outright? When you add having to scour off those clumps of ketchup that the machine bakes on, you're talking a losing proposition.

She sits down with her favorite courtroom novelist. He has a new one out, and Laura is grateful for the distraction. By page twenty, she starts flipping back to the title page to make sure this really is the new one. Every new page adds to her confusion.

The phone rings again, a distraction from the distraction.

"Mr. or Mrs. Laura Bodey?" Of course nobody she knows would actually call her.

"Yes?" she concedes, past fatigue.

The otherwise-unemployable-except-for-food-service master's-degree student at the other end hesitates, waiting for Laura to say which. "Laura Bodey?" the voice finally risks.

"This is she," Laura confesses.

"How are you tonight?"

Terse, she considers saying. "Fine. How are you?" Why can she never just hang up?

"Fine, thanks. Thanks very much for asking." She hears the voice following along on the flowchart. Point II-B-2a in this evening's script. She is his hundredth cold call so far tonight. He probably doesn't make minimum wage, even counting commissions.

The whole country has degenerated into one massive teleconferenced begathon. Police, fire, college, photo studios, tanning salons, save-the-earthers, hospitals, magazine subscription services, African relief outfits— all dependent on catching you at home after dinner. And once you've given something, then they *really* hammer you. The people already on the list are the known best bets.

She's ready to scream, but can't. Can't be a hypocrite. Everybody's in tele-marketing, one way or another. Don's only a couple of rungs up in the peck-ing order, though at least he takes his marks out to lunch. Laura too. Millennium kept her on probation for a year and a half, until she delivered her quota of new clients. For sixteen months she spent her life asking peo-ple's answering machines if they were happy with their current house.

But it's reached a point where this seems like a constitutional violation. There ought to be a law, if you could get a law passed without involving gov-ernment. This setting an alarm off in your living room, just to read you a sales pitch. It's like running an ad on the inside roof of an ambulance. Catch them while you have their undivided attention.

"Laura, we've noticed that you recently changed long-distance carriers?"

We? she wants to ask.

"Tell me, Laura. Did we really screw up somehow, or . . . ?"

Screw up. Somehow—some blip in her credit rating, the weekly perambu-lations of her charge card, the cut of her house's jib, how much she still owes on it, her soap opera of an employment history, her last three wildlife fund contributions, all those freebie magazine copies she's accepted, the number of her kids, her age at divorce—the sum of all her silicon data files must type her as a "casual." Or maybe everyone in the country is a "casual" these days. Maybe it's just too expensive to work everyone up separately, and the phone reps are told to go with the breezy best bet.

"Or . . . ?" she repeats.

"Or did our competition offer you something that made you think you would be getting a better deal from them?"

He knows what the competition offered. He knows all about the hundred-dollar check she just got for switching. He knows the exact price at which she'll sell herself. He's just waiting for her to name it, so he can tell her how shortsighted she's being.

Suddenly she wants out. "You people are evil," she says, as formally as she can make herself sound.

"We're not!" the commissioned salesman insists. "We've changed."

"Didn't you just lay off twenty thousand people?"

"That's so that we could serve you more efficiently. Give you more quality service at better prices."

"I'm sorry," she lies. And then lies again: "I don't do business over the phone."

"We can give you three free calls on your calling card for each of the next six months," he pleads.

The doorbell rings. Saved by it, even if she's just trading one evil for another.

"Someone's at the door," she says.

He does not stop talking. It's keep talking or die. Only the greater rudeness of leaving someone ringing at her door gives Laura the courage to cradle the phone.

She rushes to the foyer, shouting, "I'm coming!" She opens to a heavyset black woman carrying a stack of pamphlets. The woman wears a bright red button that reads:

> Work
> For the Lord
> The Pay Is Lousy
> But the Retirement Benefits
> Are Great

The woman takes one look at Laura and says, "You're real sick, honey."

To which Laura can only reply, "Please come in."

She stands aside. But the woman seems stuck with doubt. "You don't need what I got. You need a good doctor."

What she needs more than anything at this moment is to talk. Just talk, to a real human who sees she's sick and isn't selling anything. Words: weather, the World Series, whatever.

"Would you like a cup of coffee?"

"Always," the woman answers. Shaking her head from side to side: "Always."

Dead leaves blow brilliant orange around her ankles. She steps over their swirl and into the leafless house. She follows Laura into the living room and collapses into a chair with the force of one who has been on her feet for a long time.

"Milk and sugar?" Laura asks.

"Please. Chemotherapy?"

"That's right."

"About four months?"

"My fourth next week."

The woman stashes her pamphlets next to the end table where she sits. She nods. "At four months, my husband would bruise every time the wind blew. You heaving a lot?"

"More than I want to."

"Your skin getting thin? Hurts to touch? You bruise easily? All your hair scram at once? Ringing in your ears?"

Laura nods. It feels good. This stranger has asked her more questions in three minutes than her doctor has in three months. It feels good, if only to be fussing in the kitchen for an appreciative recipient.

"Are you still working?"

Laura pulls out the Millennium mugs. "I would be. Except . . ."

The woman nods harder. "Except healthy people hold all the cards."

"Does your husband . . . ?"

"Did my husband," the woman corrects. "And yes, he did." She laughs roundly. "Whatever it was you were asking. He did."

Laura's turn to nod. She transfers the coffee from machine to warming pot. She arranges pot, cream, and sugar on her favorite serving tray.

"What department, Miss . . . ?"

"Laura. Bodey. Department?"

"Janine Grandy. What department they have you in?"

"Oh. No, well, I'm with a real estate brokerage. Next Millennium?"

"You're sick, and you don't even work for them."

"Work for who?" As if anyone works for anybody else in this town.

"You know who. The Small Wonders people. You got *in*surance?"

Laura nods again. She serves them both.

"Good. Jimmy had *in*surance, too. Not that they ended up paying for much of anything. Funny about those people. They're supposed to spread the risks around? But they only want to play if they know they can win. In that bed for more than ten days, and, phhht." She waves her thumb like a first-base umpire. "Find someone else to catch you."

"Your husband worked for Clare?"

"Operations and Maintenance. Twenty-three years. You know what that means: O and M?"

"No. Not really."

"Me neither, sister." Janine laughs, from way down. "And Jimmy didn't either, really. It meant do whatever those folks told him to do."

"And you think that working there made him sick?"

Janine curls her neck back, a parody of surprise. "You gotta start reading the papers, honey."

"I know. I do. I mean, my daughter showed me . . ."

The cup wavers at Janine's lips. "That EPA story? That's old news. Where was the EPA twenty years ago? Thirty years ago? No. Everybody waits until the last minute. Then it's 'Okay, who didn't wipe their shoes?' "

Janine waves her hand. Human nature. Don't talk to me about human nature.

"You think your husband . . . ?"

"Jimmy was handling that stuff all the time. Chloro this and ethylene that. Pouring out paint cans full of solvent into big old drums. Drums that would sit around out back of the receiving docks until they started to rust. Then Jimmy and his gang would pile them onto trucks and haul them out to some other business's rented disposal site. Half those men are sick with something or other now. Of course, insurance had them all down as impossible risks long before they started moving drums around for Clare."

"What did your husband die of?"

"He had exactly what you have."

Laura laughs. Horrified, but she can't help it. "Not exactly what I have. Not your husband."

Janine joins in. "I hear you, honey. But close enough. Close enough for jazz, horseshoes, or dying." She looks up. "And I use that word exactly so you don't get any bad ideas."

"Of course not, Janine. I'm doing fine."

"Course you are." She sucks air and smiles again. "Somebody's got to do fine. Why not you?"

"But I never worked . . . I mean, my job . . ."

"You know what I think?" Janine says, riffling through her purse. "I think it's in the air and in the water, and now it's in the ground. Builds up in the food. Every year a little more. You don't have to work for them. They'll come to you. You don't even have to live in town."

"Oh, I don't know," Laura demurs. She pours them both another little swig. "They've run those studies. The studies never prove anything."

"Now, how you going to prove something like that? It's just a numbers game, girl. You're what's called an acceptable risk, to everyone but the insurance companies."

Laura looks down, clinks her spoon around in her cup. "Well, we can't just start shutting the world down without knowing what's causing what."

"Seems to me like we're just sitting around waiting for proof to poke us in the eye. And it's going to take a whole lot of proving to make people give up their Clean 'n Neat. Who's going to throw away all their health and beauty products on a maybe? Hell," Janine says, her eyes widening. "Not me."

They sip in silence. "You're with a church?" Laura asks, at last.

Janine looks at her askance. Everyone's with a church. What's that got to do with the price of tea in China? "Oh, you mean these." She touches her stack of pamphlets with an open-toed shoe. "I've probably overstayed my welcome, huh?"

"No, no. Not at all. I was just curious. Stop. Please. Sit."

But Janine begins to gather up her stacks and lumber to her feet. Her legs seem to know that the respite was too good to last.

"Laura, you just take about ten of these, okay? This good-word business helped me out a lot. I can't begin to tell you. But you don't have to do anything with it. You don't even have to read it. This'll just be our little secret. It would take me about forty minutes to give away another ten of these, otherwise. And a woman's got to get home sometime."

"You have children, Janine?"

"Have I got children."

"Do they eat dinner with you?"

"You dream."

———

Laura asks point-blank, at her next checkup, just before her fourth chemo. "Dr. Archer. Can cancer have environmental causes?"

"Cancer, my dear, is not cancer, is not cancer."

"Ovarian, then?"

"What do you mean, 'environmental'?" He cannot keep the tone of professional irony out of his voice.

"Can it come from something you eat or drink? Some kind of exposure?"

Slowly, as if he's very tired, Dr. Archer reaches above his desk for a large dark binder. Clearly the answer file of last resort.

"This is the latest NIH consensus paper," he says. Like she'll have to take it up with them if she has any further problem. " 'Although the cause is unknown,' " he reads, " 'some women are at higher risk of developing ovarian cancer than others. Risk factors include advancing age; nulliparity; a personal history of endometrial, colon, or breast cancer; and a family history of ovarian cancer. The evidence is inconsistent regarding the use of fertility drugs as a risk factor.' "

"Nulliparity?"

"Not your problem, Mrs. Bodey."

"What does it mean?"

"The condition of never having given birth."

"Childlessness?"

"Childlessness."

"Can you get outbreaks of it?"

"Childlessness?"

"Ovarian cancer."

"Clusters? No. We don't see much if any clustering of ovarian. Although it's interesting. Immigrants to this country do show higher incidence rates after living here about twenty years."

She knows what Dr. Archer thinks of immigrants. But she assumes he's telling her something like the truth. "That would sort of suggest an environmental reason, no?"

He extends his lower lip and shrugs. He gestures toward the NIH.

"But I'm not in any of those categories. None of that applies to me."

"There is no evidence of ovarian cancer being caused by anything you might have read about in the newspaper."

"Okay. Okay. Could I just ask one more thing, Doctor?"

He shrugs again: Go ahead. My job.

"Is there some other kind of anti-nausea pill that you aren't giving me because they are too expensive?"

He smiles his slow, comprehending smile. Patients. "Who told you that?"

She will not throw Alan to the health care system police. "I've heard that there are these pills that cost . . . The pills you give me don't seem to do . . ."

"What would you like to try? Did you get the name of something?"

She has no name. But she will try anything. At this point, she has learned to throw up at the mere sound of the food cart down the hall.

"You don't know of any anti-nausea medication in pill form that costs a lot more than the ones that you're giving me, but that works?"

He pulls out a catalog of medications. He is completely without emotional affect. "We can try something else. Here. How about these?"

"How expensive are those?"

"Would that make a difference to you?"

She leaves his office feeling a total fool. She's actually looking forward to the drip. She will tell Alan about the new anti-nausea that Dr. Archer has prescribed. See if it's the right one. She's looking forward to getting caught up with Ruthie Tapelewsky. Ruthie makes her laugh. They can compare nauseas, blacking out, other side effects. She'll ask Ruthie what kind of oral medication they give her to take home.

Twenty yards from the drip room she stops. Ruthie. Ruthie drives a forklift. There's only one place in this wholly owned subsidiary of a city where she could do that.

Laura stumbles all over herself getting into the chemo room. But Ruthie isn't there. She asks Alan, even before she asks him about the prescription. "Where's Ruthie? Did she go on another schedule?"

Alan nods, the strangest kind of agreement. "Ruthie's decided not to do any more chemotherapy just now."

THE WORLD'S DOZEN MOST LOVED VERSES
Contents

Abou Ben Adhem. *1*
Charge of the Light Brigade, The. *2*
Concord *4*
Isle of Beauty (Absence Makes the Heart Grow Fonder). *5*
Last Minstrel, The. *6*
Lochinvar. *8*
Ode: To a Nightingale *10*
Peace and Wonder. *12*
Psalm of Life, A *13*
Santa Filomena (The Lady With the Lamp) *14*
That Thing Which Death Can Never Own. *15*
To a Mouse. *16*

A Gift to You from the Clare Soap and Chemical Company.
Keep Clean, Be as Fruit, Earn Life, and Watch . . .
May Your Tribe Increase!

Peter Clare was the last company officer who did not work his way up through the ranks. After him, all the leaders of the firm, aside from the rare outsider, served their apprenticeships on the factory floor.

Peter was not the last Clare to put his hand to the Clare tiller. But he was the last to run it as a family business. And as that trading family's third generation, he possessed all the obligatory eccentricity of inherited capital.

He was a sickly child. His vague illnesses varied in proportion to how much he liked his private tutor of the moment. In Julia Hazelwood's eyes, all the unbridled promise of the American system swung in orbit around the boy. His mother's constant overvaluation resulted in a permanent sense of inadequacy that led Peter to perform beyond his natural abilities.

Yet Peter was a kind of genius: a genius of the mundane. His waking imagination obsessed upon median existence. Because he so rarely got out into the germ-ridden world, the ordinary exercised upon him all the attraction of a lurid, third-rate, mock-classical slave girl statue. The squalid public was his Arabian Nights. In his mind, the banal and quotidian took on all the desirability of unrequited love.

If the hundreds of workers in Clare's manufactories knew nothing else about the man who controlled their labor, they knew that Peter Clare kept himself sequestered, rarely seen by any but his closest aides. Even the most favored board members saw him face-to-face no more than four or five times a year. He grew in fabled reputation, a ghost of commerce. An angel.

In the general collapse of business in the 1870s, the firm fell into a downward slide. Factory soap reverted to exotic luxury. Clare's strong suit was spent, its sprint run. By mid-decade, some on the board even talked of declaring insolvency. In turning to Peter, the company was fishing shamelessly for a miracle cure.

He rose swiftly in the business, although he had trouble telling a frame from a foot press. His father, Resolve, had lived to manipulate both cash and matter. Peter's relation to the palpable, in contrast, bordered on the occult. He did not know an ether from an ester. He barely knew Sandusky from Somerville. He revered anyone who could work a shoehorn, let alone load a soap crate into a boxcar.

Yet if Peter did not always comprehend the company itself, he knew what the company promised the public's imagination. He knew, better than any of his precursors, the *purpose* of Clare Soap and Chemical.

He understood soap's destiny. He grasped the link between business and purification as only an industrious hypochondriac could. For Clare to survive, it would need to sell not just soap but Clare's Native Balm. Not commodities but familiar friends.

In short, Clare had to offer a whole new way of living. It would have to train its clients to master filth and misery. Beating squalor was now a matter of life or death, for the American, for American enterprise, and finally for America at large.

Peter began to transform the company in 1876, the year that the fix robbed Tilden of the Presidency and reduced the democratic process to parody. The year of Custer's Last Stand. The year two people independently sought to patent the telephone. The year that Silas Lapham discovered that business in this country would never be small again. The year of the American Centennial.

The scandal of the presidential election may have crushed the public belief that political ideals were above purchase. But Peter set himself the goal of crushing the public belief that purchase was beneath ideals. Yes, profiteers had sprung up in both business and politics. True, humanity's worst knew how to exploit prosperity and make a mockery of it. Yet when a man tipped over his bowl, surely it was wrong to fault the soup. What but more industry could cure these wrongs or better capitalize upon this inexhaustible land over which fate had given us dominion?

Clare turned out in force for the Centennial Exposition in Philadelphia. The firm took its place in the chorus of that vast paean to American mechanization for which Wagner himself wrote the overture. That great reviver of American hopes exceeded in grandeur the finest fair Europe herself had ever mounted. From exhibitors to foreign dignitaries to awed visitors: all proclaimed the colossus of the next century. Not even federal troops' massacre of striking railroad workers in the fair's wake could dispel the celebration's spell of opulence.

For resonance, the Otis passenger elevator upstaged most other exhibitors. The Electro-Magnetic Orchestrion gave folks their first earful of the music of the future. But Clare's Personality Diviner also managed to thrill its share of visitors. The mechanical catapult (inspired by Jewitt's old foot press) randomly doled out one of a dozen varieties of soap to anyone who survived the line.

To its industrial competition at the great trade fair, Clare showed off just enough of Walpole chemical technology to elicit envy without evoking emulation. And Philadelphia also witnessed Peter's first great innovation: the paper wrapper.

Samuel had long opposed the measure. A wrapper cheapened the product and added unnecessary cost. It was not the way gentlemen sold soap. When, just before the Philadelphia exposition, Samuel's own son broke the tie and threw in with Peter, the old man capitulated. But in protest, Samuel, infirm and increasingly powerless, refused to travel out to see the greatest spectacle in the history of American business.

The first Native Balm wrapper featured a beautiful black-and-white engraving of the familiar Brave's head. But underneath the cameo it also carried the words:

Safe—Hygienic
For country, town, city

Unwrapped soap, as it now turned out, harbored all sorts of potential health dangers that the American purchaser had never suspected. The Centennial

Exposition bore raucous witness to the rise of plumbing and public waterworks, inventions fast moving America off the conquered land and into cities. The mass hygiene movement also turned out in force, ready to convert soap from an incidental indulgence to a cornerstone of rectified living.

Big soap required bigger soap works. At the same time, the rise of a national market decimated the number of soapmakers. From thousands of cottage industries at the moment when Resolve, Samuel, and Ennis built their first kettle, the number had skidded to three hundred and was still plummeting. Before Philadelphia, Clare seemed destined to be lost in the shakeout, its Native Balm heading the way of other sentimental curios.

Peter, the White Hermit, stopped the slide. He aligned Clare's wrapped product with the forces of forward motion and decontamination: cleaner, surer, purer. Clare had for too long languished in mere technical competence. Now it began to manufacture the real seed that it was born for.

Peter launched an array of new varieties to supplement the Brave, so many varieties of soap that differences were not always apparent. The old names—Number 1, Number 2, mottled, white—no longer sufficed to supply a newly propertied class. In the olive and palm soaps alone, Peter introduced Queen, Princess Royal, Grand Duchess, Marquise, Margravine, and Contessa to those same backwoods Americans whose grandfathers had spilled blood to overthrow the monarchy a century before.

Just after the Centennial, Peter announced the first of those many outlandish publicity exercises dreamed up during long childhood quarantines. Boldly, with no fear of the odds, Peter sent his canary down into the mines of future business practice. And the fowl came back chirping happily for all it was worth.

Clare announced to an incredulous public that every tenth crate of Clare soap would have a gold dollar hidden in one of its cakes. Douglas disapproved of the circus stunt. Julia disliked marketing the element of chance. Old man Samuel smelled disaster. Such a giveaway would push the firm from ruin to damnation. Dispensing carloads of money could only spell the end of the merchandised world.

But the cloistered boy understood his beloved average mind. He dressed up recently freed Negroes in multicolored costumes to distribute handbills. And consumers flocked to the lottery. Apostate Clare customers came back to the fold, wondering why they had ever left. Those who had never before realized the qualities of Native Balm had occasion to discover the soap's many merits.

As with the best of trades, everybody won. Those cakes that bore no coins cost no more than they ever had, and they lathered as well as ever. People who bought up stocks of losing lottery tickets lost nothing: soap did not go bad, and one could never own too much of it. A closetful was, in fact, a practical hedge against inflation. And as free compensation simply for buying what you needed anyway, each buyer got that outside shot at striking the mother lode. The public scooped up crates, one hundred cakes in each. A one-in-a-thousand shot at buried treasure: the odds seemed almost too generous.

Here was the very dream that had forged a nation. The same dream could save a stagnating soap outfit without even working up a sweat. The country had been settled on speculation. A homesteading roulette: the entire mid-continent marked off into square tracts independent of terrain and sold at fire-sale prices to the nearest venture capitalist. For a hundred years, the government had lived off that sale. Now that the map had filled in and ownership solidified, the game could trickle down to all those who hadn't won the bigger one.

Shrewd shoppers thought they could detect the store shelves' heaviest cake by heft. And when they cut open their claim and came up empty-handed, they headed back to the store to roll again. Enough buyers struck a vein to keep the fire of speculation burning in the general imagination. Those who lucked into the small fortune could pour their principal back into another chance at compounding. Capital, as Karl Marx recently noted, was truly magic: value that envalued and expanded itself, like those self-renewing cornucopias of the fairy tales.

Throughout Peter's Golden Giveaway, the nation's use of all soaps expanded faster than national wealth. Clare's miniature land grab did not drive the national cleanliness craze so much as it happily exploited an already growing concern. Clare's customers might or might not have lathered longer in their race to the cake's golden core. But even after the golden lodes dried up, most customers were left with the lingering sense that they had never previously gotten as clean as they ought. Newly urban America, whatever its brand of choice, everywhere learned this upward calibration of the immaculate.

The success of the stunt surprised everyone but Peter. For he had done the math in advance. A dollar per thousand bars represented only a modest outlay for advertising, an item that Peter introduced to the standing budget. Sales had only to increase by 15 percent for the firm to recoup the expense and break even.

Sales jumped by over a fifth. The surge itself gained its own attention, and further fixed Clare's name in the public mind. As volume grew, production costs came down, making the soap even more attractive. At the end of the day, Peter's hazard paid a return that any investor would consider healthy, however one calculated return.

Clare had always set aside nominal funds for announcing its goods to wholesalers and distributors. It had long printed page circulars, trade press notices, newspaper squibs. It had even engaged a New York promotional agent to build a presence there. But permanently budgeting a tenth of a penny per bar to appeal directly to the consumer would have sunk the Roxbury works. Since then, the world had changed immeasurably, and business had changed it. Now Peter's eccentric vision was not just affordable. It was indispensable.

The need to purchase allegiance was yet another omen of the coming way of life that only Peter, in his shut-in strangeness, could read. The American was fast becoming something as far from his pioneer stock as the pioneer was from his European forebear. The rails were down, the wires up, the prairies tamed, the far ocean reached. The earth had become a factory. Humankind scrambled to emulate the productive reliability of its machines.

Cleanliness arose from its machine birth, milled to certain precise standards, packaged to preserve its integrity. Dependable, perfect, abundant: a pristine profusion. Nothing like it had ever before graced this earth. Clare soap lathered and cleansed and even softened. It helped to ensure the higher sanitation that a new pace of life required. And in its innermost core it carried a golden bonus: the prize of proper management, a rightly realized life.

Peter's next invention was the popular pamphlet series *The World's Dozen Most X Verses*. Most loved. Most stirring. Most beautiful. Grocers gave the booklets out free to their best customers. Lots of folks already knew many of these poems by heart. But no one had ever before won them as rewards.

Peter's genius seized upon the truth more easily than his asthmatic lungs inhaled the dust-filled air. He saw it written in fiery, eye-catching letters upon the future's wall. Bathing, laundering, the new craze for private plumbing, the promise of coming prosperity, direct consumer advertising—all were of a single piece. All parts of the same unlikely but adapting creature. All *Promotion*, as we lived and breathed.

———

The world trades on a foolish optimism. When Laura first started out at Millennium, she thought every person who walked through the door was a prospect. Every phone call was a sale. Every person who picked up a flier needed something by the end of the month. The mailman delivering the office mail was going to make her an offer on one of her listings in the window.

Early on, whenever she showed a place, she believed each expression of delight. She'd wrap up the deal in her head, pleasing everyone, solving all objections. She'd buy new wallpaper for her front room with the commission even before the prospect called back with a counter.

Time showed how many things could go wrong on the way to a handshake. How much of a botch the FHA could make of a simple loan application. How badly a husband and wife could disagree with each other, without knowing it. How many people could choke at the last minute, even while putting pen to the closing papers.

It took her a while to figure out just how much chaff you have to scatter on your way to making a wheat bagel. But even after a few years on the job, she always figured that things were meant to work out. You had to keep at it, of course. That kept things interesting. But every seller had his buyer, given the right agent. And in her mind, Laura was always anybody's right agent, if they gave her a chance.

The person who once thought as much is dead. She dies the day Laura wakes up and doesn't want coffee. Doesn't want to look at the morning *Post-Chronicle*. The day that she decides Lindsey is right. She wouldn't go in to the office now even if they called her back to sandbag a flash flood of clients.

Her fourth chemo makes the others seem like little starter bungalows. For the first time, she's not ready to go home by the time they make her. Alan gives her the name of the exorbitant anti-nausea pills. She tells Dr. Archer, who looks into it. But Billing says that insurance will only pay the usual and customary treatment.

Laura begs. "The customary isn't working. Don't they have to pay for a treatment that works?"

"We can give you the expensive ones," Billing says. "But you'll have to pay for the difference."

She takes a look at her savings. She calculates as well as she can: two more treatments, plus a couple rallying months, minimum, before she can think about any money coming in again. She sets a little aside, for anything else that her comprehensive insurance might not cover. Then she buys two weeks' worth of pills.

Two nights after she comes back home, her daughter throws open her bedroom door in the middle of the night. Ellen, clutching at the throat of her nightgown. Panting, *"Are you all right?"*

Laura cannot say anything. She cannot sit up. She cannot drag herself to the bathroom to retch. There is nothing in her, not even saliva anymore. Nothing to spew up and ruin the sheets. She feels light, insubstantial, emptied, yet sick beyond imagining. Too sick even to lie to her daughter. To affirm.

"Mom, you were, like, groaning. Should I call the doctor?"

"You should kill the doctor."

Ellen wavers in the doorway, paralyzed.

"I'm sorry, sweetie. No. Don't do anything. Just . . . just shut the door."

When morning comes again, she feels a little better. At least she can turn herself over, let the mattress punish some other junction of her body. She does not go downstairs. She thinks about calling Ruthie at home. She can't. Can't bear learning how things are with her.

She stays in bed until late morning. The sound of a voice downstairs gets her up. Tim. She looks at the clock. Close to eleven, on a Monday. Don was right. Who was she kidding? The kids should go to his place, permanently, until this ordeal is over.

She forces herself up and into a wrapper. Her bones push up against her ulcerating skin. Her steps are small rug burns. She works her way down the stairwell, the Sherpas lost somewhere near the summit.

At sea level, she finds what she feared: Tim glued to the computer, only five hours too early.

"What are you doing?" she demands. First words of the day. The attempt at authority comes out sounding phlegmy, fuzzy.

"Hi, Mom. I'm the Portuguese. We're just about to develop Steel Making."

"You *what*?"

"Hey, give me a break. The day is young. At least I'm wiping Rosen's butt. His Americans are still in caravels. I almost pity him."

"Timothy Bodey."

"I know, I know." He laughs. "Don't worry. I'm letting him live. I need an ally against the Mesopotamians. That's Doug Harper. He's like halfway to Fusion already. They had a great starting position, lots of minerals, very fertile lands. But I still think he's cheating his ass off, somehow."

"Turn it off," she snaps.

He swings around to face her. Like she's hit him. "I *can't*. There's seven other guys who'll kill me if—"

"What the hell do you think you're doing? You think just because I'm sick you can do anything you damn well please? Turn it off and get to school. I'm through cutting you slack. You can take detention for a month, for all I care."

"Mom."

"*Now!* I've had it with your mouthing—" She moves toward the power strip. He stops her gently, one cupped, confiding hand on her upper arm. Her first glimpse of the man this boy will be.

"Mom. It's Columbus Day."

She hangs in the air in front of him, powered down by confusion. She collapses into the hand that restrains her. "Timmy. I'm sorry."

He forgives her, as much as a boy can understand forgiveness, suffering her hold for a minute before wriggling free. Only because she is emaciated, disoriented, still in a caravel. One of the world's backward races.

She pretends to make breakfast, lunch, whatever meal she ought to be eating now. Not that Tim much cares whether she eats or not. It's Ellen, her anorexic cheerleader, who goes to pieces when Laura doesn't eat.

"Where's your sister?" she asks, shooting for a return to the proper tones of midmorning.

But Tim has already returned to the greater tasks of international progress: steelmaking, electricity, flight, the next breakout hope. He shrugs his right shoulder while holding the mouse rock-steady. "Not sure." If he does not get a job on the Joint Chiefs of Staff, perhaps he can land some hand-eye thing for the sedentarily dextrous.

She sits in the breakfast nook, wondering how to fill the day remaining to her. She should look over the insurance claim paperwork, to see what all they are refusing to pay for. She should catch up on all that personal correspondence, now that her back burner from work is all but cleared off.

But all she can do is sit. She looks out on her stubbled garden, the sparrows foraging for scraps of overlooked sustenance. After a while, the sounds of Tim's new technologies bubbling up from out of the surrounding digital buckshot grow almost comforting.

"Who's playing?" she calls out to him in the next room. He has hit some deceptive lull in the game, for he actually answers.

"Zulus, Germans, Portuguese, Babylonians. Mesopotamians, Russians, Polynesians, and Americans."

She laughs to herself, dry little stabs. "I mean, what real people?"

A puzzled interruption of clicking. "What . . . ?"

"What boys?"

"Oh! Me, Rosen, Harper, Loftus—"

"Loftus? Paul Loftus? The managing director of . . . ?"

"No, Mom. That would be his father."

"You know him? The son?"

"Never met him. He's in eighth, I think."

She wanders over to the computer, stands behind him. She watches as he boosts his research budget and throws his populace some bread and circuses to keep the Portuguese from revolting. "What's the point?"

"Point? Of the game, you mean? Build the best civilization. Cream everyone else. Be the first to the cosmos."

She samples the idea: her son, the son of the head of Clare Agricultural, and that alley rat Andy Rosen. Half a dozen other boys who have never met each other, racing one another to ever-higher levels of domination and mastery.

"Control the world?" she asks him.

He smiles without taking his eyes off the screen. "I wish. Be nice, wouldn't it?"

"Is that what happens? What the winner gets?"

"Naw. Nobody ever gets that far ahead."

"Can you talk to him? The Loftus boy? Can you type messages to him? Get him to answer you?"

"Mom. I've tried. I tried threatening him. I suggested a nonaggression pact. I even offered to teach him the secret of Rectilinear Perspective, which he doesn't have, just to keep his men out of my face. He's not responding to anything."

Trade him for Chemistry. Ask him for Medicine. Develop the secret of Justice. See if he knows anything about a man named Jim Grandy or a woman named Ruth Tapelewsky.

Who will answer what the Loftuses won't? She fishes a box of Clarity Pore Purifier out of storage in the linen closet. The bottom of the package bears the message: "For more information, write to the Consumer Products Support Center at: One Clare Plaza, Boston, MA 02109, or call us at 1-800 . . ."

She calls. It's toll-free, anyway. She has no idea what she will say. No sense of what information she needs.

That turns out not to be a problem. Consumer Products presents her with a menu. "If you have inquiries about possible health complications with any Clare product, please press seven now."

It's the closest choice available, although it doesn't have much to do with her question. They put her into a queue. The recording tells her that the people ahead of her have been waiting an average of ten minutes. While she's holding, they play various songs from famous Clare commercials. A lozengethroated narrator comes on every so often. He says things like, "Did you know that Clare's first product was a soft soap made in Boston by two Clare brothers, *over one hundred and sixty years ago?*"

Finally the history teacher breaks off in mid-recording. The music stops, and someone says, "Welcome to Clare Health Information."

"Yes," she begins. "I was just wondering if anyone there can tell me—"

But the voice on the other end talks right over her. "If your question concerns the Clarity Cosmetic line of products and animal testing, please press one now. If your question . . ."

She hangs up, anesthetized. Not even capable of disgust.

She can't say how long she has been holding, all told. In the computer room, Tim is still playing away. He's well into the Industrial Age, whatever comes after the Industrial Age. Laura checks the community calendar that hangs on the white board by the phone. The public library is open, despite the school holiday. Columbus has definitely been going downhill in recent years.

"Hey, chum," she calls to Tim, gathering her purse. "Want to go for a walk?"

"Mom, they'll take me apart. By the time we come back, there'll be nothing left of me."

"Come on. Let's go to the library. Libraries are major civilization advances."

"Tell me about it. I build one in each of my cities. They're great for boosting your research and development."

"Come on. They'll have the newest computer magazines."

"Can I just . . . ? I just have to do this one thing. Theory of Evolution. It'll give me . . ."

She looks down upon the crown of his head. The head that almost killed her in appearing. She wants to pet down his cowlick, but does not. Endless civilization advances, and we can do everything but live.

"It's okay," she tells him. "Meet me over there."

She walks the six blocks to the old Carnegie Public. There ought to be a holiday, every year, National Biped Day. A day when people have to walk everywhere. The air is cool and crisp, like those sere Octobers when she was a girl, with their brace of revealing breezes that always whispered excitedly of some approaching trip, some discovery in store for her. She walks at a fraction of her normal speed, so she can catch her breath every three steps. But also so that no revelation can slip past her without her noticing.

By the time she reaches the library, it's like she's twelve again and studying for that school field trip to Washington, D.C. Once, those field trips promised to return forever, one a year, each farther-ranging than the last. When she was young, she thought she would one day go to France, where all the schoolgirls got to wear uniforms and huddle about chanting gossipy singsong and looking like Madeline. Now she'll settle for walking across town.

Once at the library, she is lost. She browses the shelves at random, up and down the rows like a tractor, until she sees titles that seem to be about disease. She finds a big book on cancer, but it's dated 1972. A smaller but newer one has no more than a page and a half on her variety. It goes over the stages and grades, all the stuff she already knows. As far as causes, it says even less than Dr. Archer.

She has this grade-school flashback to the card catalog, the place where she should have started. She tries Cancer, Chemicals, Environment, Toxicity. A few promising titles. But nothing gives her quite what she is after.

She goes to the front desk. The librarian on duty is that sandy-haired twenty-something woman, the one Laura always thinks of as Marian. Laura studies the woman's face for the first time. Frightened, pretty, competent. A little tired, spent too soon, precocious world-weariness. It's hard to imagine her making it much past thirty.

"Could you help me?" she begins.

The woman nods, but Laura cannot think how to go on. The librarian appraises Laura's color, her scarf. Laura wants to ask her, in her own words, before Marian starts to draw inferences.

"I'd like to find out whatever I can about ovarian cancer."

The woman nods again, slower, deeper. "Yes. Here. I'll show you," she says. That simple. She walks Laura over to a table filled with forbidding-looking volumes. She shows Laura how to use the abstracts and indexes: whole, bound lists of pointers to things in print. Someone else has already done the legwork for her.

She never dreamed that such stuff existed. Beyond belief, really. A person might be able to find anything she wants, all organized, all laid out. Every entry, already an expert. You don't have to start at zero each time.

The librarian teaches Laura how to read the links and symbols. The headings zoom in more exactly than Laura thought possible. Not just cancer: cystadenocarcinoma.

Laura sees the specialist in Indianapolis's name on one of the articles. She sticks the crescent of her thumbnail just under the citation and looks up at Marian.

"Where do you keep these?"

The librarian blushes with embarrassment. "Oh. We're way too small to carry those kind of journals. You'll have to go to a real reference library somewhere. The college might have this one. But probably not."

Laura's hopes collapse again. Why stock the indexes at all, then? Knowledge is to people what small boys and magnifying glasses are to ants.

"Here," the woman says again, more brightly. "Let's try the computer." She takes Laura to a terminal, where they repeat the whole sadistic process. The electronic indexes make the print ones seem like stone and chisel. Here they just type in a few key words—ovary, carcinoma, causes—and the computer gives them back not only titles but whole pages. Actual information.

They print out two pieces that look interesting. "Where is all this coming from?" Laura asks.

"It's coming in from over the network."

"I see." She smiles to herself, more ignorant than ever. If she clicked enough buttons on this box, could she break into Tim's game? Shower her little Portuguese Alexander the Great in revolutionary leaflets?

"Can we try something else? Can we check the names of some chemicals? See whether . . . ?"

"Oh," Marian says. "Oh."

This time she does not say. Does not say *"Here."* This time she goes to a stand of gunmetal-gray cabinets marked "Newspaper Clippings Archive" and "Vertical File." She retrieves a pudgy file and hands it to Laura. "Industrial By-products and Health, Lacewood and Sawgak Counties."

Every article that has passed through the Carnegie Public, saved up and held for her in one clean folder. Laura clasps the data, debilitated, queasy with its heft.

Marian is looking at her. "That's it, isn't it? What you were after?"

It is exactly what she was after. Laura fixes on Marian's gaze and takes a chance.

"Do . . . sick people come here often?" The question that no index indexes. "I mean, do a lot of people come in looking for . . . ?" She taps the file, the top article, something about chlorinated solvents. The folder weighs down her lap. She could not stand if she wanted to.

Marian's eyes sweep upward, studying that spot near the ceiling where the human calculator tape prints out its subtotals. "Umm . . . every few days?" she tries. "Yes. I'd say pretty much every few days."

23. Burmeister, L. F. "Selected Cancer Mortality and Farm Practices in Iowa."

41. Crump, K. S., and H. A. Guess. "Drinking Water and Cancer: Review of Recent Epidemiological Findings and Assessment of Risks."

126. Henschler, D. "Carcinogenicity Testing—Existing Protocols Are Insufficient."

178. Maltoni, C., and I. Selikoff. "Living in a Chemical World: Occupational and Environmental Significance of Industrial Pollution."

293. Zahm, F. H. "Herbicides and Cancer: Review and Discussion of Methodological Issues."

———

To sidestep bankruptcy in the late 1870s, the firm needed to grow. It had to expand rapidly into the vacuum created by the collapse of cottage industry. The times required it to swell at least as fast as human expectation. But growth, as always, cost. The secret of making money, now even more than ever, was to have it already.

A firm's worth came down to how much it could borrow. Peter and Douglas devised a plan whereby the firm would borrow its way out of debt. They needed a way to placate, if not pay off, the firm's three main creditors: the railroads, their suppliers, and Clare's own employees, whom the firm had long forced to buy up obligations, dollar by half dollar.

The board approved a new, public bond issue. But the R. G. Dun and Co. mercantile agency's threat to downgrade its creditworthiness for the first time in the company's history chilled public enthusiasm. Clare had to generate some ready money, to prove itself a worthy borrower.

Douglas sold the archaic Roxbury works for a lump sum, perhaps half what the equipment and buildings were worth. In one sweep, he reduced much of the fat in the budget that had edged Clare toward default. Modern Walpole made twice the soap with half the jobs. The Roxbury soap girls, once the marvel of progressive Boston for garlanding their productivity with ad hoc factory literary journals, had to find another world in which to peddle their labor and their verse.

However much the amputation hurt, death by slow bleeding would have hurt worse. The savings in outlay did help to slow the rising tide of costs. The lump-sale sum helped to settle the most urgent of outstanding bills. But the recent, westward warehouse expansions still left the coffers cash-poor. The collapse of a good deal of commercial paper the firm was holding only exacerbated the need for real money.

Chance floated Clare a deliverance in the form of George Gifford, the Chicago grain speculator. Gifford had started life as a wheat farmer near Rockford, Illinois. When the railroad reached his land in 1852, opening its artificial corridor between city and hinterland, Gifford's existence altered utterly and irrevocably.

Rail steadied the farmer's year like a hand laid upon the turbulent heel of heaven. It standardized by fiat, without recourse to Congress, the countless different times the nation had run on. Until the train, harvest had been a wild, speculative ride in a wagon full of sprouting and rotting grain. More than once, young Gifford sold his year's labor for what could only generously be called nothing. Rail opened up a perpetual grain auction only a few hours away, and tied Gifford to it.

The train passed over Gifford's Illinois like the wave of some magic wand. New towns leaped up before it, sprung out of fields like pheasants flushed out by dogs. The Galena and Chicago Union baled Gifford's fate and bound him to the West's metropolis. Granted, Chicago paid the lowest prices on grain in creation. But at least it always paid, and in coin, not rotting promises.

Field and city fed off one another. Overnight, lakeside swamp and wild prairie turned each other into a peopled garden. Nature grew benevolent, hitched to this regulating plow. Gifford fell in love with the city now erupting from the grasslands that it had transformed. In such a place, one could do the earth's business, and more.

Gifford watched his life's capital flow through the Chicago grain market. He lived and died by that auction's smallest ripple. After the war, one of those glaringly self-evident inventions came along to transform the way that human beings organized their fate in this world. To Gifford, the new grain elevators were nothing less than giant dams that gathered the West's trickles of grain into a torrent large enough to drive the mill wheel of eternal prosperity.

In the space of a few years, Gifford watched these wood and iron hulks turn a wasteful trade in discrete seed into continuous traffic in abstraction. Corn was no longer a mere cereal but liquid cash: the silver certificate of the vegetative kingdom. Wheat was not bread alone but freely tradable chits, swapped a dozen times even before the kernels were stored.

The cut of rail through the state touched off a fever of land speculation. Mechanical reapers fed like locusts upon the newly subdued plots, extracting ever-greater yields from the rehabilitated wastes that could now be brought to market down to the last nib. Gifford's suddenly well-placed farm tripled its value in less than seven months. Smelling his future, he auctioned off the titles to his fields and headed toward cash's new Capitol.

Gifford bought into an elevator being constructed on the happy confluence of railhead and Chicago River. He jointly operated a monstrous grain ship five stories tall: fifty bins swallowing a third of a million bushels. And from his perch high up in the lucrative aerie, George Gifford began to cast his eye downtown, upon the Exchange Hall, the new digs of the infant Chicago Board of Trade.

At the Board of Trade, crops dissolved into the *idea* of produce. The Exchange promoted grain to pure exchangeability. On the trading floor, a man could buy and sell not only the amber waves themselves but also another man's ability to deliver the sheaves at some date in the now-specified future.

Gifford pushed the shape of that abstracting process to its logical extreme. 'Change did not trade in the thing so much as in the thing's price. Gifford merely extended that derivative. He decided that there must be a way to trade in the price of price itself. And in 1868, he staked his warehouseman's small fortune on finding it.

Early in that year, a messenger approached Gifford about joining an experiment in adolescent capitalism. The Lyon-Smith gang, a secret syndicate formed to corner number two spring wheat, needed an insider to report the ebb and flow of wheat supplies in store. Gifford's position gave him ownership of this information, and he saw no reason why he should not profit from its sale.

For weeks, Gifford and his syndicate cohorts discreetly bought up futures. All the while, Gifford kept his hand on the elevator spigot, evening out prices, holding off and letting out, keeping the bears from getting spooked. He waited and watched for the short sellers to wander too far from the available supply.

By June the snare was sprung. Those who had sold grain they did not possess saw the trap too late. Overextended traders returned forcibly to the facts of real grain. Gifford then squeezed the spigot tight. The bears needed grain in order to cover their positions. But the grain already belonged to the men who called those positions in.

The syndicate, holding all the buy contracts, could now name its price. Law compelled the short sellers to meet the orders by the end of the month or face prison and worse than prison. Gifford's net worth rose faster than a hot-air balloon, and by the end of June he had joined the aristocracy.

Gifford broke no laws. There *were* no laws, for the victims of capital always resist any protection that might prevent them from running the very sting that has stung them. But Gifford and friends mastered every step of the corner except how to "bury the corpse." By corner's end, the wisest course left open to him was to cash out, retire from warehousing, and get the hell out of town.

With the animal luck of the true businessman, Gifford liquidated just before the Great Fire of 1871. The inferno gutted the city. It blazed out of control for days, claiming fields, timber, and lives as far away as Wisconsin. The operator he sold to was burned out, but Gifford walked away from catastrophe untouched.

He considered tucking in his improbable winnings and calling it a day. How many consecutive spins of the wheel could one man hit? His fortune would have sufficed to keep him in his hobby—European semi-clad male torsos from any antique era—forever. But the man had been born a farmer, and grain in the ear demanded replanting.

He could not return to the Chicago grain trade without being lynched. But Gifford could still cup his hands and sip from some other spot along that golden torrent. On a raiding party to Britain in search of art treasures, he brought back two ancient Scots distillers to see what they could do to transubstantiate American corn and rye into the water of life. At first, the Scots decried the low malt percentages of American whiskeys. But the market soon helped them appreciate these so-called blends.

Gifford housed his experts in a state-of-the-art distillery on South Ashland. His first experiments hit the markets just in time to profit from the Whiskey Ring crackdown. The area's distillers had long enjoyed a comfortable system of shared tax abatements with the government revenuers. Kickbacks more than sufficed to hush up the press, retailers, and officials of all rank and stripe. When the special interests grew too numerous to placate, some poor, overlooked graftee blew the whistle, and the jig was up.

Authorities seized sixteen of the area's largest spirit-makers for tax fraud. Two hundred and forty indictments rained down nationally, resulting in more than a hundred convictions. But government pardoned the leaders, and a scandalized nation concluded that a portion of the abatements now lined the campaign coffers of the Republican Party.

Had Gifford entered the trade any earlier, he would have been more than happy to participate in the redistribution of funds. Tremendous savings, not to mention a chance to contribute to the industry's political protectors: any entrepreneur would have been a fool to pass on that deal.

But Gifford had come to the business too late, and so escaped arrest and dismantling. Having missed the party, all he could do was profit from the hangover. The punishments doled out on his competition eased Gifford's way into a tight market. G. Gifford's Blended American Double Eagle Corn

Whiskey made its infant name on honesty. It came from a clean still, one that "gladly paid its civic obligations in full." And the mash did eventually improve with the years.

When the spirits business began to generate money, Gifford plowed his returns back into an old farmer's obsession. He had long been convinced that industrial waste products, particularly his own and those of Chicago's Packingtown, could fashion a better fertilizer than the ones the prairies now employed. He bought up a fertilizer plant in the town of Lake, just south of the city, and began to experiment with its product.

Gifford promoted this work as uniting the best components of profit-making and public benefaction. After the fashion of the rich, he turned author, writing a series of pamphlets outlining his theories. What his ideas lacked in chemistry, they made up for in moral duty:

> Man must perfect those cycles of voyage and return that he has stolen from the First Developer. He must restore the ends of spent crops to crops altogether renewed, thereby teaching Nature how to revive herself . . .

One of these baroque pamphlets came to the attention of Douglas Clare. This man Gifford's goals meshed with the ones that Clare had long nurtured. The chemist Neeland had already presented the Clares with a plan for mixing used soda ash with peat and South American guano, converting the mixture to a new, all-purpose fertilizer. Complete and balanced: one that blended nitrogen, potassium, and phosphorus to revive exhausted soils and promote inferior earth to full fertility.

Certainly the products of industrial chemistry could compete with animal manure, if not in price, then in overall return on investment. The cheapest way for Clare to acquire the expertise and manufacturing base needed to enter the fertilizer trade would be to acquire this already established outfit. That way, its people could learn in the classroom of existing practice, without paying for a costly education.

Gifford Industries would also give Douglas his long-coveted presence in Chicago. The city had won the race to become the continent's great inland capital. Half the nation's rail miles terminated there, draining the frontier of its wheat, cattle, pork, and timber, and replacing these with houses, manufactured goods, and dressed meats. Chicago had become the price setter, supplier, transfer agent, and chief wholesaler to the opened continent.

More than any other single place, Chicago was Douglas's gateway to the future. Clare's sales drifted farther west of Appalachia. Clare's own plants and warehouses had themselves begun to plot an arrow that pointed at the shores of Lake Michigan. This man Gifford already had his grubstake where Clare needed to be.

Even better, George Gifford enjoyed a heavy cash position. Clare was temporarily trapped between strapped creditors. A deal with Gifford would not only pay for itself; it would bail out a fair quantity of Clare's remaining red ink.

Such a creative transfer seemed almost sleight of hand. Yet it made sense for both parties. For in return for salvation, Clare could give Gifford Industries a size, name, reputation, and distribution arm that extended well beyond the upstart's current reach. Distillery and fertilizer factory would join a far larger operation whose revenues were as good as gold, once its solvency was guaranteed. The union promised Gifford a bigger, better, wider toy train set to run his trains on. And it also gave him something that money and all the antique nude statues in the world could not buy: Eastern respectability.

Douglas proposed bringing Gifford into the firm as a shareholder, in exchange for Gifford cashing out Clare's debts. In effect, Clare would sell to the assumer of its debts that portion of the firm already owed to other creditors.

To those involved, the deal seemed preordained. It belonged to the family of charmed transactions: gain without risk, benefit without cost: the self-extending trailhead, the self-hoisting well. When all the books settled, each enterprise would be stronger and all parties wealthier than they were before the handshake. The only thing lost would be history, that fuel that business had, by nature, to keep shoveling into the boiler.

In a last-minute spasm of moral doubt, Samuel confronted the boys. Was it right to bring a liquor-maker into a business that sold soap as the measure of civilization? What would old Jephthah have said?

Douglas briefly considered the objection. In fact, there was none. His grandfather had sold ice to Martinique to fight yellow fever. He certainly would have approved selling ash to farmers to help feed the nation. And he'd ended his days in a public house. What could he possibly have against lubricating the thirsty?

That last objection met, Douglas unrolled a proposal that quickly won the approval of Clare's board as well as everyone on Gifford's side of the table. What human dared oppose the inevitable logic of a good deal?

And so the offspring of Clare brought soap's antithesis into that single-souled corporation whose charter summed to a life beyond its combined families. Samuel resigned the firm's presidency, and Douglas took his place.

Peter reserved for himself the title of General Manager, and Gifford reveled in the ceremonial moniker of Chairman. Each man attained the office he most needed and assumed the responsibilities he best fulfilled.

With the old bookkeeping trick of proliferating loaves and fishes, Peter and Douglas increased the existing Clare shares enough to leave their compliant new associate in a comfortable minority position. Gifford's flood of ready assets saw the firm through the worst of its liquidity crisis. Creditworthiness restored, Clare launched a successful bond issue. The bonds promised to finance further expansion, which in turn earned it the license to borrow more. As always, a firm's worth lay in how many outstanding loans it could generate.

Peter, Douglas, and George Gifford brought Clare Soap and Chemical into fiscal adolescence. If not an absolutely silent partner, Gifford was willing to remain deeply laconic. Douglas came West on several occasions to oversee various ventures, including the founding of the new agricultural chemical factory in Lacewood. Gifford, in turn, often traveled out to the headquarters on the glittering eastern coast.

But Peter never met with him on those visits. The eccentric Clare saw no need to complicate a good thing with gratuitous discussions. It amused Gifford to indulge his partner. For banquet entertainment, Peter Clare stories exceeded even nude antiquities. And so, for the better part of a decade, until Gifford's death, Clare's chairman and its general manager never communicated by any means more intimate than telegraph.

The two heads of the giant in embryo could not have been more inimical. The white recluse hid out in his Spartan Back Bay town house, while the statue-collector threw lavish entertainments for meat-packing millionaires in his bric-a-brac-encrusted, neo-Romanesque mansion on the north lake shore's Hot Dog Row.

Yet the two men complemented each other. Each made up the other's temperamental deficits. The stoic hermit plotted out grand strategies, while the gadabout reveled in all the unsavory flesh-pressing and shoulder-rubbing whose absence had heretofore kept the firm provincial. With Douglas as rudder between them, the company management managed to come to understand something of the heart of man. And man, after all, was the creature that all their joint labors had to appease.

Sometime during the boom year that followed the merger, Samuel passed wordlessly away. He gave out while traveling to Mount Auburn to visit the grave of his adored wife, Dorcas, a good soul who remained bewildered even in the tomb.

The entrepreneur lives and dies by ingenuity. Action enriches fortune, and fortune enables further action. But the entrepreneur's freed resources will turn on him, one by one, the way that the tin soldiers of popular verse turn on their sadistic boy generals. Trade grows steadily more efficient until it everywhere holds the day. Until, at last, it cuts out all the middlemen.

CLARE SOAP AND CHEMICAL CO.
Boston and Walpole, Mass., & Chicago, Ill.

Now that Laura looks, it seems a kind of epidemic. Not just that packed cancer room at the hospital, the ring of bodies circled around their IVs, a new batch each time she visits. Not just the neighbor's sister-in-law's father. It's everywhere. She cannot turn around without running into someone else. Everybody is battling cancer. Why did she never see these people before?

They're all over the Harvest Fair. A boy two years younger than Tim rests against a stack of pumpkins, his skin an eerie green. The bared, patchy head of a woman hoisting a papoose and swigging apple cider, clear as a brand. Laura watches as a college-age kid with a backwards ball cap and iodined arms entertains his girlfriend, mocking the townie rituals while waiting their turn to bob for apples.

She starts to recognize them on no evidence whatsoever. Something about the old guy selling the squash-mounted candles. He's nursing something in his gut the size of his fist. No proof. Laura just knows.

She has come late to this affliction. Yet they recognize her, too, despite the careful makeup that took her an hour to apply. They give her that silent salute, eyes held a fraction too long in regrettable kinship. A secret-society handshake, less anger in it than Laura would have thought. It's a best-footforward, this questioning gaze, this *You too?* They cannot help but stare a little, at all their companions on this expedition for which no one signed on.

She walks along with Ellen, pretending interest in the standing racks of needlework. Ellen fidgets, denying that their pace has anything to do with her mother's being winded.

"Aren't you cold?" Laura asks. "Don't you need a jacket?"

"Sure, Mom. Even the slugs are wearing windbreakers."

Tim spins ten paces ahead of them, afraid whatever virus that makes women women might be contagious. He cuts switchbacks through the crowd, searching for that elusive booth specializing in Amish braided bread and Mortal Kombat III cartridges.

"You think it's like this in Champaign or Decatur?" Laura wonders.

Ellen shoots her a startled grimace. "No, Mother dearest." She drops into a camp flash of Judy Garland. "We have the very best Harvest Fair in the world, right here in our own backyard!"

Illness has shown Laura at least one thing: she will lose her girl forever if she goes on taking her for a girl. Cancer has opened her daughter to her, clear as a spied-upon diary. Ellen, well over in the red zone, deep into all the illicit experiments whose outcomes could still go either way.

A year from now, Ellen will either be going to college or nodding spiked out on somebody's toilet. She'll base her choice on the available evidence, and so far, mainstream existence has made an overwhelming case for all-annihilating stupidity.

"Not the fair," Laura tsks. She whisks at Ellen, using the playful push as an excuse to grab and hold her daughter's upper arm. "I mean, look. Is it just me? Everybody's sick. It's like some kind of plague."

Ellen's already convinced. She doesn't even need to look around. "I *told* you, Mom." Adolescent delivery, a point too piercing for adulthood. "*You* wouldn't believe me."

"You think it's just here? Just near . . . ?"

"I don't know, Mom. You think they have any fat, filthy, money-grubbing capitalists in Decatur?"

Laura stops. She stares at the flesh of her flesh, this chameleon. *Ellen?* Who planted that tirade in her? It must be the time of life. At seventeen, cheerleaders can turn Trotskyite somewhere between fourth and fifth period.

The outburst feels vaguely profane, like something Laura's own mother might have washed her mouth out with soap for uttering. She feels her daughter's brassy strength, the strength of seventeen, and wants to deliver herself to its care. You think so? You think? I'm not just scapegoating?

Before they can get into the topic of Decatur industry, a man Laura's age draws up to them.

"Excuse me. I'm a counselor over at Mercy. Haven't I seen you on the Oncology floor?"

He gives his name, which Laura fails to hang on to. Wholly unabashed, he strikes up a conversation about his own seven-year struggle with leukemia, now in remission. She tells him as much about her cancer as she cares to share with a total stranger. Leaving, he says, "We have a little group that meets twice a week, if you'd like to join us."

"Oh. No thank you," Laura pleads. "No thank you. Thanks."

Ellen flees to the dried-cornstalk-doll booth in embarrassment. She drifts back only after the man leaves.

"My God, Ellen. Can you believe that? What on earth is *happening*? We were just talking . . . It's like he . . ."

"Hel-*lo*? Mother. Get a grip. He probably heard us."

Laura drops her eyes to the snickering grass. "Yeah. Well. I guess you're right." Her daughter, protecting her from the obvious.

Ellen lifts her mother's chin and looks her in the eye. "Say, hey. Baby. You come here often? What's your cell type?"

"Wanna go grab a cisplatin somewhere?" Laura mimics. The two of them hide their guilty giggles in each other's shoulders.

Laura sobers first. "Why now? I'm sure I didn't know anyone with cancer until I turned thirty."

Tim materializes at their side. He, too, eavesdropping at a distance. "Actually," he stutters. "Actually, there's been a slight decrease in ovarian cancer since 1970."

Laura looks at this child, her boy. Thirteen next month. In the basin of her lungs, a tight tumor breaks, clods crumbling into powder. And somewhere to the north, in her throat, her eyes rain down dry rain.

"You are a freak," Ellen reassures her brother. "That's what you are." She puts her arm around him, under cover of irony. More amazing still, he suffers it. Arm in arm: not since they were two and six.

"Where did you learn that, honey?"

Tim shrugs. "I don't know. The Net. Doing an oral report. Most other kinds are up, though. Skin cancer has almost doubled."

"Oh, *really*?" Ellen asks. Her Wellesley accent, almost perfect. "How interesting. Tell me more."

"Do you want something to eat?" Laura asks. Distract them back to this Harvest Fair, the last booth of childhood. Time enough for all the uglier stuff later.

Tim looks at Ellen, who looks at Tim. They shrug together, on cue.

"Come on. What do you say? Corn dog? Apple cider? It's on me."

"Y-*yum*." Ellen smacks her lips. "Sulfites! My fave."

Laura pulls them over to the open tent, into its last-chance smells of charcoal and canvas. She pushes them down on a green plastic picnic table bench, recycled from gallon milk jugs to look almost like painted wood. She takes their orders as if she were still a twenty-year-old short-order waitress in peak condition.

She gives the order to a hangdog teen, who needs her to repeat it twice. Rummaging for her wallet, she stumbles across a photocopy from the library she has filed away in her purse for no reason, for safekeeping. An article from the clippings file, another filler item buried on page 12, reading "Cancer Tracks Chemicals, Not Chance, Workers Claim."

> Three years ago, Roberto Santiago, Paula Meyers, and Willy Liu worked in the same production facility in Clare's Agricultural Products Division, just west of town. Roberto inspected and loaded stock. Paula operated a bagging machine. Willy cleaned the equipment that made Clare's BugBlaster™ seed-coating crop enhancer. They made between $7 and $9 an hour. All three felt lucky to have a job.
>
> Today, Roberto has a tumor in his testicle, Paula is fighting cervical cancer, and Willy is dead.

It's dated the year that Ellen entered high school. Roberto and Paula might even have made it to this year's fair, behind Laura somewhere in this food line, waiting for the slow woman to find her cash and pay.

Three different diseases, Laura knows. Thanks to Dr. Archer. And the three people weren't exactly working the same job. Her disease is another matter altogether. And she has never gotten closer to that plant than to drive past it in a sport utility vehicle filled with grocery bags.

The Xerox has been getting in her way for the last two weeks, floating into her fingers every time she fishes for anything. She can't bring herself to throw it away. But she doesn't quite know what to do with it. Keeping it, maybe, to show Ruthie or that Christian soul Janine, if she ever sees either woman again.

By the time the bonfire starts, it's already dark. They pull up close to it, the three of them. As close as comfortable. Don finds them out, joins them, eyes lit by the yellow-orange flame. A flame the size of a softball infield. Even Tim and Ellen start to chatter and grin.

The whole town turns out to witness this group pact of anticipation. Pledge, promise of who knows what: something about to happen, the reason behind autumn, the point of arrival for the whole calendar's long coast and collapse. The flames lift their fuel's half-spent sparks backwards, coil them up their own crazed updraft, and for this minute no one here is a day beyond eight. Community fire, older than any of them, older, still, than all of them laid end to end. And if that thrilled hint of things to come has never yet in all those years delivered, the whole of Lacewood feels, tonight around the fire, less reneged on than postponed. Any year now. This year.

The blaze's tamed threat takes even Laura out of herself long enough to quit her list-making. The branch office manager, whom she once shook hands with. Ellen's junior-high language arts teacher. That colleague of Don's. The obits in the *Post-Chronicle* that she has taken to reading now, even before Engagements and Real Estate. Who won't get sick, finally? Who won't at last host a tumor, if something else doesn't take them first? Comes with the territory. Where we live.

Whatever happens from here on, tonight excites her. Now feels warm upon her face. Don leans over to her in the oranged dark to tell her something, his peace as palpable as hers. Like some bonfire from ten years before. Like no human has ever been foolish. Like there's no such thing as forgiveness. Like there's nothing to forgive.

"Have you heard the news?" he whispers.

"What news?" Just the idea of news now seems a moving violation.

"Lawsuit against the company. Against Clare."

———

THE CHILDREN'S NEW CRUSADE

CHILD (*on the front stoop, suppliant*): "May I please have your old **NATIVE BALM SOAP** wrappers? If I send 20 to Clare Soap Company in Boston, Massachusetts, they will send me some colored pencils and a drawing pad."

LADY (*in open doorway*): "I am sorry, I cannot. For my own children are collecting those very wrappers for the same purpose."

———

Though born to run the firm, Douglas Clare I came up through the ranks. While still a child, he cleaned and swept his father's offices. Learning to write, he spent a year as a copyist. At thirteen, he drove a horse-drawn dray back and forth between Roxbury and the Boston docks. Later, he shoveled rosin at the factory for his uncle Resolve, eleven hours a day.

As soon as Douglas was old enough, Samuel farmed the boy out as an apprentice to a series of sales representatives. There, on the road, in various American cities from New York to Pittsburgh, Douglas learned the task of getting goods into the hands of the public.

Douglas's patrimony was never in doubt. But the distance he traveled, from shoveler to president, never failed to impress those he did business with.

Inside the firm and out, he emanated an authority grounded on calluses. People always remarked upon his height. Like his father, he stayed emaciated well into old age. But unlike Samuel, Douglas rarely slept. He sometimes closed his eyes for twenty minutes while seated behind his desk. But the first word would bring him back to full concentration.

Douglas was responsible for implementing the policy that required all new hires to start life on the factory floor. His own famous job history did wonders for labor relations at Clare. Because of Douglas, every wagon boy drove his team tirelessly for years, happily calculating his own outside shot at the big money.

He seemed impervious to pain. He never got cold. He walked the two miles from his house to the offices, even in the depths of winter, every working day until the day he dropped dead. In a practice that would have confounded the Clare founders, he conducted business on the Sabbath. He never took his eyes off the person he spoke with. He dispatched his few, well-chosen words like bursts of advance cavalry.

In stark contrast to the first generation, he believed in modernization's unfailing ability to justify its costs. He installed gaslights to replace the absurd lard-oil lamps the firm had clung to for five too many years. In season, he wired up even the remote offices with telephones. Then he forced his staff to use them, damn the trepidation and the costs. His Aunt Julia lived to see that first phone link between Boston and Walpole. She died proclaiming it the tool by which democracy would finally be realized.

Democracy, to Douglas, was neither here nor there. We the people, however, did interest him considerably. His years on the road convinced him that a business was neither inventory nor equipment nor licenses nor any other item in the typical assets column. Business was your employees, no more nor less. The sum total of your laboring armies. No idea, no effort, no chemistry, no freight hauling, no magic transformation of fat to cleansing foam—none of this happened without someone to do it.

The greater your human assets, the better your chance of survival. People had to feel they were part of something bigger than themselves, something growing. For Douglas Clare, growth was an end unto itself. Nothing in creation asked why bud relaxed into leaf or calf exploded into cow. Douglas had no more use for *why* than nature had. Each morning on awakening, Douglas simply thanked whoever ran the show for this chance he'd been given to preside over the firm's passage into gangly young adulthood.

Since the first Roxbury works, the Clares had pursued horizontal integration. Samuel and Resolve had delighted in buying up their strapped local competitors to grab their equipment, sack their inventory, steal their skilled labor, or simply put them out on the stoop. Laissez-faire and the rise of public companies made the horizontal game at once wider and more nuanced.

Douglas now attempted vertical integration on a vast scale. He pursued Neeland's great chemical loop, with the entire firm as but one reagent. Those manufacturers who survived the scramble to century's end would have to make their own sources and buy up their own outlets. And in between start and finish, they would need to make one process's ends into another's means.

An architectural vision of wholeness drove Douglas. Combination kept him awake and warm well into old age. Clare could make the alkali that would furnish the soap whose wastes would flesh out the fertilizer that would boost the crops that made the whiskey to feed to the day laborers who kept the alkali factory humming. What's more, in time, the company could acquire its own wholesalers and bring on board a whole sales force, breaking the jobbers' stranglehold by selling directly to the stores. Why sit still on a single link when you could grab the whole chain?

As the firm grew, Douglas liked to scout out new land purchases by faking picnics. He and two or three assistants—who all received excursion bonuses—would travel out to the prospective site with elaborate prop baskets, perfect right down to the boiled eggs and the marble-carbonated bottled sodas. Once, his own children out of reach at boarding school, Douglas even went to the extreme of renting a pair of pinafored cherubs for added cover.

The picnic ruse always supplied Douglas with a long afternoon of anonymous investigation. He'd pace through the woods with a shotgun or wander about the meadows waving a badminton racket. He wanted a chance to inspect the goods without someone inspecting him. Douglas needed to see, up close, exactly what was for sale, without the seller getting all excited and putting up the price.

In this way, he bought the land for the Allegheny soda works and the firm's big Jersey warehouses. Douglas felt no shame in this ruse. He simply preferred to play a smaller game rather than fooling around with a bigger one. Picnicking over, he could go to the seller with an offer that was both informed and firm.

Prior to every purchase, Douglas made elaborate, months-long calculations. Each new site meant corporate life or death. Growth could come neither a month too soon nor a month too late. Ten miles to the north or south of the future's rightful path, and a new site might sink them.

Douglas would figure and refigure the ledger, employing elaborate, gothic formulae. He'd hedge and waffle, qualify and demur. Then, in an afternoon of chicken wings and soda on a spread blanket, the thing was done. For in the end, no decision was easier. Long after his death, Douglas's famous take on the matter still served as one of the company's guiding phrases. "When in doubt, take two steps West."

In 1881, the firm broke ground in Sandusky, Ohio, for its largest factory ever. Douglas was there to turn the first spade of earth. The spot could not have been worse for a picnic. But it fit the spreading needs of the company to a T.

Lacewood, of course, lay too far West to haul rented children. Furthermore, the towns in that part of the world were still so small and far-flung that even the most discreet picnic basket only served to make a person more conspicuous. But by the time Clare came calling in the Midwest, many residents already knew the surname. A fair number of progressive Lacewooders used one or another of the soaps regularly, whether they needed to or not.

When Douglas Clare stepped off the train in Lacewood, he discovered to his reserved delight that he did not have to buy this land. The town put itself up for auction. Its denizens went all out to sell *him* on the place, with their dammed-up rivers and their fishing for iced, imported northern pike.

The place was determined not to remain a farming hamlet forever. Lacewood knew that what it wouldn't sell, Peoria would cash in on. Those who refused to choose the Gilded Age would be left gelded.

Douglas took a few days to size up the prospects. Lacewood lay on an exploding confluence of rails that turned the surrounding grain wastes into well-organized hinterlands for urban clearinghouses. It sat within reasonable shipping distance of several essential materials: sulfur up from Texas, lead from Galena, anthracite and petroleum oil from western Pennsylvania.

The inland seaway to Chicago opened the whole region to cheap Eastern manufacture. The East in turn needed what this West could be made to grow. Lacewood sat close to dead center of the country's agricultural future. One could not get closer to the market for Clare's new fertilizers without going past it.

Land here was still cheap, by Eastern standards. This appealed to Douglas, not so much on grounds of economy, but out of sheer business foresight. Over the long haul, a manufacturer had to lead the next burst of speculation, not follow it. Douglas, ever a long-hauler, made elaborate predictions for the way the region would develop. Most of them turned out utterly wrong.

Truth be told, the town had no great virtue to recommend it over any other prospective site. But there it was, central, vacant, ready to be made over. And more than anything else, Douglas found in Lacewood an irreplaceable asset: a labor force worth going out of one's way to enlist.

———

Clare turned fifty in 1881, to great public fanfare of its own generating. As a corporation, it was but a scant teenager. But if one dated life from conception, from the moment that Samuel hand-delivered that first two pounds of Irish widower's soap, a full half century had passed into lather.

By the jubilee year, the heavy expansion of the seventies came into its own. At last the shriek of production costs quieted to a whimper. American-made soda—Clare's included—using the cheaper Solvay process, was blowing the lid off the feeble and filthy British Leblanc monopoly. Soap proliferated, cheaper, better, and cleaner than ever.

Each dollar of income plowed back into capital investment now paid for itself in increased yields within three years. Douglas's direct volume discount plan eased Clare into wholesaling and made its consumer products competitive out West. Peter's creative kickbacks with the railroads kept carrying rates low enough that merely chasing geography could turn a profit.

The firm was again flush, thanks to the unholy trinity of Peter, Douglas, and their fast-rising protégé Hiram Nagel. Peter had discovered Nagel, a twenty-two-year-old land-grant-college boy, languishing in the Boston office answering complaint letters. Nagel had come up from Kentucky to make a buck in the business world. The young man at once demonstrated a remarkable ability to placate the common customer, an ability that threatened to ruin his career ambitions.

No one had ever handled the losing proposition with half Hy's aplomb. He could write to anyone—from Harvard divinity prof. to Sooner dung-shoveler—in his native tongue. And he could give all complainers exactly what they wanted, usually without costing the firm much more than a nickel. His letters made once-irate old ladies write back in teary contrition.

Hiram Nagel became Clare's boy with his finger in the dike. And in gratitude, the firm threatened to stick him with the thankless job forever.

So good was Nagel at what he did that word of his legendary skills of appeasement reached Peter. The White Hermit himself paid a visit to the offices to meet the man. Nagel appalled him. Peter wrote in his journal:

I would not have this man anywhere near my person, not even for short intervals. For dress, he chooses a screeching yellow plaid. His voice, while cheerful enough on the surface, is that of a farmer's, forever nagging at a curd of recalcitrant phlegm. One must suppress the urge to tell him to spit and get it over with . . .

Yet protected, say behind glass, I could have sat and studied him all afternoon. His jokes alone astonished me. His rousing inanities rolled out in an effortless stream, untaxed by the passage of hours . . .

Peter, with an invalid's fascination with the banal, had reached a conclusion too bizarre for anyone else at first to credit. The future of American business would be decided in the pages of popular print. Somehow he managed to get the board to vote the outrageous sum of $15,000 for the next year's advertisements.

Even more remarkably, he won approval for the creation of a full-time position of advertiser. Until then, the firm handed its copy over to agencies and newspaper space brokers, with perfunctory and indifferent results. Why not combine copywriter and advertisement designer into one, professional role, a man whose job it was to fit message to means and means to message?

In the yellow-checked Nagel, Peter knew at once he had found the man for the job. He promoted the complaints scribe to the position that the two of them decided to call Director of Promotion. Nagel took to the job at once as if he'd invented it, for in fact he had.

The working association between the general manager and his director of promotion was one of those fabled friendships between alien animal species. Those who knew both men sometimes figured that the chubby cherub pitchman allowed the sickly monk a glimpse of the normal, cider-swilling life that life had always denied him.

For his part, Peter recognized Nagel's instinctive grasp of the American class system. Here was a man who understood popular craving and anxiety. Nagel felt the new American appetites deep down, in the barometer of his own ample belly. Peter Clare may have known his customers the way an expert entomologist knows an exotic, collectible species. Hiram Nagel *was* the species.

Hy, as he insisted that everyone call him, made the company as recognizable as its products. Clare had long been a person in the eyes of the law. Now it became one in the minds of its customers. As he had when answering complaints, Hy spoke to the public in its own words. His bible was the serial novel, as passed through Roget's 1852 *Thesaurus*. The church of his diction held services in the penny theater.

The messages Nagel cooked up for the jubilee campaign were simple ones. For the *Ladies' Bounteous Home* and other family magazines, Hy crafted the anniversary as a Golden Wedding, with the discerning customer as the groom and those virginal bars of Clare soap as the blushing bride. For the big city dailies, he hawked the sound advice: GET ON THE GOLD STANDARD.

In *Harper's*, he claimed **Every Race Has Its Golden Age,** then let his talented stable of artists loose on imaginative and utterly anachronistic engravings of Periclean Athens, Elizabethan England, and Louis Quatorze France. The last oval showed the original profile of that high-collared, lace-shouldered, feather-capped visage that would in time become Clara Clear, America's Ambassadress of Sweetheartiness. In this, her first incarnation, Clara simply gazed gratefully at the golden cake that let her recapture an unblemished purity.

Finally, the Indian came out of retirement one last time. Nagel had the Brave proclaim, with the dignity of an ancient senior statesman, to readers of the *Saturday Evening Post:*

There *Is* Balm in Gilead
What worked for your forefathers will still work for you today.

Only in nursling America could fifty years pass itself off as venerable. Yet life in America *had* changed beyond recognition since Ennis's first slab of soap. Not one of the firm's founders could have done business in this altered world, however much their own creed of good business had brought this world into being.

The country had ballooned beyond recognition. Its inhabitants had increased almost fourfold. Where once only one in ten had lived in a city, now one in every four made their home there. Great circular flows of know-how and resource shod the barefoot boy and plunged Ragged Dick into gentility. Ready wares drove further affluence; and affluence spurred demand for ready wares.

The terms of existence had eased beyond telling. Yet ease upped the ante on the whole notion of existing. It no longer sufficed that an infant merely survive to adulthood. Now hope required that the child move from farm to fortune by fighting his patrimony of filth and disease with all the new tools at boom time's disposal.

Once upon a time, three Boston merchants had transformed a South Seas plant into a noble native cure-all. Now it fell to Nagel to market a package that looked forward and not back. His new glistening solvent had to deny all animal antecedents. Those people who had only recently lost their own art of rendering dead animal fat needed to believe that no creature ever once died for their clean hands.

In short, Nagel now had to sell the self-reliant public the virtue of the man-made and managed. He folded and glued those commodities into each Native Balm machine-cut wrapper. Soap was nothing if not reasonable regulation, the key to mankind's rehabilitation from natural squalor.

Gifford, the buyer of European refinement, showered Hy with undisguised contempt. He never understood how Peter Clare, who had been born rich, could abide even a casual business association with a man who wore yellow check. But Gifford never dared to suggest killing the prize milch cow in the interests of sprucing up the dairy.

Gifford and Nagel did conspire to produce one lasting promotional item. For many years, Clare inserted cardboard Collectible Art Cards under its wrappers: "a valued gift that outlives the purchase." A generation of Americans grew up learning their great masters from these colored cardboard squares. Proud starter homes turned themselves into domestic museums, their walls warmed by Delacroix. Rembrandt angels visited the kitchens of the working class, their dog-eared drapery darkened by the soot of coal burners.

Early in this campaign, the cards were straight reproductions of the classics, marred only by the limits of cheap printing. In later years, everything about the Gainsborough or de Hooch or Millais remained picture-perfect except for one small bar of *Clare* tucked inoffensively away, almost unnoticed, behind the matron's apron, the boy's bubbles, the hem of the Apostles' garments.

Nagel wanted not so much to sell the thing as to peddle the virtue of buying. For this, he needed more than florid images and noble profiles. He learned from Pears of London, the invader from across the seas, how the trick might be done. Pears got the drop on American soapmakers by employing the famed Henry Ward Beecher. Pears got Beecher to proclaim on record the many virtues of Anglo-Saxon rationality and foam. When attacked for this apparent conflict of interests in serving two masters, Beecher replied:

If cleanliness is next to Godliness, soap must be considered as a means of Grace, and a clergyman who recommends moral things should be willing to recommend soap. I am told that my commendation of Pears Soap has opened for it a large sale in the United States. I am willing to stand by every word in favor of it that I ever uttered. A man must be fastidious indeed who is not satisfied with it.

The genius of the move struck Nagel at once. Clare needed its own ex-abolitionist preacher to make such testimonials. If it could find one, like

Beecher, who had recently been acquitted in a long and scandalous adultery trial, so much the better.

The search was on for prominent witnesses to the virtues of sane living. By the end of the decade, Nagel had elicited sermons from Julienne Healy, the irresistible stage siren; the renowned midget Baby Alice; and World Heavyweight Champion John L. Sullivan. But Clare's prize spokesman was the disgruntled General Hancock, late of Gettysburg and the Missouri Indian campaigns, rehabilitator of Louisiana, then at an end of a long and distinguished life of public service. Hancock had recently come up a few thousand votes shy of the Presidency. With Clare, he was happy to find himself on a ballot he could carry.

All these apostles testified in print that their lives would not be half what they were in a world where Clare did not offer its commodities to a grateful populace.

———

Don starts calling her again. He calls her three times the following week. Like when he wanted to sue Dr. Jenkins for cruel and unusual optimism. Exactly the same excitement, but without the canary-yellow dress to explain his interest.

"I really think you ought to look into this case," he tells her. Two cases, really. A civil action by a handful of workers at the Clare plant, each suffering from some form of cancer. And a class action, some kind of *People of Lacewood* v. *Clare*, seeking redress for those toxic discharges in the EPA report. "It wouldn't kill you to take an interest in all this," Don says.

"What do you want me to do, Don?"

"It's not what *I* want. What I want has nothing to do with anything."

"Okay. What kind of interest should I be taking?"

"Well, I think all of this has some pretty direct concern to you, don't you think?"

Why? she wants to ask. *Why?*

"They're looking for people with any kind of unaccountable health complaints. They've set up this number that you can call—"

"What do you mean unaccountable? I've got ovarian cancer, Don. Twenty-five thousand women get it every year." And half that number die.

"Yeah. But why? You're young. You had your children young. You're on the Pill. You were on the Pill," he corrects. Giving until it hurts. "You're not an

225

immigrant. You're not an Ashkenazi. Are you? Nobody in your family has ever come near the disease."

Until now, she thinks. Until now.

"They just want you to answer a few questions," Don wheedles. "Why not let them decide whether your chart has any interest to the case."

"I'm not a chart, Don. And the last thing in the world I want is to get mixed up with a pack of jackal lawyers."

"Who's asking you to get mixed up? Just tell them the facts. Just get your name on the list of claimants—"

"Know what looks good on a lawyer, Don?" She cannot keep from giggling. And not at the stupid riddle. "A Doberman."

"Very funny," he growls. He told her that one. Over the drink they went out for, to seal the divorce. She hadn't laughed then.

"Timing, Don. It's all in the timing."

"Look, Loofa, it's not like they're going to haul your ass in front of the jury."

"What did you call me?"

Slowly, hearing himself this time: "Loofa. Loopie."

"Lo," she adds. "La. Laurish."

"I called you Laurish?"

"I always hated that one. And they will."

"What? Who will what?"

"They will. Haul my ass in front of a jury. If they like my story, that is. If they don't, they'll probably charge me $250 an hour for the pleasure of the consult."

"Laura, they won't. You want me to look into this thing? I'll look into it."

"Don't bother, Don," she tells him, not knowing why she bothers.

She makes a note to go to the library. To look up the cases and read all she can about them. Not just in what Ellen has started calling the *Joke-Comical*. She'll have a look at the Chicago and Indy papers, too. Marian will show her how to keep up with stories about this suit, without her having to deal through Don. What is it about men that they always have easier access to useful facts?

She uses an orange Post-It. Orange, the color she reserves for "Get on it."

Clare Lawsuits
Library

She sticks the note on the lower left corner of her bathroom mirror, where she's forced to see it whenever she looks at herself. It goads her to get up, get over the lethargy that pins her to her bed. It scolds her to get outside, to find the strength to make it down the block.

Problem is, she no longer has the strength to look in the mirror. Or the desire. She knows exactly the changeling cuckoo she will see there, the chick with its blasted tufts of down. She sees too much of her limp and withered skin already, without the aid of reflection. And now that the note hangs there nagging at her, she may never look in the glass again.

Her body scares her now. Alien infestation. A pink, bare, cave newt, bald down to her plastic pubes. Clammy and numb and going deaf. Her memory is shot; she cannot form complete thoughts. She weeps or rages at random. No one can tell her how much of the changes come from the cancer, how much from the chemo, how much from the meds used to soften the chemo, how much from the whiplash of coming off those meds, or how much from having her sex organs yanked out by the roots and replaced by more pills. Whatever the cause, she no longer recognizes the scraps of person left to her.

The sight of her PICC line under its swatch of plastic tape repulses her. She still blanches at the thought of that plastic tube running up the inside of her arm and into her chest. She can just bare the catheter now without feeling like the star attraction at a frat-house kegger. But she blesses the thing every time they have to stick her for anything.

She can look at the scar now, at least. The gash across her gut with its staple notches, yard markers on a football field. She couldn't bear it when she first came out. Could not glimpse the cut without feeling like something out of a slasher film, stitched together out of graveyard parts.

The scar has lightened. Once it was livid, a blood-gorged leech licking the cream of her belly. Now scar and the skin it straddles compromise on a dingy reddish-brown. The scar is less jarring than her pelvis, jutting up through her skin. She would have killed once, for this much waist definition. Now she owns the elusive grand prize: visible hipbones. She's as much of a skeleton as any jeans-ad waif, only she sports this gash in her sagging skin.

Her bones come up everywhere through what's left of her threadbare padding. She cannot sit on anything solid. Even the recliner hurts after the first minute. Taking a bath is out of the question: the spike of her tail grinds on the porcelain.

How easy weight loss is, once you know the trick. The opposite of twenty-seven, when she woke up one day and could no longer eat without paying. Slammed into reverse, after all these years of fighting. All the special diets. The pills, the books, the videotapes, the exercise cycles. The artificial-fat chips that gave her the trots if she tried to eat more than half an ounce. Now, there's your ultimate salt-water thirst quencher: substitute junk food, that you *still* have to eat in moderation.

She has to fight to put weight back on. Has to throw out the old tapes and pills and buy a whole new, opposite lineup. At first she went to the hospital shop for them. But after about two weeks she realized that she could get the exact same $14.95 diet supplement for $9.95 at Pure Succor down on Angleton. The health food store marks things up only about double, as opposed to triple at the hospital. And it carries a full line of those specialty shakes and snacks, products for the growing niche group who need to buck the dieting tide. It's mostly the same stuff the Cross Trainer store sells as "High Energy," only at the cancer section of Pure Succor the labels say "High Calorie."

She calls Grace Wambaugh, her friend the herbal Fuller Brush saleswoman. She orders the four-month booster plan, enough to see her past the end of the chemotherapy. It's more of a superstition than anything else. She can't keep most of the tablets down anyway.

She asks Grace for a pain program. The hospital stuff just stones her, then makes her edgy and paranoid when she stops taking it. It doesn't do more than muffle the anguish at most.

"You shouldn't try to mask the symptoms," Grace tells her over the phone. "You shouldn't take stuff for pain. You have to treat the causes, not the manifestations."

Laura plots to tip over the woman's pyramids and grind her crystals into little bits. No New Age court in the land would convict her.

Her old stoicism dissolves, just when she needs it. Her whole life, she's fought to win this high threshold. Even Don used to admire how tough she was. She never complained. Couldn't afford to. She never even noticed. She never had *time* to notice. Now she sees where being good has gotten her.

For months now, she's held off the fatigue, even when fatigue was so great she couldn't think straight. Every day she forced herself out of bed, even if only to crawl back two hours later, winded and depleted. She went to work on days when she could not keep her eyes from crossing in agony. She did the shopping on days when just shoving the stick shift around felt like a supermodel's aerobics video. Now she has nothing left. And the course has just begun toying with her.

"Describe the pain," Dr. Archer asks her. "Is it sharp or dull? Local or general?"

"Just pain," she says. "Bad. From the bottom of my ribs to the top of my thighs."

"When?"

She shrugs. "All the time. My chest feels heavy. I run out of breath."

"Does the pain wake you up?"

"How did you know? Sometimes the pain, and sometimes the ringing in my ears. The tips of my fingers are going dead, too. It's like I'm wearing mittens. I can't hold a pen anymore. I'm always dropping things."

"Anything else?"

Where should she stop? "Well, I've been vomiting again."

"We don't want you walking around doubled over for another two months," he jokes.

"No," she agrees.

They go ahead and work up her blood in preparation for the fifth treatment. A practiced veteran, she lets them hitch up to her catheter tap. The blood work shows her white cell count plummeting deep below the margin of safety.

"We're going to try you with Neupogen," Dr. Archer says. "Great stuff. This will do good things for you."

"What is it?"

"What is it? It's filgrastim."

"It has two names?"

"Neupogen's the registered trademark."

"I mean, what does it do?"

"Oh! I didn't get you. It's a granulocyte-colony-stimulating factor. We generally have good luck with it. A neat drug. Produced by recombinant DNA."

"My colonies need stimulating?"

Dr. Archer laughs. "The taxol and cisplatin have knocked down your neutrophil counts. The Neupogen will accelerate their recovery."

Learning that she has neutrophils plunges Laura into depression. Not only does she have the horrid-sounding things, she doesn't have as many as she should. Something is loose in her system, a runaway growth. They can try to gun down the criminal, but not without firing into the innocent crowd.

They pump her with one drug to destroy and another to rebuild. Next she'll need to take something to correct the Neupogen, and another to correct the correction. It's just like life, this chemotherapy. The cure is even worse than the disease.

She must come in for five days in a row. Five consecutive booster shots, with blood tests before, during, and after. She feels like crocheting a little doily flower to ring the mouth of her IV tap.

"Can I stay in the hospital for the four nights? It's tough for me to get back and forth."

"The point of the shots is to keep you *out* of the hospital." Dr. Archer grins. But he looks into it. The stay would not be covered. It would cost as much as half a year in Fort Lauderdale.

She thinks about asking Ken to chauffeur her. But Ken has already faded to an unpleasant memory. He is a dim stranger to her now, surely happy to be free of that bald, anemic, desexed woman with the gash across her midriff and no ass left at all. A woman whose edgy nausea and mood swings sealed him in a tomb as lonely as hers, without even the disease to comfort him. A woman who from the far edge of the bed gladly drove him, innocent, away.

Don would jump at the chance to play driver, of course. Exactly why she can't let him. Lately Laura has felt an odd concern for that twenty-something twit Don's been dating. Like the kid's got a bum deal the way it is, and doesn't need a cancerous ex-wife thrown into the kitty.

She gets Ellen to take her. Nothing makes her daughter happier than the prospect of substituting a little afternoon driver's ed. refresher for history, humanities, and algebra II. The only problem, despite what the Illinois Department of Motor Vehicles says, is that her daughter can't drive.

Her five-year survival rates are better with any cancer in the book than in this car. "Turn the radio off," Laura croaks. "Don't talk, just concentrate. Look out!"

"I see him, Mother."

"Then *stop* for him, for God's sake." They come an inch from slamming into a bumper sticker that reads: *My Dolt Trashed Your Honor Student's Ass.*

"Mother, you're making me really nervous. Just turn around. Look out the back window or something."

The back window is even more terrifying.

"I'm better off without neutrophils."

Five boosters fail to raise her count to safety. More blood work shows additional problems, problems that Laura can't quite catch and does not try to. Dr. Archer and Dr. Jenkins confer. Together, they conclude what neither wants to.

"You're not tolerating the treatments," Dr. Archer tells her. "High-dose chemotherapy has compromised your immune system. The smallest infection could finish what the cancer has started."

"I can settle for four," Laura suggests politely.

Dr. Archer smiles. "It doesn't work that way, unfortunately. You haven't completed the whole protocol."

"But didn't I have a choice, back when we started? Three or six?"

"That was then. If you can't finish all six, we have to try to move you onto another modality that you can get all the way through."

"Start from zero?" She cannot even finish this race. And they're asking her to begin another.

"We could try localized chemo washes. Or intraperitoneal radiation therapy. Pipe some radioactive phosphorus directly into the site. Or we might try another general drip. Maybe one of the newer multi-agent combinations. Try to find a mix that you can tolerate a little better. There's a new drug, topotecan. SmithKline. It's just been approved."

"I thought taxol was new."

"This one's even newer."

She goes home. The facts sit like an unbathed hitchhiker on the backseat. She does not tell Ellen, who drives back to school for a last half hour of learning things.

The middle of November, and the lilacs are budding in confusion. Greenhouse effect. Global warming probably, although that weatherman, Mr. Goddard, on the Channel 3 news says that you can't talk about climate change in such short terms.

She turns on the television, just for the sound of human conversation in the next room. Outside, in the world of broadcast, it's still raining down plenty and profusion. The catchy salsa sound of updates every eight minutes keeps her from thinking. Just what she needs from it. No worse threat now than concentration.

She plays house. Toys with the dishes, unloads them from the washer. She heats a heaping plate of pilaf, but the smell gags her and she leaves it in the microwave. She flips through the new issue of *Bountiful Living*, browsing the garden feature, the furniture-refinishing column, the entertaining hints—all the graceful pointlessness of enjoyment.

She lingers on the parting-shot article, "The Bumpy Road to the Obvious." One of those how-stupid-can-you-get lists that people love to hold up to ridicule the human race. The elusive core, hiding inside the ordinary. How long it took us to make the most self-evident things. The first two-sided record. The shift key on typewriters.

Number seven in the list stops her:

The indispensable Post-It began life as a failure, when a chemical engineer at 3M developed an adhesive that wouldn't stick. He set the whole batch aside for disposal. Another company scientist, looking for a way to mark his Sunday hymnal, asked to borrow some of the worthless stuff. Only after the two researchers painted a square of paper with the defective glue did the men realize what they had: a quarter-billion-dollar annual industry.

Distraction vanishes, reminding her of her reminder. She goes into the bathroom, careful not to look. She pulls the orange square off the mirror and rubs the reticent adhesive. The gum is fuzzy, grayed. She folds the gum over and sticks it to itself. She wads the scrap into a ball and pitches it in the trash.

She calls Don. She never calls Don. She doesn't know what she's doing. He's deeply confused to hear her. As confused as her budding lilacs.

"What's wrong?" he asks. That instant tone of professional competence. What she wanted. What she needed.

"Nothing. Nothing, really."

"How are you feeling?"

"Not the best, Don."

"Fight it. Attitude is everything, La. The mind is your best chemo. You have to picture yourself well again, and then you will be. Remember, all of this is only temporary. These treatments aren't going to last forever, you know."

"In fact, Don, in fact, I'm done for now. I don't have to do those last two chemos."

"You *what*? Sweetheart. That's fantastic. You're through?"

Fantastic, no. Through, maybe.

"Through for now, anyway. The doctors are thinking about some other treatment. We're going to have to wait and see."

Either Don doesn't get it, or he's a step ahead of her. Either way, God love him, he's off on other topics. Ellen's college applications. Tim's sudden interest in joining tech crew for the winter play. She could listen to him, listen to these things that need her interest, forever.

"Hey," he says. "By the way. We haven't figured out how we're going to handle next week. Turkey Day."

"Oh God. Already? I haven't even thought about it." At least he has never once used the kids against her. Has always made sure she got them beyond all fairness, even when they would have been better off with him. "How would you like to work things, Don?"

"I don't know." Wary; once-burned. "I don't want . . . What do you say we go out? Just the four of us, somewhere."

"No, Don. Let's not."

Silence explodes between them like a shrapnel shell. How quickly they find their way to the old hostility. She smiles a little on her end, invisible, noiseless, at the idea of two people fighting for control of a scrap of land that their battle has left cratered, wasted, worse than worthless.

But she cannot get angry now. All stakes seem inconceivable, strange.

Who can fight over something so trivial? How could anything in life be worth fighting over, when life itself is the only available win? So inexhaustibly much, so much more than anyone could spend. It must somehow drive us mad, this enraging abundance.

"No, Bodey. Let's eat here. We four. You come over."

He stops short again, flushed into the trap of kindness.

"But you can't cook. I refuse to let you."

"Refuse, Don? *Let* me?" she taunts, letting the smirk seep into her voice.

"Laura. Be realistic. You can't even stand at the counter without getting winded."

"Oh, *I'm* not cooking," she says. "I have a staff. Didn't you know about that? I've got a private chef. I've got a purveyor. I even have a maître d'. I don't have to lift a finger."

He hangs on the line, wordless.

"Come on, man. Why do you think they call it Thanksgiving?"

———

There came a year of nationwide upheaval. Everywhere, the cauldron of workers boiled over. Labor, squeezed too long, lashed back at the stamping machine. Turning the wage back on itself, line men struck for pay, safety, and survivable hours. The Knights of Labor took to the streets in every city where Clare had a plant. In two of those cities, running battles broke out and blood flowed on both sides.

But for whatever reason, agitation at Clare's plants fell below the national levels. Trade union membership at the soap works remained marginal. Even organizations more moderate than the Knights made little headway among the Clare laborers. The company headed off the unions with a two-pronged strategy. A Golden Jubilee wage hike, raising the lowest-paid workers to over four dollars a week, served as Clare's carrot. Government-subsidized strikebreakers carried the stick.

But in the summer of '85, an armed cadre of agitators from the Knights occupied the Walpole works. On behalf of all Clare employees, they demanded negotiations with the plant bosses. The loosely organized rabble quickly became a de facto democratic movement. The agitators shut down the factory and vowed to halt all soap production until such talks occurred.

To the astonishment of the manufacturing world, their demand was answered not by the plant bosses but by the *éminence grise*, Peter Clare himself. Feeble and blinking, the invalid figure appeared on the factory floor. The abashed workers' committee made the fatal mistake of letting the apparition speak first.

These are not my workers, Clare told the intruders. Where are my workers? No man speaks for my men but them.

Their recluse boss knew his own, by sight. He knew his labor force, even though they had never laid eyes on him. Peter's words so shamed his men that they voted against representation by the Knights and sent the outsiders packing.

Shortly after the incident, Peter instituted a measure giving all company employees Saturday afternoons off with pay. The move stunned labor and management alike. A paid half-holiday ran counter to the very thrift that had founded the firm. It defied all sense. No business could survive by giving away something for nothing.

Yet the move made Peter, for the moment, his workers' man. Management's popularity surged so roundly that Strasser and Gompers's new American Federation of Labor made only negligent inroads into the company workforce. The second half of the decade saw only eight production shutdowns, the longest of them lasting just ten working days.

In the year 1886, the Personal Goods plants in Boston, Ohio, and Chicago claimed to wrap, crate, ship, and sell more than thirty million units of tonic, salve, shortening, lard, candles, whiskey, and soap. The Industrial Goods facilities, by their nature, had to play their sales closer to the chest. Yet in that bumper year, the less visible branch of the operation sold enough anesthetic, disinfectant, alkali, bleach, and fertilizer to account for more than a quarter of company revenues. Industrial Goods also supplied considerable chemicals to its more visible partner, a transfer much more difficult to price.

The firm's parts now meshed with one another, cog driving sprocket, sprocket turning pinion with the precision of fine castings. Yet one could not stop oiling the points of contact even to step back for a minute and enjoy the fantastic whole. To do so would be to invite wear, breakdown, and disaster.

Clare's choice was a simple grow or die. As with other creatures in upper food ranges, its search for more fuel was intermittent but continual. The firm now made much of its own capital. Like a dirigible, the higher it rose, the fuller it expanded. And the more the blimp swelled, the smoother it rode.

But the expansion that Peter and Douglas envisioned could not wait for the slow trickle of currency from internal mints. The cousins had no patience for time in its own season. The curve of growth that the firm now tracked was insufficient to the day. To collect an advance upon the future, they needed to throw the doors open to outside money.

To make the company as attractive an investment as possible, Clare first needed a healthy, dependable flow of revenues. Investors demanded to see a reasonable earning potential before they would add their own egg to the nest.

Above all else, they needed new products. Neeland tinkered with the versatile coal tar, recently converted into saccharin by chemists at Johns Hopkins. He produced a black milled soap that Nagel promptly christened Tar Baby.

Neeland looked into the uses of linseed and lard, pointing the firm toward foodstuffs and preservatives. His labs slapped together a passable hair pomade. But the cream sold only moderately for two years until John Gale, an engineer and amateur painter, had his packaging brainstorm. Gale took the collapsible metal tube for paints invented by one of Morse's assistants, and softened and enlarged it. The squeezable tube distinguished Clare Hair Enhancer from its increasingly voracious imitators and kept it alive for a fifty-year run.

While washing dishes after the family Christmas dinner in 1887, Neeland flashed upon the idea for soap flakes that would dissolve rapidly in liquid yet remain strong enough to cut heavy grease. As simple as that idea was, it took Neeland's group years to implement. But in developing the formula for their soap flakes, they lucked into their first new runaway soap success since the Brave.

The starter recipe came from a competitor whom Douglas bought out. Clare chemists modified the soap's vegetable oil base, seeking a delicate balance of sources. Coconut lathered well but briefly, tallow poorly but long. The two would unite with soda only in the presence of palm oil. Cottonseed substituted nicely for the ruinously expensive olive. In the end, they settled upon a blend of animal, vegetable, and mineral, all artfully combined under the name Snowdrop.

In many ways, Snowdrop Toilet Soap was Native Balm's opposite. Mild, frothy, and headily white, Snowdrop mocked the herbal curative of the Brave. Native Balm bespoke a Nature pungent, arcane, and enchanted. Snowdrop delineated the *new* face of Nature: immaculate, measured, managed; purity incarnate.

The new soap threw Clare's upper brass into crisis. No one contested Snowdrop's perfection. But Native Balm still had a devoted customer base. The Brave continued to sell well, though yearly growth had slowed to nothing. Yet somehow the homemakers of New York, the Cleveland WCTU, and the Pittsburgh Girl with her bustle and five dozen buttons from the base of her blouse to her chin began to distrust its lusty unguent. The new woman seemed to call out for something more wholesome, something more elegant, more refined, *whiter*. Snowdrop was as white as any imagined future.

Clare had always sold a variety of generic soaps to a number of special niches. Men, women, the well-off, and the less-well-off—all called for unique types and grades. But Douglas did not see how one company could label and promote two such inimical household soaps. His company's name was bound up in the name Native Balm, not the name Snowdrop. How could they go on preaching the gospel of brown magic, while at the same time belying it with white?

Hy Nagel—who already had whole Snowdrop Purity campaigns worked out in his head—set Douglas straight. The company's mark could inscribe all manner of disparate brands. The nation was changing, diversifying, fattening out from desperate to luxurious. Clare meant affordable quality, and quality came in endless flavors. Native plant extract and stainless white froth were but two.

But what of sales? the fiscal-minded Douglas wanted to know. Did Clare really want to risk driving its most famous trademark out of business?

Here was the question that Peter Clare had been waiting for his whole corporate life. He laid it out for the rest of the board in the simplest possible terms.

Darwin had shown competition to be the engine by which species honed the various skills of existence. Competition had turned America, in the space of five generations, from homespun backwoodsman to the rival of European nations. Direct competition between brands within Clare could only serve to strengthen the firm in the most desirable manner: from the inside out.

Clare was not so omniscient as to be able to tell which brand best suited every niche. Only the customer's dollar ballot sufficed to describe the public's desires. Competition between brands would keep the whole firm honest, attuned, listening.

There was no fooling the market. One could no more protect a soap whose time had passed than one could keep one's body from aging by holding one's breath. If Native Balm were indeed vulnerable, better for it to give in to Snowdrop than to some ugly Colgate monstrosity. And Snowdrop would grow stronger by sounding out the weaknesses in Native Balm, as cheetahs grow faster when trained by the antelope.

By century's end, competitive progress had become Clare's product. Business was the best way to betterment, and betterment was the best of businesses. Almost by accident, the company discovered the rewards of philanthropy. Julia's will provided a lump sum for the seminary school where

Ben had found his first chemical assistants. The Samuel and Resolve Clare bequest helped build public hospitals from Roxbury to Hyde Park.

But Peter Clare hit upon the master stroke of beneficence while still alive. He dreamed up a way to attach the firm's name permanently to improvement. Clare College in Fair Spring, Ohio, was founded in 1889 by a man whose education was limited to a series of bedside tutors. With each passing year, Clare College's reputation for undergraduate education grew until there came a day when few people, even among those who went there, connected it with soap.

Soap was but one milepost on the unwinding road to fulfillment. Everywhere, companies extended the limits of what people could do and desire. W. R. Grace, who'd made a fortune shipping bird excrement back to New York, was buying up the defaulting Peruvian government. Herbert Dow began to turn Midland's underground sea of brine into bromides and chlorides. Coca-Cola, that "Wonderful Nerve and Brain Tonic," promised to cure diseases ranging from poor eyesight to vocal cord lesions. The Negro Gold Dust Twins were cleaning up in Chicago for their white owners.

Secret deals with the railroads allowed Standard Oil to force most of its competitors into mergers. Carnegie leveraged himself into a majority position in Homestead Steel. Two chemists in Spray, North Carolina, poured the sludge from a failed experiment into a stream, and up from the surprise bubbles of acetylene rose Union Carbide.

And in Cincinnati, weathering every economic storm, Douglas's enemy incarnate flourished. Douglas so frequently accused Procter and Gamble of industrial and intellectual theft that matters at last came to a head in a lawsuit that both parties lost: Procter lost the suit, but Clare received a settlement too small to cover its considerable legal costs.

If anyone should have sued for infringement, it was God. Harley Procter had raided the Bible to name his new baby, Psalm 45, verse eight:

All thy garments smell of myrrh, and aloes, and cassia, out of the ivory palaces, whereby they have made thee glad.

But the man who named his upstart from a stray sermon was not above advertising a cheat as a selling point. A batch stirred by accident twice as long as it should have been resulted in "the soap that floats." *Soap with too much air in it,* Douglas grumbled to anyone who would listen. Who would want to pay money for extra air?

The public did. For air was pure, and the public now bought into the pure air that the soapmakers made for them. Harley Procter hired a Yale professor of chemistry to come up with an absolutely scientific but totally meaningless measure of the uncombined alkali, carbonates, and mineral matter in Ivory: .56 percent by weight. Declaring these trace materials "foreign and unnecessary," Harley arrived at the bizarre, slightly huckstering, but decidedly scientific claim that Ivory was "99 and 44/100 percent pure."

The claim drove Clare to play its Harvard card. Employing the bogus purity scale, a Cambridge chemist and friend of Neeland's declared Snowdrop to be 99 and 51/100 percent pure. This was not a claim that even Hiram Nagel could now make. But his chemists assured him that ordinary precipitation always contained at least one percent foreign and unnecessary substances. So Hy settled for "Purer than the driven snow."

As the market for soap doubled and redoubled, smaller manufacturers dropped away. The public proved large enough for several large competitors, so long as growth let each one make every new bar of soap a little more efficiently than the last.

Soap *was* the burden of civilization, as well as its measure. It took considerable daily industrial tonnage just to break even against soil on the scale that expanding enterprise introduced. Cleanliness *had* to progress, if only to match pace with the steady progression of grime.

New soaps spilled forth to meet the country's swelling diversity. Chinese coolies blasting their way through the Rockies required the vilest tar soap. Ladies in the Four Hundred needed something that barely licked at their skin. Clare planned a new mild face soap, a yellow soap for dishwashing, a naphtha laundry cake, and a strong medicinal bar. The smaller the distinction, the more significant. Soap for everyone: salves, tonics, and squeezable metal tubes.

Its revenues now solid, the firm prepared to take its inevitable next step into young adulthood. A national firm, with national advertising, fighting national competitors, required nation-sized capital. There was but one place to secure the needed sums: America herself. In 1891, Peter, Douglas, their families, and associates took Clare public.

None of the firm's owners had the expertise to manage such a monstrous transformation. Peter consulted his younger brother, William, a fastidious and successful banker who had spurned the firm to spite his neglectful mother. With Julia long dead, William seized the opportune moment to return to the fold. The banker took the financial steps necessary to ensure an orderly conversion. And he took his own fee for the service in the form of new common stock.

Clare's initial public offering of 40,000 shares ran for five days. The coy brevity of the offer revealed the move to be little more than a first, strategic step. Despite its new junior partner, the company's structure remained unchanged. At the end of the day, the newly reformulated public corporation sported a board made up of six Clares and five close business associates. The existing partners held on to the bulk of the equity and, with it, sufficient votes to carry just about any issue.

And yet Clare now had shareholders. Slowly, over the years, their numbers swelled, each private citizen controlling an infinitesimal fraction of the whole operation. From California to Maine, many of Clare's owners would die with a certificate in their attic lockbox, never having stepped foot in a Clare factory.

———

This Certifies That
Mrs. Dorothea Rowen
is entitled to
ONE HUNDRED SHARES
of the COMMON STOCK
of the **Clare Soap and Chemical Company, Incorporated**

This certificate will not become valid until countersigned and registered by the Covenant Trust and Banking Company of Boston, Massachusetts. In Witness Whereof, the President and Secretary of said Company hereunto submit their signatures.

———

She gives thanks for being alive.

Not out loud, over the turkey and stuffing, Tim and Don's impossible handiwork. But in a silent prayer, her moves a bit rusty, she does mouth her life's unlikelihood. Thanks be for the lives of her children, for the shape of each of their lucky troubles. She even blesses the odd good moments with Don, today and in the past. She praises God for this dry and sheltering house, for the indelible album of years, now recovered and spread in front of her. She thinks some glad word for her asters and dianthus, her garden's constant change taking place even now, under the cold ground.

She gives thanks that she's found the pain livable so far. This much she can stand. She's still more or less herself. She gives thanks that she has made it to November able to sit up at the table. She gives thanks that radiation is still an option, and thanks again that the next consult is not until after this holiday.

Don says the grace, because he always used to. Because no one else will. "Thank you, Lord, for these, Your bountiful gifts, which we receive in a grateful spirit."

"And a special thanks to Butterball," Tim adds. "How'd they figure out how to make an all-white-meat bird? And how did you ever do it?" he asks Laura. "I mean, you know. In the old days. Dad says you had to, like, baste and stuff?" Talkative with nerves, his voice flecked with the first note of admiration since he turned twelve.

"Oh, it wasn't so bad. The hardest part was catching the damn things."

Tim laughs, tentatively.

Nobody quite knows what to do with this holiday anymore. Not a whole lot of talk about the escaped slave Squanto and his fish fertilizer these days. Even grade schools shy away from that first white harvest, now more suspect than celebrated. The Anglos with the buckles on their heads and the cone-shaped shotguns, a massive skeleton in the national closet. To Laura's kids, Plymouth's not even a car any longer.

They all eat until they feel like Laura on day three after a treatment. Even Laura, whose taxol regimen, thanks or no, is over. They watch a football game that none of them cares about. They play Monopoly. Tim wipes them all out and opens a high-rise public housing project on Ventnor Ave. where his three pauperized blood relations can end their days.

Except for a spate of profanity from Ellen, who drops a dish while trying to unload the dishwasher, the day goes by unblemished. And who can put up too many blemish-free days into store?

On Monday, Laura goes in for calibration. The peritoneal phosphorus, the concentrated chemo washes are no longer options. They will dose her with fallout, every day, for twenty days or until she can't take it. Whichever comes first.

The first flush of fear takes root inside her gut. All this time, she has stayed brave: through the operation, the discovery, the roller coaster of drugs, the poisons that killed her immune system and deadened her feet so she cannot walk without stumbling. Through all this, she's never once really been afraid.

Now she is. Fear rolls over her like breakers. It pins her arms to her sides and chills her forehead. She shies from it like a crazed racehorse. She can understand fear, but not this involuntary spasm. Death seems no closer than it did last week. Then it dawns on her: the involuntary, learned panic. She's terrified that twenty extended X rays will give her cancer.

The radiology team studies the scans. They set up the angles of incidence, map her body, mold the blocks, plot the rays, and focus their point of intersection with a precision Laura can't really believe. Faith, like nausea, only gets harder with repeated practice.

"Smart weapons," the radiologist tells her. The radiologist is a girl who can't be a day older than Ellen. She scribbles upon Laura's abdomen with Magic Markers. Ritual scarification. Runways and hieroglyphs, landing signs for aliens.

The prep takes longer than all the remaining treatments will. The actual first dose, her worst nightmare, is over in thirty seconds. Compared to the ordeal of the two-day drip, it seems a joke.

"That's it?" She giggles. "That's it?"

"One down." The radiologist nods. "Nineteen to go."

Laura goes home. There, Ellen and Tim surprise her with an ad hoc Advent calendar to mark her progress. Twenty doors, one already sprung. How small the entire scene is: two folds of cardboard that fit nicely on the end table by the sofa in the living room. Only nineteen little doors still to go through. Who could help but survive that?

Behind each flap the kids have pasted Instamatic snippets. The pictures poke through, taking the air like tenants on their balconies in the month's apartment block. Tim blowing a trumpet. Ellen trying to skate. Each Osco print struggles from behind its cardboard portal, blurry squares of underexposed existence wanting a way out.

The cardboard craftwork scalds her insides, worse than any rays. If any caustic can cure her, it will be this one. She will open all twenty doors, one after the other, and never look away. And by the end she will be healthy, well, clean. By the fifth little flap she is certain of it. No cancer in the world could survive such blasting.

The tenth door reveals a shot of the three of them falling down on cross-country skis. By the time she opens it, she cannot balance, even upon bare feet. The woman whose pelvis scraped against the bath's porcelain now begins to lose weight for real. Food no longer just repulses her. It becomes inconceivable. Even the canned weight-gain drinks marketed just for her will not go down.

For all she has been through, she has not felt fatigue until now. If she tries to take a shower upon awakening, it wrecks her until midafternoon. What she thought was nausea turns out to be some silly warm-up. She lies in bed, slammed back against the pillows, pinned to them as if to the wall of a Tilt-

A-Whirl. The carnival floor falls away, and she hangs, hurling in vacant space.

The nausea is many times worse than when she was pregnant with Tim. Only one creature could account for such morning sickness. She carries a baby beyond bearing. And marks out its term on her Advent calendar.

They load her with so many medications that it takes all her concentration just to manage the daily doses. Luckily for her, the pills are all different sizes and colors. She decides for herself what each one does, based on its appearance. Red stokes up and blue calms. On days when she feels okay, she worries that it might be just the drugs. Then she stops worrying, thanks to some other pill.

Dr. Archer suggests that she stick with the mental exercises. They can't hurt. Everything her doctors throw against the cancer needs the aid of her own immune system. And only attitude can boost that now, and only she can boost her attitude.

She dutifully repeats the chants and cheers from her cancer tapes, when she has the strength. She says them like a mantra at 4 a.m., to make herself fall back asleep. My whole life is still in front of me. Each breath I take makes me stronger. The phrases pop into her head at odd hours during the day, the way she used to hum to herself, *It's the Real Thing*, or *Wouldn't you really rather have a Buick?* She lips the words, long after she stops believing them. Just in case the syllables themselves might do some good, all on their own.

The night of treatment fifteen—she cannot remember what was behind that day's door—she wakes herself up, repeating in a blind frenzy, "My whole life is still in front of me." Twisting in darkness, all at once she washes up on an island of respite.

The night is traitless and without motion. She strains and can hear nothing: no traffic, no radios. Even the churn of life support, the air's constant generators and compressors falter from the standing background noise and go mute. The world has been evacuated, or her relaxation exercises have at last halted it.

She lies on the rocking tide of silence. There will be no more sleep tonight. Light, she hugs the mattress, throwing her favorite visualizations against the ceiling's theater screen. She has gotten good at them, now that she knows what she needs to see. Her colors are all true and her resolution infinite.

First she watches Ellen graduate from college. She summons up a commencement bulletin, complete with college seal. She follows Ellen to New York, to some kind of Fortune 500 office, where her job is to be manic and entertain international visitors.

Then she watches Tim, still apparently living at home, buy his high-school GED with a portion of his first million-dollar Microsoft contract. Laura herself seems to be sitting up in life's box seats, just laughing. The mere fact of her laughter surely means that she's clean. The scenes even come with their own upbeat sound track, music from who knows where. Maybe even her own composition.

She wants to make it. She's gotten into the habit of existing. She likes being here. She doesn't know what else she would do. Half of ovarian cancer patients can get cured. Half's a good number. No reason why she can't be in that half. Life is so endless, so anything. Limitless, the memories still lying in wait for her. And she knows this place where she can get a second set of prints for free.

Her fantasy shots pull back. They reformulate, resort to the movie metaphors that the how-to books recommend. Her grandfather pulling angry black stones out of his four hundred acres with a lever and sledge, leaving it clean for plowing. Her dad in the south of Belgium, chasing Nazi stormtumors out of hiding with a flamethrower. Her mom as a healthy, 1950s TV bobbysoxer, finding some spidery blob-creature growing in her garage and using the local college scientist's ray to purge it. She and Don as twenty-two-year-olds at the county fair, knocking over milk bottles marked with the letters C-A-N-C-E-R.

She drifts without effort to her favorite. Old reliable. The clip that always makes her feel that she is doing the greatest good for the war being fought inside her. It seems to apply, even now that she has gone from chemicals to irradiation.

First, her organs present themselves as rubbery pink cartoons, her hat-tip to the graphics in old school health movies: *Our Friend the Abdomen*. Somehow, this pretty, pink zinnia color gets tarnished. It grows speckled all over, like the bottom of neglected Revere Ware.

Then she releases a horde of animated rug cleaners, plaque fighters, scrubbing bubbles, those enzymes that come on like bug-eyed brushes, chasing the world's deviate growths down the kitchen drain. This crack regiment of mixed specialists goes over and over her cartoon insides, washing, tumbling, coursing through all her organs' nooks and crannies, until it leaves every internal surface with that see-yourself shine.

Behind door 20, a family celebrates. She looks and looks, but cannot say where they are. It seems to be a holiday, but not one that she has ever lived through. But she is there, happy, with her children wrapped in colored streamers. By the time she opens that last countdown marker, her body has become a little Nagasaki. Her skin is a field of second-degree flash burns. She cannot brush her teeth without needing a transfusion. She sleeps on the living-room sofa bed, the stairs impossible.

She lets Don do everything now. Anything he wants. She lets him drive her to the hospital.

"What happens now?" she asks Dr. Archer.

"What?"

"Now? What happens?"

Now more tests. Now another CA-125 level check. Now she must down a chalk milkshake wider than her throat. Must swill barium until she is floating on it. Lie still for another CAT scan.

"Rest up," the doctors say. Rest up, and we'll see where we are.

She cannot read them. Their words don't seem to follow. Then she realizes what they are saying. They have no more weapons to offer her. And still, in the face of this news that is no news, she wants to stay thankful and live.

———

Clare came late to electricity. It had only just gotten onto gas, so vested was it in the goods that gas displaced. Peter thought electricity as unreliable as drunken immigrant labor. Douglas pushed for it: the most powerful creature yet to issue from the hand of man. Peter conceded the beast's magnificence, while insisting that you don't use a crazed rodeo bronco to pull a plow.

When the Edison Company for Isolated Lighting electrified a block of New York, Douglas watched, enrapt. When Edison offered private power stations to all takers, Douglas wanted to sign. Peter predicted imminent disaster and asked for a moratorium.

One by one, the firms went into the light. McCormick, Marshall Field, National Tube. If disaster awaited, it was far enough down the line so that no large firm could afford to consider it. At last, Peter surrendered to the inevitability that scientific progress had become. Less than a decade after Morgan threw the switch baptizing commercial light, Walpole blazed into its own, self-contained artificial day.

Electricity took its place alongside soap in the health craze. People took current for relaxation. Large numbers shocked themselves religiously. The jolts charged recipients with scientific-spiritual energies.

The health benefits of electricity did intrigue Peter. He had taken every other cure known to medicine, for half a dozen diseases that medicine never quite succeeded in identifying. The idea of a disembodied life force played upon him. Could Clare somehow combine electricity with soap into a single product, one that would unite the two great purifying agents of the day? Peter set Neeland upon the task. The idea was too far ahead of its time to be realized.

But Neeland, inspired by electricity, leaped by analogy upon his last great contribution to the company. Somehow, he hit upon one of those uncanny inventions, the kind that anticipates another thing that does not yet exist. He toyed with a mix of tallow and rosin, satisfactory even in the hardest waters. He shaved and ground this soap, passed it through electric sparks, and gusted it in towers of hot air. After much experimentation, he hit upon a powdered soap that had no earthly use except to create new uses.

For Neeland's fast-dissolving granulated soap cleared the way for better mechanical washing machines. In their turn, the new machines made it possible for Clare to market whole new lines of powdered laundry soaps, soaps that beat back surges by Fels-Naphtha and other competitors whom electricity caught napping.

Neeland died shortly after this last innovation, a death hastened by his habit of tasting his experimental samples. Within two decades, the washing machine had become a totally electric proposition. Peter's dream of the union of electrons and lather came true, in a form he could never have imagined. But neither Peter nor Neeland lived to see their occult fantasy become an absolute necessity, the bedrock of modern existence, unless from their vantage point beyond the grave.

———

IT IS NOT A MECHANICAL LUXURY BUT A **HOUSEHOLD NECESSITY** • *Blue Monday a thing of the past*	THE NEW IMPROVED WESTERN WASHER • Made by the Vandergrift Mfg Co., Jamestown, New York	SOLD ON ITS MERITS **ANYONE CAN DO WASHING NOW** • *Sighs and Groans Turned into smiles*

———

Clare Soap and Chemical Company turned out in force for the fair of '93. In that year, Chicago, the Republic's wonder of the interior, hosted the World's Columbian Exposition, the greatest single feat of engineering and the most spectacular trade show in the world.

The rail hub by the lake, Clare's western headquarters, had risen from the ashes of its fire and taken up the gauntlet of the future. Now it challenged itself with the task of receiving the civilized world. An army of conscripts and a fleet of construction engines turned seven hundred swampy acres near the immigrant-infested South Side into a glittering metropolis. And for the space of a few months, the White City gave visitors from all nations a glimpse of that Beaux Arts heaven that awaited the industrializing earth.

During its brief run, the Exposition held almost thirty million visitors spellbound. A number close to half the population of the United States came out to gaze upon the fairyland and be transformed. The finger of endeavor reached down and animated the morasses, changing them into shimmering lagoons, bright terraces, and beauteous basins. At night, the glow of a hundred thousand electric bulbs bewitched the grounds.

And on the artificial shores, monuments erupted in a panorama of exuberance. Louis Sullivan offered to turn the Exposition into a showcase for the next century. But his designs were slighted in favor of a more princely civic vision. Magnificently fake Paris Opéras, mocked up from wood and burlap, sported effulgent plaster façades more dazzling than the marble they imitated. The whole formed a vista of snow-driven white.

"Not matter, but mind," the fair's slogan proclaimed. "Not things, but men."

A model of St. Peter's, a monster peristyle, an "Electric Scenic Theater," an ice railway, the halls of Electricity, Machinery, Agriculture, and Transportation, paint shops and log cabins, stables for private motor vehicles, a loggers' camp, grain silos, sawmills, windmills, stills, mines, Izaak Walton's house, the transplanted ruins of Yucatán—all came together in an ordered and stately frenzy, celebrating every ability known to collective man and predicting those countless skills yet to be learned.

The buildings culminated in the great Hall of Manufactures and Liberal Arts, a tenth the size of the fair itself, the largest footprint of its kind ever built. Here Clare's displays resided, among a boundless ocean of other exhibitors. The thousand displaying institutions included every famous name of the day. Diamond Match attended, and Merck, Van Houten, and Vanderbilt. Armour came over from just down the road, where it used every bit of its animals but the squeal and was even more efficient with its workers. All the

Railroads and Oils showed up, as did Smith Corning, Cunard, Crane, Libbey Glass, Westinghouse, the Rolling Chair Company, the U.S. Wind Engine and Pipe Company, even the U.S. government, still a relatively small operation.

Here, in Chicago, four hundred years after Columbus's landfall, America could see itself for what it truly was: less a nation than a collective outfit for the capitalization and development of its endless hinterlands. The fair's numerous and luminary speakers exhorted the Captains of Industry to use the power of manufacture for the uplift of all nations and the betterment of the human race.

The attending partner companies did not neglect to erect a simulated "Workingman's Home" for the thirty million visitors to examine close at hand. Labor's cabin came across as nothing less than a capitalist pavilion in the bud.

Sitting Bull's camp, too, had been taken apart stick by stick and reassembled near the entrance to the Midway, on Fifty-ninth Street, alongside the Brazilian Music Hall and the Ostrich Farm. The fair found someone to play Sitting Bull, killed three years before while resisting arrest. Buffalo Bill's Wild West Show, where Sitting Bull had until recently played himself, lay encamped to the south, between Sixty-second and the elevated railroad.

Ziegfeld's musical attractions opened for Frederick Turner's lecture on the American frontier. Scott Joplin led a band and Frederick Douglass turned away from the White City in rage to write his last great speech, *The Lesson of the Hour*. Sandow the Strong Man presented his muscles for public palpation by members of both sexes. On the Midway Plaisance, Little Egypt gained world renown for a hootchy-kootchy that she never actually danced. The movable sidewalk down the pier was a mass, smash hit. The Norwegians sent a Viking ship, Krupp previewed its most impressive new guns, and the engineer George Washington Gale Ferris debuted his 250-foot power-driven wheel.

The World's Columbian Exposition assembled in one place all the inconceivable astonishment of the industrial age. It made visible the mighty conversion of matter worked by mechanization's torrent, and rendered undeniable all the blessings unleashed by the ingenious genie over the space of three generations. It compiled an anthology of those inventions that had cracked open the globe's buried wealth: steam, electricity, telegraph, telephone, chemistry, internal combustion, dynamo: and surpassing them all, the limited-liability corporation.

Those who visited the fair had that one-time chance to walk around in the belly of a magical landscape. In one afternoon, they could witness, up close, all the elements of life that had passed away and those that would replace them. Here, in one concentrated spot, blazed forth all the wonders of consolidated wealth. The ivory Mecca's blinding white skyline proclaimed the extent of the recent strong change, while announcing all the overhauls still in store.

Henry Adams calculated that the fair's inventions, on their current curve of progress, offered "infinite costless energy within a generation." Adams came to Chicago looking to complete a lifetime's education. There he found that

> the inconceivable scenic display consisted in its being there at all—more surprising, as it was, than anything else on the continent, Niagara Falls, the Yellowstone Geysers, and the whole railway system thrown in . . .
>
> Education ran riot at Chicago, at least for retarded minds which had never faced in concrete form so many matters of which they were ignorant. Men who knew nothing whatever—who had never run a steam-engine, the simplest of forces—who had never put their hands on a lever—had never touched an electric battery—never talked through a telephone, and had not the shadow of a notion what amount of force was meant by a *watt* or an *ampère* or an *erg*, or any other term of measurement introduced within a hundred years—had no choice but to sit down on the steps and brood as they had never brooded . . . [P]robably this was the first time since historians existed, that any of them had sat down helpless before a mechanical sequence . . .
>
> Chicago asked in 1893 for the first time the question whether the American people knew where they were driving . . .
>
> Once admitted that the machine must be efficient, society might dispute in what social interest it should be run, but in any case it must work concentration.

All came to visit, for even those who did not travel to the fair were still its guests. One could see the festoons and garlands from one hundred and fifty miles downstate, in a little town whose principal growth industry had until recently been the retirement and death of farmers.

In the few short years before the World's Columbian Exposition, Lacewood had graduated from a tenuous camp on the land's unforgiving crust to a permanent settlement. Just the tiniest edge of surplus, the smallest compounding of wealth made it possible to put a little something away, to hang prints on the walls, to listen to music at the end of the day, even to make music yourself.

Clare's fertilizer factory had changed the very nature of the town's existence. Lacewood was now only two days from anywhere. Of course, two days had grown proportionately more valuable, not to be squandered, now that one's time could earn something. But Chicago itself lay only a cheap day trip away.

Lacewood came up to the Exposition, all of Lacewood. Damning the expenses, Clare plant workers spent their priceless day off looking upon what no worker had ever looked upon. They freighted their way through the rehabilitated prairies. They stepped off the platform at the specially built terminal that managed a continuous flow of tens of thousands. And they gazed out at the electric Columbian Fountains, where, in one blink, they saw their future.

While strolling the esplanades, finding their way with their indexed Rand McNally courtesy map, naturally they stopped to visit the mother company. Clare's Exposition theme, drawn up in an act of collective genius by Nagel's creative office, had soap tying together the diverse and meliorating world. Soap lay at the heart of this dizzying advancement. Soap in all its incarnations—secret earth medicine, molten productivity, recaptured pureness, evolution's highest testament—typified the best of what human effort had to offer.

So obvious was this theme that it almost did not need to be sold. Soap's theme was the theme of the Exposition itself. What was the White City but urban, collective man scrubbed clean and prepared for the coming banquet? Commerce itself crystallized around the very point. The virtues of cleanliness *were* the virtues of productivity. One did not arrive without the other. The world could unite in this insight. From the Javanese Settlement to the Indian School, from the Bedouin encampment to the Soda Pavilion, good business made good neighbors.

This message, this moment, belonged to the children of Columbus. Such, too, was Clare's implicit copy. Even mighty Pears, "a potent factor in brightening the dark corners of the earth as civilization advances," whose cakes were "the first step towards lightening the White Man's Burden," laid down that burden at the White City and asked the U.S. soap syndicates to pick up the torch.

Britain, from its lovely but modest pavilion by the North Pier, saluted its giant progeny across the Government Plaza, blessing it in this rite of passage. Clear to everyone, this spectacular assemblage of fake Beaux Arts buildings formed a great world capital calling out for an empire. America had her eye on economies of scale. Fruit, minerals, spices, tea, rubber, guano: a growing appetite for raw goods had left her chafing at her borders, snatching up those islands that the Wilkes expedition had charted for this very reason, a half century before. And even sooner than Imperial Chicago would have predicted, Illinois boys found themselves fighting Filipino guerrillas and opening China's commercial door by force of arms.

Clare's Exposition booths seemed remarkably cozy, given the size to which the whole had grown. They shed the showman's hoopla of Philadelphia and concentrated on more chemical and mechanical engineering than all but a few intrepid visitors could fathom. But in between the scale vats and dryers, they pasted up the noble "Measure of Civilization" series of placards. Each image marked off, in remarkably congruent yardstick ticks, the paired advances of sanitation and prosperity.

Small black-and-white reproductions of these posters, with their careful admonition coupled with prophetic uplift, rapidly became collector's items. Their appeal spread as deep as their reassurance: the promise of a modicum of well-being for anyone who stayed the material course and washed frequently.

That sweeping Columbian guarantee convinced everyone but Nagel, the Clares, and the bulk of their company managers. For the enchantment of Chicago could not have come at a less auspicious hour. The Exposition played out in the middle of yet another desperate depression: the most desperate yet, to those caught in it. Twenty blocks to the west of the White City, the ring of smokestacks coughing up dense columns of coal sludge were once again blinking out.

Even deeper troubles lapped at the pillars. The fair commemorated that moment when the industrial system seemed either about to transport the globe into a new Canaan or about to plunge all society over the brink. The gleam of capital, on alternate days, either hinted at marvels still to come or marked the high-water line of a spent flood.

Underneath the encrusted plaster, Chicago's celebrated promise of entrepreneurship bordered upon a bitter joke. No new start-up could take root where a corporate tree already held sway, and corporations had long since cornered every essential tract of sunlit ground. The small businesses that remained already seemed curios of another age. Cash flowed like interstellar dust falling into gravitational masses. It streamed into ever-larger, more unappeasable monopolies, trusts, and syndicates. "The day of combination is here to stay," Rockefeller proclaimed. "Individualism is gone, never to return."

For a long time, the nation's hired hands had remained mostly willing to pay the price of combination. Whatever the penalty, the vast gains in economy and efficiency poured back their blessings in real weight. Wealth's tapped wellsprings led many to expect that work conditions would steadily improve until the factory became a well-appointed health spa.

But now those who hauled the yoke of incorporation began to feel the mechanical servitude that awaited humanity. The bargain no longer seemed acceptable, let alone winnable. Seven years before the fair, labor threatened to pull the whole house of cards down around its own ears. The year before,

Homestead had run with blood: open war between the Pinkertons and anarchists. And discontent had only begun to spread.

Armies of the industrial unemployed descended upon Washington to vote their boots. Strikes across the nation demanded an end to big business's sanctioned system of theft. Pullman, once the idol of labor for his paternal and enlightened workers' village, now charged his workers more for rent than he paid them. When the inevitable uprising came, only U.S. troops, sent to Chicago over the objection of the state governor, saved the Pullman company from the wrath of its incorporated parts.

The fair's brief moment of intoxication awoke in hangover. One by one, the soaring Classical façades crumbled, their plaster-cast cornices returning to chalk and burlap. Fire destroyed much of what remained. Of the entire mock cityscape, only one exhibit building survived to see the new century. During the Great Depression, the city rebuilt the Palace of Fine Arts in limestone to house the Museum of Science and Industry. The enormous temple of technology lay just two miles from Clare's own futuristic Chicago processing plant, which finally moved offshore, to Indonesia, in 1987.

———

W ★ O ★ R ★ L ★ D ★ ' S   F ★ A ★ I ★ R

★

NIGHT PAGEANT

★   ★   ★

GRAND TABLEAUX AND FLOATS

★   ★   ★

GRAND COLUMBIAN CARNIVAL

★   ★   ★

THE WORLD UNITED AT CHICAGO

★   ★   ★

GRAND REUNION OF THE STATES BY YOUTHS AND MAIDENS

★   ★   ★

MONSTER CONCERT • GRAND CHORUS

★   ★   ★

MOST GORGEOUS DISPLAY OF FIREWORKS EVER SEEN IN AMERICA

★   ★   ★

Forming in its entirety the most
Significant and Grandest Spectacle of Modern Times

★

The lake out front is weirdly free of ice. Glaciers lock the whole town in permafrost, except for the damn landscaped puddle in front of Clare.

The thing never freezes. In all the years he's lived here, Don has never once seen so much as a wafer crust the surface. A classic joke around town. The kids at the college talk about some massive marine mammal throwing off body heat, skulking around down there in dripstone grottoes, grazing on aromatic hydrocarbons from underground sluices connected to the R and D labs. He and Laura walked down here to the waterside the night they got engaged, all giggling and silly, watching for the thing by flashlight until a squad car spotted them and shagged them off.

Years ago, he used to wonder about it. Did heat from the plant keep it clear? Proximity to all those people and machines? Some kind of thermal runoff? Flare stuff, flash powder, magnesium milk shakes—just add water. He wanted a little sprinkle of whatever it was, to keep the driveway from turning to tundra when the cold rolled down from Saskatoon around about Presidents' Day.

Every time he drove by, he'd think "exothermic," maybe the only term he remembered from college chemistry. There had to be an explanation. A town-sized tropical-fish bowl full of macabre calories. Maybe they used the lake as some kind of cheap coolant, pumped it through conduits to bathe the blistering machinery before flowing back outside, where it chilled just enough to do its sweep of waste heat all over again.

He liked to come up with different explanations, each more ingenious than the last. But nobody could tell him whether he was getting warmer or colder. At some point, he simply stopped wondering about it.

Don turns off Resolve Road and puts his car in the visitors' lot. It's all the way out by the lower-echelon, assembly-line parking. He walks alongside an inlet toward the main entrance, disconcerted all over again. How could anything liquid *not* freeze, in a week like this? Forty degrees below zero, counting windchill. Where's global warming when you need it?

His index finger froze to the lock while opening the car door this morning. He has to breathe through a paper napkin while hustling from G-13-Yellow to the Barnard Building, to keep icicles from forming in his bronchioles. The radio aired a piece last night, about a retired assembly line worker found dead in his apartment. The power company had shut off his gas over a two-month delinquency. And the lake still out there, rippling, the edges lapping away like it's high June.

Just behind the lake, everything tapers and glides. Half a million square feet of buildings tumble together in what always reminds him of a group grope of grand pianos, their lids flung open in pleasure. From across the executives' lot, he looks up and sees the place the way he saw it ten years ago. It's a softened, rounded Habitat '67, that urban-renewal dream he so loved as a kid. A flurry of curves and angles, rewriting all the architectural rules.

He thinks back a few years before Ellen was born, to when Clare decided to move its entire North American Agricultural operation here. From a regional factory to a divisional headquarters, overnight. How thrilling that skyline was, in the newpaper artist's conception. Limitless promise. Little hick town, going from prairie grass to this. And still only starting out, a mere beginner in the history of future boomtowns.

The skyline still says that, from miles down Route 47: tomorrow is the best toy set people could ask for. The splashes of teal and peach all over the dwarfing entrance still feel like an invitation. Come on in; help discover the next necessary thing. Like the whole complex is a package, an ad for itself. Better Living inside.

Especially in winter, he feels like a questing cripple approaching a cathedral. Some kind of promised sanctuary, and a little warmth, enough to catch one's breath, anyway, for the long trip home. He tries not to breathe at all now as he hustles past the garden parterre. Another few months and the whole sculpted hillside will be nuts with petunias. Laura's always hated that stand. Cheap and blowzy, she says. *Can you really trust anyplace that would plant that many petunias?* No, he decides, belatedly. No, you cannot.

Ropes click against the four flagpole stands. The clicks echo dull and cold enough to snap the fibers clean or crack the pole. Four canvas flags whip back and forth, as brittle and harsh as interplanetary space. The Stars and Stripes flaps in position one. It strikes Don as a bit of handy nostalgia. How transnationals love to play the citizenship card whenever they're looking for a protective break. But Clare is just like elites everywhere: the company keeps so many residences that it has no fixed place of abode.

On the second pole, Illinois's eagle nibbles on a red tapeworm streamer. Don only places the thing because the college flies it, too. But the banner next to that is much more recognizable and sovereign. He's known it since childhood. Like Betty Crocker, though, the company logo has had a halfdozen face-lifts over the years, various plastic surgeries to keep it looking newer than next week. Get tomorrow's style out early: that's Marketing's trick. Longer shelf life, like those newsmagazines dated ten days after they're printed.

But the logo he grew up with still hides out in the incarnation he now hurries past. The original design persists, like the Kennedy forelock or the Hapsburg harelip. It's gotten a little simpler maybe, more spare and inevitable. But Don is suddenly struck by the continuity. The boy of forty years ago would have recognized this one. Any shopper from the thirties through the nineties: name your commercial epoch, and they'd name this image.

The funny thing is, he has never been entirely sure what the shape is. They fought about it once. Well, not fought. Laura said it was a bird lifting off. He held out for some kind of atom or molecule, the company's chemical erector set. They finally agreed that it didn't matter. The thing said *Clare*, even if it stood for nothing at all.

The fourth pole is for special interests. He's seen it fly dozens of different flags, depending on who's in town. Today, it sports a black MIA–POW standard, silhouette bowed.

Above the line of flagpoles, high-tech gear thrusts itself up as lofty as possible, looking for maximum throw range. Helicopter deck, weather station, microwave relay, satellite dish: spires lift over Lacewood like Mont-Saint-Michel over its tidal flats. They never did get to France, he and Laura. Had to settle for this.

The metaphor's right: an old castle keeping watch over its village, spires towering over a civic jumble. Two office complexes, an indoor-outdoor mall with skylit promenade, a research facility, corporate theater, and conference center. He comes out maybe once a month on some fund-raising visit or another, and he still gets lost every time.

You grow up with a divisional headquarters in your backyard, and you think everyone does. Ellen, Tim: like little French kids growing up under a medieval tower whose shadow they're never out from under. They see it on the postcards and posters. They drive past it on their way to the Best Buy. A permanent and universal fixture that they hear about daily without registering. Naturally, they assume there's one of these in everyone's hometown.

He makes it inside just before he has to eat the ponies. He stands in the foyer, waiting for his frostbitten skin to revive. He kicks the snow from his shoes and loosens his coat. He has stepped from Siberia into a developer's dream of Tahiti.

Light flows everywhere. Day rebounds and ricochets, levered all over the place by louvers and polished metal surfaces. Even the sculptures and paintings pick up the brightness and distribute it free into all corners. In blocked spots, hidden sconces fill in. He's never noticed before how clever this cheer is. Ten times better and brighter than the real thing.

He passes through the range of foyers into the main terrarium. From canopy to floor, one tiered rain forest envelops the other. Whole communities of flora and fauna regulate their own heat and humidity, building up micro-climates with the aid of tunable superwindows. He looks up, four open flights, at the famous clerestory, with its double-glazed glass that darkens in the summer and lightens in winter to yield net gains in energy. Three glass elevators sweep up and down the walls, over his head. He's read somewhere that even their motor heat is recovered and put to useful work.

Living rivulets gurgle down the mossy wall faces and collect in refreshing oases. The handrail of a slinky ziggurat stairwell doubles as a stream bed, irrigating the gardens on each landing. Six flights of gently descending basins. The flowing rapids shock and delight him every time. And he's not alone today. A visiting delegation in black and gray power suits stop in mid-landing, set down their attachés, and splash about in the handrail current up to their wrists.

The babble of liquid calms Don. He finds himself shaking, and not from the cold. Best thing to do is make a beeline for the security desk, the check-point he will need to pass. He sets across the floor at a good clip. That genial, deserving expression comes over his face, the one he has made a career out of. Outward, appreciative, approving, privileged, at peace with the system: And how are *you*?

He checks in at Reception, all recessed brass and simulated cherry wood. He chooses the youngest female behind the wraparound island. "I'm here to see Deborah Pierson," he announces. Timing's a little off, a little too clipped and eager. "Public Relations."

The receptionist looks up, appraising him. He is a graceless wad of scarf and acrylic.

"Is she expecting you?"

"Yep." Trying for polite impatience.

"Your name?"

He coughs and tells her. She pulls out the ledger that lists all of today's visitors. "Bodey? B-O-D?"

He begins to regret the whole scheme.

"I'll have to call her," the woman says.

"It's extension 1737."

"Yes, sir. I've got it right here." A second later, she's saying, "This is Reception. There's a Mr. Bodey here to see you?" Another, very long second. "He says you're expecting him."

The receptionist disconnects, with that look of bored skepticism that will prove a precious professional asset for years to come. "You know how to reach the Public Relations suite?"

"Oh yes." Don grins.

"Shall I put you down for a vehicle?" She points toward the fleet of reconditioned golf carts in a corral to her left.

"I'll walk."

"Are you sure, sir? It's quite a hike."

"Thanks," he says, rubbing his midriff. "I need the workout."

He hightails it out of the main atrium before she has second thoughts and calls Building Security. West Three: he finds the right corridor anyway. He threads his way through a group of milling fourth graders on their way into the futuristic, cantilevered theater. The kids buzz in a state of high excitement, thrilled with those misconceptions still available to the very young. They love it here; the most excitement they've had since the sanitation plant outing. Some of them look ready to take a job interview.

He skirts the boardroom, a glass fishbowl secured with a checkpoint all its own. It's always struck him that the architects didn't tuck the room away in an aerie in the South Tower. A pretense at revealing the invisible wheels, bringing it all down to the small investor's level. Or maybe just the opposite: a better display of power down here.

The curtains are flung wide open this afternoon. Baring their open palms, weaponless. He slows down as he passes, as slow as he can go without arousing further suspicion. He needs a look. If there are humans at the helm, this is where they steer. As close as he's going to come to Them.

It's a great big empty room, as far as he can make out. A gaslit, Main Street feel, circa 1904. In the middle of the room is the largest table he has ever seen. A deep red mahogany, inscribed with fabulous filigrees and inlays. It looks as if it once belonged to some handlebar-mustached stock manipulator. Around this massive circle, two dozen deeply upholstered chairs. One for each of Shangri-La's caretakers. Sit down in one of those babies, and you're not going to want to get up anytime soon.

One bomb, it occurs to him. One little envelope of plastic explosive slipped into a portfolio while court was in session. The anarchist's dream: fifteen feet away from being able to change things forever. Then the imaginary dust settles, and it dawns on him. The board? The board's not even close to ground zero. Nor is the CEO's office, or the CFO's, or the majority stockholder's, or any other target that Don will ever be allowed to walk past.

How little you'd take out with one erasure, even here. Even if you synchronized the detonations and managed to bring down the whole multibuilding installation. One department, one division . . . One company, for that matter. What difference would it make? A little red ink, a local depreciation, while real commerce went on ebbing and flowing, out there, scattered, pressed thin past finding, in the shape that shared life has taken.

Real business doesn't care diddly for its regional agents. Doesn't give a squat for setback or inconvenience. Blast craters are good for it; healthy, like fires in Yellowstone. Just so long as people want what it does. Just so long as we have no real alternative. The truth of the matter is: there is no ground zero. Nothing an anarchist could ever hit, even in imagination.

He pushes on, down through the miles of maintenance-free paint. Deb's office seems way farther away from the entrance than you'd want, for someone in her line. She's explained it to him: how Public Relations is not just for front lobbies anymore. A strategy for everything, and for every strategy, its floor plan.

A fifty-foot window in one wall of the hallway opens up a view on one of the coves of production. Another strategy, Don figures. Keep the works up front and visible, so management doesn't lose touch and labor will want to step lively. He looks down two flights onto the floor of what doesn't seem anything remotely like a factory. Pastel earth tones, full of linen-textured castings to baffle the noise and cheer the equipment operators.

It's positively pleasant down there. Reminds him of a jaunty discount electronics boutique in the middle of a year-end sale. Equipment, sure; tangles of pipe and snarls of cable. Hard to tell where the supplies go in and the product comes out. But the space is agreeable, human, like the rec room in some industrious senior citizens' home.

Robots hum and whir on their mobile platforms. They whip busily about between their human allies, assisting and asking assistance. Together, the hive executes each step in the expert assembly. Don flirts with a world where robots got cancer. Wonders whether the machines would stage a wildcat walkout.

Every one of those suckers down there, their abdomens accumulating daily doses whose effects no one knows for sure or will admit if they do. But what choice do any of them have? It's rust or burn, for most of them. You're going to die anyway. Just a question of choosing what speed.

Don stands in the gallery window, shamed at his idiocy. Did he think he could see the leak from here? Some liquid spill back in the corner that he could photograph for evidence? He watches the steady activity, tons more interesting than any televised sport. The hum of a hundred people, helping to ensure the national harvest. Couldn't go back now, if we wanted to. And who wants to? No getting along without the magic additives, the super-pesticides. Especially now that we've bred a race of super-pests with them.

"Don," the sexiest voice short of commercial television calls from down the hall. Deb, come to meet him halfway. Flustered, trying to head him off. He's always wondered what this woman looks like, on days when she's not expecting visitors. But then, there are no such days. She's hosted a dozen visitors already since lunch. He's lucky, really, to find her with five minutes free. To find her at all.

He pushes back his hair and turns in one smooth motion. "Ms. Pierson. Thanks for meeting—"

"Bodey. What the hell are you doing here?" Out of the side of her mouth, mock-clandestine, but just a little flushed, and he knows he's gotten away with this.

"I don't know, Deb. Seems to me you left a pretty open invitation last time."

"Creep. That was for out-of-office hours. Ho-hum. Some women are born to be noticed only for their professional charms."

"Actually, Deb. You look stunning. Like a million bucks. And I'm talking 1970 dollars."

"Sure, sure. I can see you drooling all over your lapels."

She is, in fact, one of the most oddly attractive forty-year-olds he knows. And it only increases her attraction, that she seems genuinely not to believe it.

"Look at all your gear," she gripes, pulling at his coat. "You're lucky you have *ears* left."

"Neither rain nor hail nor sleet." He shrugs.

"So, buster. In whose name are you fleecing us this time?"

Twice divorced. Inconceivable to him. Maybe we've gotten to the point where divorce no longer needs a reason. The woman is incredibly fun, upbeat, imperturbable; a light touch, perfect timing. On business hours, anyway. But then, Laura always came off pretty good at Millennium, too. Her clients were always telling him what a lucky guy he was.

Deb walks him the rest of the way back to her office, through the customary cubbies and cubicles of Organizational Man. But even here, the layout is more airy than usual. Communal space is almost rashly generous. No desk is more than six yards from a window. And for every three networked computers, there is still a wing chair and a table for chance gatherings. More an irrepressible clubhouse than continental nerve center.

"I want to pitch the new library fund, Deb. This is really the perfect thing for Clare to be in on. Very visible. Research equals breakthroughs equals unbeatable return on investment. Everything you stand for. Exactly the folks you want to impress. I've brought you the new materials that we've just printed up."

"Don." A little shyly. It goes right through him. "Don. You could have mailed these, you know." She looks at him wide-eyed. "You came all the way out here, in zillion-below weather, without calling, to give me . . . ?"

"Figured I might try my luck."

All he can do is play the ambiguous word, and hope for the best. He's worked with six or seven people at Clare over the years. She's the best they have. And not just because of this—what?—chemistry between them. She's just good. She knows people. She likes them. Knows how to make them like her, without laboring it. Always welcoming. A good, professional flirt. Perfect Business Casual.

"Luck?" She smiles. "Gimme those. These I will pass on to the higher authorities. I'll be sure to put in a good word for you, and fail to make any mention of surprise attacks. Meanwhile, can I buy you a drink?"

"What do you got?"

She smiles. "Let's see. Nutrifruit kiwi–Concord grape. Nutrifruit melon-mango. Nutrifruit . . ."

"Can I ask you something? How come everything has to come in twos? I mean, isn't one flavor by itself good enough anymore?"

"Throwback," she taunts him. "Reactionary."

She gets them both bottles, plasticized glass wrapped in a thin jacket of plasticized foam. Single slam-back servings. Certainly the package costs more than the contents. The lid pops out when opened, so you can see if the thing's been tampered with since shipment.

She opens hers and starts to play the popped dimple like a castanet. "So are you still seeing that jailbait? Toni?"

"Terri. Actually . . . Well, it's a long story."

"Good. We love long stories. Especially with sequels."

It always amazes him, how much gets talked about in public, in places this size. "How much time do you have, Ms. Pierson?"

She bats her eyes. "Why do you ask?"

He slugs at the melon-mango. "Well. You guys are probably hopping these days. Must be totally nuts."

"What? Oh. You mean that lawsuit stuff?" A little wave of the hand, like she's trying to remember what she's read about it. She's better than good. She's presidential.

But he is no slacker either. He started in Development before this woman had even heard of a master's in human behavior.

"Yeah," Don adds. "I've been thinking about you, every time I see one of these stories. I hope none of this is coming down on your desk?"

"Not really."

And in a syllable, everything changes. She misses no beat. Just as funny, just as warm, just as welcoming. But it's like a little layer of friendly gauze has come down between them.

"I'm not really current with it, yet. There are two different things going, right? A class action, and a, a . . ."

"Civil," he supplies.

Unbelievable. They've worked together for over three years. She's paid out tens of thousands of dollars for his various college drives. She's flirted outrageously with him. Even bad-mouthed the company, indirectly, after hours. Don and Deb. Two people who like each other as much as you can like each other and still work together.

It's not like she's desperate for this job. She's told him how often she gets head-hunted, even about flying up to Minneapolis to scope an offer she turned down. She can't possibly feel loyalty toward this blob, this amorphous jellyfish of fifty thousand people who don't care if she lives or dies. She can't possibly *like* that Nutrifruit shit.

But it's not even a contest. It's over before he can even ask her to make a choice between Clare and him. Over, and the amorphous blob has won.

"I sure hope there's nothing in it," she says, earnest.

"Me too."

"And I hope those people get better," she adds, her eyes moist around the rims.

They exchange a half-dozen more idle topics: kids' snaps, plans for Christmas. To get the timing right. To pretend that nothing just happened.

"I'll get that material to the right people," she says, handing him what might as well be his hat. "I'm sure we'll be there for this library. Those plans look awfully pretty, Don."

He finds himself standing inside the double doors, the last barrier between himself and Midwest bitterness. He wraps his coat back around him and prepares for a race to the car through air that is now both forty below and midnight at 4 p.m.

He arranges his scarf to cover as much skin as possible. As he fastens his coat buckles—last year's stupid fashion—his glance plays over the dedication plaque. Right there at eye level, in front of him, eternally unread except by accident. The site's christening slab lists the architects. It sucks up to the company president, proclaims the date and circumstances of the dedication as if the place were the damn Capitol, and sends all pilgrims back out into the pitch-black vacuum by quoting Churchill: *We shape our buildings. Thereafter they shape us.*

———

A Message from Clare North American Agricultural Products Division
CLARE INTERNATIONAL

December 17
For Immediate Release

Recent and somewhat misleading media coverage of the Environmental Protection Agency's annual Toxic Release Inventory has generated concern in those communities near Clare's three downstate Illinois agricultural chemical facilities. While public concern over health is never unreasonable, we would like to take a moment to address these concerns and to reassure the residents living near our plants of their complete and unqualified safety.

In order to understand fully the EPA's routine inventory figures, one first needs to look in greater detail at the government-directed reporting procedures. Manufacturers are required by law to supply the EPA with information about a wide variety of substances, including some that have never been proved unsafe in any clinical trial. The inventory itself makes no statement about any risks posed to health by these substances.

Concerned residents should conclude from this annual report that Clare is once again well *within* the stringent limits imposed by both state and national regulations. Some chemical emission is an unavoidable by-product of any vigorous and viable economic activity conducted on so large a scale. The important factor to consider is not the existence of a trace substance but rather its concentration. The levels of hazardous material coming from Clare's plants are negligible and pose no significant risk to anyone living in the vicinity.

We welcome the added safety that a system of government review can supply. But our own internal guidelines are even more stringent than those required by law. Our team of scientists and chemical engineers constantly monitors flue output at all three area plants. Monthly levels of emissions at these sites have not changed for the last four years. Regular samplings of both water and soil reveal no concentrations of either toxic or carcinogenic substances that merit concern.

Misunderstanding over the EPA results has resulted in inappropriate alarm in some quarters. In particular, suggestions of systematic health problems among our workers are unfounded. We are not aware of a single worker who has been exposed to a dangerous chemical or who has suffered adverse health effects as a result of such on-the-job exposure.

We at Clare remain as committed as ever to a safe and healthy environment, both for our own workers and for those with whom we share this region. We will strive to work closely with the area's news sources to ensure a complete and accurate understanding of the impact of our operations here.

We deeply appreciate the support and appreciation that the people of the Sawgak Valley have always shown us, and we will continue to do everything possible to remain a valued and respectful neighbor.

———

Lucky it had been, and it had lived right. But not even Clare could dodge the same bullet forever.

For half a century, the economy had pitched and yawed between boom and bust. Oversteering had become a standing feaure of American capitalism. Three generations of Clares weathered half a dozen such cycles. And every time through the millrace, they watched their competition make the same mistake.

A rival factory, failing to keep up with orders, would go in hock to build a machine base that quickly flooded the public in goods. With the market glutted, the bosses would start laying off workers. Unemployment crept up and disposable income vanished. At this point, the bank that had extended all the initial expansion loans would panic. The creditors would harry the plant into failing. All the shiny new machinery then went to ruin, bringing down another chunk of economic activity with it. Recovery took years.

Panics and depressions grew so frequent that bad times now outnumbered good. Advancement seemed a matter of eternal contraction and collapse. Industry began to resemble those cities situated in an earthquake zone, constantly rebuilding from their own rubble. Throughout the century, the business failure rate topped the three-quarters mark. Even in good times, death was more likely than survival.

Every cataclysm, every descent into wholesale misery produced its economic theory. Boom and bust were self-correcting cycles. Massive layoffs and the collapse of industrial production were but inefficiencies weeding themselves out by trial and error. Its ponderous boom coming about, each tack of the full-sail system unavoidably knocked some unseaworthy soul into the deep.

While the world went to Chicago to gaze on its future, across the entire continent the present rose up visible. Strikes set off others. The victims of competition demanded redress, with all the violence that competition had taught them.

For a precarious moment, all society hung in the balance. Chicago's answer—the reaffirmed American system—was to stay the course. There were four thousand millionaires now, in contrast to the fifteen when Ennis had taught the Clares how to make soap. Did that not mean the odds of breaking into privilege had vastly improved?

No matter that one in five lived without means and that the top one percent controlled more assets than the bottom 99. Forced to pick between liberty and equality, the market had no choice. Production was already a sealed contract, the factory a foregone contest. Wealth's job was to make more of the same, let the chips fall where they may. The best people could do was get out of machinery's way. No turning back now, short of a second flood. But year by year, that flood drew closer to its return engagement.

The race went to the fit, the fitness of those who survived. Clare pulled through '37 and '57 and '73 and the other panics partly on dumb, industrious luck. A Yankee skinflint temperament kept the Clares from getting caught with somebody else's bills in their pockets. Their slow ascent unfolded with lucky timing, expanding in step with productivity. They kept down their fixed capital costs, the equivalent of carried debt. They made their product panic-proof, selling soap as an answer to recession and hawking economic recovery as the proper reply to good hygiene. Not all could afford riches yet, but everyone could be clean.

Mostly, they had learned how to make more for less. Advances in production made up for retreats in economic confidence. Soapmaking had changed beyond recognition, boosted to unbelievable yields on the shoulders of its forebears. Cadres of mechanized steel kettles boiled in one night what had once taken a whole month and twenty men, although it still required a kettle man tasting a finger's worth to tell when the brew was done. Each 150,000-pound charge filled fifty semi-automated frames. Steam-powered conveyors now moved the items along each step of the process, from the boiling house to the framing house to the wrapping girls and the stock-hauling boys, on out to the rail-drained shipping docks.

The lives of Clare's thousand employees had grown both lighter and darker. Work grew to fill every hour of the year. Boiling-house temperatures rose an average of fifteen degrees in as many years. The heat of the works climbed with each boost in output and power. The stench of animal fat curdled in the living cauldron, dissolving in the perpetual sea of human sweat and sticking forever to the skin of the soapmakers.

Plant mortality remained low, given the national average of one hundred industrial deaths a day. But few who worked at Clare for a year or more left with much hearing or concentration intact. Electricity, hydraulics, chemistry, and metalworking, each with its countless small improvements, combined in an environment more deafeningly hostile to life than the center of Verne's hollow earth.

While machines did steadily more of the work, there was, now, vastly more work to do. Every manufacturer of any size adopted the same mechanical advantages. In order for a company to remain competitive, wages per item had constantly to fall. Prosperity depended upon selling as much as possible for as little as possible above cost and keeping the human outlays to a pittance. Salaries fell to a forty-year low.

Douglas, who had shoveled rosin as a teen, began to make his own time and motion studies of the factory. He formed crews to compete with others. He laid out shorter paths between rack and cooler. He cut the number of steps a girl needed to fold a wrapper. He invented the "spurt." He improved and enlarged the stampers and the slabbing machines, allowing the operators to work at twice their former speed. He redesigned the rosin shovel, increasing each scoop by 7 percent.

His men took to calling him the Nigger-Driver. Most workers left after a few months. But an endless supply of stopgap labor waited to replace the discontented. It came from other restructuring industries and from farms driven into foreclosure by mechanized harvest. The draining countryside bought Clare no end of time. Douglas's move to Lacewood, one of the firm's shrewdest gambles in those years, bypassed in one swoop all the evils of unions, pay raises, and coordinated strikes.

Of the thirty thousand strikes involving several million workers in the century's last two decades, Clare suffered only six serious stoppages. The lone appearance of Peter Clare had once startled the Walpole men out of organizing. But as Peter's mysterious, nonspecific ailments became more pronounced and less treatable, he withdrew from corporate life, leaving no other figure powerful enough to scare up submission.

Those who found life hard during the fat years simply gave up hope during the lean. A few generations earlier, when one had not lived by wages, there might have been some alternative labor to stock one's table and reward one's days. But the wage system now fenced in the entire available working world.

On April 13, 1895, a bomb exploded in the old lard oil factory. The child of hopelessness who planted the device never surfaced. William Clare, that practical accountant, scoured the rolls of recently severed laborers who had worked in the building. But the lists were long and led nowhere. Douglas always blamed the bomb on some nameless, crazed anarchist, the kind that cared nothing for the consequences of his actions so long as civilized life suffered.

The blast ripped through the north soap house, wounding five and killing a twelve-year-old boy. The instant that word of the explosion reached William, he telegraphed Clare's buyer on the Chicago Board of Trade as well as agents in New York, New Orleans, St. Louis, and everywhere else that red oil was traded. Any explosion at the lard plant threatened the underground ocean of red oil in the reservoir beneath it. William moved boldly to secure a replacement stock, before world prices skyrocketed on news of the detonation.

By fluke, Clare's underground sea of red oil escaped intact. Furthermore, William's quick action led to a virtual corner on the good. Clare made more on reselling its surplus than it spent to repair the damage to its plant. As far as the books were concerned, the anarchist bombing of 1895 resulted in a tidy profit.

Profit was short-lived. Stirred on by that violence, over one hundred Walpole workers struck in mid-June of that year. The stoppage almost emptied the plant before the warring parties reached a shaky agreement. Another two-week walkout hit the Ohio factory in high summer.

Not even the highest tariffs in American history helped to stabilize the situation. A worldwide Red revolution seemed just around the end of the next breadline. The fate of the firm depended upon finding a more lasting resolution to the disenchantment of its own muscle.

Douglas proved unequal to the task. He considered the strikes incomprehensible, a moral affront. Clare had laced its works with flower gardens, bright lunchrooms, even a baseball diamond. It gave its entire force Saturday afternoon off with pay. Yet still the workers struck. They simply failed to understand that a manufactured good had to cost less to make than it sold for. It was as if labor somehow expected the waters of deliverance to flow uphill.

Solving the labor crisis fell to William, the astronomer of cash. Perfect happiness, for William Clare, required only that the day have thirty hours. William was forever at war with the rest of the firm. His job was to hold at bay their various urgent requests for outlays: Nagel for advertisements, the chemists for research, Douglas for expansion, the newcomer stockholders for their dividends, and labor for more pay. William's permanent crisis was to finance a company that wanted to shoot up faster than its capital allowed. He sought a way to grow the firm without venturing too deep into the quicksand of speculative credit.

More than any previous Clare, William understood money. Money was the salt of human activity, its refrigeration. It retarded the spoilage of your day's efforts. It deferred your lien on material experience until you elected to deal with it. It moved you from consumption to accumulation. It let you stock up not just what you could eat today but a whole, long winter's worth of larder.

In his years with the company, William learned to put his fiscal knowledge into soapmaking terms: money was the great enzyme, society's zinc catalyst. It allowed any source material to be turned into the product of your choice. It was your one war chest. It let you talk about the running balance in the abstract.

Money was a theory of universal conversion. Everything was procurable by the sacrifice of x units of any other object, effort, or interval of time that you might care to sacrifice for it. The history of humanity was the history of higher and higher orders of convertibility. Barter, money, insurance, corporations: equivalence for equivalence, transfers for transfers, until all cogs turned every other in the self-replenishing whole.

William never doubted for an instant that the solution to the labor upheaval would have to come down to money.

He attacked the issue like an algebra problem, operating simultaneously on both sides of the equation. He encouraged the company's European agent to help raise immigrant interest. He subscribed to a consortium of companies whose posters in eight languages proclaimed how easy it was to find lucrative work in the booming American economy. The posters promised nothing. Nevertheless, they fed the growing frenzy of exodus from Europe. And as millions bolted for the far shore with nothing, wages in America fell proportionately.

But ultimately, William knew he had to deal with the workers' demands. The cost of retraining replacements every eight months was itself breaking the bank. William thought long on the problem. He took it apart into its basic bits. Why would these men refuse to work with the same force that had made William Clare's own ancestors rich as Croesus? Somehow labor had been split off from its results. Workers no longer believed in the ends of their own efforts. Another free hour, another twenty cents a week would do nothing to reinstate them. He had somehow to bring labor back into the fold, to sell it again on its role in the dream of expansion.

Full of method, checking his figures from every possible angle, William perfected a radical plan. He presented it to the board. The basic idea was absurdly simple, and the bookkeeping only slightly more complex. The workers had to be rejoined to the consequences of their own actions. Every adult male who worked for the firm for more than a year and who made more than five dollars a week should be allowed to participate in the company's profits.

The idea burst upon the board with the force of a second anarchist's bomb. The notion was nonsense, and worse than nonsense. It was out-and-out Red. It flew in the face of all that Clare, business, and America stood for. What kind of outfit would need to add such a ruinous cost to its books? The best way to keep the unruly workers in order was to show them the long line of hungry men waiting at the gate.

William, unruffled, took out his slide rule and calmed the board down. Profit-sharing would not increase cost but lower it. The men would only be earning a share of their own increased efficiency. By reinstating the incentive of self-interest, Clare could make labor see that the welfare of the firm was labor's own welfare. The men had to start working not for some overgrown and insensate corporation but for themselves. If the bosses paid out bonuses in proportion to increased profit, then workers would take their destinies back into their own hands and align themselves with the interests of productivity.

The company would keep its own share, of course. Profit would be split between labor and the firm in the same ratio of wages to total manufacturing and marketing costs. If better work made more dollars, there would be more for everyone all around. If not, the company would not be out anything. At last, even the most scandalized on the board saw that this was a no-lose proposition.

William expected an easier sale to the workers. But suspicion among the hourly wage earners outran all of management's objections. Profit-sharing was a ruse, a scam, a way to compromise and further enslave labor. William addressed the workers' representatives, showing how the idea was actually a bit Red around the edges. And so it was: a plan as conflicted in interests as the mother impulse of profit herself.

The workers remained wary right up until the initial disbursements. The first annual Profit Picnic took place concurrently at all Clare locations, on the new national Labor Day holiday, in 1897. Workers turned out in their weekend white. Brass bands filled park gazebos with "Columbia, the Gem of the Ocean" and "Turkey in the Straw." The company supplied the lemonade and peanuts, and Clare officials handed out the envelopes with theatrical fanfare.

Suddenly the abstraction of participatory capitalism began talking real money. Some folks made an extra dozen dollars, already nothing to sneeze at. But others pulled down hundreds: significant sums, enough of a boost to float the earner out of poverty and keep him there.

For the first few years, the bonuses were a resounding success. Profit Picnics remained enormously popular, both for the envelopes and for the social diversions that began to mark the holidays. But within half a decade, the annual premium began to seem an entitlement. The source of the payouts vanished in antiquity.

Productivity settled back down to indifferent levels, spurting up just a bit before the Labor Day fest, for ceremonial reasons. When profits fell and the sums shrank to nothing, workers complained bitterly about the loss of their money.

William hit upon a new plan to restore the sense of personal incentive. All workers were to receive annual review ratings based on performance, loyalty, seniority, and attitude. Those workers earning an A rating would receive a double dividend, B's would get a single, C's a half, and D's nothing. This system played for some years, but grew increasingly Byzantine and cumbersome.

In 1910, William launched a motivational scheme that the company continued to use, with slight variation, for the rest of its existence. The year's performance would be rewarded in company shares. These the shorter-sighted employees could sell for cash. But those who held and worked hard could watch their investment bloom in proportion to a job well done.

In this way, labor came on board more fully than ever before. Employees began to work for themselves, in every sense of the phrase. The company became theirs in a bankable manner. Profit-sharing at long last succeeded, so long as William and his successors each year made sure to dilute the shares paid out to labor with ones paid back to management.

———

. . . Finally, it must be said that uncountable men and women are better off, and generations of children will be born into a healthier world because of the work that he, in his fastidious life, managed. No man could seek more.
—*from Peter Clare's obituary in the* Boston Transcript, *1900*

The unseasonable cold lessens, leaving them in just Christmas.

Laura hasn't had the energy to prepare, or the time either, though she's not doing anything now but recuperating. She's simply let the holiday catch her unaware. And so, for once, Christmas doesn't plunge her into the depression of good cheer.

Millennium invites her to the office party, knowing full well she has to decline. Happily, for that matter. Horrible thing; horrible idea, the office Christmas party. All those would-be dieters slamming down cream cheese wreaths and pecan-cholesterol nuggets, listening to disco-synthesized CDs to honor the birth of the world's Saviour.

Didn't Jesus say to turn our backs on all this? Store up treasures some-where else. Give Caesar back his trinkets. How did He wind up here, official state sponsor of our chief retail season? It's as if buying and eternal life were somehow flip sides of the same thing. Christianity's genes must be as supple as a wolf's, breeding everything from chihuahuas to great Danes. And there's no help for us now but a little hair of the one that bit us.

She's going to no parties. Just rolling over in bed is a full morning's activity. The three steps to the downstairs bathroom exhaust her. Fortunately, she's almost stopped producing bodily waste. She can walk, but with great pain. The hospital sends a wheelchair, which she rapidly learns to need.

She looks like the Ghost of Christmas Yet to Come. She knows she's scary, because the kids start asking if they can do anything for her. Something to eat? Something to drink? But all she can get down is the canned vitamin shakes. Tim pours one into the Christmas crystal for her, dressing it up with a Santa swizzle stick.

Don calls every other night. "It's going to get really cold tonight," he warns her. All these years, and the temperature still panics him. The original Chicken Little. Always a killer heat wave, a polar storm. "Make sure to leave your taps open a little," he nags.

Always the outside threat, the perpetual vigil of maintenance against the world's danger. She would rag him back, tease him a little, if she could find the strength. But he's right, he's right, and he has been forever. Now she barely raises the stamina to thank him and hang up.

Her old friends call, too. Those who can stomach the awkwardness. Steph breaks down on the phone. "Hey, Lola. I can come out right away. I already have a reservation."

Laura tells her not to be silly.

Hannah, the other third of the once-inseparable Three Sheets, can't even talk about it. "Down one for me," she instructs Laura.

"Two olives," Laura growls back the password.

Brother Scotty is in periodic touch. He's a comfort, most of all his absolute, unspoken assumption that she's on the mend.

Ellen takes to studying near her. Crawling up to the foot of the sofa bed in the evenings with a beat-up copy of *Romeo and Juliet*.

"Oh," Laura says, remembering. Remembering the play, and that Montague she read it with. "Oh. What do you think of it?"

"It's okay, I guess. Too many clichés, though. I thought Shakespeare would be, like, you know: a little more original?"

They watch TV together, the three of them. A family again, if only because Laura has pitched a permanent base camp in the living room. The kids pop microwave popcorn. The smell of the seared fake butter disgusts her. But she says nothing.

They sit through all the old specials. A bankrupt Jimmy Stewart readies to jump into an icy river. Edmund Gwenn goes on trial for deeply inappropriate conduct at Macy's. She, Ellen, and Tim look on, stunned, like hurricane victims huddled over a cellar crystal set.

"If you've recently received a serious diagnosis," somebody like Kirk Douglas tells them between reels, "then this invaluable series of medical reference videos can give you knowledge and peace of mind. Try Volume One, *Living with the News,* for thirty days at no risk . . ."

She tries to imagine thirty days without risk. Even thirty seconds, with peace of mind, or anything that could remotely pass for it. We must be mad; that's the only possible explanation. Thinking we could housebreak life, beat the kinks out of it, teach it to behave. Complete, collective, species-wide insanity.

She wants them to have a tree. But there's no way. She doesn't want to impose on anyone, and she can't ride with Ellen, even as far as Prairie Orchards. She dreams of the kids reverting to pioneers, dragging one back for miles across the snow. She should just call Don, but then he'd want to decorate, and she cannot bear old times, not just now . . .

Then it happens, as in the best and worst of scripts. Tim, taking the trash out one night after microwave dinner, returns with a scared little grin. "There's a tree on the back steps."

"Liar," his sister calls out, so fast it can only be reflex. But she's out on the porch in a flash, that old fallback habit of checking. She comes back in gentle, a little spooked. "It's true, Mom. It's just lying out there. What should we do with it?"

"What do you *think*?" Laura laughs, pain flecking her insides. Guilt, gratitude, relief, maybe even a little remorse. But she will take this gift, no questions asked. Like a child's petals in a forgetting pocket. They have a tree. Sap in the house. They're good for another year.

She can only sit up in the recliner and direct them. "Make it nice," she scolds. "Turn it a little. No, the other direction: bald spot toward the wall. More red up top, I think. Don't we have another string of lights? That pretty tin angel belonged to your nana. It's very old. Oh, that one! I knitted that when I was pregnant with you, Ellen. It's supposed to be a shepherd. God, it's time to put that one out to pasture."

This once, the kids refuse to do as she tells them, although they do mercifully cover the wretched ornament with tinsel. Tim gets a chair, steadies it for his sister with the star.

She calls Don, on the cordless, now kept next to the sofa bed. "Thank you," she tells him. "It's beautiful." All she has strength for. "Come see."

She blows the wad: presents by mail order. Amazingly, the money she set aside to get her through spring is almost gone. She has lived so many years without worrying about cash that she can't quite believe real need. She cannot bring herself to imagine being without, despite how much closer to without she has come.

When it's gone, it's gone. The kids can go live with Don. Beyond that, she doesn't care. She doesn't need anything more.

For Tim, she gets a 3-D video graphics accelerator with two megs of VRAM. She has no idea what it is, except that he wants it more than he wants friends. For Ellen, she gets that long-coveted boutique leather skirt and vest whose worst consequence Laura hopes will be pregnancy.

They open the presents on Christmas Eve. The kids—God knows where they have gotten the cash—shower her with small things. Chocolate-covered peanuts to fatten her, books on positive thinking, long spy stories, more visualization tapes. She opens them one after the other, smiling and thanking without respite, trying not to look at either the gifts or the givers.

"Can we go to the carol service?" Ellen begs. Unlikely request, stricken with eagerness. The girl locks on her mother's eyes, and neither can let the other down. Laura grinds her dry shoulders together and upward: *How?* "Let's try it," Ellen says. "Oregon Trail. You be the wagon."

Tim eyes his present hungrily. "Can I just . . . ?"

"Sure, Slim," his sister tells him. "It's all rerun numbers anyway. We'll hum them for you when we get home." She gives her bro a peck on the head. He parodies smooching sounds as she heads for the door.

Laura reaches back into a hidden reserve and makes it upright as far as the driveway. Ellen is waiting for her there with the chair. They roll on the twisty and obliterated sidewalk. The wheels, hardened rubber, slip against the fossilized snow. It's hard going, in the frozen dark. Each curb is a sheer cliff face. The way is blacker and slower than they bargained for. They fight the sidewalk for blocks, Ellen battling each slush-up and jam. Laura tries to help, walking, kicking, and skiing by turns, until she is limp and expended anyway. Then the sidewalk ends altogether.

The later it gets, the worse the going. "Damn it," the girl curses the world's redesigners. "You can't walk anywhere anymore." They are both iced over now, Polartec coats or no. Too far past the halfway point to turn back, but too late to make any service tonight or anytime in the near future.

Ellen slips and bloodies her nose on the chair's handgrip. "Damn it," she says. "Damn it. I'm bleeding." And breaks into tears, tears at her failure to get her mother where they *always* go on Christmas. Her failure to bring this night into the stable of continuous years.

Trapped in the chair, Laura cannot reach her. How to tell her daughter, redeem her with the lesson of all defeated plans? This, these are our terms of credit, uncertain, unsecured, unmanageable, and therefore past price. The very opposite of all we hope for. We lose, finally. We don't even get to roll.

"Look up," she tells her. She does so herself, and it's like singing. Funny, how well you can see it all, and even better, seated way down here. Fuzzy, dispersed, uncollectable, polluted with all the light that this frightened crust is desperate to generate.

"Put me on the ground."

"Mom? Don't be crazy. I'm freezing. I'm bleeding. I can't take this anymore." Ellen stamps in place, slaps her sides, slipping into panic. "*Please.* Don't go nuts on me."

"I'm fine, sweetie. Really. Put me on the ground. I want to make an angel."

———

Business has destroyed the very knowledge in us of all other natural forces except business.

—JOHN JAY CHAPMAN (1862–1933), *Practical Agitation*, 1898

The Sociology Section of the Personnel Department saw that only those workers who lived decent, clean, and well-regulated lives qualified for profit-sharing. And the workers' best model for orderly living had to be their parent employer.

William's insights into the workforce compelled a radical rearrangement of the way Clare did business. Times had again changed for business, or rather, business had worked another change upon time. The days of people working for other people were over. The company was no longer a band joined together for a common purpose. The company was a structure whose purpose was to make more of the same.

Labor had long since come to realize certain truths about its standing in production. The job position filled the person more than the person filled the job. Now it was time for the firm's structure to admit what its constituent parts had long ago gathered.

The national hysteria following McKinley's assassination confirmed that the age of empire needed an overhauled structure. Closer to home, Peter's death marked Clare's own timely torch-passing. The way was clear for the firm's long-overdue reorganization.

The upper brass, behind Douglas, set about revamping the corporate hierarchy to accommodate life in the new century. Douglas and his men subdivided the old geographical job definitions into functional ones. It no longer made sense to govern the firm as if it were a loose set of physical outfits. Walpole, Boston, Schenectady, Albany, Sandusky, Chicago, and Lacewood were not independent cottage industries, each with its own guild governor. Clare was not a set of plants; it was a set of purposes.

The world had grown both more specialized and more concentrated. No person could do his partner's task any longer, or even know what his partner did. But every hand was bound more tightly than ever into the complex task of making ever more and more elaborate products.

The structural solution to this dilemma revealed itself to be a company that was both more centralized and more diverse. Revamping simultaneously strengthened the core nervous system and increased the number of limbs:

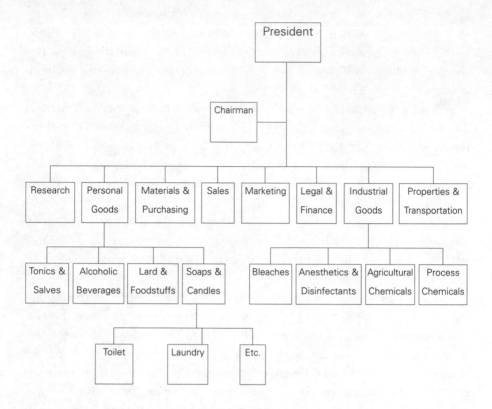

From the first, the new structure distinguished between those responsible for guiding daily operations and those who directed broader company objectives. At every gauge, each man now either directed or implemented. Each of the many functional departments included both an executive planner and a day-to-day manager. Collectively, the committee of executive department heads planned the policies and set the direction of the enterprise as a whole.

Authority ran from the president to each departmental executive, then on to his departmental manager and staff, downward through each works manager, group supervisor, and team foreman. Each department held regular meetings of plant managers and staff. At these brainstorming sessions, people at all levels of the hierarchy traded ideas on how to save costs, eliminate inefficiency, and increase production.

Clare had become a vast man-of-war, if not a small armada. The new organizational chart demanded a new managerial class. On down into the less visible levels, freight managers, personnel managers, and credit managers all turned their trades. The hierarchy itself provided for its own replenishment. Word went out: be aware of those among the skilled laborers who showed a predilection for leadership. Douglas himself often made promotions without ever once watching the soul at work. A good secondhand description was all he needed to know when a man possessed the will to organize.

Whatever the source of his ability, Douglas showed frightening skill in promoting those persons who best understood the new gospel of centralized departments. He enlarged the powers of this new stratum of middle managers, while also increasing their accountability to those above them. He himself abhorred the need to intervene in any branch of the concern that he had hired other people to attend to.

The rainbow of restructured levels had to appear both delineated and continuous: a peaceable kingdom where lowliness and power drank from the same stream. The system would work only if a person who filled one level of responsibility could be raised in time to another level as fluidly as the industrial process plants promoted salt to bicarbonate and then to soda ash.

Clare's lowliest workers—according to Douglas, the concern's only bedrock resource—had to believe that the operation did not just spend human capital but also invested it. They had to feel that Clare needed them, that the endeavor molded their efforts into something of greater worth, the way vats transmuted dead animal parts into hygiene or Sales converted soap into more capital. Labor, too, had to feel it might be infinitely improved.

Douglas raised his novice managerial class on a system of incentives— *credits,* as the protocol called them. Chits paid out for seniority and performance were converted, by an indirect formula never entirely available to the rated workers, into rewards of rank and pay. Paperwork recorded the merits and demerits of every employee. Folders dutifully rated all personal accomplishments, just as careful sales figures now tracked the fate of each Clare product. Formal accounting ensured that, in time, the well-sown seed would rise and the seed that fell upon barren ground would die of its own accord.

The restructured company looked for a way of doing business that was worthy of its new profile. That meant reinventing the old channels of distribution as well. After much introspection, and over the vocal alarm of his board, Douglas hatched a plan to circumvent the old network of corrupt jobber sinecures that the company had dealt with since Resolve, Samuel, and Ennis first sold soap by the generic pound.

It made sense for the Industrial Goods Department to deal directly with those purchasers who made up the majority of Clare's bulk chemical customers. What money it lost on small lots it more than made up for in realized savings. Yet the Personal Goods Department still depended upon whole-salers. No firm could hope to build an internal sales force enormous enough to replace such go-betweens. Trying to sell to every store in the burgeoning West would be an expensive catastrophe.

Nevertheless, Clare could offer its largest urban retailers volume dis-counts, if the stores would bind themselves contractually to sell at list price. And through remote warehouses and small regional sales offices, Clare could still undersell, by a few fractions of a cent, its closest competitors in the most lucrative city markets.

Clare offered the same laddered discount scheme to its old jobbers. And to keep the game fair, it fined all stores that violated price contracts. But its internal sales forces—first five men, then ten, then twelve—took to the out-field to plug the jobbers' gaps and push its distributors to the fences in all areas of the map.

In effect, Clare now competed against its own jobbers in getting Native Balm, Snowdrop, Gifford's Double Eagle Whiskey, and all the rest of Clare's beloved line into the stores. Some of their oldest customers grew furious at the move. Some cried foul and refused to carry Clare any longer.

But Douglas ventured to bet the entire eighty-year family excursion that the greedy would shrink from pauperizing themselves in an escalating war of spite. All parties lived off the fat of the spread banquet. The slighted jobbers would settle for selling the still-lucrative scraps, rather than lose everything. Pride was a quality no businessman could afford.

And he bet right. The public called out for its familiar brands. If a store dropped Clare, some of its shoppers looked elsewhere to find the name they had grown to trust. One by one, the apostate merchants came back into man-ufacturing's fold. The transformation of American business was complete.

The company reorganization would live or die on the character of its hired representatives. Clare's internal sales infantry had to sell the salesman him-self as much as the salesman's samples. Douglas and Hiram taught their sales managers how to choose these new foot soldiers. The instructions were explicit, arriving in a steady barrage of handwritten memos:

> If a man reeks or sweats, if his shirt is stained by food or his collar yellowed, you do not want him going out to meet the public in our firm's name. He is not the man for the style of life we are now merchandising . . .
>
> Our fellow must make the people feel he has come from the same place as they, prayed in the same church, worked in the same office, but has gotten on a shade more cleanly, more efficiently . . . "You, too," the man's face must say. "You want to go where I have gotten. I am what you could be, if your life was a little better managed . . ."

Clare's new sales force offered quantity reductions, not just on its stock of goods but on the entire package deal of ordered existence.

Honesty and simplicity turned a brisk trade, for the world had grown keen on purchasing those quantities that it most sorely lacked. *The Soap Maker's Journal* decried the passing of those very values from the trade. A brand of "No. 1" no longer had any real reference to process or material. Soapmakers disguised inferior or spoiled runs with heavy perfumes and additives. Soap might contain anything: flour, chalk dust, paste. The new science of advertisement produced its very own free-for-all. Cheap fly-by-night brands such as Kickapoo and Sapolio built small empires on nothing but pretty words and pictures. The volley of claims that drove the new century forced even manufacturers of decent wares to escalate in kind. The avuncular Nagel's response was to tempt the wholesome and ordinary on to ever more dizzying heights of self-defense. Hiram's posters and jingle campaigns partook of a genial, ingenious populism on a scale beyond any Boston Clare's wildest flight of normalcy:

> You would not eat the meat of diseased cattle, and no sooner would you wash your plates in the fat of those same unfortunate beasts. Protect yourself. Use only soaps made from the purest vegetable oils. Snowdrop Soap comes entirely from the goodness of plants . . .
>
> In this increasingly complex and volatile world that we all share, at least one thing remains certain: You get what you pay for, unfortunately. If you have found a bargain that seems too good to be true, it most probably is. Weigh your soap, and do not settle for an ounce less than the figure printed on the wrapper.

Countless icons of legendary camp and nostalgia flowed from Nagel's bottomless imagination. He gave birth to the little black boy, rolling his eyes in ecstasy at how sparkling Pearl Tooth Powder left his remaining baby teeth. He announced the Suds Party as "New York's latest fad this season." He let the Modern Woman run, jump, swim, cycle, and throw a softball, her two million three hundred thousand open pores calling out for a gentle body soap.

And Nagel let loose a flurry of babies. Babies everywhere. Infants by the dry ton, in pictures, paeans, and prayers.

> The happiest product of the Lord's imagination is the oval face of a newborn child. It is like the most delicate of blooms. You would not wash the blooms of your garden in harsh chemicals. Neither should you let them touch the skin of your babe.

He penned the tune and lyric—beloved of rakes everywhere—that demanded to know, "What do you need more than anything else?" He credited himself with coining the phrase "Squeaky clean." He taught the country the three essentials of a healthy breakfast and how to prepare them. He devised the Snowdrop Soap bracelet charm, coveted by as-yet-unmarried girls across the country. And he gave away in holy matrimony to a grateful nation Clara Clear, America's zaftig Ambassadress of Sweetheartiness, whose copyright Mary Pickford cheerfully if anemically violated.

The new volume discount scheme that Clare offered to its biggest retailers inspired Nagel to extend the offer to the customer herself. Buy twelve, he told America's housewives, and you will get one free. Store them on end, in darkness, for they will only improve with age.

> It may strike you as counter to our own interests to tell you how to extend the life of every bar of Clare soap that you purchase. But in truth, our interests are best served by serving yours. This is how we have done business for eighty years, and how we intend to stay in business for at least that much longer.

Amid these prosaic claims, Nagel inserted leaves from the sainted memory of Peter Clare. Now that the poetry-lover was dead, the man of verse was free to trot. His anonymous poets—whose nimble feet were easily the match of Kilmer's or Kipling's—graced the pages of *The Atlantic*, *The Century*, and *The Ladies' Home Journal* with stanzas of sentiment and humor.

Each poem came to life through its own litho or woodcut. Nagel insisted on hiring the day's top artists and writers. At first, all art went unsigned. But as public enthusiasm for the works grew, artists and writers alike gladly attached their names to what often became their most popular and lasting creations.

Jackson Stimpke, the portraitist, produced a series of colored inserts, including the famous beauty in shining finery titled *Arrayed for Conquest*. Georgette Garner Roberts chipped in, painting *Baby's Ablutions* and *The End of the Day*. For ten wrappers, a reader could get any one of these color paintings on fine, coated paper, ready to frame.

The *Chicago Tribune* did not know which service to praise more: the steady inspiration and delight of these poems and pictures, or the astounding new factory that threatened to produce half a million cakes of soap a day:

> Such a plant in itself provides an inspiration that no Poussin nor self-respecting Virgil of any age would let go to waste . . . Whatever one's personal habits, all must admit the astonishing force for health, wealth, and happiness that this firm now

represents, both in its manufacturing might and in the face of mirth and moral betterment it presents to the world.

The poems and illustrations grew so popular that any attempt to substitute another form of testimonial in their place produced overwhelming hue and cry. The Clare mailbags began to swell with amateur submissions, so many that they practically forced a brilliant idea upon Hy Nagel.

Why pay famous and high-priced folk to do what the public craved to do for free? Nagel began to run the best of the unsolicited verse, crediting the authors and citing their daytime line of work. This only fueled the interests of the nation's versifiers to see their name immortalized in print. At last Nagel ran a continent-wide contest for the best poem commemorating the virtues of any Clare soaps. He offered two thousand dollars, a sum set in honor of the new century.

The company received 39,472 submissions. Hiram himself wrote the galloping rejection sonnet, mass-mailed to all the losers, whose send-off lamented:

> That ever we did suffer so much woe
> In telling forty thousand beauties, "No."

The winning poem came from Mr. Herbert Kalksteen, an insurance salesman in Lincoln, Nebraska. Kalksteen's submission was titled "The Blessings of Time."

> Praise we the souls whom the harsh years once tested:
> Pioneer spirits whose moil and pride
> Would craft from their leftover drippings and potash,
> Gelatinous masses, saponified . . .

There followed two stanzas on the extreme difficulty of making soap from scrap while at the same time having to clear forests, hold off native attacks, farm by hand, and bury dozens of children.

> We who can speak 'cross unthinkable distances,
> Who thunder on iron, who take to the air,
> We who, galvanically, drive back the darkness
> Cannot begin to conceive of your cares . . .
>
> How much, in that darkness, your cleanliness mattered!
> How laden with brambles the way that you came.

The war that you waged for the spotless and decent
Puts all of your latter-day scions to shame.

And on through four more equally inspired stanzas describing the inconceivable increase of human health and declaring how much luckier life had become than any of the past's pathfinders could have supposed. It closed on the chorus:

Had you but dreamt what Advancement would bring us,
Our utter advantage o'er soil and grime!
How large life has grown, how complete the ascendance
That we have achieved through the Blessings of Time!

Hiram chose the poem in part because it was one of the few out of all the thousands of entries rhyming "soap" with "hope" that didn't mention Clare by name. It seemed time to capitalize on all Clare's preexisting advertising, to unite the firm with inevitability's other nameless forces, and to render all mention of the grand manufacturer conspicuous in its absence.

The first runner-up, vastly more popular with the public, resorted to the tragical-pastoral-comical:

Amaryllis does the wash,
Cursing Colin soundly.
Skin is ruined, day is lost,
And fabric reeketh roundly.

She, 'midst boiling and much mopping,
Waxing furious, mad-hopping,
Scolds her swain,
Forsooth, for fain,
She'd rather far be shopping.

Clare's Powdered Yellow Laundry Soap for Mechanical Washing Devices arrives by line eighteen, to get our girl to town with skin and lower back intact, while at the same time astonishingly preserving the meter.

The director of promotion gathered together the best two dozen contest entries and published them as a twenty-four-page booklet. This Clare gave away to wholesalers as yet another promotion. Such booklets of ad reproductions would take the firm up through the Great Depression: woodcuts for coloring, poems to laugh at and savor and recite, lithos for collecting or framing. All free.

The winds of a new era also called for a coordinated change of packaging across Clare's growing product line. The archaic Indian head belonged to the dead century. He no longer served to proclaim all the goods the firm now trafficked in. Nagel commissioned one of his stable of artists to capture in an image this fresh breeze, clean and bracing, transfiguring all that it blustered over.

The anonymous engraver drew upon the original, stylized image of the *Utilis* bud that Clare had once stamped upon its crates for trade protection. He worked it into a circle of twisting vines, gilded in profusion. Clare registered the new trademark in 1911, the year that the Supreme Court busted up the Standard Oil trust.

———

Two Irish washerwomen with overflowing tubs, decrying soaps that employ harsh chemicals.

A moonstruck young heir telling his sweet young croquet partner that he lost his concentration in the glare.

A herd of mud spattered cows eyeing a bull who has just scrubbed himself clean with a trade-stamped bar: "He doesn't know his own kine."

A black baby bathing himself closer in tone to the white baby sharing his suds.

A sultan who proclaims that his entire harem must wash their hair with the formula his newest and youngest wife has just discovered.

Automobile mechanics agreeing that there is only one product strong enough to get them clean.

Two muttonchopped stockbrokers in a brilliantly appointed train compartment complaining about chapped hands.

A young couple savoring social success and business promotion brought about by their radiant table covering.

Santa stuffing soap cakes into fireside stockings.

Uncle Sam distributing free samples to baffled but eager Ellis Islanders.

An Indian and his wife, strolling with a bar of hard white soap on a leash, above a two-stanza poem entitled "Reclaimed":

> We once were factious, fierce and wild,
> To peaceful arts unreconciled,
> Our blankets smeared with grease and stains
> From buffalo meat and settlers' veins . . .
>
> But I——Y SOAP came like a ray
> Of light across our darkened way.
> And now we're civil, kind, and good,
> And keep the laws as people should,
> We wear our linen, lawn and lace
> As well as folks with paler face.
> And now I take, where'er we go,
> This cake of I——Y SOAP to show
> What civilized my squaw and me
> And made us clean and fair to see.

———

She gets a letter stamped "Personal and Urgent." Her address is typed right on the heavyweight bond envelope, so rare with her mail anymore. The return address is also typed: the Cancer Research Institute. Her first, frightened thought is that they want her to go to Houston or New York or Bethesda, some monstrous facility for special treatment.

But it couldn't be that, she thinks; it can't. Her doctors here would have told her about any plans on her behalf. Then she realizes: it must be this lawsuit.

The news has started to spread. The big, national groups must be trying to make a test case of it, for some reason. Don has sent them her address. They must be trying to get all the local cancer cases to turn out in support. To do their bit for the collective health.

She opens the envelope, her fingers shaking. Already, she is writing the apologetic response letter in her head. She's not the woman they're looking for. They need someone else, someone who knows what's what, who understands what's going on. Someone who can speak well. Someone who can say what everybody in this town is feeling.

Dear Mrs. Bodey, she reads.

She plunges into the first paragraph. But right away, she has to turn around for a second read. Please send $25. Or anything you can afford.

It doesn't make sense. Solicitation letter. Why would they single out cancer patients? What kind of fund-raising drive is this, where they pass the hat not for the victims but to them?

It takes her a minute. A full, real minute, a pretty considerable unit of time these days. She's not being singled out. It's the same old list. The master database. The mass mailing to everybody.

She flips back to the envelope, the typewritten return address. A trick to make this piece seem like real mail. Hide all the tracks. Get the thing opened at least. Keep it from being pitched in the trash sight unseen. Maybe a letter that looks like first-class mail increases the chances of a contribution by another one percent. And one percent, on the scale things get done now, must come to millions.

A whole new art form: the protectively disguised bulk envelope. Like that one she got last week, a torn magazine page, pinned with her exact color Post-It note. "Hey, Laura! Check this out! Susan." And she spent all afternoon tossing on the sofa, trying to reassure herself that she'd never had a friend named Susan in her life. Convinced that the cancer, the chemo, the rays were getting to her memory.

Avoid meat and fat. Don't smoke or drink. Limit the time you spend in the sun. Don't expose yourself to toxic chemicals at home or at work. Do not indulge in multiple sexual partners. And send twenty-five dollars.

Well, she's had sex with three men in her life, and one had trouble with intercourse. Sure, she drank a lot in college, with the girls. But these days, she could probably have had half a dozen more glasses of red wine a week and still come in under the guidelines. She smoked for maybe three years, now and then after dinner, just to be sociable. But, ludicrous or no, she never really inhaled. Her diet's not perfect, but because of the kids, she's always been more careful than anyone else she knows.

Don't expose yourself to toxic chemicals at home or at work. There's the catch. They might as well say: Don't get cancer. Well, she hasn't exposed herself. She hasn't, knowingly or otherwise, as far as she knows. She hasn't even *been* exposed. No Love Canal under the house. No Three Mile Island just across the river. Whatever she's getting by chance or proximity is no more than anyone else in the known world is getting.

She looks over the simple list of do's and don'ts, counting in her head all the things she's done wrong in her life. All the little carcinogenic amenities, the dangers she's known but risked anyway, because the odds seemed so small or so hard to work around. From hair spray to charred barbecued burgers. The paints and paint strippers. The hair color treatments, so crucial to her self-image. The maraschino cherries she used to reward herself with, for being so good. All the diet sodas, which she loved, because they made her feel that she could drink as much as she liked while burning more calories consuming them than she was consuming.

She sends Ellen to the library, and tells her to ask for Marian. Ellen comes home with a book called *Shopping for Safety*. Laura reads it in tiny increments, in those moments when her head is clear and her eyes can focus. As far as she can make out, nothing is safe. We are all surrounded. Cucumber and squash and baked potato. Fish, that great health food she's been stuffing down the kids for years. Garden sprays. Cooking oils. Cat litter. Dandruff shampoo. Art supplies. Varnish. Deodorant. Moisturizers. Concealers. Water. Air. The whole planet, a superfund site. Life causes cancer.

Lying awake at nights, afraid to take even those universally prescribed milligrams to help her sleep, she thinks about going clean. Cold turkey. Here is all the checklist anyone needs. With it, she could learn to buy only those goods that are above reproof. How hard could it be, to change a few habits? No beef, no chemical toothpastes, the right brands of polish . . . Nothing she would miss. Buy her way back to health, by choosing the recommended items.

The brief fanatical fantasy dissolves on her like pixie dust. She'd need a lot more health than she has to pull it off. And every plastic bottle of water she bought would just spew poisons somewhere else.

Another letter arrives to take her mind off the first. This one's not really to her, either. It's an open letter, a larger database. It takes up a quarter page in the Sunday *Post-Chronicle*. In the Public Notices column of the Classifieds. To anyone living in the area bounded by Base Line, Kickapoo, McKinley, and Airport Road—pretty much all Lacewood and Kaskaskia Heights, and most of the little farm towns and tax-evading subdivisions that hug them.

If you are suffering from any ailment that you or your physicians believe might have an environmental basis. If you have an interest in the current class action suit being lodged against the area's largest manufacturer. If you would like to be considered for inclusion in this suit. Please respond to the following post office box no later than March 21.

It has the look of some paid advertorial. Serious text in a black box, the kind that Laura sometimes mistakes for public service announcements. Mass tort, punitive damages: the kind of products that her edition of *Shopping for Safety* fails to rate for danger. It's the law firms' best product anymore, so of course they're going to hawk it. One efficient and profitable institution against another, both competing within the rules of the game that have made everyone rich.

She clips the open letter. She puts it up on the fridge so she won't forget the due date. After two days, she gets sick of looking at it. She moves it to the ceramic letter holder on the hutch, wedges it in next to her quarterly payment vouchers. But she's afraid she might forget about it there. She puts it on the dining room table, where no one has eaten for months. It keeps blowing off each time the kids walk past, so she weights it down with the money cowry shell that Ken gave her when she broke into the Million Dollar Movers Club.

Don comes over to clean the flue, fix the stuck window casement, and do a couple other things the kids can't manage. "How are you doing?"

"How do I look?"

"Better than I expected. You see the notice in the paper, by the way?"

She gestures at the table, where the thing still nags at her, unanswered.

"You going to do it?"

"Do . . . ?"

"Come on. Get in on the claim?"

"Don. It's hard for me, hard to think of *this* . . ." Her hands cup inward and sweep back over herself, her wasted torso. "As a claim."

"I'm sorry. Bad choice of words."

But he can't leave it alone. And she doesn't really expect him to.

"Does it have any interest for you? There's not a lot of time . . . I mean, March will be here faster than we know."

He never meant anything but well, maddeningly well. "What would you do, Don? I mean, God forbid, if you were me?"

"No question," he says. "Absolutely no question."

But she has lots of questions. "It's just not something . . . cancer's not something that I really want to profit from."

She sees him fighting down the agitation. "It's not a question of profiting, Lo. Do you want to just stand aside and let *them* profit, while everybody else picks up the tab?"

She wants to say: *Whose tab?* Who ordered this meal? Who chose this life? Who invented these rules? Instead, she says, "Well, I doubt that my joining or not joining will have any bearing on the outcome at all."

"You don't know that. The numbers may help things. There may be something about your particular—"

"Don. My *doctors* won't even guess why I got this."

"You're part of a cluster."

"Ovarian cancer doesn't cluster, apparently."

"Oh, there's a cluster here. Believe it. Haven't you seen the statistics the paper's been digging up? We're way above average, for all kinds of cancers."

She wants to say: The whole country is way above average. She says, "The old Rowen marksmanship." For years, he compared the way her family argued to a kid who scatters buckshot against the barn wall, then draws a bull's-eye around the densest concentration of hits.

He grins at her, clearly irritated. "I just think you deserve some answer. Somebody owning up. Some compensation."

There can be no compensation. No owning up, no answering to something as common as she has.

"They can't possibly make a case," she says. "Think of what they'd have to show. That there are carcinogens somewhere loose—"

"There are."

"—in a concentration that could cause people to get cancer. That Clare put them there."

"Piece of cake," Don says.

"That the victims were in contact with it. That they got their cancer *because* of the stuff they touched that the factories put there. That they wouldn't have gotten cancer if—"

"I don't know, Laura. If it's as tough to win the case as you think, then why are perfectly shrewd law firms sinking so much money into it? It must have cost them half a million just to get it this far."

"I don't know." And she doesn't. "Publicity? Maybe they think that the company will settle rather than go through the hassle of defending?"

"If the company settles, for whatever reason, you will kick yourself for not getting what's due you."

She is due nothing. No more than anyone else with a body. No more than anyone who will get sick, which is everyone. As bad as she has it, millions will have it worse. She is on her own. She has always been on her own. Everyone who lives here is on her own. And anyone who promises otherwise is selling a bill of goods.

He putters about a little longer, shimming up the washing machine, which has begun to dance across the basement floor. He tries to fix the broken 5-CD changer, getting angrier and angrier, while she tries to tell him that it's okay. She can listen to only one disc at a time anyway.

Before he leaves, he comes back to her chair-side. "It's not just you," he confides. "You have to think of the kids."

"The kids?"

"If there's any kind of settlement. Anything at all . . ."

"Oh." She hears what he is saying. "Oh." For the first time in the argument, she falters. His words set off her worst fear, her primal hope. He knows the nerve, the one that life has hinged on since she turned adult. The one contest that justifies any aggression, any tactic, any fight. She would steal for them. She would push any other kid out of the lifeboat. There's nothing she wouldn't give them. Except what gave her this.

She moves her mouth twice before the words come out. "Sometimes I wonder if those two don't already have more than they know what to do with."

"Oh, for God's sake. Laura. Listen to me. Don't you think you have a stake in any of this? Don't you even want to *know*?"

She looks at the man. His earnest, irrelevant soul must be forgiven everything. She cannot remember now what she ever held against him. Nor can she remember why it mattered so much, or how they ever thought they might raise a family together.

She does remember trailing him for months, collecting the evidence even while he denied everything. She remembers pressing for divorce, not because he had had an affair and lied about it, but because he took the pitiful creature to such grimy places. Because he did the thing in such a discount way.

She looks at him and smiles. At least it feels like a smile, from inside her face's withered sheet of muscle. "A court is not going to tell me what I need to know."

"That's not true," he hurries out. "A court's the only place that *could* tell you . . ."

She reaches out, rubs her tired arm on his. The hush, the interrupt of human touch. "Don. Don. What difference does it make now?"

———

A flat, narrow, rufous-colored box bears the sober Courier caption Certifast. *Along one edge, the hint of an anxious female profile holds a test strip up to the light. $19.95*

The name Engender *flows across an ampler coral-colored carton in Corsiva italic. Upon the pastel, country-craft highlights, a rapturous couple cuddles their newborn. $29.95*

The fine print on both reads:

A first trimester colorimetry home pregnancy test. This exam may produce up to 12 percent false positives and 10 percent false negatives. Consult your doctor for professional confirmation.

CLARE DRUG AND PHARMACEUTICAL

In the first year after reorganization, sales reached ten million dollars. The members of the new managerial class now threw themselves against the problem of unused capital, the most pernicious cost confronting any life, let alone the corporate one. In the fiercely awakened markets of the twentieth century, inefficiency could end only in death. Every ingenuity that the human spirit could throw against it, every strategy of rational management had to be enlisted in the fray.

Competition within the firm, between the different teams and departments, began to produce the same benefits that winnowing produced in the market at large. Clare got out of old lines in time, and into new ones even before it needed to. Whatever was too wasteful to survive did not, and good ideas spread like a plains fire in August. With the right corporate structure, decisions practically handled themselves.

Prosperity no longer meant inevitable subsequent shutdowns. When the water rose in the harbor, all the boats indeed went up. Yet when the snow came down the mountain, those at the foot still got buried.

"If we can continue to produce high-quality merchandise," hoary-headed Douglas urged the firm's cohorts in his annual Profit Picnic address,

> the public will continue to buy, and it will keep right on buying. And we who have joined together for this purpose will continue to enjoy the fruits of our efforts . . .
>
> But as you all well know, we can't spend the profits until we earn them. And every one of you here is sharp enough to see that we have to hold back a certain portion of the gains. We have to plow them back into improved equipment, better distribution, and more jobs. That way, we can distribute even more gains tomorrow.

In truth, neither William Clare nor anyone in Finance could say just how much his profit-sharing scheme actually contributed to the steady gains in efficiency and the drops in production costs. Modern machinery and power, coupled with the highly cost-effective reorganization, might have made it unnecessary to pay out any more to labor than it had at the end of the last century.

Then again, workers stayed employed longer, and retraining costs fell dramatically. And when strikes broke out in Fall River, when the Mine Workers came above ground, when the IWW and the International Ladies' Garment Workers' Union took shape, when the Supreme Court turned the Sherman Act against organized labor, Clare's factories stayed remarkably quiet. Even the renewed agitation inside the plants for an eight-hour day was met with hostility among those who wanted to keep their bonus dividends flowing.

For the first time since its earliest boilings, the company found an answer to the chronic problem of overproduction. Peaks and crashes in the demand could be met by easing out the throttle of direct sales and boosting the budget for advertising. Douglas toyed with fine-tuning the whole system, as if he were a backyard mechanic timing the firings of a primitive internal combustion engine. And for a while, his tuning attained the unthinkable Olympus of American business: guaranteed full employment without layoff, overtime, or any other whiplash.

The board voted two new public share offerings, one to fund a new seed-crushing mill in Georgia and another to build an expanded Kansas oil-making plant that began milking a new hydrogenation patent. Both lots of stock sold out quickly. The issues continued to trade actively on the New York Stock Exchange, for whom the company had opened its books in 1902. Dividends rose and remained rock solid. The public proved as eager for Clare shares as it had always been for Clare soap.

The name Clare now stood for valued things. People needed the goods Clare made. Any number of competing groups had gotten together for the shared purpose of meeting those needs, groups that sought ways to make those goods with incalculable industry. These groups would have picked up the slack in no time at all if Clare ever failed to meet its share of the public demand.

A national Pure Food and Drug Act came into existence in those years. For a long time, the law had trouble discerning between the desire to mislead and the desire to be misled. But it did hunt down products claiming secret, curative ingredients. In 1913, the amended law finally shut down the last production run of Native Balm tonics and soap. Government lawyers discovered there was nothing Indian about the extract, and nothing medicinal either. Douglas pulled the plug with deep regret, and the original magic name disappeared from circulation.

Government also struck at the company with the first significant tariff reductions since Resolve Clare's death. The United States, now the home of two fifths of the world's manufacturing, suddenly absorbed a tidal wave of cheap imports. The time had come to see just how good for business natural selection really was.

In the end, Clare kept its share and competed, by making sure that nothing went to waste. Its chemists learned how to make the same old things out of cheaper and surprising materials. They studied Carver's ingenious uses for peanut oils and cotton sluff. They began to convert refuse materials, turning the expense of disposal to a little bonus profit.

Clare thrived in the Progressive Era. Its products liberated women from drudgery and elevated the general level of health and cleanliness even among the poor. And its factories and reclamation businesses provided a model for the proper conduct of commercial exertions. When Teddy Roosevelt said he wanted to apply the principles of good business to the new endeavor of public conservation, he had the Clare model in the back of his mind.

The mountains had been cut for easy passage and the valleys raised up for richer cultivation. Summers ran chilled for longer shelf life, and winters warmed to extend the season of useful work. Light bulbs lengthened the intervals of productive day, allowing still more timesaving tasks to be completed in less time. Soon death itself would be brought into the process, made to occur at the optimal transfer points.

"THINK," read the new letterhead over at National Cash Register. Douglas ordered that the Clare letterhead imitate the slogan. "Manage wisely, and wisdom will manage." Not as succinct, but it made its point. That desperate readiness for new solutions, even at the eleventh hour.

Everywhere, the corporation proved to be the greatest extension of human prowess since the spear and the most flexible one since the baseball mitt. Ever-larger institutions began to spring from the corporation's brow, giving birth to one another: the Federal Reserve System. The Consumer Price Index. The first national income tax.

Each new human structure launched more inventions than raw meat launches maggots. Ten years into the century's experiment, and entrepreneurs everywhere were breeding radio, motion pictures, the box camera, the mass-production automobile plant, telegraphic transmission of pictures, the mass-market phonograph, cellophane. Edison even promised a machine that would communicate with the dead. An infant industry sprang up to meet every imaginable human desire, and several arose to meet desires that were not yet human. Clare could not spend its way forward fast enough. There were too many sure bets to invest in.

Even the humble store reinvented itself. After a test run with Filene's on Washington Street in mother Boston, Clare jumped wholesale into the new block-long, ten-story beehive monstrosities, with excellent results. Shortly after, it put its stamp of approval upon mail order. Of the third of a billion packages the U.S. Parcel Post shipped in its maiden year, 12,396 originated at Clare. Between Sears, Spiegel, and Montgomery Ward, universal availability came to visit every flyspeck town that ever sullied the map. What's more, catalogs taught the public the invaluable lesson of how to buy goods blind.

American-built, gasoline-motored, heavier-than-air vehicles lifted off the surface of the earth. The last real barriers to the universal shipping of goods collapsed everywhere. And now that America had its own nursling empire, Clare raised its eyes from trade's old borders. Fats from the Chicago slaughterhouses joined coconut oil from the American Philippines and palm oil from the Belgian Congo in the same kettle. Why couldn't the company emulate its own products?

The firm stood ready before its next stage of existence. It would take its magnificent mills of wealth and export them, process for process, into new climates. Start the whole seed again, from scratch.

The choice for Clare's ambassador for international start-up operations quite literally made itself. Young Douglas Clare II had taken a First in History at Trinity College, Cambridge. He'd returned to the States to work in three different company plants, first as lineman, then as foreman, then as plant manager. Even after he rose to direct the Materials and Purchasing Department, he never lost his taste for travel, art, architecture, or his beloved far side of the Atlantic.

After five minutes in any cathedral from Ulm to York, he could recite the details of the nave's elevation and bays blindfold. He could recount the lancets and mullions of the tiniest parish church in photographic detail. He bought Cézannes when the man was still considered a boorish laughingstock. He took the waters at Spa and Baden-Baden, speaking to most anyone he met in whatever language they addressed him. It was as if the man's entire vita had been groomed in advance, for the very opportunity the company now threw him. And in fact, it had.

Douglas the Elder packed his most successful son off to Europe with detailed instructions for investigating rights, privileges, and potentials in Britain, France, Germany, and the Low Countries. The plan was to use Snowdrop Soap to run advance interference, a kind of flying wedge. Then they'd get the other products downfield by using America's newly invented forward pass.

Douglas II stepped off the boat in Le Havre in the first week of April 1914. In four months, the business partners he courted began to slaughter one another. In three years, the unthinkable went inevitable: Doug Jr.'s compatriots died by the tens of thousands, to salvage the same international system of loans that was supposed to have rendered war obsolete.

At the end of the four-year, static, stately bloodletting, ten million lay dead, four empires had vanished, a quarter of the world began to renounce the market system, and Clare had chosen a short list of plant sites on the Continent and in Britain.

———

Reluctantly, she refinances the house. She knows it means paying for the present by mortgaging the future. But at least it's paying for the present. Cash in hand, first things first. She'll figure out how to make payments down the road, after she figures out what's down the road.

Lindsey, at work, pulls some bank strings for her. He seems almost eager to. As if money's cheap, after what he's done to her. And she'd rather take the favor from him than from Don, because the bastard owes her.

Each day she gets a little strength back, now that the atomic devastation lets up. Her body, not knowing any better, rallies. She's like a tiny science-fair seed planted upside down, spinning, righting itself by the laws built into growing things.

One day, she wakes up wanting a scrambled egg. The next morning, while the kids are at school, before the visiting nurse comes by, she tries the stairs. A third of the way up, she crumples. She has to rest twice, but at last makes it to the top. The second floor of her house is like another country. She has forgotten even the color of the walls.

Her mind clears a little. She starts generating small surpluses of thought again. A false spring of February's doing, flushing the ice pack into puddles. *Don't you want to know?* Don's words nag her more, the better she feels. At last she hits that week when she's lucid enough to want to. Want to know, know *something*, while knowing is still a going proposition.

She tries the books that she gets from Marian. The short ones, anyway. She might need to Cliffs Note the more difficult ones. She gets to the point where she can read the word "adenocarcinomatous" without needing to call it quits for the day.

The stuff is worse than poetry. The more she reads, the harder it gets. She reads enough to begin to suspect that the real experts want to know the same things she does. Technicians, as TV in her girlhood liked to say, are working on the problem. Each level down gets stickier, requiring ever-bigger institutions full of scientists and administrators to unfold. Every new ten-syllable Latin word requires another million more twenty-five-dollar contributions to root it up.

After reading for several days, she still does not know what "cell type" means. And when she looks hers up, it tells her less than nothing. She'd have had to start ten years before getting sick, just to know what hit her.

On Presidents' Day weekend, she tells the kids, breezily, "Why don't we head to the Historical Society?" They give her a bewildered look. "You know. The Riverton Mansion."

"Didn't we just go there?" Tim whines. Five years ago. This from a child for whom thirteen milliseconds is an eternity.

"Sure, Mom," Ellen says. "I'll drive."

"Let's walk."

"You sure?"

"Yep."

"I can wheel you, you know. If it's my driving you're worried about."

Laura pleads with her in silence. The mansion is not so far as it was. It gets closer, each day that the treatments recede into bad dreams. Please. She needs to walk outside again. Now. Today. Ready or not. She begs her daughter with her eyes, until Ellen relents.

Just being outside is the greatest source of stamina she could ask for. Ellen walks alongside her, mocking her baby steps. "Go for it, Mama."

Tim walks five yards ahead, placating his Game Boy, pushing all the buttons it wants pushed. He does fall back when Laura gets winded. One child under each arm, while she catches her breath.

The Riverton Mansion has grown since they last came out. Or Laura has shrunk more than she realized. Ellen starts for the stairs, takes three, then turns around, remembering.

"Go on, honey," Laura reassures her. "I'm fine." Her daughter disappears up to the attic dolls and dresses, a secret regression that the crowd at school never needs to know.

Laura tries to interest Tim in the old machines. "Look at this, honey. It's an old mechanical corrugator. They used to . . ."

He tries to listen. She can see him struggling. But he cannot sit still for it. He buzzes the rooms at high speed, pauses briefly at the old radio gear, then retires to the foyer, where he sits on a 1920s love seat, blasting the unbeatable twelfth-level boss on Wonky Dong.

Laura heads for the Clare collection, the rooms she has always skipped on past visits. All the boring bric-a-brac of company history that Mr. and Mrs. Riverton collected during his thirty-six-year association with the Lacewood plant.

Some people collect glass paperweights or telephone pole insulators. Some collect books or brocade or bad debts. Mrs. Riverton collected dolls and

clothes. During the week, her husband collected subsidiaries. And on week-
ends, he collected every scrap of memorabilia that ever bore the name Clare.

Rooms full of it: stationery, shipping cartons, drink trays, presidential cita-
tions. Goofy public health primers. Tape clips. Stereoscope cards of factory
christenings. Bills of sale. Ancient dentifrice powder tins with embarrassing
logos of beaming golliwogs that you'd think any good company man would
have wanted to bury.

Why? she wonders. To fill the house with the stuff. To build a collection so
impressive that it forces your kids and grandkids to extend it, with taxpayer
help. To show it off to crowds long after your death.

The rooms fill up with display cases, each devoted to a slew of packaging
and ads. Some of the slogans ring like old nursery rhymes in her ears: We
make the impossible happen. Making your life a little simpler. One and the
same thing, at this point. She finds herself humming all the tunes, too. Every
familiar phrase, its melody.

Each glass showcase gets a little older than the last. The Me Decade
reverts to the Summer of Love, which fades back into the Golden Era. But-
terflies in a box. After three or four cases, she realizes she has entered the
loop backwards. But she's in too deep to leave and start again from the beginning.

Time pulls off, layer after layer. The company strips in front of her, like
someone getting undressed for the night. Factories shrink; equipment goes
rickety and primitive; the official company portraits grain and blur. The Oakland addresses on the labels vanish, turn back into Kansas City, then Lacewood, Chicago, Sandusky, Walpole, Roxbury: a reverse Pilgrim's Progress,
back toward Plymouth Rock.

"There *is* Balm in Gilead," she reads. A glass wall cabinet proclaims,
"Native Balm soap with secret extract of Healing Root will cure several cuta-
neous and dermal disorders." And everywhere, the scalp of a long-suffering
Indian Brave, whom she vaguely knew about but never suspected.

Soon she's too far back for anything that might help her. But the goods are
like an ambulance on the interstate: against her own will, she has to slow
down and look. She wanders back into the next room, then the one beyond
that. Time unthreads; profits shrink with each step. She relives the sale of the
first two pounds of soap, delivered by hand, at a disastrous loss of cash and
hours.

The famous Clare logo grows backwards before her eyes. The icon unsim-
plifies. It branches and embellishes itself until finally, after all these years,
she makes out what it is: the bud of an ornate plant.

She's known the thing her whole life, but never would have guessed. A lush weed, nothing that could ever take root in her garden. In fact, the thing looks like nothing that grows on earth. Tropical. Foreign. Martian.

The plant earns one whole case of its own. She traces its discovery by the brother of the company's founders, on some early research voyage to the South Seas. Letters in the naturalist's spidery hand fan out, one on top of another. Below the letters, a caption announces how much Mr. Riverton paid for the papers in public auction.

Of the visible lines, she can read only a few. How the islander King kept the living root in his healing pouch. How only this man Clare recognized the root's odd smell. How the native name meant either *strength* or *use*. How powerful taboos prevented the plant from hurting anyone, by binding the soul of the injurer to his victim.

This last bit curdles on her lip like alum. Just what she needs. But the letters fail to go into detail.

What tiny roots that plant once had. How was anyone to know? She pushes on, article after article, slogan after slogan. She reads all the lore, how much the sale of those first two pounds of soap lost them. She studies the simple formula: a pound of fat makes two pounds of soap, one of which will trade for the next pound of fat. A simple enough thing, and nothing can keep it from covering the earth.

She ventures back through the audit trail until she reaches the docks of Boston, desiccated. She washes up exhausted in front of a cardboard calling card that reads, *"He that hath clean hands shall grow stronger and stronger."*

What else did anyone ever want? Here it is, the thin thing pulling life on, the value-added thread tying salve to salvation. She sits down in a refinished chair in the corner. She closes her eyes, wiped out. She pictures a crippling class action suit, the next microscopic bit of corporate history laid out in a last, empty display. A settlement big enough to close down the whole, ancient operation.

She has a month to join this procession. A month to decide where to sign. But it will take her longer than that, will take a whole, eternal afternoon just to walk back home.

"Thank you, guys," she tells the kids, halfway to the finish line.

Tim shrugs. "For what?" Ellen asks, almost snapping.

"For doing this. For bringing me."

"Jesus, Mom. Don't make us ralph."

Laura calls Marian as soon as they get home. She still has fifteen minutes before the library closes. "Can you tell me where a certain line came from? It sounds like a quote or something."

"I can try, Mrs. Bodey. How does it go?"

"He that hath clean hands shall grow stronger and stronger."

The librarian pulls up and scans the electronic full text of four thousand famous books at once. "Got it," she replies, half a minute later. "It's from the Book of Job. Chapter seventeen. Verse nine."

WHAT DO WE DO NOW?

A wide-angle pan along the decimated horizon. A sober female, public-television-voiced narrator intones:

The town of Muinak, in the former Soviet Union.

Not that long ago, Muinak was a thriving inland port on the coast of the Aral Sea. Now it sits in the midst of a vast salt desert.

Aralsk. A different town, the same fate. Its people once fished for a living. Now they don't know how they will continue to put food on the table.

How did this happen? And why? It happened because people in other towns in Kazakhstan and Uzbekistan needed to eat just as badly as the people of Muinak and Aralsk. To grow their crops, they diverted the Syrdarja and Amudarja, the great rivers feeding the Aral. Yields soared. Water fell. Now the entire region is stretched to the breaking point.

Intercut black-and-white footage of varying stock quality rolls by to a Berio sound track.

In Japan, forty-four nuclear reactors sit on the unstable boundaries of tectonic plates. In northern Europe, crucial fisheries collapse from overuse. In China, a rapid growth in the standard of living is about to flood the world with greenhouse gases and CFCs. In the United States, fat-soluble PCBs concentrate more densely on each rung up the food chain. In India, industrial pollution is already the leading cause of hospitalized illness. Throughout Africa, AIDS, famine, and runaway birthrates have become a way of life.

The images culminate in a robed mother and child, sitting quietly in a dusty doorway. Berio has slowed to Brahms: andante, piano and strings.

There is a time for every purpose under heaven.

Right now, it's time for the best that the human race can do. Right now, it's time to think.

The Advanced Research Group
CLARE MATERIAL SOLUTIONS

War wrought more changes at home than it did in Europe's trenches. The new reality of total warfare maimed the Progressives and machine-gunned the last holdout opposition to big business. All talk of closing down the monopolies ceased well before Armistice Day, and it never started up again after the signing.

For the war not only proved the impossibility of beating the giant corporations. It showed how much the public good now depended upon them. The electrified, biplaned, broadcast, synthetic, pharmaceuticaled, plasticized human project could no longer last a week without those vast, syndicated pools of capital.

General Motors and Union Carbide saved the world for democracy. Du Pont fired one shell in every five, laundering its windfall millions by expanding into paints and polymers. Government had no choice but to join hands with industry in the nation's interests. In 1919, when four million strikers threatened to rip society apart, only government's residual wartime powers finally forced the last militant miner back to work. Debs went to jail for violating the Espionage Act. The business of America would never again be anything but business.

The trusts now came out from behind their protective machinery. They did away with their grosser tactics, rendered obsolete by triumph. Corporations no longer needed to fear anything from the public. For the new stockholding public was squarely behind them, ready to sign for anything printed on the proxy ballot.

"War baby" stocks hit the roof and then kept right on rising. Their swell carried a raft of related equities up with them. The taxi drivers of New York became self-styled brokers. Maids and butlers took to speculating on 10 percent margins. Kids cried at Christmas when they got toys instead of Type A Preferred.

Clare's employees had been spoon-fed the pleasures of stockholding long before the public at large discovered them. Their steady willingness to put aside wages to purchase shares at discount prices kept demand firm and the performance of Clare Common flawless.

Even as the firm's equities began to take off, Douglas Sr. succumbed to the Spanish influenza. Worldwide, the end-of-war pandemic claimed twice as many lives as had the conflict. No one at Clare thought the chief would ever succumb to anything, least of all something as absurd as a microbe. The old raw rail still walked coatless to work, daily, even through snowstorms. But Douglas died all the same, despite long hours, an iron constitution, and the most expensive doctors money could buy.

His unplanned death left a vacuum at the top of the organizational chart. Douglas Jr. seemed singularly uninterested in any job that would interfere too much with a life of galleries and triforia. None of Douglas's other sons had risen above the level of inept assistant plant manager. Peter had left no children. As the senior Clare in either branch of the family, William figured the company was his for the taking.

But it had been decades since the firm had been a genuine family concern. Hiram Nagel, the handpicked prodigy whose sweaty folksiness had held Peter Clare in horrified fascination, chose to fight William for the run of the company. Nagel had learned, over the years, to forgo the yellow-checked suits. He'd mastered the difference between the soap you sold to the common man and the self you sold to your business associates. He'd done as much with nothing as anyone in his line could have. Now he wanted one more sale.

William outgunned the upstart Nagel in percent of equity controlled. But the treasurer, despite his magic name and large block of shares, hadn't a chance against the advertising genius when it came to promoting himself to both board and stockholders. All William's handpicked inside men elected to pass him over. They called him too old, too frugal, too tied to the past.

Had bitterness been cost-efficient, William might have let himself get bitter. Instead, he settled for a ceremonial Chairmanship. He strengthened his profit-sharing scheme through several overhauls. He implemented a guaranteed-work plan. He found ways to finance the greatest period of expansion the company would ever enjoy. And he commenced a gradual, decade-long sell-off of his own stock into a climbing market.

And so the Jazz Age opened with no Clare at the helm of Clare. The soap cake that the family had crafted succeeded beyond anything any one of them could have predicted for it. The shape had outlived the sum of its shapers. The peddler now owned the production line.

The company structure that the vanished generations had jointly fashioned seemed only to have been waiting for the twenties to vindicate it. The nation was a silent-film showgirl, giddy with confidence, one step ahead of the censors. Yet for all its Charleston-shimmying out between the struts of biplanes, the age raised management to absolute ascendancy. As Capone summed it up: "This American system . . . call it what you like, gives to each and every one of us a great opportunity if we only seize it . . . ." To this businessman's credit, the protection rates that Capone charged Clare's Chicago warehouses were never anything but competitive.

Radio linked all peoples in an instant community. Couéism promoted self-improvement to the level of religion. Millions of people took to chanting to themselves: "Every day, in every way, I'm getting better and better." "All Races," Clare proudly declared, "are learning new and improved ways to fight harmful body odors."

Charles Ponzi's postal voucher scheme paid its early investors a 100 percent return on investment, with money obtained from later investors. After ducking out early from his jail sentence, Ponzi slipped down to Florida and briefly turned a brisk trade in underwater lots. For all the age's losers, for all the hedgers, for all those not yet flush enough to invest, Clare offered something "Greater than Riches: that grade school complexion."

Prohibition shut down the Double Eagle Whiskey Distillery. Two years later, the law lured the subsidiary to test the waters with a magnificent site near Windsor, Canada. Never more than a mama-papa sideline, the Alcoholic Beverages Department grew sea legs while abroad. Soon enough, it was doing a far healthier business than it had in the years before America went dry. Ads were mostly word of mouth.

American per capita soap consumption continued to rise as rapidly as the national appetite and fortune. Yet soap was fast becoming the most competitive good then being sold. No article was advertised more heavily. Even the floating soaps required a constant buoy of new promotions to keep from sinking. The prosperity revolution left America awash in a glut of goods. The business of manufacturing necessities now fell behind the broader effort of manufacturing needs.

Marketing experimented with coupons: "Take this clipping to your grocer, along with two cents . . ." "I want to take the two-week New-Dawn test. Mail me my absolutely free trial bar to: . . . Only one sample per address."

But war had matured the public. It had grown sophisticated, jaded. Homey poetry and sentimental art no longer sold it on anything. Nagel, his hands full with other expansions, accepted the inevitable and professionalized all promotional materials. Clare's old space broker, Thompson, now wrote all its copy as well. The story of Clare would henceforth be handled by frustrated New York novelists who had never set foot in a factory, who didn't know their acids from their bases, and who couldn't make a soft soap to save their lives. In these hands, Snowdrop went snazzy, out there on the biplane wing, knocking its knees together alongside all the other jazz babies.

"Queenly Beauty for One Thin Dime," the Thompson Agency promised:

The same mixture of sumptuous and unguent oils that graced the palaces of Egypt, Crete, and Babylon is yours in each bar of Cleopatra Beauty Soap. All the arts this ancient queen of beauty commanded come together to cleanse, protect, heal, and smooth your modern-day skin. Cleopatra Beauty Soap blends together only the finest and most expensive oils of coconut palm and olive to bring you the luxury that formerly only queens could afford. By importing these rare oils in massive quantities, and by working its factories day and night, Clare can offer you this costly luxury for only ten cents, no more than plain soap. The gigantic volume and great popularity of this exclusive blend thus benefit all its users, bringing the world of exotic beauty secrets within easy reach of everyone.

Shrinking profit margins and the rising costs of relentless competition forced the company to diversify on all fronts. The Industrial Goods Department began to lose its ad hoc quality and acquire the rational organization and volume distribution that Personal Goods had perfected. The bleaches and disinfectants groups were reorganized under the Consumer Goods unit. The Georgia seed-crushing enterprise as well as Lacewood's fertilizer and pesticide plants entered the age of galvanized steel and modern management. The firm dumped its uncompetitive process chemicals efforts, while the smaller drug and medical lines were brought together in their own department.

While soap still floated the bulk of the enterprise, the existing Consumer Products Department began to expand so roundly into other operations that it bewildered even the knot of new college whiz kids who organized the expansion. The plan was simple enough: a pyramiding scheme that really worked, because the pyramid was theoretically infinite.

First, an analyst whose full-time job it was to scout the industry would identify a promising consumer good that bore some relation to an existing Clare line. The company's experience with lard, for example, prepared a jumping-off point for shortening. The scout would locate some small shortening firm, one that was earnest, expert, but utterly hopeless when it came to market share. The target's business prospects meant little or nothing.

Clare would acquire the small company, usually through stock transfers that did not reduce available cash. Then it would ship its engineers and managers out to the newly acquired plant, anywhere from Jacksonville to Walla Walla. Clare employees descended upon the little outfit like exchange students on the Sorbonne. And they would proceed to run the new toy train set not with an eye toward profit but for the pure technical experience.

Once Clare's men learned, in this lab school, all the do's and don'ts of the new process, it was time to scale up. They would salvage what they could of the existing physical plant and sell the rest for scrap. They would transfer the best of the old skilled workers to a new, state-of-the-art plant erected in an ideal location, one that benefited from Clare's golden name, executive experience, and growing distribution arm.

Within a few years, the careful training and groundwork generally paid off. The new plant would begin earning enough to defray its own costs, generating enough surplus to launch the process all over again. So shortening would lead to oleomargarine, and oleomargarine to emulsified ice cream. And each new adopted child inherited all the contagions of fitness and fortune that the name Clare had come to stand for.

The factories in Liverpool, Lille, and Münster rooted in their transplanted soils like native growths. The suave and cultivated Douglas II went abroad to become Chief of European Operations, splitting his time between the factory towns and his villa in Vézelay. The plants belonged to Clare, but bore only material resemblance to their American cousins. They operated on local principles and employed local labor. And for legal and cultural reasons, all Clare's familiar brand names assumed different European identities.

Europe's polyglot stew presented intractable problems on this score, until Douglas II hit upon certain synthetic names that had sonorous, neutral associations in most major tongues. His happiest invention, Clarea, played well across all borders. Nothing in those years gave Douglas greater pleasure than making a soap in Germany that the Germans thought was French, and one in France that the French thought was Italian.

The possibilities of expansion spread before the firm without limit. In 1927, Nagel snatched up Sparkle Soap of Oakland, a familiar if aging household name. The acquisition completed the expansion of Clare's manufacturing facilities into total continental coverage. And overnight, the move left them a key player in the burgeoning mouthwash business, a twenties epidemic among the newly rich. Clare's little antiseptic line, languishing since the Civil War, erupted with the invention of a market for germ-free breath. Thompson sold the gargle with what looked like hospital public service announcements.

The Sparkle takeover was expensive, but Clare's soaring common stock gave it considerable leverage. Patience, pruning, and several excellent packing plants promised steady and swelling yields for as long as Clare cared to harvest them. But Hiram Nagel was not a patient man. No matter how fast all the individual slices were growing, he wanted the whole pie.

With close-kept secrecy, Nagel steered his board into the deal of the century. The plan originated at J. P. Morgan's rival house, National City, and it grew to maturity over at Clare's great rival, Colgate-Palmolive-Peet. Although most companies still paid lip service to competition, many had begun to tally up what competition cost them. Clare and Colgate had spent hundreds of thousands over the years in a fruitless attempt to best each other. At last, Colgate came to Clare with a very simple suggestion: if you can't beat them, why not join them?

The plan was nothing if not bold, a fitting climax to the flashiest decade in American history. It aimed at building nothing less than the largest and most powerful food, drug, and personal hygiene corporation in the United States, perhaps the world. Kraft-Phenix Cheese, at 38 million, was already in. So was Hershey Chocolate, at 25 million. The group was working on the Great Atlantic and Pacific Tea, Hormel, and a cannery worthy of inclusion in such company.

It was, by all vantages, a match made in heaven, albeit packaged and marketed in an angel-free zone. Manufacturers and retailers, linked together to take the goods right from the factory to the consumer: horizontal and vertical integration on a scale that would stun even boom-time America. The plan seemed the perfect extension of the trajectory that Clare had been following for decades.

Clare's stock had risen at an annual rate close to 30 percent over the previous five years. But not even that run-up compared to what happened the week word of the merger leaked out to the Street. The stock traded throughout that spring between a low of 38¼ and a high of 43½. By the beginning of fall, it had touched 70.

The merger participants gathered together to sign their names to the agreement on October 20, 1929. That afternoon, the markets began to sputter. Nine days later, a cascade of margin calls wiped away a tenth of the market's worth. When the slaughter ended, enough wealth to pay for another World War had vanished in a cloud of smoke and mirrors.

Among the Crash's lesser casualties was the monster merger contract. Clare's stock fell from 69¾ to a long and obstinate 13. Colgate dropped from 90 to an eventual 7. All parties scrambled to extract themselves from the rubble of the collapsed tower. The contract now meant nothing, for meeting the agreement would require even more fiction than the fiction that had just exploded.

And on November 1, All Saints', Hiram Nagel, the hick kid from Kentucky, the farmer-voiced, silver-tongued, complaints-letter answerer whom Peter Clare raised to greatness because he sweated just as profusely as the great unwashed, was found behind his president's desk, dead. No contemporary newspaper or subsequent corporate history ever adequately explained the circumstances.

———

A rocky prominence, like a volcanic cone, teems with a continuous carpet of people. Mostly we see their hats, although here and there a body manages to hoist itself up onto an outcrop. Top hats, felt hats, berets, porkpies, tam-o'-shanters, caps, fedoras: the whole socioeconomic gamut surges as one toward the summit in the distance, where a tiny suited figure holds up a celebratory bottle against the halo of a sun whose corona reads: "HEART'S DESIRE." To the lower right, a small insert shows a neat dresser top with comb, brush, perfectly folded towel and washcloth, and bar reading "SOAP."

A KIT FOR CLIMBERS

Hard work, courage, common sense will prove stout aids on your way up in the world. But don't overlook another, one that is tied up with good manners—cleanliness.

Any way you look at it, clean habits, clean homes, clean linen have a value socially and commercially. How many successful men and women do you know who are not constantly careful of personal appearance and personal cleanliness?

In any path of life, that long way to the top is hard enough—so make the going easier with soap and water.

For Health and Wealth use SOAP & WATER

PUBLISHED BY THE ASSOCIATION OF AMERICAN SOAP AND GLYCERINE PRODUCERS, INC., TO AID THE WORK OF *CLEANLINESS INSTITUTE*

(*Ladies' Home Journal*, August 1928)

———

No longer her home, this place they have given her to inhabit. She cannot hike from the living room to the kitchen without passing an exhibit. Floor by Germ-Guard. Windows by Cleer-Thru. Table by Colonial-Cote. The Bodey Mansion, that B-ticket, one-star museum of trade. But where else can she live?

She vows a consumer boycott, a full spring cleaning. But the house is full of them. It's as if the floor she walks on suddenly liquefies into a sheet of termites. They paper her cabinets. They perch on her microwave, camp out on her stove, hang from her shower head. Clare hiding under the sink, swarming her medicine chest, lining the shelves in the basement, parked out in the garage, piled up in the shed.

Her vow is hopeless. Too many to purge them all. Every hour of her life depends on more corporations than she can count. And any spray she might use to bomb the bugs would have to be Clare's, too.

Who told them to make all these things? But she knows the answer to that one. They've counted every receipt, more carefully than she ever has. And wasn't she born wanting what they were born wanting to give her? Every thought, every pleasure, freed up by these little simplicities, the most obvious of them already worlds beyond her competence.

The newspapers, Don, the lawyers: everybody outraged at the offense. As if cancer just blew in through the window. Well, if it did, it was an inside job. Some accomplice, opening the latch for it. She cannot sue the company for raiding her house. She brought them in, by choice, toted them in a shopping bag. And she'd do it all over again, given the choice. Would have to.

And if some company got together, came up with something for her, for what has happened, some fruit-scented spray that would return her to all those blissful, carefree assumptions: well, they could name their price. Cancer-Be-Gone. She'd sell just about anything but the kids to get it. If the cure lasted for only, say, ten years, at the end of which the vendor wanted the most unthinkable item in trade, she'd still sign.

She cannot watch television now, even old movies. The radio is a painful shaggy-dog joke. Magazines and newspapers know what has happened to her, and they bait her with page after page of full-color burlesque. Her own kids now seem like walking billboards to her, their legible clothing proclaiming, Kiss Me, I'm Current, I'm Knowing, I'm Pliant, I'm Lost.

She never knew what this place really looked like while she was living in it. Now that she lives elsewhere, she cannot believe what she sees. Once you learn a new word, it's everywhere. The world is a registered copyright.

On her way to the bath—surely it cannot hurt anyone if she bathes—she goes to the linen closet. Linen closet, that last refuge of her mother, the pristine hangout of buttons, thread, tissue, hot water bottles, all that is innocent and obsolete, now crawling with trade names like crabs in a bucket. She simply wants to fetch a clean towel to dry herself off. But she can't find one that's not already spoken for, that isn't embroidered with someone else's monogram.

Shoving aside a stack of facecloths, she stumbles by archaeological accident on a small stockpile of yellowing soap. Siamese triplets. Three bath-size
bars. The $1.79 suggested retail price is crossed out and overprinted, by the
same press, with a red 99 cents.

She stares at the archaic, nineteenth-century brand. When could she possibly have bought soap? Soap, which everybody now knows is the worst possible thing for your skin. She graduated to scrubs and exfoliants and gels
years ago. Someone has come into her house and planted this thing without
her knowing.

Then it comes back to her. She bought it in a back-to-basics fit, about six
months ago, when she first began to wonder whether her cancer might come
from products. When she thought it might not be too late to go clean.

She pulls open the old-fashioned paper wrapper and slides out the white
casket. She takes it up close to her face. It seems scraped all over, gouged by
some glacier, some cranky whittler. The perfect cake is not perfect at all. If a
machine cut this, the machine was drunk. The bevel drifts down one edge
like a sand castle's seeping parapet. The soap's skin is everywhere dimpled,
scratched all over by the factory's fingernails. A tiny piece of one corner has
come unchunked, flaked off like shale, leaving a rough, clayey pocket against
the polished white.

The impression of the paper wrapper folds across the two ends. The back
harbors two rectangular incisions, variable depths, mysterious as Stonehenge.
She has never looked at soap before.

Across the front, a single word calls her back to Sunday school:

Lux

She sets the bar down, returns to the wrapper for more explanation. The
Pure Beauty Soap. Four point five ounces. 127.6 grams. A bar code clumps
up in irregular strands, like stringy wet hair, held taut. Questions or com-
ments? Call toll-free 1-800-598-5005. Made in USA, copyrighted the year
she probably first got sick without knowing. Distributed by Lever Brothers
Co.

Her dad's old brand. The one that bought their house, fed and clothed
them, put her and her brother through school, paid for her folks' retirement.
She can't remember choosing it.

To hell with VCRs and garage openers and microwaves: how do you make
this, this little block of angel lard? She knew what this stuff was, once. She's
sure she knew, instinctively, before she even thought twice about it . . .

Days pass without her help. March comes in. The month when she needs to get back out to restart the gardening. She's already six weeks behind on the forcings and indoor beddings. She must start the valerian and forget-me-nots, prune her butterfly bush, divide and propagate the euphorbia and phlox. She putters in the basement, under the grow lights. She wants to get better. She will make this deal, any deal, if they will just let her grow these plants. She will give up flowers. She will go to 100 percent vegetables this year: only useful things, for canning and preserving.

Dr. Archer orders a second-look surgery. Because the procedure is available to them. Because it is all that's available to them. Because we have to do all the things we know how, do anything that might help, however little. Because we cannot stop until we have done all we can possibly do.

———

We know that sometimes when the trail of history leads through dark valleys the traces of cleanliness along the road are scarce, but when the trail leads along the ridges in the sunlight the evidences of cleanliness are many . . .

We live today in the sunlight, one sign of which is our increasing use of soap and water and our growing knowledge of the joys and benefits of cleanliness. It has been suggested that historians of the future looking back to our times will mark this as one of the outstanding contributions we have made to the advancement of civilization. It may well be that they will call this age in which we live the "Age of the Bath."

—GRACE T. HALLOCK, *A Tale of Soap and Water*

———

Lacewood's sole moment of legatee's doubt came during the summer of 1932. Men gathered in barbershops and soda shops, forgoing haircuts and Cokes, for such frills had long disappeared into luxury. Women milled about at the A & P or at the fountain in front of the courthouse, each scared soul searching the other for explanations and shushing any brave individual who dared to speak the unspeakable.

But a few folks did say what everybody else wondered: Lacewood was better off without the damn factory. Better off before people had come off the land. The town was no better than a bunch of domesticated rabbits, living it up and praising the good life until the fattening hand came down on you with a club. That's what the "free" in free enterprise meant. Free to be the stooge of any enterprising crook who knew the system.

Others gainsaid the gainsayers. Depression wasn't Clare's fault. If it was, why were all those dust bowl Okies pouring *off* the land and heading here? Two score more of them every day, lining up in front of the Lacewood factory gates. Philo, Homer, Mantooga—all the neighboring farm towns were bellying up even worse than Lacewood. Farms failing left and right, all by their lonesome. At least the factory gave Lacewood some buffer, a little bit of mooring in the cyclone.

Debate went on throughout that summer and fall. Half the town damned the company and the other half fled in fear from the words that, spoken out loud, would surely bring down a real curse upon them. Those who lifted their eyes past the town's borders saw that the source of their damnation had, if anything, spared them half the misery of the wider world.

By Independence Day, four fifths of the wealth traded on the New York Stock Exchange had vanished into the thinnest of atmospheres. The Jazz Age took a quick refresher course in the imaginary value of equities. Clare's stock tracked this average drop downward with all the tenacity of a bloodhound puppy. By summer's end, the worth of the entire, far-flung manufacturing empire was less than the book value of the Illinois factories four years before.

Alone among the corporate brass, William Clare had seen the shape of things to come. The careful financier knew all about bookkeeping by mass hypnotism. Throughout the twenties, he sold off his shares in steady, disciplined lots. By the peak, he'd gotten far more than fair market value for his portion. When all hell broke loose, he dumped the rest of his worthless paper, enjoyed a year of ship-spotting off Nantucket, and returned to business to serve briefly on the board of Gillette just before his happy death as a traitor to his family in 1931.

Douglas II was less hurt by the plunge in his net worth than by the reception of his monograph, *The Dream of the Romanesque*. Scholars laughed at the work because it was written by a businessman. And businessmen by and large failed to read it because it appeared to be about old stones. Douglas retired from the firm to the Greek island of Soundetos. There, in comfortable if reduced circumstances, he took to financing his own amateur forays into classical archaeology.

Everyone else whom the company bound together went to the cleaners.

And the folks in the khaki shirts got cleaned longest and hardest of all. All the sorters and sifters and gauge-tenders and packers and haulers who had been forced into buying company shares at a discount now watched helplessly as their precious nest eggs cracked into the national omelet. Workers who had built their retirements for forty years came up empty-handed, the victims of the distributed pyramiding swindle of capital.

The Clare Guarantee of Full Employment worked right up until the moment that it stopped guaranteeing anything. Direct sale no longer absorbed overproduction, for there were no longer any buyers with credit left to absorb direct sales. Ten by ten, then hundreds by hundreds, workers got their walking papers. Each salary that disappeared cut by another small fraction the disposable income that might have lifted Clare from its slump.

Prosperity turned back into potash, on no provocation except whiplash and mob psychology. Those who lost their jobs, who were now losing their balloon-frame homes, began to wonder how else disaster could have happened if not through the faults of ownership itself. The map in the Lacewood Titles Office had been filled in. The world had gone fully professionalized. And the result was a third of the adult male population sporting sandwich boards that read "Will Work for Food," in the middle of the richest cropland in the world.

By the fall of 1932, Lacewood was as radicalized as a conservative farm town would ever get. Folks who would not have stooped to slip bread and water under Debs's prison bars lined up to vote for Norman Thomas. And the revolution would have prevailed, society would have transformed itself at last, had not Roosevelt come along and stolen the best lumber out from underneath the militant Socialists and turned it into mainstream party planks.

First, the President brought back booze, that distraction beyond value. Then, almost instantly, he went on a shark hunt. Two successive, sweeping securities acts lowered the boom on all the clever riggers of the big money. It was time, Roosevelt declared, for business to play by the rules and remember the original purpose of doing business. What that purpose was, neither Roosevelt nor anyone else ever ventured to recall.

Clare, which had always held its cards close to the chest, at first chafed against the call for additional disclosure and registration. In the chaos of Hiram Nagel's death and the retreat of the last founding-family partners, some of the board pushed for getting out of the game entirely rather than playing by Roosevelt's new rules.

But even at bargain-basement rates, a cash-poor Clare had too much outstanding stock to buy back and go private. The company simply couldn't afford to go unlisted. Control slipped, at least temporarily, from the discredited children of Nagel back to the next generation of desperate dike-pluggers in Finance. Finally, Kenneth L. Waxman, the most capable of William's bean-counting protégés, arose to steady the helm and get the firm back on a production footing.

"Our product," Waxman was fond of saying, "is confidence." He ran his own version of Roosevelt's jobs creation programs, reopening whole sections of his idle giant factories on subsidized apprenticeships. He figured out how to turn Roosevelt's business meddling into a company asset, on both sides of the ledger. In short order, Ken Waxman learned how to run Clare on a shorter leash as if the whole yard were still theirs to bury bones in.

For its part, Lacewood labor continued to assemble all the packaged confidence that management fed it the specs for. Forced by law, the workweek fell to forty-eight hours. To the dismay of desperate families, children were swept from the factory floors. The Wagner Act legitimated the process of collective bargaining. Now the strapped factory could deny its employees as a group as well as individually.

For the first time in history, working Lacewood had an ally in the White House. By '36, if desperation had not yet lessened, it was at least under attack with enough governmental vigor that Lacewood turned out to help the once-despised poor little rich boy from New York to the biggest landslide in history. Landon, decrying the new infringements on American liberties, got trounced. Yet the New Deal marked little more than the latest corrections in a maturing market.

Suffering brings out the showman in a person, and the Great Depression turned America into the world's great performer. Sound propelled cinema into a heavy industry, the Depression's Native Balm. In the year that Lacewood sent FDR back to the White House, the Cinema on Lincoln and the Rialto on Main combined to outgross all other town concessions, not counting Clare. All unemployed Illinois lined up to watch Charlie Chan go to the opera, Mr. Deeds go to Washington, Fred and Ginger follow the fleet, Nick and Nora reprise the perfect marriage, Weissmuller and O'Sullivan cavort half-naked through the jungle, Kern and Hammerstein take the show on the boat, Errol, Nigel, Donald, and 597 other brave souls ride into the valley of death, and Duke Mantee, "the last great apostle of rugged individualism," make life miserable for everyone.

Modern Times opened to a greatly amused factory audience. Roughshod rode the assembly line for weeks following the run, as every joker and his oil can perfected his Charlie imitation.

But the happy invention that kept the town from banding together to follow

Charlie's red flag was yet another Clare promotion. The company's new hit product was at least as amusing as the talkies, and incredibly, it came free to any home that could afford a radio. As most homes in Lacewood would have sooner gone without running water than forsake this free gift, the listening audience quickly grew to include almost every home within the city limits.

No minutes ever recorded just which underpaid executive genius first came up with the idea for *The Henry Happel Hour*, although several stepped forward over the years to claim the honor. The show seemed to emerge intact from out of the oaken radio cabinet itself: unscripted, full-blown, and from the first as rich and capricious as one's own life was empty and dull. And yet the very emptiness of Lacewood's existence itself formed the basis of the *Happel Hour*'s endless caprice.

At 8 p.m. every Thursday, the town would go dead, even deader than the usual background static of small-town deadness. Lights in the diners would go out. The bowling alley fell to a hush so profound you could not hear a pin drop. Homes pulled themselves together around the receiver like a shawl on pinched shoulders. Only the second shift at the factory showed any signs of continued life, and even these men had sets installed here and there around the plant, awaiting the rich and jocular baritone announcer's rolling tones: "*The Henry Happel Hour*. Starring . . . *Henry Happel!*"

Perhaps the gales of laughter from the sophisticated New York studio audience were what so vindicated Lacewood's prosaic existence and turned it into the stuff of brilliant burlesque. For Henry Happel and his hopeless family lived in none other than Dunnville, Illinois, a thinly disguised Lacewood, recognizable even to those who had never heard of the original. Through the miracle of wireless broadcast, Lacewooders could see themselves in their own mind's eye, raised from blandness and redeemed by high myth.

Luckless hero Henry worked as a "shift-fitter" at the nearby fertilizer factory, a gag that never failed to reduce profane, tobacco-spitting, tattooed, three-hundred-pound clean-and-jerkers to tears of defenseless mirth. Henry's relentlessly status-conscious wife, Marge, though finally good-hearted, hatched a continuous scheme for getting and staying one fashion step ahead of all the other yokel wives. Daughter Betty lived only for getting pinned, while her beefy-sounding brothers, Biff and Hank Jr., who attended the Big U on a football scholarship, pretty much failed to follow the action in an infinite variety of creative ways.

Greater Dunnville was a complete menagerie of types: the last bastion of a vanishing communal America looking in one another's windows and living in one another's pockets. To most listeners, the Happel microcosm felt denser and more real than the universe it mimicked. "Brought to you by Snowdrop Soap. Untouched by human hands until you break open the wrapper." Marge loved Snowdrop, because it was cheap and classy at the same time. Betty thought it upped her odds of getting pinned, by making her smell "Franch." Biff and Hank Jr. liked to toss wet cakes of it around in the yard. If you could catch one of those slippery little white things, no pigskin in the world was going to give you trouble.

While Lacewood had never made Snowdrop per se, it worked for the same logo. It made the fertilizer that grew the corn that fed the cow that sacrificed the fat to the company kettles that cooked the soap that put funny little Dunnville on the map of American consciousness. And of that, Henry Happel's real-life models were abundantly proud. They made Clare, and Clare made soap, and soap made radio, and radio made Lacewood famous. And so the town basked, happy in its haplessness, held up to the loving ridicule of a nation.

Brought to you by Snowdrop, Gristo, Tar Baby, FlapperJack Pancake Mix, Mentine Gargle and Breath Repairer: as if these things themselves were doing the bringing. Through radio, these names grew as easy to flesh out as any phantom, as real as the Shadow, Jack Armstrong, Jack Benny, Ma Perkins, or Kate Smith.

Each brand was a wooden puppet longing to be a little boy. The best of them grew lives of their own, until not even their most devoted listeners could say who made them anymore. America knew what Gristo brought you, but not who brought you Gristo.

Behind this happy front, the world economy lay in ruins. Clare's capital value contracted to a third of its pre-Depression peak. Junior executives banded together on graveyard humor. They bet on who would be next to the gallows. They started office pools to guess the day and month when the firm would go under. They began clamoring for a strong man, someone who'd have the strength to lower the massive hatchet their common salvation required.

In a dark time, soap learned the supreme selling tactic of fear. For fear boosted the desire for the protection soap offered. Americans learned to keep their soap dish dry and press the last slivers together for a few extra uses. Some even reverted to the atavistic knowledge of making their own.

The same desperate parsimony trickled up through Clare's corporate ranks. Janitors were instructed to extinguish all unneeded lights and unplug all frivolous appliances. Clerks had to turn in old pencil stubs in order to qualify for new pencils.

These years scarred the next generation of company leadership, branding the firm with a frugality that would last for another three decades. The managers who did best were those who learned to squeeze every last penny until it sang. All departments cut back their budgets to the bedrock. All except for marketing and research.

For existence now depended upon scraping together enough capital to launch an eleventh-hour invention. Backs to the cliff, the Research Department garnered more patents in the period 1932–39 than the company had filed for in its previous hundred years. New chemical revolutions began to cascade from one another: hydrogenation, nitrogenizing, and most important of all, synthetic detergents.

The Germans, as usual, were first into that virgin realm. Henkel produced a proto–commercial detergent back in 1907. Clare's chemists found it only natural that this most rational of races would come up with the first scientific improvement for soap since soap itself. A synthetic replacement for fats and oils promised to break nature's last bottleneck and bring hygiene into its dreamed-of scale. When aromatic compounds were treated with sulfuric acid and salted out with alkali, they produced a sticky paste that could wet any surface and strip it of dirt in the hardest or coldest of waters.

Detergents represented a lasting victory through chemistry. By any measure, they were a miracle surfactant, the greatest breakthrough in health and cleanliness for millennia. They sudsed beyond all reasonable expectation, and what "our girlfriend, Mrs. Housewife," wanted more than anything else was suds, suds, and more suds.

As the economic desperation receded, Clare became one of detergent's American licensees. The company built modern, stripped-down plants in New York and Los Angeles, plants that could deliver ten times more work with only four times as many hands. It developed its own clever spray-drying process, and it plugged the resulting tiny spheres as "hollow cleaning nodules, exploding on contact with dirt."

Soon the miracle Oxygon had its own radio program, a crime show called *The Racket Breakers*. Lacewood, whose most egregious crime in recent memory involved a quartet of hoodlum-capped fourteen-year-olds defacing the motto on the Belleau Wood monument, listened weekly, entrapped and entranced.

Clare touted its "all-scientific" detergents at the Clare Centennial Exhibit at the 1939 World's Fair in Flushing Meadow. Stocked with the full larder of goods that the company now made, garlanded with stylized images of benzene rings, the exhibit depicted a busy humankind "Making the World We Imagine." NBC televised the fair's opening for a few hundred experimental viewers. Before the Clare exhibit officially closed that fall, Oxygon's licensing country was rolling into Poland.

Within three years, the Lacewood plant went from stuffing sacks with fertilizer to stuffing artillery shells with explosives. In the same year, an aging British botanist who escaped the South Pacific just before the outbreak of hostilities published a squib in *Botanical Studies* declaring that *Utilis clarea* was not a distinct species at all but a bit of early American scientific overzealousness in renaming an obscure, unusual, but previously documented succulent lily.

———

Are you unpopular with your own children? Nidoritis rarely announces itself to the victim. Do your colleagues avoid you in the workplace? Science has shown that most cases of halitosis are accompanied by "coated tongue." Perform this simple test to see if you are suffering from "coated tongue" syndrome. Are you the unwitting victim of harmful B.O. (Body Odor)? You may not be able to detect it yourself. And your closest friends may be too polite to tell you. "Gosh, Lil, I hate to say this, but I guess I really ought to." Science tells us that a full 83 percent of all cases of detrimental B.O. can be cured by simple preventative hygiene. Don't let your body tell people more about yourself than you want. Do your children refuse to bring their friends home to visit? Is your blood starving for essential minerals? Do you look older than you are? Is your scalp leaving behind flecks you cannot see? Is stress making you ill? Tired of those unsightly stains? Are your husband's yellowed shirts holding up his career? Would you knowingly take chances with your children's health? Do your pots and pans tell tales out of school? Do your friends talk about you behind your back? Are you always the last to know? Is your world cracking up around you? Could your loneliness have a reason? Research has found a way. Science can teach you how to relax. Four out of five doctors agree. You may not know what you need.

———

A simple procedure. Tiny incision across the midriff. Absolutely routine. All over by one o'clock, quarter past one at the very latest. Only: it's two-thirty now, and nobody has come by to tell them word one about anything.

Of course, the doctors started late. Didn't even put her on the gurney until past twelve-thirty. And who knows how long it took them to get started, once they knocked her out. It's like O'Hare in there: once they scratch your sched-uled departure, it's hard to get back into the queue. The assembly line goes on without you: Jenkins, Archer, the surgeons all running around, booked to do four procedures at the same time.

Don can feel the kids starting to twitch. Tim paces around in front of the Coke machine, punching the buttons in studied sequences, trying to beat the level and win a free game.

Ellen slams through the stack of ancient *Mademoiselle*s and *Vogue*s, twice each. She's rubbed herself up against all the aging perfume inserts and now smells like a civet with mumps.

"I just don't see why we have to sit here like idiots," she repeats for the third or fourth time. "It's not like she knows we're here or anything."

"You want to be here when your mother wakes up."

"Fine, Daddy. I'll meet you back here on Tuesday." She buries her face in the cover story, "Ace Accents with Affordable Accessories."

He's making it worse on everybody. Don knows it, but he can't help him-self. Every time any medical-looking person comes anywhere near the wait-ing room, he's on his feet and over at the information desk. And if ten minutes goes by without anyone coming through, he's on his feet and over there any-way. Ellen's gone from flinching each time he leaps up to registering soft dis-gust on the roof of her mouth.

A tiny incision, shorter than your pinkie. They feed some kind of fiber-optic cable up in there, pliable, like a plumber's snake. Like those robotic arms in Tim's favorite sci-fi film, only more amazing. A TV camera and a mechanical scalpel attached to the end. The surgeon performs the whole operation by steering things around on the monitor screen. Maybe that's what's holding up the show. Bad reception. Channel on the fritz.

"Sit down," his daughter berates him. "You're stark-raving me. What floor's the loony bin on? I'm going to go see if they take walk-ins."

He sits. And when a bedraggled woman in surgical scrubs enters the room, Don doesn't respond. He doesn't even recognize her, at first. He's looking for someone pretty, young, lively. Dr. Jenkins. The canary-yellow dish.

But it's her. She recognizes them, comes over. Don looks up, connecting at last, ashamed at finding her so haggard, here on a subsequent viewing.

"Hello, Bodeys," she greets them, cheerful but spent. She focuses on Ellen and Tim. "Your mother's fine. She's going to be a little while yet, waking up. We had no trouble with the laparotomy. Here." She hands a videotape to Ellen. "It's a film of your mother's insides. Everything we saw when we were looking around in there."

Ellen examines the thing in helpless panic. She hands the cartridge to Tim, for explanation.

"So what did you see?" Don manages to ask. Casual, curious, mature.

"We need to wait for some other results. We want to follow up with some scans."

"What do you mean? How come? What kind of scans? Did you see something?"

"I'm sorry, Mr. Bodey. Can we talk about this when we know what we're talking about?"

They go to see Laura in the recovery room. "Hey," she tells the kids, her words still slurred from the anesthetic. "Cheer up. Cheer *up*! It's not the end of the world."

The cancer has come back. It's now sprinkled in her abdomen. Don sees it on the tape, confiscated from Tim. He watches it late at night, with the kids asleep upstairs and Laura in her shared room at Mercy, across town, suckled by a plastic bag on a metal pole. Little dark peppercorns, visible even to an amateur, once he learns how to read the pulsing pink masses. They must start all over again, from nothing.

Dr. Jenkins finally calls him, with the results of the scans. Two new nodules. Remote colonies, delayed growths that Laura's old tumor has planted, even after its surgical removal. "There is a shadow on her liver and another one under her armpit."

Don lays into her. "This is the fault of the surgery, isn't it?"

"Mr. Bodey, surgery did not cause—"

"The knife spread the cells around. How else could they have gotten—"

"Mr. Bodey, I know you're upset."

"Upset? Why? Just because what you're calling her treatment has practically killed her? And for what? What did all the torture do for her but speed up her—"

"That's enough, sir. I'm not going to talk to you like this. When you're calm, we can discuss Laura's medical options."

The options are more of the same. Dr. Archer comes to Laura's bedside, to lay them out. "We can go after the secondary mets with another operation," he tells her.

Laura, in bed, doused in bladeless surgery, smiles up at him apologetically. Shadow on the liver. What exactly is it that the liver does?

"We can follow that up with second-line intraperitoneal chemo. We'll try some other drug combination. One that you can tolerate. Carboplatin, doxorubicin, cyclophosphamide . . ."

They can transfuse her. They offer her bone marrow transplants. Another try at radiation. And maybe it's the operation, still. The stuff they have given her, coming in through her wrist. Maybe it's not her at all but all these chemicals making her wonder, but she wonders: Why so many decisions? Shouldn't things be getting simpler, now, at their most visible? Surely she's reached the obvious stage. Only, still nothing is obvious. Doctors, lawyers, Indian chiefs: everyone wants a decision from her.

She thinks back over the last year, the one she has just gagged on. They seem to be saying: now gag on another. More time, time at any cost, even at the cost of time. She hears trucks rumbling through the hospital double-glass, and she thinks it might not be hard to leave so choked a place, a place with so many choices.

She goes home without deciding. Don, the doctors, Tim, Ellen: each takes silence to mean what each needs it to mean. Days pass without her electing any treatment from the menu offered her. Then the day passes when it's clear, the kind of time she's chosen. And still no one names her choice out loud.

Back at home, the phone starts to ring off the hook. Each ring is a big, circling desert bird. The word goes out. Nervous, excited, almost. Every day around 2 p.m., she gets a call from another one of the Realtor girls. A perfectly arranged round-robin. Independently, each of her old colleagues volunteers, "Now, if you aren't feeling up to a visit, you just say so." She says so.

Lindsey calls. "You hurry up and get better, babe. We need you back here, but bad. It's getting to be crunch time, you know."

Her brother calls every week now. "How about if Jen and I come out at Easter with the kids?"

"That would be great," she tells him. "Or June, if you can stay longer then."

Stephanie and Hannah hook her into a conference call. "The Three Sheets," Steph manages to say. "United again by high tech."

Hannah snorts: "New York, D.C., and . . . tell us where it is that you live, again?"

"One of us has to remember our roots," Laura banters. And quieter, "I always said you two would make it big."

Hannah's a rock. "Listen, hick. We're coming out on the twenty-seventh. Me and Steph are meeting in Indianapolis at four and we're renting a car. We'll be at your place by . . ."

"Please," Laura begs. "Please don't. I need you guys. I need you to be . . . what we *were*."

They fight her feebly, but hear. Hannah seems to get it; Steph is close to hysterical. They hang up, nobody saying goodbye.

Neighbors come by with pies. How many of them will be at her service? Will there even be a service? If she still went to church, if she had brought the kids up in some congregation . . . Not for the faith so much as for the routine. Religious people would know what to do now. Janine, that door-to-door witness: for her, this would be like going to the PTA. Atheists are not damned but lost. Lost in too much possibility.

Marian sends her a book about the importance of preserving a positive attitude. *Cheer: Your First Line of Defense.* Well, actually, it's your immune system that's the first line. And a bad attitude is this fifth column in the cells' trenches, working the immune system to give in.

Cancer is a mind disease. She has brought this disease on herself, by being unhappy. And she didn't even know she was unhappy. Now she must fight it mentally. The book calls her back to her old visualizations: picture your immune cells fighting the tumor. Only now she no longer knows which of her countless immune cell types to activate.

Even now, she is responsible for her own, ultimate cure. And if she dies, it'll be her own fault. It'll be because she doubted, took her eyes off the road, let negative thoughts poison her.

Somehow, everyone's read this book, or one just like it. People tell her three times a day: hold your body together with hypnotism. Ellen won't let her watch any old movies except comedies. Don refuses to help her sell the car. Dr. Jenkins cannot mention the word "death" for fear of malpractice. There's not a person she can talk to about what's happening.

The thing she needs most is to make some arrangements. But she must do this herself, in secret, so no one can see her shirk the responsibility of living forever. She takes the plastic three-ring binder she used to keep the kids' after-school schedules in and labels it neatly: "Funeral." She fills it with hymn numbers, poems she likes, the names of her favorite charities.

She manages the papers so that the kids get everything that's left and Don gets the bills. She calls Casey Brothers to come flush out the gutters and remortar the flue. She finds Tim a good summer camp and Ellen a therapist who might be able to help with the transition. She gets an estimate from the church and arranges for the crematorium's cheapest package, a double-sealed sanitary hardened-polyethylene urn.

She can deal with whatever happens. What are things to her, that she can't live without them? But she cannot, cannot begin to think how she can leave her children without a mother.

Everything else, she learns how to shed. It's weight off her, almost. A clarification, a spring cleaning. How exhilarated it makes her feel some days, when the pain holds still and she flies out from under this live burial. Things will do their work without her. Things will do their work without her.

All except her one good thing. She can no more relinquish it than she can leave her own children. If she could just get the soil ready again, sink her hands in wrist deep, she might still be all right. She lies in bed, twelve feet away from the plot. She obsesses over that perfect ground, the richest soil in the world, lying there going to waste.

The ripples in her plaster ceiling deepen into furrows as she studies them. She drifts from visualizing her T cells, finds herself getting the visualized poppies in. She decides to do all blooms this year, to leave the vegetables for another life. On good days, when a sprig of breeze leaks in through the casements, she imagines hearing herself turning over spade after spade. Then, one spring day, a day when it smells as if no one in the world has ever sinned, she *hears*. Hears herself digging.

It takes Laura a moment to be convinced: real. Real. She rises and makes her way to the window, looks out. Her daughter, wearing her boots and gloves, jumping clumsily on the heel of the shovel. God knows where she has gotten seeds. God knows who told her where to put them.

She holds her breath, watching. The stumbles and breaks, the spastic damage and scatter, the rare, glancing good done with every shovelful. Like a four-year-old baking clay balls of bread. If one in a thousand of these seeds grows, it will be a miracle. She holds back in perfect quiet, until that awful telepathy no mother or daughter can silence gives her away.

Ellen snaps her head up, enraged. "You're not supposed to look." Looking will break the spell, whatever the spell is. Whatever this ritual is supposed to bring off.

Laura retreats from the window, back behind the shroud of her room. The shovel starts up again, scraping, shushing. In a minute it stops, and a voice like her daughter's calls, "Mom?" She goes back to the window. Her daughter's eyes stare at her, red with effort and confusion.

"Am I doing it right?"

Yes, she feels herself nodding. Yes. Perfect.

The hospital sends her a staggering bill for the chemotherapy, the treatments she did not even finish. Her insurance has decided that the overnight slow drip—the difference between massive nausea and total devastation—is not considered an essential service. Everything had seemed okay, handled. But now they want her to pay the difference.

"What do I do?" she asks Don. "I can't afford this."

"Contest it," her ex tells her.

"How?" She doesn't even know where to start. She has never understood how to do the simplest thing in this world.

"Maybe Kogan and Lewis can have a look at it for you."

"Kogan . . . ?"

"The firm handling the Clare class action. They . . . they want to see you, anyway."

"They want to see me? Me? They said that?"

"Well, actually, they want to know if you want to talk to them. But that's how those guys do things. Always covering their asses."

"What do they want?"

"More ovarian cases. They're extending the cutoff for ovarian cases. They've gotten hold of your records . . ."

"My *records*?"

"Apparently, they have two scientists. Epidemiologists. Expert witnesses."

She hangs in the air, on these Martian sentences. Waits, small, for explanation.

"The theory is that certain ring-shaped molecules"—he shrugs—"ones with chlorine in them, get taken up into the tissue of women. The body turns them into something called xenoestrogen. Very long-lasting. These fake estrogens somehow trick the body, signal the reproductive system to start massive cell division. There's a new study out."

She shakes her head, already miles away.

"The thing is, these ring-chlorine things are found in certain pesticides." He waits for her to respond.

"And . . . ?" she says.

"Don't you see? That's what they're making down the street."

Also what every pristine cow pasture in the Northern Hemisphere is floating in. It doesn't make sense to her. Like asking *Who had the egg salad?* after a free-for-all buffet.

"Their stock is going through the basement," Don offers. Coaxing her back, against her will, to the things of this world.

"Why doesn't the company just, just . . . ?"

"Just settle? Hon, the case involves scores of people, each asking for a lot of money. It's cheaper for them to fight on. They've got very deep pockets, and lots of lawyers who can throw smoke from now until Doomsday. Apparently, the fertilizer that Clare makes depends in part on chemicals that it buys from another firm. There's some confusion about liability. It's all a bit chaotic."

"But the scientists? The fake estrogen?"

"Well, the company's gone and gotten its own expert witnesses, of course. Scientists who say these other scientists are wrong. That the evidence doesn't amount to anything. They have other studies. Ones that show that estrogen, even real estrogen, doesn't even cause breast cancer, let alone ovarian . . ."

His words are like lights on mountains, out an airplane window at dusk.

"You mean, no one knows anything?"

Don lifts his chin to correct her, then drops it. Incontestable, our total ignorance.

"Don," she gentles him. "How do *you* know all this? About the epidemiologists, and all? The papers haven't mentioned any of this. Unless I've missed it," she falters.

He shrugs again. "Sources. They're also going after Clarity Nature-All hair dye, and that Sof 'n' Sure talc powder they used to make. Apparently, women who use it on their . . ."

"I'm pretty sure I've never . . ."

"Also, a very common herbicide called Atra- . . ."

Her plot of earth. Her flowers.

Sue them, she thinks. Every penny they are worth. Break them up for parts.

And in the next blink: a weird dream of peace. It makes no difference whether this business gave her cancer. They have given her everything else. Taken her life and molded it in every way imaginable, plus six degrees beyond imagining. Changed her life so greatly that not even cancer can change it more than halfway back.

She must go before the end of the month. Before whatever new deadline they've set for her signature. She must become as light as she feels. As light as this thought. Cease eating, cease turning nutrient into mass. Start to convert flesh back into air and vapor. Recycle her body, return it to the breath that seeded it.

"All right," she tells him. "Okay. Anything."

———

Ford and U.S. Steel hammered Daimler-Benz, Krupp, and Mitsubishi. Dow ravaged I. G. Farben's killer chemical works. Merck swallowed Bayer, while GE and Union Carbide blasted Mitsui and Sumitomo. The *zaibatsu* and the *Wirtschafts-Verwaltungehauptamt* hadn't a prayer against the American assembly-line worker holding his hundred shares of Common.

Clare, with its allies Lever, Colgate, and Procter and Gamble, scrubbed out of existence those German and Jap cottage industries that had hoped to convert the world to a soap made from unspeakable sources. Clare Soap and Chemical won the war.

Or rather, Mrs. Consumer did. She won it in the pantry and on the stovetop and in the medicine chest. She fought the flat-out campaign, just as in that poster for the Fats and Oils Salvage Reclamation Drive: whacking that giant Kraut in the head with a greasy but indispensable frying pan.

For with the onset of world holocaust, soap sprang up paramount. Wartime industry starved for it, to clean millions of uniforms, lubricate machinery, and pull off K.P. on a scale never before imagined. More important, after the Japs grabbed Malaya and Indonesia, soap kept the Allies in rubber tires, treads, floats, and gas masks. For the reclamation of old, ground-up rubber required emulsification with soap. One pound of soap reclaimed almost twenty pounds of essential war matériel.

Glycerin, too, the ancient Clare by-product, shot to the top of the procurement list. Paints, dynamite, smokeless powder, and nitroglycerin, not to mention plasma and sulfa drugs, all clamored for their fix of the stuff. There was no end to what the war asked for, or what destruction needed.

Keeping the soap business in business grew into a matter of national civil defense. Everyone had to do his part. Roger Shacklehurst, Clare's general manager for manufacturing, joined the directors of the Fat Salvage Committee. Disney released the film *Out of the Frying Pan, Into the Firing Line*. Clare's radio programs hammered home the drive relentlessly. And patriotic families everywhere were conscripted into production. They saved their every used fat dripping, to return to their butchers, who surrendered it to the national renderers, Clare among them.

By collecting a billion pounds of fat and supplying a good 13 percent of needed grease, the country's housewives saved the soap industry. *Ladies!* the radios teased. *Get your fat cans down to the grocery store!*

The resulting steady supply of recovered materials prevented the government from having to ration consumer soap. With coconut and palm oil impossible to come by, the wartime quality of Clare's home brands did fall noticeably across the whole product line. "Snowdrop Soap has gone to WAR!" Any complaint would have been treason.

Mobilized Snowdrop made a virtue of necessity and a business of shortage.

Lard-o helped extend expensive meat and make it more digestible. Pearl Paste changed its tube, "For the Finer Effort." Wartime was no time to waste precious fabric. Oxygon helped extend the life of wartime clothes: "One wartime secret Uncle Sam wants you to tell everyone!" Wartime colors, too, were more valuable and needed more protection. "Don't waste soap!" Marge Happel scolded her listeners. "Use only high-lather brands. Get more suds from less bar, saving precious fats for the front. And that way you'll also save our boys' precious lives."

With its own rallying cry, Clare returned the favor of the wartime drive. It held a national soap-carving contest on patriotic themes. Contestants applied in one of four categories: children, artists, amateurs, and wounded veterans. The winner collected in war bonds. When, in 1942, the Department of Justice charged the Big Four soapmakers with price-fixing and controlling raw materials, Clare settled by giving away an extra $20,000 in bonds to government causes.

The company also donated rafts of supplies to the Red Cross and helped stock home-front canteens. It cheerfully surrendered more than three thousand of its finest and strongest workers to uniform. And like the country at large, it made its own material sacrifices, scrapping its multimillion contracts with Axis companies like so much silk stocking scrapped for parachutes.

Clare's draftees entered the fray at all levels, from potato peelers to government advisers. Kenneth Waxman himself was rewarded for his remarkable turnaround tenure during the Depression by being named assistant secretary of commerce under Jesse Jones. When the Germans razed Clare's Lille works in the sweep to Paris in 1940, Waxman was still Clare's CEO. Three years later, from the highest circle of government, Waxman gave his unequivocal support as the Air Corps bombed Clare's Münster factory into rubble. The Liverpool plant survived, only to be shut down by raw material shortages.

And when the Army Ordnance staff approached the firm in top secret about making a further sacrifice, the company's acting executive committee did not hesitate. "We will do whatever the country needs," their joint letter declared. What the country needed was a major facility for loading medium-caliber artillery shells.

The Army, in its massive expansion, looked to Clare as a logical affiliate. No one had more experience in mass-manufacturing and packaging small units. Clare had the experience and the know-how. And it possessed an even greater military asset: skilled management. As Waxman put it, "A man who can juggle apples knows exactly what to do with an orange."

Clare management took to war work as it had to the Depression. The Clare training school—promotion up through its mobilized ranks—turned out talent by the trainload. A ladder more powerful than the sum of its rungs, the company hierarchy harnessed and coordinated its every constituent skill.

The Army asked for a sweeping new factory fitted out with state-of-the-art belt-assembly lines. Clare's Defense Facility team studied the arsenals in Jersey and Georgia and Texas. It performed reams of time-motion analysis and shot reels of film. At last it decided that it could outperform the military's requested output by 40 percent, simply by retooling the existing Lacewood plant.

While the factory was being overhauled, the line workers practiced stuffing shells with a mix of fertilizer, cotton seed, and brown sugar that perfectly matched the consistency of explosive powder. Clever automated component assembly kept to an absolute minimum the number of feminine hands that the line required. Clare chemists refined a process for reclaiming TNT, and X-ray quality control on casings helped reduce costs even more. When the first 60 mm trench mortar shell rolled off the line months ahead of schedule, a patriotic Clare delivered its product for half the price that the Army had specified.

War settled on Clare the new structure that expanded affairs demanded. Taking a cue from the Allied Command, the company went floridly decentralized. Clare birthed up vice presidents even faster than the Italians bred generals. The pyramid broadened at the middle: more executives, more operators, more divisions: food products, paper products, drugs, toiletries. Its streamlined phalanxes forged a new aggressiveness, both in making products and in moving them.

Forced wartime efficiencies left the firm slim, trim, and ready for the atomic age. In part because there had been so little to spend it on, Clare's cash surplus, by Nagasaki, was almost twice what it had been before Pearl. For four long years, the nation had held itself in check, rationed, a seed of winter wheat under snow. By the last blast, it broke out buying, ready to bury the past in a new era of long-promised prosperity.

When Waxman tried to return from the war cabinet to commercial life, he found a business that had moved on by its own accord. The old internal battle of succession had flared up again in his absence. Palace revolution deposed him in favor of Robert Kaufman, head of Marketing. The sons of Nagel were back in charge, and would stay there throughout the coming glory years.

Chronic shortages in fat continued to hamstring soap production after V-J Day. But by then, quotas and rationing had taught the housewife the many virtues of synthetic substitutes. Consumers were turning eagerly away from nature toward something more reliable. Buyers were ready to embrace a product built specifically for their needs. When an R and D fluke called tripolyphosphate proved to have inexhaustible building action, Clare labs turned the molecule inside out until they got it to do their bidding. A quarter-million man-hours later, they announced the first truly successful, all-purpose, all-synthetic soapless soap. And with it, they turned the age of deterrence into the age of detergent.

The tower-blown, spray-dried, immaculate molecules truly consummated an ancient aspiration: Resolve's reverie, Benjamin's dream, James Neeland's vision of a perpetual chemical engine. A race that could make everything from scratch would be beholden to no one. All bottlenecks would vanish. Life would be at nothing's mercy.

Yet freedom carried a crushing sticker price. Soap was now made with staggering efficiency in gleaming steel continuous hydrolizer plants. Conversion to new phosphate detergents would require junking much of that investment and starting all over again. The executive committee debated whether Clare could afford an outlay on that scale. But of course, it could afford the outlay's alternative even less.

"If we don't do this," Robert Kaufman declared, "someone else is going to make us wish we had. Better to go down swinging than get beaten to the punch." The result was all-water, all-purpose Awe, Clare's most successful new introduction of the twentieth century.

Awe plants rose one by one, their profits plowed back into the next groundbreaking. Gleaming detergent-drying towers rose in Albany, Greensboro, Detroit, Rapid City, Kansas City, Los Angeles, Turin, Vancouver, Caracas, and Mexico City. Castro would confiscate the Havana works shortly after the fall of Batista.

The capacity of any one of these proliferating germ centers exceeded the entire production of the firm just thirty years before. And not one housed anything remotely resembling a kettle. Fats and crutchers and drying racks vanished, replaced by continuous sprayers and coolers and huge field tanks of alkylbenzene and other petrochemical derivatives. Scarcity no longer dictated how people would live or what goods they could make. Freedom was within easy reach.

The two-tiered design of the firm—personal and industrial—now paid off in spades. Clare became its own chemical pipeline, one that supported simultaneous vertical and horizontal integration without limits. Once more retooled, the modern agricultural division took off, enjoying all the advantages of a late starter and aided by Lacewood's increasingly central, well-serviced location. As the family farm, forced into new economies of scale, vanished into agribusiness's combine, Clare was there with a series of packaged solutions: Capsure, Pest Ban, Lariat, Hoe-down, HarVaster.

Each additive secured a new round of record crops for less human capital. Some part of each bumper harvest made its way back into Clare foodstuffs, at ever-better prices. And as the dollars flowed into Lacewood, so did the hospital, the college, the secondary businesses.

Advancements in corporate management and merchandising kept pace with the rush of new technologies. Douglas Sr.'s old scheme of internal promotion responded to the exploding demand for talent. The best and brightest, those who most understood the rising tide of goods, rose rapidly into the niches that needed them. One could advance from salesman or engineer to brand manager to divisional head to VP almost as fast as the new fatty alcohols could be sulfonated.

Robert Kaufman, only fifty, ascended just that meteorically. But the hour had unquestionably found its right man. Kaufman exhorted his forces, "We must sell our promotions as vigorously as we sell our products." Vigor spread across the country in a series of stunts, from scrubbing national monuments to showering cities with free samples from the air. "Our line is desire," Kaufman asserted, "every bit as much as it is manufacturing. We are in the 'Awe' business in more ways than one."

Throughout the golden era, Clare's product lines grew tenfold. The pruned company tree burst forth in new branches. There was Glow, the magical white toothpaste for those who couldn't always brush when they wanted, and Chlorocleen, the verdant, wintergreen, bacteria-killing wonder. There was Liquid Sun dish soap and Mista shampoo in an unbreakable tube. There were hair-altering formulas for every race, color, creed, and trichological conviction. There were home permanent kits, kits for medium, tight, loose, sprightly, or insouciant curls and waves. There were mother-daughter kits, kits with neutralizers, kits for frizzled and sizzled hair, quick and convenient kits, kits requiring rods, pins, coils, and foil, all delivering yesterday's, today's, and tomorrow's styles.

There were facial cleansers, creams, masks, spreads, and lotions. Pure washes, washes with miracle XR-50, and washes whose chief virtue was their $10 million rollout. A floor cleaner and a glass cleaner and a tile cleaner and a counter cleaner. Detergents for dishwashers. Detergents with fluorescent additives and optical brighteners and free tea towels right in the box. High sudsers and low sudsers, for durables and dainties. Synthetic soaps for each new synthetic fabric. Powders and sheets and shavings, blue and white and yellow, that left no curd and needed no rinsing. Fluids that simply proclaimed, "It's here, It's clear!" And that sufficed.

Skill in manufacture, the technology of making things were no longer the issue. The issue was fitting the itch to the scratch: bottling thirst's salt water. The old war of material efficiency became a war to make and convey everfiner distinctions. Clare could answer just about any of the public's needs. But doing so required figuring out how the public saw and thought.

A team of eager consumer brand managers got together to found the Market Research Department. The new science entered the merchandising loop from the opposite end. Clare could reduce the risk and expense of marketing a new product by learning, in advance, what would sell without needing selling. It made no difference how good or useful a product was. What mattered was what the populace thought it needed.

Like the best of fifties gumshoes, MR wanted just the facts. It aimed not to influence but to observe. It sought data over desired results, method over merchandising, and statistics over wish. The best way to decide what might be was to learn what already was. Toward that end, MR built its carefully controlled test markets—less markets than measuring tapes. It did not care whether Devota or Claretone sank or swam. It simply counted the bubbles.

Marketing, then, could work no end of wonders with the indifferent data. But the greatest merchandising prize to come from the Market Research Department was the idea of market research itself. By the time Sputnik left the earth, the industry of needs creation had learned to see the blind taste test as its own product. The men who gave us the bomb and cured polio were more than a match for the problems of daily existence. Science had to sell science, scientifically. And the resulting combination serviced huge sectors of the psychic economy.

"The modern woman," the modern ad declared, "is no longer the slave of the laundry room. Chemistry has freed her, giving her time to concentrate on those things she really wants to do, like looking great. And behind that dynamite party dress, our drudge turned diva feels pretty good about everything she got done this morning!"

Product research scientists looked great on television, conscripted into advertising's new arms race. And market research was there to help Clare pick the best spots of the emerging national folklore to sponsor. Narrative's mafia, Clare bought up huge pieces of Jackie Gleason and Lucy, *Crimebusters, Quiz Me,* and the Flying-A Ranch. Snowdrop babies mobbed *The Steve Allen Show.* One could not see talent without thinking *Talent Hour,* and one could not think *Talent Hour* without thanking today's modern toothpaste, with Fluoroguard. "Speak your piece without a care. Sing your song out, anywhere: Glow, glow, glow!"

Clare's sixty-second spots ran the gamut from animated, chattering cream canisters to anguished sufferers from chap, psoriasis, or worse. The saga of grease and grime passing through the kitchen pipes or the epic journey of indigestion through the esophagus were much more entertaining and elegantly produced than the twenty-odd minutes of prosaic filler they came wrapped in. The ads took more takes, more tech, more ingenuity than the shows they hosted. They crammed into half a minute more implicit history and adventure than their parasite shows lingered over for the better part of half an hour.

All day long, these free streams of surplus delight flowed into the homes of any worker who could afford a set. Clare's jingles and cartoons weren't a tariff. They weren't even a luxury tax. They were little lagniappes, much-loved gratuities that people chuckled over together at work the next day. One hundred million notions, planted every evening and harvested each a.m.

Market science also made the surprise discovery that ad outlay had to remain proportionate to sales, or the product would wither in the surrounding shouts for attention. The leading brands required more promotion, simply *because* they were the leading brands. Whole new television shows had to be invented and filmed just to provide a showcase exciting enough to goose an aging product.

Being seen cost orders of magnitude more than being heard, a truth Clare discovered even as it abandoned its onetime savior, radio. Now and then Clare VPs got together with their P&G or Colgate equivalents to hash out informal cost-holding armistices. But such cartels were unstable and tended to be broken by any party that thought it could get ahead. By the time the hatless boy President took office, Clare's TV expenditure exceeded all other promotional budgets combined.

Unprecedented plenty and perpetual low-level panic produced fertile hybrids. A spate of Korean War hoarding spiked the company's revenues. Groundless buying seemed driven by the desire not to be caught soapless following a nuclear exchange. When the Soviets exploded their first thermonuclear device, sales of household goods surged by 12 percent. Peaceful, prosperous, precarious beyond comprehension, Americans turned to the only safety left. Clare products were just the thing to stock that second, underground larder.

Panic's windfall provided the foods division with the cash to buy a broader toehold in new food entries. Clare's seed-crushing experience earned it a place in the heated arena of cooking and salad oils. From edible oils to peanut butter was but a small hop, leaving Clare positioned to charge into the erupting snack food market.

Upper-level executives, keen to make their mark on company history, repeatedly faced the same decision: to buy or to invent? With its massive distribution and promotional arms, Clare could make a go with just about any item that a sufficient number of humans wanted. The question was whether to start a new life up from scratch or reach down and animate some sleepy, stunted, mom-and-pop brand that enjoyed only local presence.

This dilemma was part of the larger, philosophical challenge of an expanding commission. Should Clare concentrate on doing what it did best, steadily refining its technological expertise? Or should it plunge ahead into new challenges, learning, as it went, how to make newer and better things?

Kaufman's answer, formulated in executive chambers, became official corporate policy. "A company that stops growing is dead. Clare has a charter to go make whatever people want and need. More than a charter: we have an obligation. We will find out each niche where we can compete, and apply our proven methods to making our contribution."

As Clare's new anchor product proclaimed, *Awe works wonders*. Sales crept steadily up the staircase of fiscal quarters. Earnings tripled in the fifteen years following Hiroshima. Capacity at Lacewood alone was up a hundredfold since its inception. And the number of new factories doubled every other presidential election.

Television made for mass demand, which led to larger factories, which led to cheaper goods, which led to more consumption, which paid for more broadcasts, which led to a lower cost per consumer message, which brought all the accoutrements of a freer, fuller life. Profits boomed, though margins shrank to nothing. The whole trick was done on volume.

A hundred years before, a family's soap cost twenty days of work each year. Now two days of effort paid for the whole year, leaving pots of cash for purchasing cleaners whose mere existence lay beyond the power of bygone ages to conceive. Half of Clare's profits, by decade's end, came from products that hadn't even been on the market before the First World War.

A share of stock purchased at the end of the previous century was now worth two hundred times its initial offering. Group life insurance, retirement funds, the forty-hour week made life better at every level of corporate existence. Round and round the wheels of human effort ran, the enhanced circular flow leaving a little surplus for more improvements each time through the loop. The human race had graduated from a handful of extra seed corn to extraplanetary satellites, all on the simple trick of compounding reinvestment. Mankind had all but won.

WE'RE WAGING WAR ON THE WORKING CLASS

Not that we want to hurt anyone. Just the opposite. As far as we're concerned, most people have been working too darn hard for too darn long. And we're fighting to change all that . . .

Wouldn't it be nice to put your feet up for a spell? Let a machine lift that barge or tote that bale. Let a robot do that dangerous welding. Make a thinking machine manage those books. It's a dirty job, but who says some *body* has to do it?

Thanks to remarkable changes in human industry, we're now embarking on a new age of free time and opportunity. Rising salaries and lightening loads, greater automation and smarter factories mean that we are getting more and more work done with less and less . . . well, *work.* And that's a very good thing, whatever class you're in . . .

The last few hundred years have witnessed the advent of unparalleled laborsaving devices, each helping to lift mankind's oldest burden. And the more we come out from under the yoke, the more energy we have left over to make the next generation's lives a little lighter and more interesting. Modern business is intent on freeing people for what they do best: thinking, creating, relaxing, enjoying . . .

Class warfare? You bet! And we won't stop fighting until everybody's a member of the leisure class.

(ANIMATED FILM, 1963)

The hospital sends a nurse to her home every afternoon. It's an afterthought, a kind of apology. Why they call it managed care. First a scared one named Maria, then a brisk one named Catherine, then a condescending one named Hope.

Overnight, the sciatica in her leg shuts down all walking. The least weight shoots a column of liquid fire up her spinal cord into her brain. Her doctors cannot say why this is happening, and she doesn't make them guess. One week later, her left arm no longer has the strength to roll its side of the wheelchair. She can still move, but only in slow counterclockwise circles.

They install a hospital bed in the den. Motor-controlled: the head rises, propping her until she can look out on the newly turned earth where her daughter has scattered an awkward potpourri. She sits up in bed and watches a squirrel unbury a nut from a tiny pothole in the middle of the road, a hiding place so cagey even he forgot about it all winter.

They outfit her with a Porta Potti. She reads or listens to the radio or dozes. Ellen sits at her bedside, amusing her with tales from the vortex of high school: who's up, who's down, who's in, who's out.

"Anything you want me to look up for you on the computer?" Tim asks. "Anything you want printed out?"

The room turns into a crazed curatorial collection before her eyes. All day long, she names the eight hundred objects she can see. She excuses each one, ticks them off against the checklist of her existence: wedding gift, birthday, emergency replacement, mail order, free sample, garage sale, something the kids dragged home. The world is her spent purchase, by turns sweet, sour, pointless, urgent, refreshing, dull . . .

She studies this plenty. She looks on it at dawn, midday, dusk. Vertical light filters in through the blind slats at 4 p.m., settling the hodgepodge into a still life of inscribed beauty. Each thing, a mute and vulnerable need awaiting its annihilation, and how can she go on breathing?

She presses the button on the bed motor and lowers her head to the horizontal. Then she can see nothing but her own confinement and a thin crack of sky through the window's corner. She studies the little patch of sky, searching it for clues, for additives that shouldn't be there: diffusing, invisible, a stealth air force.

Bored, frantic, amused, appalled, miffed, distracted. Why this odd persistence of expectation, these bursts of unthinkable pleasure? Nothing seems to add up, to join itself to anything bigger, anything large enough to keep pace with what's happening. The sheets chafe her skin. The metal springs of the hospital bed cut into her rump. Her body feels like an impulse purchase, two days after the free return period.

People call. Some people even come by. If they call first, she tells them it's not a great day. Maybe next week, when she's feeling a little better. "Keep your spirits up," people tell her. She tells them she will.

She watches the daytime soaps, but she cannot follow them. In the station breaks, she collects herself. Human temperament is not only its own jury and executioner. It also writes the criminal code, runs its own slate of judges, and railroads them into office on bought votes.

The hospital installs a device to load and unload her from the bed. A personal crane, an ingenious combination of design and new alloys. Don comes by to learn the seventeen steps required to lift her from lying to upright. He slips the canvas sling under her, hooks the rings, winches her upright, locks the cross braces, raises her from the bed, removes the wheelchair arm, swings her in a gentle arc, and lowers her down into the chair, shaking from the ordeal.

He wheels her into the front room, now farther than Paris. So many exhausting diversions. By the time they get her staked out in a corner, ready for a chat, talking has become too great an effort. The words don't catch anymore. They slide out of her throat on little bubbles of phlegm. Don tries not to make her repeat anything, although she knows he's not catching all she says.

They try to eat dinner together. Don rushes around preparing, dolling up the TV trays with sprigs of parsley and pocket carnations. She grows hungry again, against her will. She struggles to balance the tray on the arms of her wheelchair. She cranes the food to her mouth, each bite a labor of complex engineering.

The spoon falls from her hand, of its own accord. She watches it in slow motion, tumbling end over end, cascading down her front, bouncing off her immobile leg, and delivering its payload of gazpacho to the ivory rug. Don is up in a flash, chasing remedies, cold water, salt, stain removers. She watches him, a comedy of manners whose plot she can no longer follow.

"Don. Don." She feels her face from the inside, wet, slurried, broken. Forget about the rug. Fix my *hand*.

The outing is over. Don cleans up after her as best he can. He wheels her back to her bower. In the room, he stares despondently at the personal crane, all the steps it will take to get her back into bed.

"To hell with it," he says. "Who needs this piece of crap?" He slats his arms under her and lifts her, over the edge of the bed, as he once did. They bump against each other like strangers on a bus, despite themselves, forced together by circumstance.

He has lifted her before, no end of times, back when there was some substance to her. But he underestimates how much harder it is to dead-lift a rag doll that cannot adjust its center of mass, cannot assist even by shifting. Harder than a sprawled sack, for she is splayed. He scoops her from the chair, takes two steps, staggers. They start to go down together. He pins her to the side of the bed, his back ruptured. He struggles underneath to hoist her, half–fireman's carry, back to safety.

She lies where he manages to place her, furious with shame. What are they waiting for? She's sick of the long lesson. She knows everything; she's ready to graduate. She looks up, fixing him in her gaze. Her eyes are big, inverse to what they can see now.

"Why does it have to be this hard?"

She has felt pain before, but never like this. Tenderness flares into a gouge grinding deep into her bone. Each breath is a band saw; there's no longer enough space in her chest for any more air. Some hours, agony blinds her: in her leg, in her belly, her lungs, throat, brain. Soon enough, she loses whole afternoons to sharp crescents of black. The pain digests her. It smelts her words back down into a slag of vitreous thought. She calls out in her sleep, biting her pillow when she comes to, to keep from waking anyone.

A little Baggie of diced oregano materializes one morning on her bedside table. She whiffs it; it smells like college. It seems to be there for a reason, the postscript of an ancient conversation she can't retrieve. It must have come from Ellen. All the old nightmares about her daughter revive: the various slides to disaster. Even worse, her girl might settle into her mother's naïve good citizenship. No place, no useful, middle place to live. She puts the Baggie in a bedside drawer, for safekeeping.

Instead, at Dr. Archer's suggestion, she skips right to morphine. Doseless doses at first; 5 mg orally in the morning, when things get bad. And then again at night, if she needs it to sleep. Somehow, despite everything, she still wants to be clear. But untreated pain is even harder on clarity than the drug.

She tries to reach Dr. Archer, but cannot. She leaves a message with the nurse. Some lives later, the nurse gets back to her: she can go as high as 10 mg every four hours, if she needs to.

She saves it up. She takes to counting. All sorts of calculations. Times since her last pill. Since her last bowel movement. Minutes until the nurse or Don will show. Seconds until the kids get home. How many miles, how many feet she is away from her mother's grave, her father's. Calculates for as long as she can, to prove to herself she is still lucid. She asks for a calculator and a number two pencil, keeps them ready on the equipment rack, next to the Porta Potti that Don has rigged up for her.

She watches TV, but cannot concentrate on it. The news stories don't make sense. People who blow up buildings to keep them out of the hands of Big Government. A conditioner that knows exactly how much conditioning your hair needs. Even her beloved old films, a jumble: Hope and Crosby on the Road to Damascus.

Don seems to be around a lot. "Are you sleeping here?"

He shrugs. "Sometimes."

"Where?" she asks, amazed.

He bares his palms. "Upstairs."

That's right; she doesn't sleep there anymore.

"Don't worry," he assures her. "I'm changing the sheets."

Where did we think we were? What did we think we were doing? She issues all the parts of a laugh, but her throat won't assemble it.

She learns to save her voice for the essentials. "Is it time for my pill?" she whispers to Don one evening. She's pushing it, but hopes he'll spring for the fifteen minutes.

"Say again?"

"Is it time for my pill?"

"You just took it."

"Just? No. Are you sure?"

"Maybe an hour ago."

She gets lost on that word, "hour." Soon enough, she loses the day. She's pretty sure about the month, still. Then she's not sure about anything.

"Laura?" Don says to her, another evening. So politely, she knows she doesn't want to deal with it. But it's not what she thinks. "Lo? Clare . . . has offered a settlement. Out of court. It's not . . . not what it should be. And there's no . . . admission. But they've mentioned a significant sum."

"Settled? What does that mean?"

"It means they want to stop things. It means they don't think they can beat the suit in court."

It means no such thing. It means that the common stock has fallen to unacceptable levels. It means an offer is the more cost-effective solution.

She looks at this man, his diligent dispatches. He wants her to be happy. Has worked for this. Lobbied. She wants to be happy for him. The survivors always have the hardest row.

"Thank you," she tries. "For everything."

Outside, the night is howling. A night that makes you bless the invention of houses.

"Don't you want me to tell you how much?"

She cannot. Cannot want to know. Even for him. Even for the children. She's done with how much. She lets her head rock from side to side, like a lullaby. It hurts her throat to move, even a little.

"I don't understand you," he whispers. "What do you want?" Gentler still: "What do you need, Lo?"

She thinks how she would say it, if she could still say things.

"I want the president . . . I want the . . . chief to come sit here. In my house. Tell me why this happened." She wants what it promises, in that naturalist's log: the wrongful users of the magic plant, answering to her.

———

Hock it, **Sh**ock it, **S**queeze it, **T**ease it!

Infiltrate, **C**onfabulate, **E**quilibrate, **D**efibrillate!

Knead it, **Pl**eat it, **S**eed it, **E**at it:

KNICK-KNOCKERS!

(Now with a quarter of your RDA of Beta Carotene,

not to mention a whole grit brickload of other celebrated antioxidants)

———

Throughout most of the 1960s, Clare faced a persistent cash flow problem. It did not know what to do with all the cash flowing in. And for most of the 1960s, the best answer anyone could come up with was to spend it.

Even this was easier said than done. Corporate HQ raised salaries and hiked dividends. Marketing and Sales saturated the available advertising outlets. There were no more improvements in equipment or machine base to make. Advances in engineering actually encouraged "factory build-down," shrinking the number of plants for the first time in the corporation's history. And, of course, saving money.

Research and Development ate what grain was thrown at it and continued to lay golden eggs. But its cost-per-hatch rate faltered with each additional dollar spent. Production already pretty much pressed up against the wall. Soap turned over as rapidly as possible. America simply could not buy cleaning products faster than it already did, no matter how much more the price fell or the quality increased or the packaging improved.

Nothing was big enough to absorb all those revenues but more increase. And so Clare, freshly reorganized for the space age, turned its hand to acquisitions. The new breed of up-and-coming Clare executive was neither salesman nor bean counter. He was a scout, a whiz kid of the Quotron and the annual report, scouring the great foothills of American light industry for pretty geodes, ones that went well with the swelling collection.

The watchword was *synergy*. The perfect purchase added extra value to Clare's existing lines, even as it took its own advantages from them. Of course, a soap and lotion firm needed a lustrous cosmetics line. Clare bought one run by a former Chilean fashion model who passed herself off as Spanish émigré nobility. The marriage filled the fashion and business pages alike: a newsworthy match made up in heaven. Clare's name also turned a mediocre deodorant line into a bastion of surety and protection. It got into the congested shaving cream and gel market by buying up a popular Western European brand and migrating it to the American market.

The Travelot Motel chain converted to Clare toiletries after purchase. Lucy Day Kitchens brought coffee and cake mixes and powdered fruit drinks into the fold. CaliMills, picked up to round out the faltering paper products division, proved a gold mine at the onset of the disposable diaper industry. A controlling share in Grizell, a small drug company, brought the company its first new medical products since the nineteenth century.

Not all the pieces in the conglomerate fit quite so cleanly. Portfolio diversification at times turned gratuitous. At first, Clare concentrated on friendly takeovers. But as the pool of available prospects began to dry up, the top brass began to okay hostile attempts that were both increasingly exciting and expensive.

Somewhere late in the decade, things crested for Clare. America woke one day to find its greatest lakes dying or already dead. The culprit was eutrophication, the aging of waters through biological enrichment. This natural process had somehow begun to accelerate, collapsing a thousand years into ten. Some supernutrient fed the aquatic plants, speeding up the lake and choking it on its own growth. That something, the public concluded, was Awe and all its fellow phosphated detergents.

Clare stood firm in contesting the verdict. Company scientists proved, in experiment after experiment, the complete safety of phosphates. Phosphates were common, natural ingredients found everywhere, even in human food. The real culprit, the company claimed, was untreated human sewage reaching lakes in unprecedented concentrations.

The public rejected the company's evidence. By law and choice, it turned to phosphate-free formulas, eagerly provided by Clare's competitors. Such alternatives did not clean as well; they were potentially even more harmful than phosphates. But the battle for public opinion was lost. By the early 1970s, Awe was history.

Hard on the heels of this blow came another, much more devastating. A shocked executive committee watched, helpless, as the Clare name began to be crucified on college campuses for a negligible contribution that its Agricultural Products Division made to a defoliant the Army used in Southeast Asia. No amount of public relations damage control seemed to make any difference.

The student protests polarized Lacewood. When Sawgak College turned out to picket the factory, the factory workers turned out to bloody the pickets. Bumper stickers, legible clothing, and posters chose their slogans like so many fifteen-second spots. A photo of naked children fleeing an air attack in terror read: "Clare: Making Your Life a Little Simpler." A cartoon of a weed-smoking, fungus-garlanded hippie transformed into a clean-cut bank clerk declared: "A little defoliation never hurt anyone." It seemed a wound the town might never recover from.

Shortly after the defoliant disaster, the courts ordered the company to hire more minorities. Recruiting officers already had a contingency plan in place. The forces that had for so long scoured the leading business schools for the best and brightest men now turned their attention toward locating women and blacks. Although they found some, and made their hires as visible as possible, the new recruits never went as far or stayed as long as their counterparts. Once again, Sawgak joined the nationwide protest, circulating fake bars of Snowdrop, the famous stamped name now reading "Lily-white."

The Clare brass failed to fight this collapse in reputation, because it couldn't comprehend it. The public had turned not just against Clare but against all industry and enterprise. Now that business had delivered people from far worse fates, people turned against the fate of business. Like the careless grantees in fairy tales, they forgot the force that freed them to complain in the first place.

But when OPEC's cartel capped the world's holiday font of oil, Clare stuck by Lacewood. When the Japanese expeditionary forces landed, able to make better versions of just about everything for less, Clare kept the town from the worst rust spreading across America from Pittsburgh to Denver.

The dollar began its slow turn toward the imaginary. The market fell apart. During the decade's stately decline, Clare's best play seemed to be to spin off unprofitable businesses to smaller companies who could manage them better. But the company held on to its profitable core, a core with a century and a half of expansion and know-how behind it.

The game seized up so gradually that no one could say whether the run was all over or only regrouping. Three short-lived chief executives tried to revitalize the corporate image. They scrounged about for something up-beat, something eighties. They launched new, clashing, teal-and-grenadine-colored soaps and soap products. Now self-adjusting. Now with DNA. They hired popular androgynes to make thirty-second rock videos plugging their high-dose caffeinated water. They got four famous basketball players to fake pickup games with one another on film, paying this dream endorsement team half the salary of the entire Lacewood plant. They became the Official Redi-Wipe of the Olympics.

Nothing quite worked. Despondency descended upon the Boston HQ, a gloom that radiated outward to the divisional operations. Further growth seemed to depend on externalizing costs. In private, away from the water-cooler, managers began to ask whether the late-day industry could really keep yielding interest, or whether it was just a pyramiding scheme that continued to work only so long as the world had a little more principal left to liquidate.

Despair traveled high up the food chain. The disenchanted, bright young Director of Holdings, whom many thought was being groomed for bigger things, quit the firm in 1983 to take a position at Harvard Business School. There he made a name for himself with a carefully worked-out theory that American business could work once and only once, with a blank continent in front of it to dispose of.

Franklin Kennibar, Sr., longtime SVP at Coke who was passed over for the ultimate promotion, came in to become Clare's first outside CEO since founding. For a starting annual remuneration of two and a half million dollars plus incentives, he saved the company from despair with two words: "global," and "green."

Kennibar broke down Clare's last vestiges of parochialism. He swept out the residual shirt-and-tie manufacturing mentality and replaced it with the new, aggressive blood of the raiding eighties. He knitted his executives into the emerging corporate elite, that interlocking international membership whose directors all served on one another's boards. He brought a new slogan to the twentieth floor of One Clare Plaza, a quote attributed to Locke: "Private vice makes public virtue."

The most visible company head since Kenneth Waxman, Kennibar was born to stump. He lived for it, doing for the company what Nagel's stable of artists and poets once did for the company's products. He canvassed the country like the most tireless of candidates. Everywhere he went, from college commencement to charitable banquet, he gave some variation on what he called his Corporation Speech:

The corporation has been so debated, demeaned, and vilified that we have lost sight of what it has done . . . In fact, it is, without qualification, the most remarkable and successful invention in the history of democratic peoples . . .

Corporations pay for a quarter of public undertakings at all levels, provide half of all jobs, produce two thirds of all payroll, and an even greater proportion of total national wealth. In this century alone, corporations have generated the capital, invented the tools, marshaled the labor, and produced the machinery needed to win two world wars, curtail disease, extend the human life span, harness the atom, and put men on the moon . . .

The market cannot be "corrected." It cannot be "wrong." The market is just a chalk mark on a wall, a mark of what we want and how much we're willing to do to get it . . .

The very notion of "consumer advocacy" is a well-meaning mistake, for there are as many consumer interests as there are consumers. Only by leaving consumer interests to the market have we managed the whole mind-boggling transformation of life since the days when Americans boiled dead animal scraps on an open hearth to make a little liquid soap.

The consumer's best advocate is her own dollar, a franchise given her over every aspect of her existence. By scrambling to win consumer votes and avoid consumer censure, business becomes the best tool we have for building the world that people want.

Remember that business is not some autonomous machine, hell-bent on making us do its bidding. It is no more than a group of people, gathering their abilities together to meet the needs of other people, needs that could not be met by separate efforts . . .

Yes, the corporation's goal is to raise the expectations of all humankind, to raise them to shameless, unmeetable levels. And then it must meet those expectations. Whatever we may yet achieve as individuals, the corporation will underwrite that achievement . . .

Kennibar's internal corporate message was a more pointed variation on that theme. The world was still full of unfilled vistas. One simply had to look farther afield. The Philippines was awash with people who craved Clarity Pore Purifier. Isolated Indonesian villages swarmed the Clare Lady who came selling shampoo samples out of her motorboat. Already Brazilian Partifest sales were growing twice as fast as North American. Eastern Europe had a hundred million young adults ready to swap their Trabis for a year's supply of Compleet and Viva-cleanse. The Indian middle class would soon outstrip any in the world. In China alone, one billion people had never tasted fat-free fruit snacks made with real fruit. And by the time Clare filled all that map in, even Africa would be ready to provide additional new markets.

When the market crashed in October of '87, Kennibar engineered a sizable stock buyback at bargain basement prices, strengthening management's freedom of movement. And after the fall of Communism's Wall in '89, the "prophet of enterprise" could no longer fill all his speaking engagements. A revitalized Clare set up provisional shop in Moscow by the second quarter of '91. A year later, it began bidding for factory site licenses in Vietnam, helping to replant the country it had once helped defoliate.

At the same time, the overseas campaigns led to new domestic savings. Ecuador offered startling tax incentives. Samoa, an unincorporated possession, sported several interesting legal benefits. Malaysian workers underbid American machines. All those advantages meant a cheaper, better product back home. More: it meant that "home" was everywhere. A company couldn't afford to be bound emotionally to any one address.

But even the filled-in, exhausted American continent still had new frontiers. The trick was to continue delivering that next new lifestyle still struggling to be born. Once upon a time, good chemistry sufficed for good business. Then Clare expanded into the evolution line. For a long time, good business meant peddling a progressive sociology. At the end of the day, the business to beat became ecology.

Clare went green, inside and out. Internally, several factories instituted paper, glass, energy, wood, and plastic recovery cycles in their manufacturing processes, realizing savings of several millions. Company-wide, energy use declined 30 percent in the five years following the oil crisis, twice the Department of Energy's mandated goal. This performance then became the subject of ads all its own.

To the consumer, Clare sold ecology in all sizes. Brand managers built the extremely popular "Environomic" line. Their chemists came up with the first ever Environmentally Responsible polyurethane, marketed by an irresistible parrot who flew about the fume-free cans croaking, "Pretty Polly." Clarity hair spray was among the first to dispense with CFCs. All Weather Gravel-Grippers, made with 15 percent post-consumer recycled materials, came with a "Save the Earth" bumper sticker.

This was Kennibar's flash of saving genius: to see that anything—anything at all—could become good business. Business had to shed its every association, its every product and process and purpose in favor of another, better one. Green, too, was a need, the same as any that has faced the species. And nothing met human need better than concerted human industry.

As Wall Street binge-purged its way through a decade of junk bond, leveraged debt, shotgun merger, hostile buyout, bankruptcy, and overvalued startups, Clare, too, reequipped itself to play the radically changed game. The key lay in lifting the whole entrepreneurial cycle to ever-higher playing fields.

Clare's new merchant banking wizards built the financial portfolio, moved quickly, juggled their exposures, timed their strikes, and turned profits simply by taking the right trading risk at the right time.

The company increased its political profile. The new strategy for the times was not to fund either side of an election with the purpose of buying a victory. The idea was to spread the seed moneys, like a terrace of philanthropic grants, among all the contenders. That way, they supported whoever won.

Even as Clare Corporate built the war chest and played the paper-value game, it continued to make new things, or at least new packages. It introduced Solva, a laundry detergent for acid-rain-damaged clothes. It set up the Cow's Common Farms subsidiary, to make and sell health foods to conscientious label-readers who would never have bought from a multinational conglomerate. It enjoyed huge success with a PVC-bottled, highly purified water.

And all the while, its chemists chipped away at the problem of material existence. Fats and oils had built the company. Clare had already driven them out from all detergents and many cleaning compounds. Now the company staked its future on replacing these evil esters all together. The day's holy grail was the simplest thing in the world: something that behaved like fat, cooked like fat, smelled like fat, tasted like fat, but had none of fat's sinister qualities. The substance—whose ultimate existence no chemist doubted for a minute—would join the calorie-free sugar, the cholesterol-free egg substitute, and the nondairy creamer to serve up all of the pleasures of eating with none of the consequences.

Clarene got its FDA approval in record time, during a period of economic jitters. In test markets, a small portion of users suffered severe cramping and diarrhea. Some rival scientists warned that the substance might have invisible long-term health effects, leaving the body susceptible to infection or worse. Never doubting that its chemists would eventually hammer out the kinks, Clare simply marked all Clarene-based foods with a warning label about limiting consumption, and pressed on with its biggest new food breakthrough of millennium's end.

By the mid-1990s, before the spate of unrelated lawsuits hit, Clare was again a remarkable success story. A *Wall Street Journal* poll listed it as one of the most admired corporations in America. It managed the combination of consumer and industrial enterprises with rare efficiency. Its clean balance sheet was a favorite with mutual fund managers and other institutional investors.

Clare brands continued to command a loyal client base. Its ads—assembled by three of the big ten agencies—provided the backbone of shared culture, from playground to dinner table. *Adweek* judged its healthy eating campaign, "Have a Good Meal,"™ to be one of the decade's most recognized. Old Native Balm engravings now went for thousands of dollars at auctions. A novelization of a series of commercials for Clare's leading over-the-counter painkiller ran for twelve weeks on the *New York Times Book Review* best seller list, and even made money as a film, if one counted its international and video releases.

———

On a brass plaque, darkened by air, at eye level just off to the right of the main doors:

The renovation of this hospital and the extensive modernization of its patient-care facilities were made possible by a gift from the Benjamin Clare Charitable Fund, established by Clare International.

The effects of this generosity upon our community will be lasting and incalculable.

George Garmon, M.D., Chairman, Mercy Foundation Hospital
Gerald S. Rawlings, Mayor of Lacewood

August 1978

———

Tim comes home from school to find her gasping. In that shortness of breath, a waking dream of live burial. Air will not enter her. Panic sucks her down into the black.

Tim rushes into her mouth to check for obstructions, just as the films say to. There are no obstructions. He calls his dad at work, who calls an ambulance. Just that quickly, Laura is back in the hospital.

Don, Ellen, and Tim stand around her new bed, forming a cordon with their bodies. The boy is shaken, now that the immediate danger has passed. "She was fine when we left this morning. The stupid nurse was supposed to be there at . . ."

"Hush, sweetie," Laura croaks. "You did everything right." He must lean against her to hear.

"It's just as well," Dr. Archer adds. "We can keep a closer eye on her, for a few days."

And so she comes back to this receptacle, the place she'd prayed never to enter again. Her room is a harsh coral. She shares the suite with an older woman who cannot talk and does not hear her. The two commune silently about where they are going.

Whenever Don and the kids come, they pull the flimsy curtain around on its little runner. Privacy. It exhausts them to make out what little she can bring herself to say. Mostly they just sit quietly together, or the kids will read out loud to her their schoolwork.

Reading is over, and she can't hold a pen. She feels opaque, flattened by the morphine, now 50 mg over her waking hours. It should bother her. She can't eat. She won't, because the drug has constipated her.

The nurses are kind. They come by at all hours to feed her pills, take her vitals, fiddle with her drip. They ask her how she is. She makes cheerful noises.

She can still watch the news. She still has a little taste for it. Maybe even more than when she could understand it. She asks her blighted roommate if the TV bothers her. But the woman doesn't reply.

She watches the headline channel. She watches the local news, the state news, the national news, the international. Trawling. Something still out there, something she mustn't miss. But the stories scatter before her, as senseless as her own. The Clare class action drags on. The lawyers for the plaintiffs aren't happy with the settlement that the company lawyers offer. The two parties work the local news like hagglers in a street bazaar.

Through the morphine, Laura dreams that her own daughter crashes the local news cameras. Strange fantasy, where kids from the local high school take to the streets. Then Ellen is there at bedside, thrilled, telling her it was real.

"Then we set all our Clarity stuff on fire. Mom, everything. Hair gel, lip balms . . ."

Laura finds herself, searches for *Good girl,* but pain annihilates even those syllables.

Tim is there, too. She doesn't see him at first. So small. She never noticed before how small he is. Why he lives on the Net. In cyberspace, no one knows you're small.

"I figured it out for them, Mom. Fifteen girls, and they needed me to figure it out. How to get it to catch on fire and stay lit. We had to juice it a little. Petrochemicals. But once we got it going? Man: clouds of black smoke. Perfect for the cameras."

She wants to ask: *Are you in trouble? Will they punish you?* Then she remembers: there is no trouble. No punishment bigger than living.

"That stuff is really weird, Mom. Can't believe I wore it every day. You should have seen what color it turned when it burned. And it doesn't really taste like apricot, you know? Mom? Why would anybody want to have apricot lips, anyway?"

A knot breaks in Laura's throat. Her words gurgle up blood from her vocal cords. The tear widens, and muteness drives deeper through it. Her lips move, but Ellen can't hear. Only air in smoothed-over drumlins.

Ellen puts her ear on Laura's mouth. There, up close, words are still rustling. Laura tries again. "People want everything. That's their problem." Speaking wears her out. She closes her eyes and dozes a little. When she wakes, everyone is gone.

She dozes often. Constant catnaps, without her even knowing. So funny of the body, as if there's still some point to these spot restorations. From her perch high above town, she can see Northlake Mall, the college, Clare, the Mercer Small Business Park, Millennium's main office. Inside, in her coral chamber, all is chrome and pastel. The gear of survival. The landscape left her.

Sometimes in the catnaps, she is a little girl. She helps her mother make her father's birthday cake, tiny bars of Lever for the candles. She and her brother help carry canned goods down to the crawl space under the basement. Or her father explains gravely to her the ins and outs of the tax-sheltered plan that one day, very far off, will send her to college.

All day long she lies in bed, these chapters in front of her. They are clearer now, more sharply focused than when they happened to her. As if she's filed them away, put them up in the pantry for emergency. Now the emergency comes home, and she does not know how to use them.

She wakes up one afternoon to see a pamphlet left for her on the rolling table arm. *Putting In a Good Word for You.* "Thank her," she tries to tell her daughter. "Janine Grandy. Thanks."

"No," Ellen cries. "I can't get it. Can you speak louder?"

The pain gets smarter. It scouts out the wall that her pills erect. It tests every brick and pushes on the loose ones. Soon it learns how to skirt the barrier all together. The hospital fights back. They open her vein to fit more painkiller in her.

On the morphine drip, she is an angel. Untouchable; enormous; most of all, clean. Paul Loftus, the head of the Ag. Division, visits her. He sits on the edge of her bed and offers her an apology. Franklin Kennibar, the CEO, flies out from Boston. No one knew anything. They will clean everything up. They have to, of course. No company could stay in business if it caused people harm. The market wouldn't let it.

Clare comes to take her out for dinner and dancing. A male, in mid-life, handsome, charming, well built, well meaning. He comes with an armload of flowers, thoughtful gifts, even a poem. He comes again and again, always finding her at home. But always, the night of romantic dancing turns by evening's end into desperate caresses, a brutal attack, date rape.

Some days, she feels a little breeze, even through the sealed plate glass. Life is so big, so blameless, so unexpected. Existence lies past price, beyond scarcity. It breaks the law of supply and demand. All things that fail to work will vanish, and life remain. Lovely lichen will manufacture soil on the sun-roofs of the World Trade.

She can do this. It is not so hard. She feels the good that goods only hint at. At dusk, she hears the hollow bark of barnacle geese passing over her head, like the creak of a gate's rusty hinge. Her eyes follow their shapes to infinity, their bodies bobbing like buoys in the sky. They ribbon off, streaming to a high place where nothing costs anything. One by one, each takes his turn at the difficult tip of the V.

———

After twelve days, the billing and payments officer at Mercy approaches the family. Laura is reaching the end of the emergency hospitalization period. They will need to find some other solution. She can go into a nursing facility, and 50 percent of that cost will be paid. Or she can go back home, where 80 percent will be covered by hospice.

They hold this conference on the second floor, miles below the room where Laura lies. But on that same day, she takes a sudden turn away from them, out of the theater of all decisions. Her lips still move, but without air. Her eyes move to take in her loves, but the muscles around them no longer register.

Her body recedes just by being looked at. It shrinks as Ellen pushes on the bed to get next to her. The daughter is waving a letter, too small and faraway to see. "I got into college, Mom. I'm going." Laura's mouth, a rictus of puzzled medication, tightens a little at the edges. *A smile,* Ellen tells herself, for the rest of her life. *Mother, glad for me.*

Tim sits silently at bedside, fidgeting at the floral curtain. For days, he has said nothing past yeah and no. His eyes retreat into the protective undergrowth of bangs and glasses. Now he stands and goes to her. Puts his hand on what remains of her shoulder.

"It's okay, Mom," he tells her. "You don't have to do this anymore."

She looks at him. Her face startled, relieved. I don't? I really don't? He shakes his head. No. We'll do it for you.

The kids slip down the hall, leaving Don alone with her for a minute. A little space, all the myth of the private that's left to anyone.

"Lo," he says. "La. I love you?"

Who knows what she hears.

———

It all starts in sun. The cardboard case, the instantly pitched packaging: a sunny upland stand of southern yellow pines. A thing that once lived for light.

Somewhere on the coast of British Columbia, machines receive these trees. Pulper, bleacher, recovery plant, and mill synchronize a staggering ballet, juggling inventory from calcium hypochlorite to nitrogen tetroxide, substances ranging from Georgia clays to the South Pacific guano.

Timber, scrap, and straw cook together in the maws of enormous chemical vats. Black liquors and white liquors—spent and new infusions of caustic soda and sodium sulfide—swirl the raw chips downward into the continuous digesters. Screened and washed of sodium brews, the pulp proceeds to beating. Micro-adjustable blades tease out the fibers. Into this smooth mash mix sizers and fillers and dyes. Calcium carbonate, aluminum sulfate, aluminum silicate, titanium dioxide, hydrated silica, hydrated alumina, talc, barium sulfate, calcium sulfate, zinc sulfide, zinc oxide, cationic starch, polyacrylamide resins, locust bean gum, guar gum, and asbestos combine to make any kind of paper the world wants made.

As the creamed blend dries, subatomic van der Waals forces assert a new mat of tentative filaments. A Fourdrinier machine forms the wet stock, presses the draining sheets between felts, and carries them through a series of high-energy furnaces and dryers. Every pound of paper takes sixty pounds of heated air just to drive off the birthing fluid. The sandwich of myriad paperboard layers paste together to a thickness just under one millimeter.

The outermost layer is manila-coated and impregnated, by thermoplastic extruder, with an invisible skin of polyethylene plastic. Molten resin flows through a heated cylinder under high pressure. A die heats the resin to a precise temperature and viscosity, squeezing it into a film of absurdly controlled thickness. Hot film slips onto the rolling stream of paper so perfectly that paper and plastic bond permanently into a weird, third thing that, within the last few years, has become another universal given.

All this for the box, the throwaway. The product's one-piece pup tent is also a self-contained sales-rack display. A series of machines cut, fold, and glue the cast around the finished camera. Powdered glue for sealing the carton arrives at an assembly plant in Guangzhou in whole railway cars, by the metric ton. The double crucifix of cardboard still bears the kerf of the complex jigsaw that cut this continuous contour. Parallel paper mold marks run down its inside surface, invisible except in slant light. A person could go to her grave not knowing that blank cardboard is so striated.

The thing that Canada ships to Guangzhou for gluing is already an orchestral score. The chipboard must be perfect, to hold the vibrant stripes and bursts of look-at-me words that promise a life that will not fade prior to expiration date. The product calls itself after a youthful West Coast city. The trademark scrawls across package front in a childish rainbow of noisy graffiti. Variegated promises of well-behaved euphoria dance on a white background. The inks and resins smell musty and antiseptic, like an obstetrician's waiting room.

Dyes stain the front with a photographic transfer of the enclosed camera, itself ensleeved in a dye-transfer rainbow re-creating the design of the outside box. Down one side, text identifies each machine feature with an arrow. A golden star bursts above the scene, reading: "New: With Eye-Glare Elimination. Ultra-thin profile. Drop in your pocket!"

Stamped onto the bottom, a disclaimer states:

> Liability for any product found to be defective in manufacture, packing, or shipping will be limited to replacement. As color dyes will change over time, this film bears no warranty for accuracy or fidelity, either implied or expressed. Not responsible for any damages consequent upon the use, misuse, failure to use, or inability to use this product.

Next to these words stands a broken-toothed comb of bar codes, precise enough to be read by wands the world over. Next to that, the "Recycled" triangle and the words "Develop Before 12-99." Ten more digits hide under a folded flap: GB72-020-001. The number means something to someone. At the bottom, in the smallest of fonts that will not smear, the manufacturer discloses its address: a town in a state where people assemble things made elsewhere.

The high-tech paperboard encloses a vacuum-packed camera-in-a-bag. Hermetic foil pouching extends the thing's shelf life, as if it were a slow-ripening fruit. The bag is part aluminum alloy, part plastic, part space-age oilskin. Inside, the camera itself: "Thinner than 'n inch." On its inner cardboard wrap, the camera wears its own unlosable instructions. Explanatory icons lighten the labor of reading. All across the intricate machine, pointers identify the salient features: the electric flash, the ready light, the film counter window and ratcheted thumb wheel, the pressed lenses more exact than whole workshops of Dutch Golden Age scientists could hope to grind.

The smooth, black plastic of the camera's right side is impressed with a dimple the size and depth of the median human thumb: a composite grip averaged from several thousand hands by painstaking research. Another research team orchestrates the eyepiece, a third the flash. An army of chemical engineers, fresh from school, selects ingredients for the plastic casing. Perhaps management has a grasp of the general theory, a cartoon notion of what you'd need to rig up color film from scratch. But when the strained chains of infrastructure next crack, history will return to those long centuries after the Empire packed up, when a farmer's scythe falling down a well meant permanent farewell to iron.

Plastic happens; that is all we need to know on earth. History heads steadily for a place where things need not be grasped to be used. At a shutter click, a bite-sized battery dispatches a blast through a quartz tube filled with halogens. Excited electrons, falling back down the staircase of available energy states, flash for a second, to dissipate the boost that lifted them briefly into rarefied orbitals. This waste energy bounces off the lines of a grieving face and back down the hole of the aperture, momentarily opened. Inside, reflected light ruffles the waiting film emulsion like a child's hand impressing a birthday cake. Years from now, metal from the flash battery will leach into runoff and gather in the fat of fish, then the bigger fish that eat them.

The camera jacket says: "Made In China With Film From Italy Or Germany." The film itself accretes from more places on the map than emulsion can cover. Silver halide, metal salts, dye couplers, bleach fixatives, ingredients gathered from Russia, Arizona, Brazil, and underwater seabeds, before being decanted in the former DDR. Camera in a pouch, the true multinational: trees from the Pacific Northwest and the southeastern coastal plain. Straw and recovered wood scrap from Canada. Synthetic adhesive from Korea. Bauxite from Australia, Jamaica, Guinea. Oil from the Gulf of Mexico or North Sea Brent Blend, turned to plastic in the Republic of China before being shipped to its mortal enemies on the Mainland for molding. Cinnabar from Spain. Nickel and titanium from South Africa. Flash elements stamped in Malaysia, electronics in Singapore. Design and color transfers drawn up in New York. Assembled and shipped from that address in California by a merchant fleet beyond description, completing the most heavily choreographed conference in existence.

On the label, the manufacturer warns: "To avoid possible shock, do not open or disassemble." And still they will be sued, by someone, somewhere. These words hide a feat of master engineering under the hood too complex for any user to follow. What makes the sale is transparency. Set to go, right out of the package, and ready to disappear when used. No anything required.

The instant camera lies forgotten in a drawer by the side of a hospital bed. Its pictures, too, began in sun: day's finger painting, where every product starts. A girl sowing a garden. The Million Dollar Movers Club, dropping by with chocolate and flowers. A woman blowing out the candles on a cake, the IV just visible beneath the sleeve of her robe.

A nurse's aide throws it out, prior to the next occupant. For the entire engineering magnificence was designed to be pitched. Labor, materials, assembly, shipping, sales markups and overheads, insurance, international tariffs—the whole prodigious creation costs less than ten dollars. The world sells to us at a loss, until we learn to afford it.

Such a wonder has to be cheap enough to jettison. You cannot have a single-use camera except at a repeatable price. Buy it; shoot it; toss it. As mundane as any breakthrough that seemed our whole salvation once. A disposable miracle, no less than the least of us.

———

From up in his glass-skinned executive aerie, Franklin Kennibar, Sr., gazes down twenty-five stories upon Fort Point Channel and the replica of the Tea Party ship, and contemplates a world without Clare. He locates the microscopic India Wharf, where Jephthah's *Rough Bed* put in with its seed cargo of stoneware plates. From the other side of the sumptuous suite, he can just pick out the public dock where the pauper Irishman landed, the dock where the Irishman's wife died.

That minute of his wandering nostalgia costs the firm twenty-seven dollars. Nor can he really afford the time himself. For this afternoon he will be interviewed by Public Television for its survey of American business. And two days from now, at the monthly meeting of the board, he will set forward a repurchase and reorganization plan that will put the entire company into play.

We speak of bitter, he thinks. *We speak of sweet.* We speak of bounce, we speak of body. Of hold and shine and nonstick and pine scent and quick-acting. In reality, there is no bitter, no sweet, no bounce or body. There is nothing but a series of chemicals, each distinctly shaped, stretching on forever into the Void.

None of this is his choice. Neither the interview, nor the board meeting, nor the plan that will rock the future of these two centuries of business. It has always amused him, drawing the salary he does, how little say a CEO has about anything. The corporation's point man, the passive agent of collective bidding.

We speak of profit, we speak of loss. We speak of cost, we speak of revenue. Of debits and credits and downsizing and expansion and layoff and stock split and reorganization. In reality, there is nothing but a series of little Clares, each with its own purpose, spreading down the fiscal quarters without end.

This interview, for instance. It could not have happened at a worse time. But Clare is not a company that ducks the public, not a company that breaks appointments, not a company that misses a chance to represent itself in a large and sympathetic forum.

"Part one," the producer has written him, "will examine business at the most fundamental level. What is its purpose? What do we want it to do?" Smirking a little at the questions, which would not survive five minutes in the real world, Kennibar sets his three-hundred-dollar fountain pen to canary yellow legal pad and begins to scribble:

To make a profit. To make a consistent profit. To make a profit in the long run. To make a living. To make things. To make things in the most economical way. To make the greatest number of things. To make the greatest things. To make things that last the longest. To make things for the longest possible time. To make things that people need. To make things that people desire. To make people desire things. To give meaningful employment. To give reliable employment. To provide workers with a steady income. To give people something to do. To do something. To provide the greatest good for the greatest number. To promote the general welfare. To provide for the common defense. To increase the value of the common stock. To pay a regular dividend. To maximize the net worth of the firm. To advance the lot of all the stakeholders. To grow. To progress. To expand. To increase know-how. To increase revenues and decrease costs. To get the job done more cheaply. To compete efficiently. To buy low and sell high. To improve the hand that humankind has been dealt. To produce the next round of technological innovation. To rationalize nature. To improve the landscape. "To shatter space and arrest time." To see what the human race can do. To amass the country's retirement pensions. To amass the capital required to do anything we may want to do. To discover what we want to do. To vacate the premises before the sun dies out. To make life a little easier. To make people a little wealthier. To make people a little happier. To build a better tomorrow. To kick something back into the kitty. To facilitate the flow of capital. To preserve the corporation. To do business. To stay in business. To figure out the purpose of business.

Kennibar thinks of adding: "To beat death," but he's afraid he'll forget what he meant when the cameras roll this afternoon. He cannot concentrate. His heart is not in this commission. Already he feels that the floodgates have opened. Two weeks ago, the Masters of Tobacco, all innocence, taking Kennibar to dinner at the Union Oyster House, mentioned, in passing, the many advantages the two companies might enjoy by getting together.

Tobacco has no desire to "get together." Tobacco means to eat Clare on the half shell with a squirt of lemon. Here was the nightmare scenario Clare has feared for months. What with the Common languishing down around 40, for no real reason aside from unfair concern over a few unrelated and easily addressed lawsuits out in the boonies, the company has become a steal. But neither Kennibar nor any of his field marshals have any intention of being stolen. And so they go into the fire drill they have prepared for just such an emergency.

The management group will make an offer to spin off much of the company while bringing the core industry private once again. Chopping up the firm will horrify the board; it may choose any other fate over such an end. Sprinkling the bloody pieces on the waters may make the sharks even hungrier. Or the move may prove a kind of starfish solution: each severed limb regenerating a whole new viable body.

Whatever the outcome, change will be massive and massively expensive. That is the nature of markets: the loser's auction, throwing good money after bad, bidding things higher until whoever ends up with what is left of the company will be saddled with a lasting legacy of debt and downsizing. Debt that gets shouldered by the fifty thousand people who work for him in one way or another. Debt that gets passed on to the consumer, *All My Brood,* as the old Clare soap opera called them.

Five floors below him, middle managers teem, trying to make sense of their little corner of the numbers. The order goes out to bug Tobacco's offices, down South. They will use the same people who tapped the phones of their own labor organizers, last year.

Out in Oregon, at a new plant site, environmental testing consultants stun the fish in the adjacent river to make a head count. Acquisitions has paid to have the river graded class five: do what you will to it. The soil of a pristine neighboring farm turns out to contain massive doses of heavy metals concentrated by cows processing their feed, poisons that the purchasing company will have to clean up.

Down in New York, one of his jingle writers rags the other: "Will you quit with that 'convenience' already? It's like 'Baby' with you." Three offices down, the ad firm's accounts supervisor arranges with the networks to show its finished handiwork on programming that is guaranteed free of offensive content. Already they have arranged for the country's second largest retailer to drop a competitor's stock in favor of this new entry.

A team of twenty analysts looks over the management team's buyout proposals and financing schemes. They have been doing this for four days, without sleep. Every two hours now, they scrap their last two hours' work and start again. *Raiders, poison pills, goal-line defenses, porcupine provisions,* one of them thinks: didn't we use to make things?

On the line in Rapid City, a woman with raging Type II diabetes picks defective wrappers off a belt as they try to slip past her. She converses with the woman next to her over the din of the conveyor, neither of them taking her eyes off their tollgate. "He was supposed to be paying maintenance on the mortgaged lot, okay. But before they could transfer the title, okay, he had to . . ."

A truck driver in Karachi inches his load of Snowdrop through a particularly vicious snarl of city traffic at the crack of dawn. Each month, the jam starts ten minutes earlier. But this month three years from now, he will be free. Barring a bolt from God, he will have saved enough money by then to buy his own twenty-year-old two-ton grain truck and begin driving for himself.

The semiannual reviews come out in Dallas. A young chemical engineer, only three years out of school, reads her evaluation in mounting anger. "They can't do this to me," she tells her organic flavorings project partner, who nods in sympathy. "This is an insult. I don't need this. I can get a job anywhere. I have three of the best new citrus scents in existence in my portfolio."

The Clare Agricultural Muck Shuckers look over their new uniforms: gray flannel with red stripes, and a blue shovel as logo. Tonight they begin defending their citywide sixteen-inch softball championship. Their only potential competition is a group of twenty-year-old upstart ringers from Sawgak College.

A public relations agent shakes her head over the latest spin challenge: a former Greensboro employee who claims to have been beaten and raped for telling the local paper about management-approved product adulterating. Out in the refrigerated warehouses, fork drivers slap their shoulders for warmth. A regional buyer whose territory spreads over four square states juggles his stock figures. A trio of R and D analysts in Detroit, L.A., and Kansas City get together via teleconferencing. They conclude that the company's molecular toolbox ought to be producing a new product once every forty-seven days.

Team bosses at the Knick-Knocker packaging plant in Caracas come to reprimand the new nineteen-year-old hire. They told him when he joined a month ago that if he could manage a hundred packs an hour, that would be fine. By dint of discipline, practice, and hard work, the boy has gotten up to a hundred and twenty. "You don't understand," the shift foreman says gently. "A hundred would be just fine."

In Lebanon, Ohio, a Ph.D. in music composition from Columbia repeatedly hits the BACK button on his CD remote, replaying a strain from a Shaker hymn. His last steady job was playing accordion at age fourteen for his friends' bar mitzvahs. He has bounced from waiter to radio programmer to delivery man, landing at last as an adjunct professor at the close-security prison college just ten miles down the road from the vanished site of Mother Ann Lee's failed utopian community, where he gives the Western culture survey to lifers.

Almost by accident, a Clare creative director has heard the composer's variations for solo viola on the old fuguing tune *Idumea*, performed in a Chelsea loft the year before. Now the composer has been given the offer of a lifetime, the chance to earn more for one half-minute scrap than all his other music combined has earned in his entire life.

He must set to music a digitally rendered ad sequence that makes the viewer feel present at the day of creation. He cannot help but grin euphorically, watching the rushes unfold. In the takes they send him, every human possibility flies up, freed, while doom morphs into dahlias, crop-filled fields flow like rivers of delight, and the sky rains contentment.

This is the vista that needs his thirty seconds of consummate tune. They ask for "something American, something Coplandesque." Something yawping, praiseful, embracing. Again and again, he replays the old Shaker lines, *'Tis the gift to come down / Where we ought to be.*

And on the top floor of One Clare Plaza, this year's CEO readies himself for his latest television performance. "Be prepared to speak a little about the history of your firm," the producer has written him. To this end Kennibar is cramming, consuming thumbnail biographies of the first five Mr. Clares and all that they assembled. The ruined merchant family. Their rescue of the lost Irishman. The first sale, a five-cent loss. One and three-quarters centuries of product improvement.

He stops and gazes out the window again, musing on the story of the Clare who once searched for a hole at the Pole. *They only looked,* it occurs to him. *We made one.*

Years later, the thing he remembered most about the funeral was how many people came. He'd always thought of his mother as more or less alone. It shocked him, going into the church. The place was full.

He couldn't imagine where all the people had come from. Yet he recognized most of them. Friends of his parents before the split. Colleagues of his mother from the real estate office. Neighbors. People she'd worked with on fund-raising and charity drives. Her best friends from college, from childhood. Aunts and uncles and cousins that Tim hadn't seen for four or five years. His dad's friends. His sister's friends. His own friends. His friends' mothers: all the sorry women who used to suffer with her, up in the soccer stands. People from the hospital. Her old chemo nurses.

The only person in that church who didn't know his mother from Eve was the minister. The man talked for twenty minutes about a total stranger. His father and sister sat fixed in the pew, standing for the hymns but not singing, silent even during the prayers. Only, when the minister read that bit from the Bible, about God making man in his own image and telling him to be fruitful, and multiply, and replenish the earth, and subdue it, his father had cried, loud enough for the five rows behind them to hear, "It's subdued."

That much Tim always remembered. Afterward, a lot of people came back for a reception at his dad's. He spent the afternoon eating little sausages on toothpicks and eavesdropping on the adults. Everybody either had cancer or knew three people who did. That was the afternoon when his dad met Hannah, his mother's best friend from college. Hannah, who would become Tim's stepmother for seven years, more than half as long as he'd known his own mother. Seven pretty rocky years of power struggle on behalf of a woman whom each loved better than the other.

A week after the funeral, Tim and his sister and father returned to his mother's house with the packing boxes. His mother's old boss at Millennium offered to sell the place at reduced commission and was optimistic about an asking price. Ellen found the first note. She was cleaning out the cedar chest upstairs. On top of the pile of winter sweaters was a yellow Post-It: "Wash these in cold water, on gentle. Lay them flat on a towel to dry!"

It seemed a fluke, until the next one. Tim found it on a bird feeder in the basement. "If you leave this out over winter, make sure to keep it filled." A moment later, Don turned up a green one, in the deep freeze: "Feb. Ellen's favorite ratatouille. Thaw the day before. Heat at 350, about 20 min. Very good batch."

Maybe a hundred color-coded notes, throughout the house. All the things none of them knew how to do. They sold the other house, his father's, and moved back to the one with all the instructions.

They had all moved back in when Clare announced a massive corporate reorganization involving the sale of the Agricultural Products Division to Monsanto. The high bidders didn't really want the division, but even less did they want it to fall into the hands of American Cyanamid. Two years later, the new owners moved the plant to a *maquiladora,* several hundred miles from the nearest fertilizable ear of corn.

After the move, the town more or less shut down for a long winter's sleep.

Ellen never touched a dime of her settlement money. She didn't want to give the company the gratification. But she never returned it either. She studied botany at Sawgak, answered phones for a design firm for two years, went to Chicago to get her LPN, moved back to a dying Lacewood, and worked at Mercy. She fell for and married the sporty Tom of Tom and Al's Sporting Goods, who wanted nothing more than to give her everything she wanted.

The only thing Ellen really wanted was to have kids. She and Tom tried for years: concentrations, harvesting, implanting, in vitro. Nothing worked for them. But because the doctors were perpetually in there looking, they saw her ovarian trouble early, and gained her many years.

For a time, Tim, too, did nothing with his lump-sum buy-off. While still in high school, he purchased a pretty fast rig and some decent software for it. As he saw things, that machine got him into MIT.

In his junior year of computer science, he fell desperately in love. The woman toyed with him for two months before upgrading. Thereafter, he stuck with the dependable. He worked late at night, in the subterranean caverns, on self-propagating learning routines and distributed processing.

Burnt out by graduation, he went to work as a data processing pack animal for a firm down at Lewis Wharf. He fell in love again, tentatively, then floridly, with a married woman who used him to hurt her husband, to whom she finally returned.

He lived in a hole in the wall near the North End, a two-room apartment he refused to furnish. He bought only secondhand clothes, and he ate only fresh vegetables from the Haymarket stalls. On those rare occasions when he resorted to manufactured goods, he always checked the labels. Nothing made him happier than going without. For three years running, he marked the anniversary of his mother's death with hunger vigils on One Clare Plaza.

After some time, he went back to Cambridge, to graduate school. There, curiosity slowly got the better of bitterness. He hooked up with an interdisciplinary research group working on a computing solution to the protein folding problem. They sought to write a program—a whole library, in fact—that would take any amino acid sequence and predict exactly how it would fold up. For if they could find the folded enzyme's shape, they would know how the molecule behaved. And knowledge of enzyme behavior was the key to a cell's life and death.

The problem was intractable, as adamant as creation. Tim's program lines ran into the millions. The monster grew eternally bigger, slower, more brutish and bug-ridden. It threatened to collapse under its own weight.

Then one year, under constant heat and pressure, the eight of them managed to dissolve the problem. The trick relied upon a chunk of code whose ambidextrous data structures looked out Janus-faced to mesh with both raw source and finished product. The result was a transforming algorithm that worked in two directions. The program told how a given protein sequence would fold up and behave. But for any given enzymatic action, the program also supplied a sequence recipe.

In such a vat, people might create molecules to do anything. The team found itself staring at a universal chemical assembly plant at the level of the human cell. Together with a score of other machines just then coming into existence, their program promised to make anything the damaged cell called out for.

And no one needed to name the first cure that would roll off their production line.

It was then that Timothy Bodey mentioned a healthy bit of capital he had tucked away, untouched since childhood. The sum had been compounding forever, waiting for a chance to revenge its earning. The figure was now huge, a considerable bankroll. And softly, Tim suggested that it might be time for the little group of them to incorporate.